THE LOCKER

Emily –
Here's some cop
humor for you!

Ted
Nulty
'23

THE LOCKER

Ted Nulty

Braveship
BOOKS
Aura Libertatis Spirat

THE LOCKER

Copyright © 2014, 2016 by Ted Nulty

Braveship Books

www.braveshipbooks.com

Edited by Sara Jones

Selected graphic elements licensed from 123RF.com

ISBN-13: 978-1-939398-80-2

Printed in the United States of America

I would like to dedicate this book to all the Marines I have served with, and to those who will carry on after me. I have to mention these few especially:

1st Sgt John McNulty USMC- Recipient of the Navy Cross, two Silver Stars and Purple Heart in WWI.

Hubert E. Nulty US Army- Recipient of the Silver Star and Purple Heart in WWII.

Thaddeus M. Nulty USMC- WWII. VFW Post 471 is named after him.

Thomas G. Nulty USMC- Recipient of the Silver Star, two Bronze Stars, and Purple Heart with two Gold Stars in Vietnam.

Pamela A. Nulty USMC- My mother and a Judo champ beyond compare.

These people left me with some awful big shoes to fill...

Semper Fidelis

PROLOGUE

It was ninety-four degrees at the San Ysidro border crossing, and people's tempers were getting short as they waited in their hot cars for over an hour and a half to cross into the United States. The slow moving cars and trucks were subjected to dozens of street vendors selling all of the standard Mexican tourist wares on the sweltering Sunday morning.

Juan Alfaro stood next to one of the vendor booths and watched as a pickup truck approached the flat area before the customs booth. A slight bit of movement caught his eye as a US customs officer and her dog came out of the air-conditioned building and began to work their way through the crowded vehicles. A slight nod of the head and four children took off into the same area.

They began a finely choreographed pattern of moves designed to place them between the dog and the pickup. The children each had a handful of souvenirs, one of which was full of cut-down cocaine. As they passed each other, they would pour tiny amounts along the ground in front of the dog's scent cone. The small trails were laid out in such a manner as to lead the dog to another pickup, which had been prepped by some of Juan's operatives while it was parked in a garage in downtown Tijuana.

This truck was being driven north by two San Diego State University students who had no idea that the underside of their truck had been dusted with cocaine. The two college kids had been drinking in one of the bars on Avenida Revolución. One of Juan's employees had tagged the vehicle and dusted it with enough powder to set a dog off, then a small baggie of cocaine was taped up in the wheel well of the truck. Juan's pickup and driver had then waited patiently for the two twenty-year-olds to head back north. When they did, they were shadowed a good ten car lengths back.

The first clue Josh Steeple had that something was wrong, was when his truck was surrounded by US customs agents and he was waved forward into secondary inspection. A path had to be made through the other waiting cars and caused quite a commotion. By the time they reached the edge of the crowded entry plaza, Juan's driver was exchanging pleasantries with the inspector for his line.

"What do you guys do with them?" Richard Levy asked the stern-faced Filipino customs agent who had asked him his citizenship and was waiting for the computer to finish clearing the truck's license plate.

"Well, it was the dog that got onto them, so their truck will be pulled apart, and they'll go to jail." Efrain Yuong had retired from the Navy and was working on his second retirement. The little Philippine agent was usually very distant to the uncountable numbers of people who came through his checkpoint, but the friendly young man was staring with such wide-eyed wonder that he almost smiled. "You can't beat the dogs; they'll get you every time." He handed Richard his passport. "Have a good day, Mister Levy."

"Thank you, sir!" Rich said in his best Wally Cleaver voice and pulled slowly through the booth area past the two dazed and uncomprehending students, who were being led away in handcuffs. *Well, not every time,* he thought as he pulled onto I-5 north bound.

Four hours later, the truck was parked in the garage of a house just off of the I-10 in LA. A crew of several young Hispanic men easily stripped the vehicle of the twelve million dollars' worth of cocaine hidden in it. They replaced the bundles of powder with Saran wrapped bundles of cash. The truck was refueled from several gas cans that were kept in the garage for that purpose, and two guards were posted, one inside and one outside of the garage.

Meanwhile, inside the house, Rich grunted and sweated as he thrust himself into the beautiful Latina girl who had been arranged for him by El Jefe. The entire crew knew that Rich was a very important part of the network, and they were under orders to keep him happy and safe. Since Rich's boyish good looks made it tough for him to get women his age, he settled for the young sixteen- and seventeen-year-olds who were supplied to him while he waited overnight before heading back down to San Diego.

The following morning, Rich drove the truck back down to the city of Chula Vista, just north of the Mexican border. He drove the truck into a nice East Lake neighborhood and pulled into a driveway. He hit the garage door opener and pulled into the middle of the two-car garage. He was again met by several young Hispanic men, who began taking the truck apart.

Rich walked out to a Honda Accord parked at the curb and was driven to the Plaza Bonita Mall. After going into the mall and watching a movie and doing some shopping for things he didn't really need, his phone rang. He glanced at the caller ID and slid his finger across the face of the phone to answer the call.

"Hey, what's up?" he asked.

"When are you coming home, baby?" the female voice on the other end asked.

"I'm on my way, babe." And he hung up. Having been given the *all clear* by the team of teenagers who were assigned to his back trail, he went out to his car, which had been left there earlier by those same teens, and drove home to his apartment in Downtown San Diego.

Back at the drop house, the cash was removed from the car and carefully counted and bundled. It was then placed in a cardboard box with millions of other dollars and sealed. A coded label was placed on the box and it was driven to South Bay Self-Storage. There it was placed in the back of Locker Number 38. Some other boxes containing neatly folded T-shirts were shuffled around and the delivery boys made a big show of going through the boxes and holding up shirts in case anyone was looking. Then, with the boxes of cash stacked in the back, and plenty of boxes of low-quality tees in front, the locker was sealed and the crew drove away, not noticing the auction sale sign posted near the entrance.

It was Monday. The auction for unpaid units would be held on Friday.

CHAPTER 1

"Honey, what are you going to do with that storage unit? They sent us the notice that they're going to sell it if we don't pay for it today. We owe $450.00 in fees. Has it been three months already?" Carol Price asked her husband as she shuffled through paperwork on the kitchen table.

"Is there really anything in there we want? I mean, it's just old kids' toys mostly, right? I've been meaning to clear it out, but I just haven't gotten around to it."

"Well, I think Rick's bike is in there, isn't it?" She leaned back from the table to look at her husband, Alan, who was firmly entrenched in his reclining chair for Monday Night Football.

"No, we got that out. I think it's mostly old linens and stuff from the cabin."

The Prices had owned a small cabin up in Big Bear until the economy put them in a pinch. Alan had been laid off and was only recently able to get part-time work. Unlike the rest of foolish America, though, Alan and Carol had been smart about their savings and resisted the urge to encumber their home. The cabin had been used sparingly during the year and they had rented it out through a management company during the busy ski season and the somewhat less busy summer camping season. In fact, it had been a money-maker until the economy had gone south and the rentals dropped off.

The cabin still had enough equity in it to pay off their home when they sold it. With both of their boys in college and no real bills, they had packed all of the things that accumulate in a second home and put them in a small locker at the self-store a few miles away. The little locker up on the third-floor interior hallway had quickly become a dumping ground for family items that had just enough sentimental value to not be thrown away.

"Shit, babe, I say we just dump it. Someone will buy it for $50 at the auction and probably just give that stuff to the homeless."

"Alan!" Carol's voice took on a faux indignant tone. "That stuff is worth at least $60!"

Alan glanced over his shoulder through the archway and shrugged. He then turned back to the game, which was just starting; Carol knew further discussion was pointless. She thought about the items briefly, and then shrugged herself. She threw the statement in the trashcan next to her desk. The notice read, "Your unit, #3B, will be sealed and the items sold to cover any late fees or charges."

Well, good luck with that! Carol thought and turned to paying the rest of the bills.

CHAPTER 2

Brad Stone was hot and didn't like having to sweep the storage grounds during the day. He was sweating profusely and it was just 9:00 am. He wanted to get out of the sun, but that wasn't happening as long as Tina was on the property, getting ready for the auction, which started at noon. She was going through the place like a mad woman, making sure every little detail was taken care of. That included having the place nice and clean for the auction.

"Brad, do you have that list of lockers ready?" He looked up to see Tina's head poking out of the upstairs office window. He winced at the thought of all his air-conditioned coolness flowing out of the open window.

"Yeah, the handwritten one is on the right side of my desk. I was going to e-mail it to you."

Tina's head disappeared for a moment then popped back out with an arm waving a sheet of lined notebook paper. "This it?"

Brad rolled his eyes and nodded in exasperation. Tina looked at the horrible writing and shook her head. She distinctly didn't like Brad and his creepiness. There wasn't much she could do about it though since he was the nephew of the owner. He got a small apartment adjacent the office and a small salary to manage the 420-unit facility. At 80 percent occupancy, it was just enough work to keep Brad from doing things that would put him back in rehab.

The job had kept him away from the hard drugs, and he very rarely slipped on the drinking. The Kiddie porn on his computer would get him in a lot of trouble though if he ever got found out. At 6'5" and a whopping

165 pounds, he was emaciated thin. His asymmetrical face had kept him from any real social interaction almost his entire life.

His one real romance to a girl ended when she found some disturbing images on his computer by accident. Ellie wasn't planning on saying anything since Brad was the only real romance she had ever had. She was his physical opposite, being short, overweight, and having a large, round, oversized head that didn't get her asked to any dances in high school. A week later, when she saw him staring at some children on a playground and playing "pocket pool" with himself, she was so horrified, she left and moved back East with her parents, changing her number and refusing all further contact with him.

Tina typed up the list of lockers that were to be auctioned off and printed it out for Jerry, the auctioneer. The auction company handled everything for a percentage of the total take generated by the sale of the unclaimed units. They supplied the advertising, cut the locks, ran the auction, supplied security, and even made sure the bid winners cleaned up after themselves.

By 10:30, the first buyers were parking their trucks outside the gate. At 11:00, Jerry and his assistant, Bill, were collecting the bidders' registration fees and getting ready for a relatively calm day. There were only seven units for sale, one of which was a trailer being stored at the facility, and the auction should be finished by 4:30 ... 5:00, at the latest.

At 11:55, registration was closed and everyone went out to the first locker. Bill, who served as the lock cutter/security for the auction had a pair of large bolt cutters and an industrial grinder in his truck, which was the only vehicle allowed inside the gates during the auction.

Unit #12 had some furniture and other household items that were in decent shape. The locker was purchased by one of the local thrift shop owners for $450.00.

Unit #27 had some model airplane kits visible and sparked a bidding war that ran the price up to $1200.00 before a young man won it. He managed to piss off both the pawnshop owner he was bidding against and his own wife. She wouldn't stay mad long when they discovered several model kits new and in the box with their radios. After selling the items he didn't want, he still turned over twenty thousand dollars profit. The new car he bought her with the profit went a long way towards the makeup process.

Unit #38 was opened to a lukewarm reception from the crowd. The only thing visible was a bunch of T-shirts and sweatshirts that were obviously packed into the boxes, which filled almost half the unit. The bidders were not allowed inside the unit, but they could see that several of the shirt logos were crooked and it was immediately apparent that this was just storage for misprinted and non-saleable shirts.

Tom and Sheila Stanford were casual buyers who sometimes bought things for their church rummage sales. The church also sent boxes of clothing down to Mexico for the children there when they did missionary work. Several of the other bidders heard them discussing the unit and how it would clothe some disadvantaged children. They only had one other person bid against them, and he backed out at $130.00, due more to the public peer pressure than lack of funds. Tom and Sheila won the locker for $140.00 and moved on after putting a cheap padlock on it. They had come looking to bid on a nice travel trailer that had been advertised for sale.

The travel trailer was twenty-four feet long and slept four comfortably, six if you converted the dinette. It was in decent shape and the Stanfords wound up paying $2,300.00 for it. It needed to be cleaned up a little, but it was still a great price for the trailer. They were so excited about it that they agreed to pay an additional day's storage fee for the locker so they could come back the next day and finish cleaning it out. They hooked the trailer up to their truck and loaded almost half of the boxes from the locker into the truck bed. Once it was full, they started storing the boxes in the trailer.

"You know, we could fit all those boxes in here if we wanted to." Tom looked at his wife as he shoved another box into the trailer. "I mean, we aren't going to clean this thing out till next weekend anyways. We might as well just take it all home right now."

Sheila plopped a box down and sat on it. They had looked through a couple of them and found nothing but the same items they had already seen, but Sheila could swear the last few boxes had been substantially heavier. These were thoroughly taped and they had not bothered to look into them.

"I think you're right, hon, but they sure are getting heavy."

"Yeah, I noticed that too. Probably more shirts stuffed in them or maybe they're vacuum sealed or something." Tom had sat down on one of the boxes as well. He leaned down and thumped the side of the box, which gave off a solid-sounding thud. "Let's do this; I'll load all these heavier ones into the trailer, and you put the lighter ones into the bed of the truck. That way, when we get home, they'll be easy to take out and stick in the garage. We'll leave the heavy ones in here till we can deal with them after the weekend."

"Ugh, okay, but what about the lock on the trailer? They broke it to get in." Sheila pointed to the broken device.

"Well, if someone wants a bunch of T-shirts that bad, they can have some. Besides, I'll pick up a new lock from the RV dealership tomorrow, so it'll only be unlocked for one night. The rest of the stuff will be done at Doug's."

"Okay then, let's get to it." Sheila got up and began separating the boxes as her husband continued to load the heavier ones into the trailer. They stuffed some of the loose shirts into other boxes to reduce the total number they would have to store and threw away the spare boxes in the already overflowing dumpster at the end of the aisle. They rolled out of the gate at 7:05. In the bed of the truck were several boxes of T-shirts. Each box worth about $12.00. In the trailer, they had another eighty boxes; sixty-four of them contained ten million dollars each, in carefully wrapped hundreds, fifties, and twenties.

They drove the seven miles to their house and spent twenty minutes trying to back the trailer into the space alongside their garage. After unhooking the trailer and unloading the bed of the truck, they both collapsed on the couch. Tom barely had the energy to call for takeout.

After consuming the Chinese food at an alarming rate (they hadn't eaten since breakfast), they showered together quickly and fell into bed still damp. A kiss and a murmured "I love you" and they were both out cold.

Inside the garage, a couple of hundred dollars' worth of T-shirts sat in relative safety. Outside, 640 million dollars of the cartel's money sat in an unlocked trailer.

CHAPTER 3

Albert Castillo was moving up in the world. He had just gotten a new two-bedroom apartment, and he was driving a decent car. The boss was paying him two grand a week, cash, for about twenty-five hours' worth of work.

The boss had some weird rules about work and the lifestyle he was allowed to portray, but the benefits were awesome. The crew received bonuses in the form of all-expense paid trips to Vegas, where they were allowed to "Roll Heavy," meaning they could wear some bling and flash their cash. They rode around in limos and stayed at the best hotels.

These things were strictly prohibited when working. As was using product and driving cool rides, both of which got you kicked off the crew in a heartbeat. Their cars had to be three to five years old, the registration and insurance had to be paid, and they could not be luxury-type cars. In fact, the boss had put out a list of cars that were forbidden and a list of recommended models. No fancy rims or tires, and the car had to have factory paint.

Albert's job consisted of driving large amounts of cash to the storage unit and providing counter-surveillance for Richard and Gilbert when they came back from runs. He also had to do one shift a week at the stash house as the standing guard. For this, he got to drive a 2009 Nissan Altima and live in one of the better apartment complexes in town. Another promotion, and he was going to start saving for an ultralight aircraft. The father of one of his high school friends had given him a ride once, and he was hooked. He knew that flying was in his future.

Albert met up with the crew to deliver another couple of boxes of cash to the storage unit. He knew it was cash because he helped unload it from the various vehicles that made it to the stash house. He didn't know how much it was, but he knew it was a lot. There were always four of them assigned to deliver boxes to storage, and he was pretty sure that they were watched by people in another vehicle. He often saw one of three SUVs following them to the storage unit. Not that he cared; it made him feel safer.

They loaded the cardboard boxes into the bed of a plain white Ford Ranger pickup and headed to the storage unit. Jose and Julio followed in Jose's five-year-old Honda Civic. Albert noticed that it was the gold Tahoe following them this time as he drove a very specific route to the storage facility.

Another car was pulling out as they approached the gate, and they were able to drive right in without entering their code. They pulled up at Unit #38 and Albert immediately noticed the lock was gone. He got the first twinge that something was not right. He walked up to the garage door but didn't touch it until the other three were standing next to him.

"What the fuck, man?" he said to Julio. "I'm calling Rich!"

"Fuckin' chill, homie," Julio said as he grabbed the door and lifted it to reveal a swept-clean locker. "They might have had a new crew come pick the shit up."

"No fuckin' way, man!" Albert whispered forcefully at the others. "They always leave the boxes of shirts and shit. And they have never taken the lock with them!" He was shaking the key in all of their faces.

"He's right, bro," Jose said, looking around at the ground. He saw something shining under the lip of the adjacent garage door and bent down to pick it up. It was the half loop of the padlock hasp that had been cut off.

"Shit, man, we better make that call!"

As Albert was dialing, Julio looked around and noticed the security cameras posted at the end of each aisle. The facility was clean and in good repair, so he figured that these cameras probably actually worked. He noticed the overflowing dumpster at the end of the aisle and walked over to examine one of the boxes sitting on top. He pulled it out and brought it back to the others.

"Dude, do you think another crew stole our shit, man? Look." He held up the cardboard box with the familiar printing logo on it. "No one who was ripping us off would take the time to clean their shit up, would they?"

"He said he would check on it and call me back," Albert said as he closed his phone and rejoined the group. "That from the dumpster?"

"Sí, homie."

Back at his condo, Rich was also getting that sinking feeling in his stomach as he dialed Juan's number on a special throwaway cell phone. The entire distribution side of the cartel's operation was overseen by Juan, who was the southern California operations manager and decided all policy for the distribution network. He picked up on the second ring.

"Sí?"

"Sir, I received a call from the transport team at the storage place and they say that the shirts were moved. Some of the things are not the same as when they were moved in the past. Also, the fabric was removed. The entire room is empty." Rich paused for a deep breath then continued on. "The lock had been cut as well."

"Tell them to return to the house." Juan's eyes began to squint. Anyone knowing him knew that there was a storm brewing—a deadly one. "Guerro will be there shortly. They are not to leave."

"Yes, sir. Do you need me to do anything else, sir?"

"Yes, I would like you to meet Guerro there and help in anything he sees fit."

"Yes, sir."

"And Richard ..."

"Yes, sir?"

"You knew nothing about this, right?" The implication of the statement sent rivers of ice water through Richard's veins.

"No, sir." Richard waited for a moment before he realized the line was dead. He slowly closed the phone and took out the battery; it could be used in the next phone in case of emergency.

He spent the next twenty minutes straightening his apartment and packing a duffel bag. The bag had some clothes and a shaving kit. It also held over $800,000.00 in cash. Although Richard had not been involved in stealing the money, someone, somewhere had screwed up. If any of that screw-up was laid at his doorstep, he would try to run. He didn't believe for a second that he would get away, but he would sure try.

He also logged into his E-TRADE account and put in the sell order for 75 percent of his holdings and had the check sent to his secure P.O. Box. That money would put him over the two-million-dollar mark in liquid cash. A man could find a pretty deep, dark hole for that much money. He debated calling his mother or sister but knew that would just expose them to more danger if someone was monitoring his calls. If he had to run, he would call them and send them money. The explanation would be a little harder, but they could deal with it later.

Finally, he went down to his car and pulled out of the garage. He didn't notice the blue GMC SUV that was coming down the street towards his building. In fact, he was so distracted by this morning's developments, that he didn't notice it following him all the way to the mall. He got out of the car and headed to the entrance.

He didn't even make it into the mall when he was picked up by Julio. Richard got all of the details from Julio as they drove to the stash house. Richard actually felt better when he got there. He was sure that an outside entity had ripped them off. He had left his duffel in his car, knowing it would be safe there. Jose had the keys and would drive it to a secure warehouse, where they kept all the work vehicles under guard.

Richard walked in the front door and saw Albert sitting on the living room couch. He sat down next to him and got pretty much the same story as Julio had just told him. Albert was nervous though, and Rich tried to put him at ease.

"Okay, so you didn't have anything to do with it, right?" he asked.

"No way, man! I'm not stupid. The last time I was there was when I dropped off your stuff on Monday." He was starting to sweat a little. "Everyone was there and we came straight back here, man! Besides, you can look at the pictures from the place, man. I swear, I'm not on it."

"Okay, easy, easy. I had to ask, Albert." Richard could see the fear on Albert's face, but it didn't feel like he was lying. "What pictures are you talking about?"

"The cameras, man. The place has like fifty cameras all over it! There's four of them pointed right at the door to the unit, man!" Albert's voice had gone up an octave. "You look and I swear you won't see me there except when I'm supposed to be there."

"All right, relax. We'll get it figured out. Now, next thing. Have you ever heard of any of your crew talking about work shit outside of here? Any slightest thing. Even something at the taco shop, eating lunch when you guys thought no one else was around."

Albert thought long and hard about his answer, carefully going over the last month in his mind, trying to recall every instance that he and his crew were out together in public. The boss had strict rules about talking out of school, and they all tried to follow them carefully. The truth was that there wasn't much to talk about work wise. They all knew what they were doing, and until now, nothing out of the ordinary had happened.

"No man, I ain't never heard them guys talkin' 'bout nothing." Albert shook his head. "Fuckin' Jose don't talk to no one, anyways, and Julio is too wrapped up in his kids and shit, man. We don't really hang out together 'cept for when we go to lunch, but we stay cool with that."

"What about Julio's woman, you think he talks to her?"

"Shit, man, I don't know. I mean he's really into her and stuff, but he's said a couple of times that she don't know shit, and he's gonna keep it that way."

"And you? You got a woman?"

"Shit!" Albert barked out a laugh. "Man, I fucked three different bitches last week. Ain't one of 'em even know what I do! I'm not even close to tellin' them ho's nothing.'"

"Okay. Well, Guerro will be here soon and your stories better match up because that dude has a very small tolerance for foolishness."

"Oh fuck!" Albert almost wailed. "Ah man, that dude is fuckin' crazy, man! Ah shit!"

"Relax, Albert. We're just going to find out what happened. If it wasn't you, then it wasn't, okay?" Richard sounded confident even though he was also feeling like a very dark cloud was on his horizon. "We'll go down there and find out what's up ..." The sound of car doors slamming caused Richard to turn towards the front door. The deadbolt clacked back and the door opened to reveal a 6'2" hulk standing in the doorway.

Guerro was followed by three other men as he came into the room and sat down opposite Rich. The other three, all of whom were also quite muscular, spread out through the house. He looked at Albert and then seemed to dismiss him from his mind. He turned to Richard and looked at him for a minute before speaking.

"I don't think you guys had anything to do with this. We watch you pendejos all the time. I think someone else stole our shit. We need to find out who and why." Guerro had a habit of speaking in sentences that were curt and to the point. "Where do you want to start?"

"We need to see the films, man!" Albert blurted out. Guerro slowly turned his head to look at Albert and fixed him with a steady, yet not quite threatening stare. "They have security cameras at the storage place, man," Albert said in a much more subdued tone.

"Okay, let's go." Guerro started to rise.

"You mean now?" Albert was looking at Rich.

"Yes, now. That money isn't sitting still. Every second, it's getting farther and farther away! We need to find that shit and get it back before it's gone!"

They all trooped out and got into Guerro's black Suburban. They drove to the storage unit, and after looking in the still unlocked unit, they went to the office. Five of them went inside while one of Guerro's men stayed with the car.

Brad looked up at the men as they walked into the office. At first, he was a little taken aback by the amount of muscle that walked in, but he recognized Rich right away as one of his tenants and smiled at him.

"Hey, good morning!" he said, getting up from behind his desk and going to the counter. He addressed his speech to Rich as he looked the group over. "How can I help you folks today?"

"Hi. Brad, right?" Rich put out his hand and shook Brad's hand as he nodded. "I thought so. I rented my unit from you over a year ago for my printing company. We store extra stuff here, unit #38. I just came from there and someone broke into it and stole all my extra T-shirts and sweatshirts."

"Oh shit! Really?" Brad looked totally confused for a second. "I haven't seen anything out of the ordinary. But we can look at the security tapes. Do you want me to call the police department?"

"Well, let's look at the tapes first," Rich said. "There is a chance that one of my shippers came by and cut the lock without telling me, in which case, I don't want to call them out for nothing. If the tapes show something, then we can call." *Like I'm ever gonna let that happen!*

Brad went over to the computer monitor at the end of the counter, which was dedicated to the security system. It was divided into sixteen small panels with views throughout the complex. Brad referred to a chart several times as he enlarged two of the screens.

"This is your aisle. When was the last time you were in your locker? The recording is web based and stored offsite. The recordings are stored in high definition for ninety days and then they get compressed or something, and stored for another ninety. After that they get deleted." Brad was turning the screen so they could see it. "Just give me a date and time and I can enter it and we can fast forward through until now."

Guerro finally stopped staring intently at the man. If he was a part of this, it was unwitting. He was far too cooperative and apologetic. He moved closer to the screen and began watching it.

"We were here last Sunday, storing some stuff, and everything was fine." Rich looked at Albert, who nodded confirmation. "So could we start at 11:00 last Sunday, please?"

"Sure thing." Brad looked at the calendar and began typing in the date and time. Guerro watched this closely to make sure it was accurate. Brad entered the correct date and time and the two cameras showed remarkably clear pictures of the front of the unit. The cameras showed the delivery crew coming in and delivering the last shipment. The crew did everything they were supposed to, including holding up a few "off-printed" shirts for show in case anyone was watching. The camera clearly showed Julio locking and Albert double-checking the door before they left.

"Okay, was that the last time you were in there?" Brad asked.

"That was it I believe," Rich replied.

"Okay, I'm going to fast forward and we'll slow down whenever we see someone at the unit."

They watched as shadows swung by and an occasional person, usually Brad himself, passed near the unit. Every time anyone, even Brad, was in the frame, he would slow it down to real time and they would watch until the figure was gone. No one so much as looked at the locker until a big crowd gathered around it on Friday. They all watched as the lock was cut off and the bidders started looking at the boxes.

"Hold it right there!" Rich stared at Brad with a look of total disbelief on his face. "What is that? There's twenty people there!"

Brad, who had immediately realized what had happened, was walking over to a file cabinet at the back wall.

"Oh, your locker was sold at auction. We sent out notices to everyone who was more than ninety days late on their rent." Brad turned to see Guerro staring daggers at Rich, who was visibly wilting under the glare.

"What?" Rich almost screamed. "We pay every year in advance!" He turned to Guerro. "I have the receipts! I can show you!"

Brad was starting to feel uneasy, as he seemed to recall that Rich had paid in advance. He forgot about the file cabinet and went to his desk. He called up the list of units sold at the auction and sure enough, #38 was on it.

"Sir, I am very sorry! I don't know what happened, but we'll figure it out. Could your check have bounced? Cause if it was returned, then Tina would have put it up for sale. I ..."

"We paid with a cashier's check, dammit!" Rich was beyond furious.

"Easy there, mijo." Guerro gestured to Rich to calm down. "Who is this Tina?"

Brad was shuffling through some papers, looking for something. "Señor!" Guerro said in a much louder voice, causing him to freeze and look up. "I asked, who is this Tina person?"

"Oh, uh she's the operations manager for the company. She's the one who does the final list for the auction." Brad gestured to the pile of paperwork on his desk. "I'm trying to see why your unit was put on there."

"Could we perhaps call this Tina and have her come down here? That way we can get this all sorted out." Guerro was again using a reasonable tone of voice.

"Sure! You bet. Let me just call her right now."

Brad pulled out his phone and scrolled through his contacts as he leaned back in his chair. He held up the phone to show that he had it and hit the send button.

CHAPTER 4

Tina was driving back to the office after meeting with the merchants' association of one of the malls that the Flynn Family Trust owned. The plumbing company had messed up installing a fire sprinkler line, and the resulting water damage had been extensive. The storeowners had been (for the most part) understanding, but Mrs. Burns, who owned a small candy shop, had been extremely difficult.

She just wanted to get home and soak in the tub. So she almost didn't answer the phone when she saw it was Brad who was calling, but since he almost never called her, she figured it was probably important.

"Hey, Brad, hold on a second; I'm driving and need to put my Bluetooth in."

"Ahh, okay."

"All right, it's in. What can I do for you?"

"Uh, Tina, I got some guys in here that say they been paying their bill, but their unit got sold Friday."

"Well, I used the list you gave me of people you sent notices to. Did you look at the list on the computer?" It was hard to not use a condescending tone with him.

"Uh, yeah, but they say they paid in cash checks, and their bill was paid. I didn't know if their check was bounced."

"Cashier's checks don't bounce, Brad." Tina was only a few blocks away and sighed as she made the decision to handle this forest fire. She was beginning to feel like a duck. "I'll be right there. Go get your list of units to be sold from the desk upstairs. I left it in the right side top drawer."

"Okay," Brad said to a dead line.

"She's on her way here," Brad said to the men on the other side of the counter as he put his phone back in its holder on his waist. "I'm gonna go get a list from upstairs real quick, and I'll be right back." He stood up and went up the stairs at the back of the office.

Guerro almost sent one of the paisas with him but whispered for him to call the other guy outside to keep an eye out for Brad if he did try to run. He told them to look for the Tina woman to show up. He wanted a make and model as well as a license number on her car. He went outside to call El Jefe and to keep an eye on the front of the building. He glanced up at the office window and saw Brad bent over what he assumed was his desk. After a brief conversation, he went back inside just as Brad came down the stairs.

"Okay, I have the list that they sent over from Tina's office of the people that were late." Brad was waving a tattered piece of yellow notepaper. "I can compare it to the units in the computer and we can sort this out."

"I'm sure we can, but I want to know where my shirts and belongings are," Guerro said as he walked around the counter to look at the screens again.

"Hey! I'm sorry, who are you? I believe that this gentleman is the renter of that locker. And I can't have you back here. You have to go back around the other side of the counter." Brad stood up and approached Guerro.

As soon as he was within arm's reach, Guerro's right hand shot out and up to Brad's throat. Although Brad was almost three inches taller, Guerro out-massed him by ninety pounds. As Brad choked and sputtered, Guerro grabbed the back of Brad's neck and brought his face down by the keyboard.

"Listen, fucker! I need to know what happened to my shit! If you do not get me some answers right-fucking-now, I will carve you up!" Guerro emphasized each word with a slight shake of Brad's head. "Now zoom in and show me who got into my stuff!"

Guerro released Brad's neck and left him choking and bent over the counter. Two of the crew had also come behind the counter, as well, and one of them had a black pistol in his hand. Brad began to shake uncontrollably, and he could barely bring himself to type the commands into the keyboard.

"I'm sorry, guys, really! We can replace your shirts, sir!" Brad's eye drifted over to the crumpled piece of paper next to the keyboard. "Hey, wait! Look! Your unit isn't on my list!" He held up the list of delinquent lockers. "Look here, see … your unit isn't on the list!"

Guerro snatched the list from his hand and smoothed it out on the countertop. He ran his finger down the list and stopped it at #38. He turned and held the paper up to Brad's face.

"What's this, puta?" Guerro pointed at the line. "Looks like '38' to me."

"What? No, no, that's 3B. See? Look closely. Ahh, man, I swear that's 3B!" Brad was shaking his head and his gaze kept wandering over to the guy with the pistol in his hand. "I swear; we'll get your shirts back! Now please let me call Tina and find out where she is. She was the one who typed the list ..." A look of realization dawned on his face. "Holy shit! It was her! She was the one who typed up the list! She is the one who handles the auctions and she hires the auction company. If anyone was going to rip you guys off, she's the one that could do it!"

"You sit here," Guerro said, shoving Brad towards a chair. "Where is this woman? I thought you said she was coming here!"

Guerro was looking at the paper more closely, and now that he did, he could see that it was actually a B. He was digesting this when a sports car pulled up next to the office. A quick nod and the guy with the pistol was standing right behind Brad. Richard moved over to one side of the door and waited. Tina strode in and came to an abrupt halt as she took in the scene before her. Richard quietly pushed the door closed and stepped in front of it.

"What's going on here?" Tina's eyes scanned the three men who were still behind the counter. "Brad, what is this all about?"

"We were wondering why our storage unit was sold at the auction the other day. You see, we have never missed a payment and yet you still put our locker up for sale." Guerro came out from behind the counter and approached Tina, who took a step back as he invaded her personal space. "You see, Brad here has been a great deal of help, and now we need to know why our locker was on the list you typed up."

"All of the lockers we sold were units that had been abandoned for three months or longer." Tina tried to sound firm and in control, but there was something about the man in front of her that radiated violence. "We only sold units that were in default. It says we can do that if ..." She fell silent as she saw Brad shaking his head at her.

Guerro glanced over his shoulder at Brad and nodded to him. "You explain it to her."

"They paid with cash checks, like I told you on the phone! Their unit isn't even on the list I gave you!" Brad started talking slowly, but his speech began to speed up. "I wrote down Unit 3B and you typed in Unit 38. Their locker was sold at the auction. I told them we could get their stuff back."

Tina got an uneasy feeling in her stomach as she remembered the unit. "Those weren't all T-shirts in those boxes, were they?"

"Bitch! It ain't none of your business what was in those boxes! You just better tell me where they are!"

"Just a minute, sir! I'm sorry if there was a mistake made, and if there was, we'll find your belongings and make every effort to recover them." Thinking she might throw a little fear the other way, she added, "I'm sure if I called the police, they would be interested in helping you out. There is no need to swear at me!"

Realizing that she had just signed her own death warrant, Brad began to try to save his own ass. He was about to speak when he saw the look on Guerro's face and closed his open mouth. He hung his head and remained quiet.

"Tina, right?" Rich said, stepping from behind her. "You see, we have no desire to speak to anyone but the people who are in possession of our property. Now since you and your friend here are responsible for our loss, we are going to hold you accountable."

Tina had turned when Richard began speaking to her, allowing Guerro to come up behind her. She had just opened her mouth to speak when her head was wrenched back by the hair, and she found herself staring up into Guerro's eyes. A hand clamped down on her throat and she was bent over backwards. Unable to breathe, she began to panic but the eyes staring into hers from inches away took the fight right out of her.

Brad looked at the way Tina was being held and couldn't help staring at how her blouse was stretched tight across her chest. The violence in the air, and the helpless position Tina was in, excited him. So much so, that he eagerly leaned forward to get a better look. The man behind him thought he was trying to be a hero and slammed the pistol into the back of his head, sending him sprawling to the floor. His head hit the concrete and he was out cold.

The disturbance only distracted Guerro for a second. He turned back to see Tina staring at the pistol in Buto's hand. He tightened his grip on her throat, causing her to look back at him with startled eyes. Guerro walked her over to the chair that Brad had occupied only moments before. Kicking it away from the legs of the unconscious man on the floor, Guerro then sat Tina down in the chair by her neck. He nodded at another of the men and Albert, tilting his head at the door to indicate that they should go outside and be lookouts.

Tina had recovered her breath by now and was looking at the telephone on the counter. Her gaze tracked left and she saw Buto looking at her. He gave a very slight shake of his head, telling her she would wind up next to Brad if she reached for the phone.

"How are you going to find out who has my property? Hmm? I need to know where my things are. Now, I look at this list here and I see that you were supposed to sell Unit #3B. Is my stuff up there?" Guerro's foot bumped into Brad's unconscious form, and he looked at Richard. Rich and one of the other men grabbed Brad by the arms and pulled him over to the corner of the wall and counter. They propped him up as the movement caused him to come around.

"Where is this Unit 3B?"

Tina was leaning back away from Guerro's face, which was now inches from hers again. The smell of his cologne and his breath were distracting because, for such a terrifying person, he was surprisingly well groomed, with even white teeth and pleasant breath. She shook her head to get focused and returned his stare. "Flavio, go and find it. Check it out!" One of the muscle-bound men turned and left.

"Look, I'm sorry about the mistake. I only copied the list as Brad gave it to me. We can go look at the other unit. If we sold your unit by mistake, our insurance will cover it. I can even get the auction company to get a hold of the people who bought the unit and return your stuff. I'm sure they'd understand. I realize that you must be upset and I didn't mean to be threatening or anything. I just think you people are going about this the wrong ... urgk!"

Tina had grown more confident the longer she had been able to speak. Guerro didn't want her getting too cocky though, so his hand flashed out and latched on to her throat again.

"Bitch, I don't care what you think! I care about what you know! Now who are these 'auction people' you are talking about? Who are they and do they know who has my stuff? You have their number, right? Where's your phone?" The vise on Tina's neck released and Guerro looked around and spotted her purse on the floor where she dropped it when he had first grabbed her. He walked over and picked it up. After dumping the contents on the counter, he picked up the phone and waved it in her face. "You do a lot of business with these people, right? Is their number in here? What's their name?"

"Jerry. I can call him and explain everything. He can tell us who the buyer was. They have to register and pay a bidders' fee. He can get a hold of the buyers and make ..." She stopped talking as Guerro's palm was held up in her face. He was looking at her phone.

"Unlock it." He shoved the phone into her hand.

Tina slid the unlock symbol on the screen and touched her numeric security code when the keypad came up. Out of habit, she began touching the phone symbol on the app screen. She had just called up the contacts section when the open-palm slap spun her out of the chair, landing her on the floor next to Brad's legs. She looked up at him, but he kept his eyes lowered and his left hand pressed to the bleeding gash on his head. He was using his right hand, which was behind him next to the counter, to hold himself upright.

"I don't think you understand our relationship. So I will explain it to you once. Just nod your head yes or no. You will do exactly what I tell you to do, nothing more and nothing less. If you do not follow my instructions to the fucking letter, I will carve the skin from your face. Do you understand?" Guerro was staring intently into Tina's eyes.

Tina nodded and began to speak again. The slap was so fast that she didn't have time to move her head more than an inch to avoid it. She began to sob as tears rolled down her cheeks. She nodded again, but wisely kept her mouth shut.

"Good, now Jerry is his name. Do you know the address of this Jerry?" Guerro watched as she shook her head no.

"But you have his number." It was a statement. Guerro was looking at the phone. "Ahh, here we go; Jerry ... auctions!" He held the phone up for her to see. "This is him, I take it?" Tina looked at the screen and nodded her head yes.

"Good, you will remain quiet now. Do you understand?" He leaned in over the terrified girl, who was nodding her head vigorously. Guerro pressed the send symbol and put the phone up to his ear. After ringing several times, it went to voicemail. Guerro touched the end symbol to hang up.

"Well, now we have a problem; he's not answering. Is this normal?"

Tina nodded again and then flinched, fearing retaliation for the negative implication of her answer. She wiped the tears from her face and asked, "Can I speak? Please."

"Go ahead." Guerro was still scrolling through the phone's contacts.

"Sometimes he turns it off when he's doing an auction. I can leave him a message and he will call back when he's done."

Guerro thought about this and turned towards her. After considering her statement, he shook his head. "I don't think that will be necessary. In fact, I don't think you can be of any more assistance to me. I am going to ask you a couple of questions though, and you should answer them very truthfully. Do not lie to me because you don't think I will like the truth. Understand?"

Tina went back to nodding her head because her eyes were watering again. A low sob came out and she tried to regain her composure. Guerro gave her a minute to get it together, and then leaned in closely.

"Okay, did you know what was stored in our unit? Have you ever known what was in there?"

"No, never."

"Why did you put that unit up for auction?"

"It was on the list. I swear, I thought that was a 38, not 3B."

"So this was all just one big misunderstanding?"

Tina nodded again, not answering.

"Now, knowing what you do about this auction, how would you go about recovering the boxes which were removed? I need you to think carefully on this because it could save your life."

"I would call Jerry and find out who the winning bidder was. Then I'd just call them and ask them to return the property. We'll reimburse them, sir, I promise." Tina watched as Richard manipulated the security feeds.

"So you don't know who these people are?" Richard said, pointing to the screen.

Tina leaned forward and looked at the image on the screen. Richard was pointing to a middle-aged couple holding up some of the sweatshirts. The female was clearly visible in the frame, but the man was turned partially away and the top of his head was cut off from view by the upper edge of the door opening.

"I don't think I've ever seen them here before, either as customers or as tenants. Maybe Brad has, but I haven't." Tina gestured with her head to Brad, who was still sitting in the corner, but glaring at her now.

"How about it, puto? You seen them before?" Guerro gestured for Brad to get up and take a look at the screen. He rose slowly, only using his right arm, while keeping pressure on his head with his left.

"Yeah, I've seen them at other auctions before. They belong to some church group and usually buy lockers with clothes and stuff for kids down in Mexico." Brad looked around at the others. "They don't have a unit here though, so we don't have any records on them. He used to be some military guy or something. He's always wearing some kind of Marine Corps shirt or Army shirt. She's really quiet, at least around me she is. They bought the trailer that we had up for auction."

"What trailer?" Guerro's attention switched from the screen to Brad.

"They were here to buy a travel trailer that we had up for auction. They won the bid."

"You have the records on this trailer?"

"Umm ... not anymore; we gave them to Jerry. He gives them to the buyers."

"Well, I guess my business is with this Jerry now."

"Yeah, and I'm really sorry too. We didn't mean to mess up your unit. We'll pay for any costs to recover your shirts ..." Brad stopped talking as Buto put a pistol to his head.

"Oh, don't be sorry; you will most definitely pay." Guerro nodded and the pistol went off. The 9mm bullet plowed through Brad's skull and blew out a flap of skin on the right side of his face in front of his ear. There was no dramatic spray of blood, but a solid chunk of gore popped out the hole, bounced off his shoulder, and plopped on the floor. The body collapsed straight down.

The shot startled Tina so much she froze in place. An arm snaked around her neck from the guy standing behind her and pulled her to her feet and off balance. She attempted to grab the arm that was choking her when Guerro stepped up to her and pulled up her blouse. He placed the tip of a folding knife against her side and began to slowly push it in. She could only manage a choked gurgle as the knife broke the skin and slid into her body. She attempted to kick out with her feet, but the feel of the knife sliding back out and pushing through the skin next to her left breast caused her to try to twist away from the cold pain that was shooting up her side. The knife went in four inches and slid back out again.

Tina's left lung began to contract from being perforated, the diaphragm contracting and drawing air in through the wound. Since her airway was 90 percent obstructed by the chokehold she was in, blood and air were pulled in through the hole in her ribs. Another slow push, this one from under the ribs up into the diaphragm, caused it to spasm and her breathing to stop. One last thrust into the chest cavity and the corpse was dropped where it was.

Guerro dropped Tina's phone into his pocket and turned to leave. He looked at Richard tapping keys and lifted an eyebrow in question.

"I'm erasing the last ten days of footage. We're on here today. I don't know where their offsite storage is; it could be anywhere, so I'm gonna erase this, just in case."

"Well, wipe that shit down for fingerprints, just in case." He turned and walked to the drawer labeled "Cash Drawer" and pulled it open. He took all of the bills out and dropped a few ones on the floor. He took a Kleenex and used it to scatter a little change on the floor. He looked up to see Rich grinning at him. "Just in case."

"Yeah."

CHAPTER 5

Jerry Parks was driving his lifted Chevy Silverado back home from his mechanic's shop when his phone rang. He looked at the caller ID and was going to answer it, when he saw the CHP lookout on the overpass ahead of him. The news had shown how they were using spotters with binoculars to catch people talking on their cell phones while driving. He set the phone in his cup holder and let it go to voicemail. After passing the overpass, he saw the CHP motorcycle officer on his BMW off to the side of the freeway. Feeling smug about dodging that bullet, he turned up the radio and began thinking about his trip to the desert the following weekend. He and Bill had done three successful auctions in the past week, and he was looking forward to some desert time.

After pulling into his driveway, he went to the back of his truck and opened the camper shell. He pulled out the box of parts that had been replaced in his front wheel hub and put them on a shelf on the side of his garage, where they would sit until his wife made him get rid of them. He always made the mechanic return any replaced parts because he had once worked in a shop where they had a policy of "paint it black and put it back, or paint it blue and sell it new." He also planned to check under the car as soon as he was done unloading the quad parts he had picked up on the way home.

While unloading the parts, Bill called. Jerry tried to get to the phone before it stopped ringing but was too late. He picked up the phone, looked at his missed calls, and decided to call Tina back first. He selected her number from his missed calls list and hit send.

Guerro was talking on the phone to Alfaro as he was driving back to the stash house when the phone in his pocket began to play music. He pulled it out and glanced at the screen. He immediately slid his finger across the bottom of the screen as he said, "Uno momento, Jefe."

He put Tina's phone to his ear and said, "Hello."

"Hey, this is Jerry. I was calling Tina back. Who's this?"

"Ahh … Hi, Jerry, yes, this is Ben. I am one of Tina's friends. She's doing something downstairs and will be right back up. We are here at South Bay Self-Storage and we had some questions about the auction. You see, one of the units was sold by accident, and we were hoping to get a hold of the person who bought it. It had some valuables in it and we would like to have them returned to us. We would be willing to compensate whoever bought the unit for their time." Guerro flinched and covered the mouthpiece as a horn honked outside the car. "Tina told us that you would be able to put us in touch with these people."

Jerry had heard the car horn in the background, and he had the feeling that the person he was speaking to was in a car as well. This made him feel a little uneasy, as it meant the person he was speaking to was lying to him.

"Well, if that's the case, I think we could contact them. Where did you say Tina was? I'm sorry, but I can only give that information to her."

"I understand completely, sir. She'll be back here in just a few minutes. Is there someplace we could meet you and give you the paperwork? There was a computer error, you see, and my unit was sold by mistake. Tina will be with us."

"Umm, okay. Just come on by my house. The records are here. I'll have to make the phone call though. I'm not comfortable with giving out our client information." Jerry still didn't feel comfortable about this conversation, but if Tina showed up with the guy, and she was willing to take the blame for the mix-up, he was cool with it.

"And where are you located, sir?" Guerro was praying that Tina had never been there. If she had, then Jerry would expect her to know the address.

"I'm at 2131 Enterprise in Lemon Grove."

"Thank you very much, Jerry. I'm thinking we can be there in about forty minutes, if that's okay? We would really like to recover our items before they get scattered to the wind." Guerro had programmed the address into the Suburban's navigation system and was pointing at the screen for Buto to follow the directions.

"Well, I can't help you with that; most of our bidders have pawn or thrift shops, and the stock hits their shelves pretty quickly."

"Oh, I don't think so. Brad here says that it was a husband and wife that purchased the unit." The other cars followed as the Suburban got on the 805 North.

"Ahh, yeah. Well, it's either the Stanfords or Browns. They were the only two couples there, I think. The Browns got the model airplanes, and the Stanfords got some clothes and a camping trailer. I'll call them when Tina gets here and I see her paperwork."

"Very well, we will see you in a bit. Thank you for your time." Guerro hung up the phone and called Richard. He picked up on the second ring.

"Yes, sir?"

"I want you to go back to the house and get on the computer. The name of the couple who bought the unit is S-T-A-N-F-O-R-D or a similar spelling. As you know, they are involved with a church. I want you to Google search the name with the following key words added: Church, Mexico, Donation, Missionary, and any other words you think might link to a newspaper article that would tell us which church they go to." He paused to think. "If we can work this right, we may be able to get our stuff back without a problem."

"Yes, sir," Rich said as he mouthed to Albert to head back to the house. "I will call you the moment I have anything."

"Gracias."

Rich didn't even wait to get to the house. His phone was Internet capable, and he immediately called up his browser and went to Google. The search revealed several articles that mentioned members of the Christ First Church doing missionary work in Mexico. The Stanfords were mentioned in three of the articles and there was even a picture of a group of missionaries and one of just the Stanfords by themselves. Rich sent the information to Guerro's phone and called him back.

"That was fast. I just got what you sent me."

"I was able to look it up on my phone. What do you want me to do? It's Sunday, do you want me to go by the church?"

"That is a good idea. Go ahead, but just sit back and observe if you can. If you see them, follow discretely. I want a home address. Also, look for the trailer from the auction. I saw them loading the boxes into it on the security cameras. If they are using this trailer at the church, then it might be there and we can just get our property back." Guerro looked up as the car switched over to the 94. "We will call you when we are finished with our friend Jerry."

CHAPTER 6

Alicia Pinero walked to the office of the self-storage and pushed the call button. The dumpster had been left in front of her aunt's unit again and she needed to get into it. Her aunt owned a small restaurant and they kept their extra catering utensils in the storage unit. After banging on the door a couple of times, she went over and looked into the window. The shade had been dropped, which was odd, as she'd never seen the shade down during posted business hours.

As she looked through the slice of an opening between the shade and the window frame, she saw a woman's purse spilled all over the counter. Alicia was having a funny feeling when she noticed a reflection on a computer screen. The screen had been turned so that someone in front of the counter could see it. It was angled down slightly, and although the security images were clear, Alicia could make out the reflection of a body on the floor. She immediately looked around, and not seeing anyone, walked quickly back to her car. Once inside with the door locked, she dialed 911 on her cell phone.

Detective James Cooper was sitting in Blue's Sports Bar when his phone played "The Charge of the Light Brigade," telling him that dispatch was calling him. He hit the answer tab on the screen and said, "Hold on a sec," as he made his way outside so he could hear. "Yeah, what's up?"

"Hey Jim, it's Martin. We have a multiple 187 at South Bay Self-Storage. Reporting party is a young Hispanic female who saw a body on the floor through a crack in the blinds. Parnell was the patrol unit that responded. He went in and found two victims in the office. I'm texting you the address right now."

"Don't bother; I know where it is. Did you call Brian yet?" Jim was digging cash out of his wallet so he could cover his tab.

"Cindy's on the phone with him now. You want me to relay anything to him?"

"Yeah, tell him I'm in my work car and have the kit with me if he's away from his. I'll meet him there."

"Copy; I'll show you en route at 1137."

"Thanks." Jim hung up the phone and went inside. His brother and father looked at him and frowned. His brother threw what was left of a potato skin at him as he came back to the table.

"I'm telling you, Dad. He does this shit to get out of watching his team get their butt kicked."

Jim slapped the missile out of the air and flipped off his brother. He tossed the cash on the table and picked up his sweatshirt from the back of his stool.

"You know, some of us do real work that requires skill and intelligence to catch the bad guys. I'm not just a 'Thursday Warrior' who gets regular days off," he said, referring to SWAT's regular Thursday training days. "My sacrifices are many!"

He gestured at the big screen TVs. "You didn't want me to gloat as Green Bay had a fish fry, anyways. I just caught a multiple 187 at a storage unit. I'll see you guys."

"Stay safe, son." Harold Cooper was a retired US Border Patrol agent. He was wearing a Dallas Cowboys jersey. It was almost a ritual that the three Cooper men would be found at their favorite sports bar every Sunday during football season. Their wives usually were with them and tolerated the massive amount of testosterone-fueled horseplay.

"Yeah, you good?" Charlie Cooper was also on the department but was a senior patrol officer with SWAT. He was wearing a Miami Jersey.

"Yeah, Parnell took the call and Brian's on the way." As he walked towards the door, Jim tossed over his shoulder, "Good luck with that game, loser. Miami sucks!" He ducked as a substantially larger piece of potato skin was thrown at him.

Harold looked at his son and then up at the TV, where the score was already 24-3 Green Bay.

"They do suck, you know."

"Yeah, yeah, I don't need it from you too, Pops!" he said as he got up to go clean up his mess after receiving the evil eye from one of the waitresses.

Jim climbed into his "G-ride," the take-home Crown Vic that the department issued him. He got on the road and headed to the scene, which was less than two miles away. He called up his wife's cell phone number in his contacts and hit send.

"Hey, babe." Kelly Cooper was visiting their daughter, who was starting as a freshman at SDSU and was attending cheer camp. The noise of thirty girls practicing in the background made Kelly yell into the phone just to be heard.

"Hey, hon. Just calling to let you know that work called, and I caught a multiple homicide. I don't know when I'll clear the scene. I'll call you when I get free."

"Oohh, I bet that went over well with the guys."

"Actually, aside from my bother throwing some food, it wasn't that bad." Jim hit the Bluetooth button and the phone synced to hands free. He set it in the center console. "Green Bay was kicking butt, anyways."

"Oh great! I'll tell Caroline to be ready for a grumpy husband!"

They both laughed then said their good-byes just as Jim pulled into the driveway to the self-storage lot. Another patrol car had pulled up and was parked at an angle across the driveway. There was enough room to pull around and Jim did so, waving at the cop, who was pulling some crime scene tape out of the trunk of his marked unit.

Just as Jim got out of the car, he saw a news van pull up and marveled at the response time. He turned and saw Parnell talking to a young Hispanic girl a short way up the aisle between units. He walked over to them and introduced himself to the young lady.

"Could I take some things out to my uncle, please? I was here to get some things for my aunt's restaurant, and they have a Quincinera to cater today. I know you need me to stay, but my aunt really needs this stuff," she said, lifting up some stainless steel utensils in her hands.

"Sure thing. Do you need some help?" He gestured towards the front gate. "We'll help you load it up, if it's a lot of stuff. We would prefer it if no vehicles came through the gate until we process the scene."

"Thank you. That would be great."

After seeing to it that she was allowed to deliver the equipment to her uncle, Jim got a detailed statement from Alicia and let her go. While he was doing this, his partner, Brian, rolled up in his personal car and walked through the gate. He listened as Alicia finished giving her statement, and then went to the trunk of Jim's car and got out the initial crime scene kit. He went over and set it next to the door to the office, which had been pried open by Parnell upon arrival.

"Hey, Brian, I only checked for a pulse. The door was locked. I took a photo of it, then I just had to pry the bottom lock. It looks like whoever did it just twisted the lock thingy and closed the door. I went straight to the bodies and checked for a pulse, then came straight back out. Female has multiple stab wounds in the torso. Male has a single GSW to the left temple."

"Suicide?" Brian turned to Parnell with a look of longing in his eyes. If it was a murder suicide, the case would close almost immediately. The investigation would receive a lot less pressure from the brass.

"You're not that lucky. They were both roughed up prior to death from what I could see. Looks like a 211 gone bad; the register was emptied." Parnell walked over and pushed the door open gently. "The wounds on the female are under her clothes. I had to pick up her blouse to see where all the blood came from. The male has grey matter in his lap."

"Okay, thanks." The crestfallen look on Brian's face made Parnell let out a short bark of laughter. "You see any weapons?"

"Nah, but I didn't move anything. Just touched their necks and picked up her shirt to see the wounds. Clearly edged, not GSW." Parnell pantomimed a stabbing motion.

"All right," Brian said as Jim joined them. "Once more into the breach."

They carefully walked into the office, making sure not to step on any blood spatter. There was a large pool of blood next to Brad's head where the head wound had drained once he was slumped over. There was almost no blood on the floor next to Tina's body because her clothing had soaked up most of it. The clothing, however, was drenched from the stab wounds.

Brian began to do his approach photography, snapping the large area pictures as they moved closer to the victims. Both victims showed signs of pre-mortem trauma. Because death had occurred so soon after being slapped, the bruising from being struck did not show on Tina's face. The swelling and redness, however, were still visible. Also, the choke marks on the neck were plain to see.

Jim bent down next to Brad's body and began to look at it. As he was getting ready to move his arm to look underneath it, he saw a Sharpie pen lying under the edge of the counter. He looked over there and saw writing under the overhang created by the cabinet. He noticed it was from the Sharpie and appeared fresh. In fact, he could smell the alcohol scent of the marker when he put his face down near the writing.

"Hey, Bri, look at this." Jim was now lying down with his face right next to the scribbled writing. "It says '#38 Rich bad guy, Jerry danger, Stanfords D-A-N-G.' I think this was meant for us!"

Brian got the camera down next to the writing and took pictures at several different angles. A quick check of Brad's hand showed some fresh ink from the marker. No other obvious clues were visible. He did have several other Sharpies of various colors in his back pocket.

"Okay, let's find out who these people are. If someone is in danger, then we need to get ahead of the game." Jim stood up and looked at the contents of Tina's purse on the counter. A cardholder had several business cards showing her to be the operations manager for Flynn Investments. On a hunch, he looked through some drawers until he found paperwork showing the Self-Store to be part of Flynn Investments, LLC. A look in Brad's wallet had an ID card showing him to be an employee of South Bay Storage.

"Okay, these two worked here." He glanced at the open cash drawer and the small amount of money on the ground. "Are you buying this as a 211, Brian?"

"I sure am ... not! The cash is missing out of the drawer but none is gone from her wallet ..." He bent over and opened Brad's. "Nor is there any missing from his," he said, holding the billfold open so Jim could see the cash inside.

Brian glanced up and saw a Rolodex by the computer, on the desk that was set back from the counter. He walked over to it and started to flip through it. He got to the J's and found a card for Jerry's Auction Service. He pulled the card out and held it up to Jim.

"What do ya think?"

"Better call it now."

CHAPTER 7

Guerro had the two remaining cars stop short of Jerry's house. They pulled into a strip mall parking lot and parked next to each other. They huddled between the cars and planned their next move.

"This *puta* is going to know something is wrong when we show up without the bitch. We have to get close enough to get inside the house before he can make any noise. Julio, I want you to drive by and look the place over, sí? Drive past and then let us know what is going on ... What are you doing?" Guerro was looking at Flavio, who had a mapping app open on his phone. He had a satellite view of a house showing on the screen.

"This is the house," Flavio said, hovering his finger over the picture, being careful not to touch the screen. "It will be on the right as you drive by from here."

"Very good," Guerro said with an appreciative nod. "Okay, Buto, we need to find out where these Stanfords are, so as soon as we get into the house, we need to look for an office, but ..." He held up a finger. "If they just put the records into storage, it may be in the garage or something."

Julio took off in his white Ford Ranger. They discussed who would search where for another three minutes until he came back. He pulled into the lot and stayed in the driver's seat.

"There is a white 4x4 truck in the garage, which is open. There is a man lying under the truck. He has the music up very loud, Señor Guerro. We could walk right up on him and he would never hear us."

"Julio, I want you and Buto to approach him. Get as close as you can. We will park on the street, but will be ten seconds behind you." He turned to Buto. "Take him as quietly as you can, my friend, but take him, and quickly." The immense man nodded.

They piled back into the vehicles with Julio driving Buto in the truck. Everyone else climbed in the Yukon and began pulling out various makes and models of pistols. After a few clicks and clacks, the car was silent. They watched as the white pickup pulled into the driveway and Julio and Buto got out. They could see a person standing by the front of the truck. It was on such big tires and had such a tall lift, that they could clearly see his legs from the other side.

When Buto rounded the back of the white truck, he saw that Jerry was standing and talking on the phone. The panicked look on his face was all Buto needed to see. He drew his pistol and rushed to the garage.

As soon as Jerry hung up the phone with the strange guy on the other end, he looked at the missed call log, which reminded him that Bill had called. Recalling the creepy feeling he had, he used the phone's redial function and called his pal back.

"Hey, sorry I missed your call. I was under my truck. Did Tina call you about a mix-up with one of the lockers we sold on Friday?"

"Nope, not yet. What did she say happened?"

"She didn't. I got a missed call from her, and when I called back, some guy answered it. He said that there was a computer error and their unit was sold by mistake. He said Brad ID'd a married couple. The only two couples who won lockers were the guy with the model airplanes ... Browns, right? And the Stanfords. I hope it's the Stanfords; they're good folks and will probably return the stuff no problem. It was just clothes and stuff."

"Yeah, they won't put up too much of a fuss. Shit, they're so Christian they might just give it back free!" Bill was fond of the couple, who were always going to the auctions just to buy stuff for underprivileged kids. "They only paid like $130 ..."

"One hundred forty but, yeah, you're right. They'll be easy. That guy who got the airplanes was happy as a pig in shit with his locker. He was crowing like a rooster about how cool all that stuff was, once he got inside." He leaned back against his truck. "But I got the heebie-jeebies from the guy I talked to. I can't put my finger on it, but I got the feeling he was lying to me or something. Anyway, he and Tina are coming by and we're gonna get it all straightened out."

"Coming by where?" Bill asked with a little alarm in his voice.

"Here, man. He said they wanted to get their stuff back right away."

"Dude! Really! You told him to meet you at your house? When did the creepy feeling set in? After you talked to him?" Bill was shaking his head. "Why didn't you tell him you'd meet him down at South Bay?"

"Shit, it never came up. He just offered to come to me with Tina."

"Okay; well, you want me to come over? The game is almost over."

"Nah, it's cool. I mean, the guy didn't sound mad or anything. He didn't cuss me out or make threats. I'll just see what Tina has to say and make the call. But I'm not making it if she isn't cool with it."

"Well, call her back now. She's on her way over, right? Ask her what's up before she gets there." Bill had a feeling that something wasn't right either. He'd known Tina for almost five years and in that time he'd never known anyone but her to answer her phone.

"Yeah, okay. Maybe I'll do that. If she's alone in her car she can tell me if the guy is a weirdo."

"No *maybe*. Do it!"

"Okay, okay. I'll call right now. You gonna be ready for the desert?" Bill was Jerry's riding partner.

"Yeah, just came back from Alba. I picked up the LED light bar for the Rhino. It'll look badass!" Bill had the high output lights in his hand. "That's what I was calling you about—to see if you wanted to come over and wrench with me."

"I'll see how long this takes and I'll call ya back. I still want to check out this hub before I four wheel it."

"Okay, call me back. And call Tina!"

"All right, sheesh!" Jerry disconnected and tried Tina's phone. It went to voicemail. *She must be driving,* he thought and crawled back under the truck.

He was still there a few minutes later when the phone rang again. He looked at the caller ID, but it was a blocked private number. He considered ignoring it but then figured it might be this guy about the locker. He tapped the answer tab and pushed himself partway out from under the truck. He put the phone to his ear while he was still lying on his back.

"Hello."

"Hi, is this Jerry?"

"It sure is. May I ask who's calling?" It wasn't the same voice as the guy who answered Tina's phone.

"Jerry, my name is Detective Brian Doudt of the Chula Vista Police. I'm calling in regards to South Bay Self-Storage."

"Ahh, shit. Hey, look, I already talked to the guy whose unit we sold and he and Tina are on the way over here right now." He stood up and leaned against his truck. "We only sold the units that were on the list we were given. Did they file a police report?" Jerry turned as a white Ford Ranger pulled into his driveway. "In fact, I think they just showed up."

"Jerry, listen very carefully; I am at a crime scene here at South Bay Self-Storage. Tina Cincero is dead and so is Brad. If you do not recognize the people who just arrived at your location, get somewhere safe! Where are you?" Brian's voice had gone up in volume as he gestured frantically at Jim. He put the phone on speaker and shoved Jim out the door and towards the Crown Vic.

"Ahh, shit! I'm at home—2131 Enterprise in Lemon Grove! There's two guys getting out of a white Ford Ranger. The guy on the phone said his name was Ben before when he called me!" Jerry started scrambling backwards and Buto could see the look of panic in his eyes as he rounded the back of the Chevy. Jerry turned and stumbled towards the door to his kitchen just as he heard a loud *bang* and felt a searing pain in his side. "Fuck! They just shot me! Help! There are two of them!"

Jerry stumbled through the door as another shot went off, missing him by inches. He slammed the door and twisted the button lock. Realizing that the flimsy hollow-core door wasn't going to slow down his pursuers for long, he ran through the house to his bedroom. He slammed this one closed as well, but it was the same type as the interior garage door and wouldn't hold anyone for any appreciable amount of time. Especially the WWF-looking bubba who had just shot him.

"Fuck! They're here. I'm holed up in my bedroom, but the door isn't going to last long!"

The sound of the garage door being kicked to splinters could be heard clearly from down the hall. Jerry was pulling down a shoebox from the top shelf of his closet. He pulled out a Smith & Wesson .357 revolver with a four-inch barrel. He ripped it out of the nylon holster he kept it in and tore open the box of .38 hollow points he kept in the shoebox with the gun. He had been holding his phone against his ear with his shoulder while he opened the box, but the activity caused him to drop it. He also dropped the box of shells, trying to get into it. He came up with three.

Jerry dropped down to his knees on the floor and began picking up the cartridges that had fallen into and between his shoes. As soon as he had six in his hand, he flipped open the cylinder to the revolver, causing him to drop two of the shells again, and began loading them. With four in the chambers, he was hunching forward to get some more when he heard a loud crash from what sounded like his dining room. After finally getting the pistol loaded, he scooped up some more shells, stuffed them in his pocket, and fumbled the phone up to his ear again.

"Hello! I'm in my bedroom and I have my gun! Where are you guys?" Jerry could hear the siren in the background of the phone.

"We just left the self-storage, but we called the sheriff's department and they will be there any minute. Can you get somewhere safe?" Brian was yelling into the phone over the siren, which was blaring.

Jim had the Crown Vic over 100 MPH, weaving through the light Sunday traffic. "If you can defend yourself, great, but put the gun away when the deputies get there, okay? I'm going to tell them you are armed; I'm also calling for an ambulance. How bad are you shot?" Brian met Jim's eyes and nodded. Jim had been on the radio, alerting dispatch to what was happening while Brian tried to maintain an open line to Jerry. He continued to repeat Brian's instructions to the dispatcher.

"I ... um ... oh shit!" Jerry looked down to see a red stain on the front of his shirt. He had been lucky in that Buto had standard ball ammunition in his pistol. The round-nose bullet had punched through his side, making a clean entry and exit wound. The fact that the damage was minimal was lost on Jerry, who immediately felt nauseated after seeing his own blood. "Oh God! I'm gonna be sick!" The statement was immediately followed by the sound of retching.

Brian glanced at Jim and they exchanged worried looks. They were both relieved when Jerry's voice came back over the phone.

"Oh shit! You know, it really doesn't hurt that bad. It just looks really scary."

Jerry staggered up, hobbled into his bathroom, and again closed and locked the door. "I'm in my bathroom now. I can hear them going through stuff in my house. That Ben guy said he was looking for the records from our auction on Friday. He said we sold his locker by mistake. He wanted to know who bought it. That's what he said he was coming here for." Jerry slid down into his tub. "He wanted to know the names and addresses of the couple that bought his locker."

"Jerry, was the name of the people *Stanford*? Brad left a note saying 'Stanford' and then D-A-N-G. We think he was writing 'Danger.' Could that be what he was talking about?" Brian held on to the Jesus handle as the car drifted through an interchange.

"Oh, it for sure was. We only had two couples win lockers. One was a guy named Brown and his wife. They bought unit #27. The Stanfords bought unit #38 and the travel trailer that was for sale. It wasn't a unit—"

The sound of multiple gunshots cut off the rest of his sentence.

"Jerry!" Brian was yelling into the phone, but there was no response. "Where the fuck are those SO units?"

"Central, David Two, any word on sheriff's ETA at the victim's location. We have more shots fired at that location." Jim was speaking calmly into the microphone as he one handed the car around the corner at the bottom of the off ramp.

"David Two, standby." They waited for almost a minute. "SO shows they are 97 at the scene."

They made the final turn onto Enterprise a minute later. They could see a sheriff's patrol car angled in front of a house up ahead on the right. They could also see another patrol car about four blocks away, heading towards them. They swerved around the marked unit and slid to a stop. Jim stopped the car so Brian could get out of his door while using the patrol car for cover. They both met at the trunk, which Brian had popped with the interior release as they were coming to a stop. They both threw Kevlar vests over their torsos. Jim had to hike his Green Bay jersey up over his concealment holster so he would be able to get to his pistol, then he picked up his M4 Carbine. He inserted a full magazine, pulled the charging handle to the rear, and let it return before tapping the forward assist.

Brian threw his vest on and pulled out his Bennelli M2 shotgun. His vest had special shotgun shell holders attached to it, containing a variety of ammunition. He stroked the operating lever back and pulled an additional buckshot round from one of the holders. He fed the extra round through the action and into the tubular magazine.

They both looked at the front of the house as the second sheriff's car stopped about twenty yards on the other side of the home. The deputy saw the two detectives with the long guns out and grabbed his Remington 870 twelve-gauge shotgun. As he was taking a cover position on the far side of his car, he saw the body of the other patrol deputy lying in the driveway.

"Eleven ninety-nine; officer down! Officer down! Sixteen Paul one is down!"

Jim and Brian hadn't seen the body, but as soon as they heard the call, they both rushed to the rear of the Ranger.

"Central, twenty-nine this plate: California 6-Nora-1-2-7-3-9." Jim had popped up to look at the interior of the truck. It was clean; the only thing out of the ordinary was the open glove box. There was a tool bag in the bed of the truck. "We are at 2131 Enterprise in Lemon Grove with a sheriff's unit. We have shots fired and an officer down. We also have at least one civilian inside the structure who is also shot. We know there to be two suspects that arrived in the vehicle with the aforementioned plate."

"David Two, Central copies all. Lincoln Two is en route to your twenty. SO reports receiving an 11-99 and is making a SWAT callout."

Just as the transmission finished, they heard a groan from the other side of the truck.

"Shit! He's still alive! Let's go! Cover me!" Brian was around the car first, moving like a running back. Jim rolled out from the front of his Crown Vic and put the holo sight of his carbine on the front door. He began panning the rifle back and forth to cover the front door and garage.

Brian let the shotgun fall and hang from its sling. Then he scooped up the downed officer, whose uniform shirt looked like a bear had mauled it. He picked him up under the arms and carried him back around behind his patrol car, having to weave between the truck and the unit to get behind some decent cover. The deputy was lucky in that his vest had stopped eight of the nine bullets that had struck him. He was unlucky in that the ninth had hit him on the inside of his left arm and severed the left brachial artery.

Just as they were checking out their wounded comrade, they heard a scream and two shots.

"Ahh, shit! That sounded like the next street over!" Jim had to yell at the end as two more black-and-whites roared up. The deputies un-assed their units and got out their long guns. "Central, we have more shots fired!"

"We've got at least one shooter still active in there," Jim said, bringing the new arrivals up to speed while Brian assessed the wounded deputy. "We just heard two more shots, but I think it was the backyard. We need to get a perimeter set up before this guy gets mobile."

"Fucking great timing! We were right in the middle of shift change. Benson here is our cover/overlap unit," one of the new deputies said, gesturing to the man lying at his feet. "Any idea how many suspects?"

"We were on the phone with the victim, who is still inside as far as we know. He said that two men got out of this white Ford pickup and started shooting at him." Jim was watching the front of the house for movement. "We're working a double homicide out of South Bay; one of the victims left us the name of the victim who lives here."

"National City or Chula Vista?"

"Chula Vista PD," Jim said as another patrol car came flying up from the opposite side. It was followed moments later by two CHP officers, then three SDPD cars. A sergeant from the sheriff's department arrived and began to coordinate a perimeter. Over the next six minutes, thirty-seven law enforcement officers, including two helicopters, converged on the scene. All of the major news networks had vans as close as they could get them, and three more news copters were circling above the low-flying police choppers.

The sheriff's SEB unit (SWAT) arrived and they tried to contact anyone in the house. Receiving no response, and in light of Jim telling them that they had a wounded innocent victim inside, they made entry. Jerry was found dead in the bathtub with multiple gunshot wounds to the head and torso. A search of the neighborhood revealed that a female neighbor to the south, who shared the rear fence with Jerry, had been gunned down in her kitchen with two shots to the face.

Brian was briefing a circle of brass that included his lieutenant, an SDSO captain, two sergeants, and a deputy chief from SDPD. Jim was with the crime scene crew when his dispatch called him.

"David Two."

"David Two, go ahead."

"The twenty-nine on that plate comes back as registered to a Julio Paez, 615 East Street, Apartment 212, Chula Vista. The plate is twenty-nine, with no wants or warrants associated with vehicle or registered owner." Jim wondered about that but then probably figured it for stolen, and the owner just didn't know it yet.

"David Two copies." Jim walked over to the group of officers just as they were telling the sheriff's public relations officer what to release. He pulled Brian aside and was filling him in on the truck when a shout caught their attention.

"Hey Doudt!" One of the crime scene techs was jogging towards them from the front of the house. He was waving a piece of paper in his hand. He stopped in front of the two officers and held it up in triumph. "You said you were looking for anything with the name 'Stanford' on it. Well, here's a bidder registration form from earlier this year. Address is in East Lake. He handed it over to Jim, who wrote down the address and handed it back.

"Okay, we have to check this out," Brian said as he rushed over to tell their lieutenant. Jim hopped in the driver's seat again and pulled up next to his boss.

"The truck is registered down on East Street, Lieutenant. We were going to go down there and see if this guy had any idea his truck was stolen."

"How do you know it's not the suspect's truck?"

"Comes back twenty-nine; no wants or warrants for both the truck and the RO. I doubt someone with that clean of a record is involved in this shit, but we'll be careful just in case."

Brian shook his head at the chaos that had enveloped the neighborhood. Emergency vehicles were parked for blocks, the SWAT team was conducting a house-to-house search, and both the sheriff's helicopter and several news birds were circling the area. "We'll do a drive-by and check it out. If anything looks odd, we'll call before knocking."

"You guys did not fire your weapons here, correct? I can't let you go if you did." Emmerson stared at them as they both shook their heads no. "All right, let me know what's going on."

They slowly wove their car out of the mess and headed back down to Chula Vista. Jim called his wife to let her know everything was all right but got her voicemail. Brian did the same. Once that was done, the conversation went back to the case.

"We need to sort out this whole storage thing," Brian said, looking at his notes. "Someone wants whatever was in that locker pretty fuckin' badly."

"Gee, ya think?" Jim sent a sideways glance at his partner. "We're up to four dead bodies. All of whom appear innocent, although I think that Brad guy was a creeper. I know we got a complaint about him somewhere. I don't think it's related to this. Probably drugs. If that storage unit was full of drugs and the cartel is involved, that would explain the level of violence."

"I'm gonna have them send a K9 unit over and see if the dog hits on the unit. If he does, then we'll swab it for type." Brian started typing on the unit's VDT keyboard. "And I really want to find these Stanfords and see what this is all about. Let's swing by this address after we visit old Mister Julio here."

"Okay."

They were outside the apartment complex ten minutes later. A slow drive-by showed kids playing in the driveway and on the front grassy area. Several adults were sitting in folding chairs under an umbrella and patio set, chatting and watching the kids burn calories.

"It looks pretty peaceful; I'm going to call us in for the contact." Brian typed a message to the dispatch center as Jim drove the car around the block and pulled into the parking area behind the apartments. This area also looked quiet, so they got out of their car and walked through to the front side of the building, looking at apartment numbers along the way.

"Up there," Jim said, pointing up to a door.

One of the women sitting in a chair under a patio umbrella noticed and stood up. "Can I help you?" The woman had a pretty Latina face that was filling out. "That is my house."

"Hi, ma'am. I'm Detective Cooper and this is Detective Doudt. We are looking for Julio Paez. Is he here?" Jim and Brian both flashed their badges.

"He had to go to work early today. He works construction, and they called him in for overtime. I'm his wife, Luna. Is everything okay?" The look of concern on her innocent face was enough to get them both thinking that the truck probably was stolen.

"Well, we think his truck may have been stolen and used in a crime. Do you have any way to contact him to check?" Jim was pulling out one of his business cards and writing his personal cell number on the back.

"Sí, I will call him. I hope he didn't leave his phone in the truck." She walked back over to the table and picked up a cell phone. A little girl with some sort of chocolate residue ring around her mouth ran up to Luna's leg and grabbed onto it, shooting a curious look at the two detectives.

"Aaaiiee, mija!" Luna began chastising the child in rapid-fire Spanish as the little girl rubbed her grimy face against her mother's leg. Luna limped back over to the two men with the child still stuck firmly to her leg. She was attempting to wipe the uncooperative child's face with one hand while holding the phone to her ear with another. She spoke into the phone for a brief moment in Spanish then clicked it closed as she made it back over to them, shaking her head.

"He is not answering. That's not unusual though when he is working. I left him a message to call me." She bent over and finished the clean-up job on the little girl's face and sent her off with a playful swat to the fanny. "You said his truck may be stolen? He has a white one he uses to carry his tools in."

Brian recalled seeing some tools in the bed when he had checked it in Lemon Grove. "I saw some tools in the bed of the truck at the scene. Do you know where he is working?"

"Well, he works at different job sites, but I've visited him at the new Convention Center building down by the Bay. He does electrical and drywall down there." Another small child, this one a slightly older boy, ran up to her and tugged on her blouse. "Go! Go! I'm busy. Go on!" she said, shooing him away. She took the card Jim offered her and put it in her pocket. "I will have him call right away as soon as I get a hold of him."

"Thank you very much, Mrs. Paez," they both said and began walking back through the complex to their car.

They had just come out from between the buildings and were walking between two cars when they noticed a black Suburban pulling into the driveway, followed by a blue SUV of some sort. Both cars were travelling a little fast and braked abruptly. Three doors on the Yukon swung open and three men stepped out. They noticed the two men in front of them and everybody's eyes locked onto each other.

CHAPTER 8

Buto had seen the look of panic on Jerry's face as he walked up the driveway. As soon as he realized that he was trying to escape into the house, he fired at him. The hit caused the man to stumble to the side, making Buto miss his follow-up shot. The door slammed shut and the lock clicked just as Buto got to it.

Julio had peeled off and gone to the front door. He saw a shadow flash by the window and could hear the person yelling into a cell phone. Realizing that stealth was no longer an option and that the police were definitely on the way, if not from whoever Jerry was talking to, then definitely from the sound of Buto's gunshot, Julio kicked in the front door.

Buto had already kicked the garage door off its hinges and was stomping through the archway from the kitchen. They both turned and were heading towards the back of the house when Guerro came through the front door. He looked at the mess and raised an eyebrow at Buto.

"He knew, Jefe; he took off as soon as he saw us. He was on the phone with someone and the policia are on their way for sure now." Buto shrugged as if this was just the way of life. "I think he might be responsible for the boxes being gone; he was afraid."

Guerro motioned for the rest of the men to get on with their search and gestured Buto down the hall. After turning a corner, they came to a locked door. They could hear panicked talking and rustling noises. Then another door slammed.

Julio made a circling motion with his finger and went out the back door. He walked to the bedroom window and peered in. He noticed the closed door to what he assumed was the bathroom and went over to that window. This window was smaller but open. He moved a patio chair underneath it and stood on it to look in. He saw the guy from the garage sitting in the bathtub talking on his cell phone.

Julio stuck his pistol through the window and opened fire. Jerry saw the arm coming through the window and started shooting at it and the wall below it. Both men hit their targets.

Jerry's .38 special +P jacketed hollow points punched right through the drywall and hit Julio in the gut twice out of the five shots he fired, knocking him off the chair and on his ass. Julio fired his Glock five times as well. The .40-caliber hollow points struck Jerry three times, once in the cheek and twice in the chest. The other two bullets went through the wall and narrowly missed Buto and Guerro, who were still standing in the hall outside the master bedroom. They both fired several rounds each through the wall, most of them striking what was now Jerry's corpse.

"Guerro!" Flavio yelled from the front room. "I have the papers!"

Guerro came around the corner from the hall and yelled, "Let's go!"

Flavio went out the front door first and pulled up short as a young deputy was just coming around the front of his patrol car. Buto almost collided with his back. Guerro had a little more space and was able to step to the right side of his two companions and see what had caused them to stop. A young sheriff's deputy was clawing at the pistol holstered on his right hip. Guerro's pistol was already in his hand, and he calmly raised it and pulled the trigger.

A pistol in the hand wins a quick-draw contest every time. Guerro fired three rounds, all of them striking the deputy in the chest. Buto stepped to the left side of Flavio and fired six more times, driving the young officer back until he collapsed. The engagement happened at a range of eight feet. All three men calmly walked past the downed officer and headed to the Suburban.

"Shit! Where's Julio?" Flavio asked as they passed the Ford on the way to the Yukon. "He never came back out from the backyard!"

Buto and Guerro exchanged glances.

"He's down; the vato had a gun and they shot each other up!" Guerro gestured for them to get in the car. "Let's go!"

They were turning the corner at the end of the block when Julio staggered out the front door with his hand pressed to his stomach. He saw the SUV roll out of sight and then looked at his truck, which was blocked in the driveway by the patrol car. The sound of approaching sirens told him he'd never get out of there in his own truck so he staggered back into the house.

He made it into the kitchen and dialed Guerro's number as he heard screeching tires out front. He staggered over to the kitchen table and sat down. Guerro picked up on the second ring.

"You fuckers left me!" he wheezed into the phone. "My fucking truck is blocked in!"

"Shit! Sorry, ese! Can you make it out the back? We thought you were dead!" Guerro had Flavio pull over. "We're just two blocks away. Can you get here on foot?"

"Are you going to wait? I'm shot bad, man. I can't run." Julio got to his feet and went out the sliding glass patio door and looked at the fence. "I'm going over the back fence. I'll be one block over going to the south, got it? Back towards the freeway!"

"We'll come get you in one minute; after that we rolling.'" Guerro hung up and had Flavio drive around the block. "He'll be coming out on this street. Watch for him. He says he's shot bad."

"We should leave him, Jefe. He got himself shot!" Buto was not known for his compassion or team spirit.

"No, my friend; too much of a chance he will talk." Guerro pointed to his left. "There he is."

Julio had scaled the rear fence between Jerry's house and his neighbor. After falling flat on his face in the backyard on top of two piles of semi-dried dog poop, he pushed himself unsteadily to his feet and stumbled in the back door of the house. A woman was just walking into the kitchen from the living room to see what her two small dogs were barking about. She saw Julio, who was covered in blood and dog feces, and screamed.

Julio didn't hesitate. He fired two shots right into her face and continued out the front door, kicking at the two frightened Shih Tzus along the way. He left a bloody streak down the hallway from leaning against the wall. He nearly fell trying to walk down the front porch steps but made it out to the street just as the Suburban pulled up.

Buto pushed open the rear door and pulled him into the seat as Flavio kept the car rolling. They went to the end of the block and turned right, leaving the neighborhood at a normal speed. They were passed by a dozen police cars, all heading in the opposite direction. They slowed and pulled over for each one, then calmly headed back to the freeway.

"I have to get to my house, man!" Julio said through gritted teeth. "My fuckin' truck is back there! They'll be at my house in no time!"

"Sí, compadre, we will take you to your house. You must gather your wife and kids. We will take you across the border right away. You will stay at the Los Rocas house." Guerro was referring to the large house that was kept on the beach for the cartel's guests. "You will be well taken care of. Can you hold on?"

Julio looked down at his hand pressed over his bloody shirt. He lifted it away and studied the wounds. The two bullets had been slowed by the wall they passed through. One of them had collected debris in the hollow cavity at the front of the bullet and had passed right through his side, just nicking his intestine along the way. The other round had expanded inside his stomach and slammed up against the inside surface of a rib. Although both wounds were painful, neither one was debilitating. He was, however, hemorrhaging internally.

Guerro called another team of men, who met them at the stash house. They took Julio in and patched him up as best they could. It took them thirty minutes to get the bleeding under control before they drove over to his apartment, followed by the extra men in the blue GMC Acadian.

CHAPTER 9

Sheila Stanford was helping clean up after the last services at the church. She and the pastor's wife, Ellen, were washing the coffee service and silverware, drying everything and putting it all away. The two women chatted about their men and the latest church gossip, although Sheila wasn't much into that. They began setting up for a Boy Scout banquet that was going to be held there later that night.

Tom left with Doug, another member of the congregation, right after the services ended to take the trailer to Doug's house. Although he hadn't intended to work on the trailer until the following weekend, Doug mentioned that he would be able to fix the trim on the Stanford's trailer early because another client had canceled their appointment.

Tom and Doug hooked up the travel trailer to Tom's truck and towed it over to Doug's yard. As soon as it was unhooked, Doug gave Tom a new door-lock kit in a box and got some tools to fix the trim on the driver's side corner of the roof. The previous owner had bumped it into an overhang and torn off a piece of the molding.

Tom had the old lock out in a jiffy and was installing the new one when Sheila called; she was going to the Costco and asked if he needed anything. After giving her his wish list, he turned back to repairing his new trailer.

They didn't finish until 4:30. But when they did, the exterior of the trailer looked almost new. Tom tried the door lock one last time then pocketed the keys. He was going to leave the trailer in Doug's yard and work on it during the week. Doug's fee for this was dibs on one of the beds while they were down in Mexico doing their missionary work.

After saying goodbye, Tom headed back over to the church. He pulled into the lot and got out of the truck. He noticed a young man looking through the window into the banquet room. He was walking up to the young man when a slamming door in the parking lot caused the boy to look around.

"Can I help you? Are you here for the Boy Scout banquet tonight?" The young man looked to be seventeen or eighteen at the most.

"Oh, uh—yeah!" Richard turned to see the man from the photograph on his phone standing right in front of him. He had looked all around the church complex for a travel trailer but hadn't seen one. He had then started looking around for the Stanfords. The six-foot-plus tall man with broad shoulders standing in front of him was not what he expected. "We have some stuff to deliver. The guys will be along in a few minutes. I just got here early."

"Well, the closest door to the stage is that one over there. You just let me know if you need anything." Tom smiled as he gestured at the door. He walked inside to see his wife taping paper tablecloths to the folding tables, which had been set up throughout the room. A pile of groceries and other goods from Costco sat by the door.

"Hey, honey. We took Ellen's car to Costco. Could you please put that stuff in your truck?"

Rich went back out to the parking lot and met Albert. It was him slamming the car door that had warned Richard of Tom's approach. They both climbed back into Albert's car and waited.

"Guy thinks we're here for some Boy Scout meeting. The wife is inside the hall there." Rich pointed to the building. "She's working on setting stuff up. I'm going to call Guerro."

He took out his phone and dialed the number. As soon as it was picked up on the other end, he said, "We found 'em."

"Stay with them. We are on our way down now. We are stopping by the house for a first-aid kit, then we're going to Julio's to get his family headed south, then we will be there. We have to go through these boxes for the home address still. Did you find the trailer?"

"No, and I looked all over the property."

"Okay; we'll be there in about half an hour. Do not lose them!"

"Okay, you got it," Rich said as he watched Tom come out the door, carrying an armful of groceries and headed for his truck. Both he and Albert stared at the man, who looked at them right back. After loading the box into his truck, he paused to again look at the two men sitting in the Nissan. The one he had spoken to looked like a nice enough kid, but the Hispanic male sitting next to him sure didn't look like a Boy Scout. He committed the license plate to memory and went back inside.

"Babe, I have to run home real quick and get the big coffee filters I picked up but forgot to bring. I'll be back in just a minute." Sheila was passing him on the way out. She had some milk and other cold items in her arms. "I'll just put this stuff in the fridge and then you don't have to worry about making a trip home right away."

"Are you sure, hon? I can just do all this at once."

"No; Ellen is going to need you to use those Gyrine muscles to move some more stuff around." With that, she shoved open the door and began striding out to her Audi. She put the groceries in the passenger side foot well, and then climbed into the driver's seat. The S5 sport sedan purred to life, and she drove rather quickly out of the lot.

Richard had to make a command decision and told Albert to chase after her.

"What about the guy?" he asked.

"Dude, if she leads us to the house and we can find the trailer or money without having to deal with him, then we've got it made. Besides, we know where he is and Guerro will be here soon. If she leads us to the house and we find the money, we can call him and have them meet us there."

"Okay, it's your call." Albert put the car in drive and peeled out trying to get out of the lot in time to not lose sight of the receding Audi.

Tom was halfway back out to his truck with more groceries when he noticed the Altima speeding out of the lot. He got the first twinges of something not being right. He put the items in his truck and went back inside.

"Hey, did you notice the two guys in the Nissan Altima?" he asked Ellen while he picked up the last load of stuff for his truck. "Young, good-looking white kid and a 'wanna-be' tough-looking Hispanic kid?"

"Nope, didn't see anyone in a car, but there was a young man in a dark shirt and khaki pants wandering around earlier."

"Yeah, that's him." Tom paused in the doorway. "He just took off in a blue Altima pretty quick. If I didn't know better, I'd say they were following Sheila."

"Well, do you?" Ellen paused from setting up the tables.

"Huh?" Tom gave her a baffled look.

"Do you know better—that they're not following her?" Ellen was now standing with her hands on her hips and a Sunday school teacher expression on her face.

Tom paused in thought for a second.

"You know, I really don't." He set the groceries on the floor and pulled out his cell phone. "The kid I talked to said he was meeting the other kids here for the banquet. But now that you mention it, I was carrying the groceries out and they both just stared at me. I don't think any of John's boys would see that and not offer to help."

"She's going to be back in a few minutes. Call her and tell her to look for the car on the way back."

"I'm just going to do that," Tom said, mimicking his tone from earlier. He hit the speed dial for his wife.

"Hi, hon, what's up?"

"Hey, babe; did you notice a blue Altima behind you on the way home just now?"

"No, nothing that jumped out at me. Why?"

"Ahh, I just saw a car follow you out of the lot, and it looked like they were trying to catch up with you." Tom started to relax a little. "There were two guys and they gave me a funny feeling."

"Didn't notice them. Blue Altima, you said? I just pulled into the garage, and I don't see any blue cars on the street." Sheila panned her head around to look out the open garage door. "Nope, don't see one."

"Okay. Probably nothing, but be careful."

"K, babe; I'll see you in a few minutes." Sheila climbed out of her car and left the door open as she ran around to the passenger side and grabbed the groceries. She just planned on running into the house, putting the refrigerated items away, and grabbing the items she needed.

Albert pulled his car up across the street from the Stanfords' house. He'd had a hard time keeping up with the woman, who was obviously a NASCAR fan. He had been unable to keep up and was delayed by red lights twice. He was lucky that the house was so close to the church because he would not have been able to tail her for any appreciable distance. In order to keep up, he would have had to swerve around slower traffic and run lights to maintain a visual.

"Shit! There it is. Look—the boxes are right there!" Albert was pointing excitedly at the open garage door. "There's our boxes right there!"

"I'm calling Guerro." Richard was scrolling through his contacts.

"Look, man; alarm panel near the inside door." Albert was staring closely at the interior of the garage. "If she leaves and we have to break in, we won't have time to load everything up before the cops get here."

"Fuck, you're right!" Then into the phone. "No, sorry; I was talking to Albert. We have the boxes in sight! They are in their garage just sitting there, but they have an alarm panel. If she leaves and sets the alarm, we'll never get all the boxes out before the cops come."

"Look, we're almost at Julio's. Don't let that shit out of your sight! I don't care if you have to kill that bitch! Do not let her leave. And try to do that shit quiet, man! I'm tired of loud fuck ups today, got it? But get control of that shit!"

"Okay, but Albert's car won't hold all the boxes, even just the ones with the money. So you'll have to bring the SUVs here quick." Rich was waving Albert out of the car.

"What's the address?"

It took Richard a second to figure it out and describe the house.

"Okay, we're on our way!"

Richard disconnected and dropped his phone in his pocket. He took out his pistol and pulled the slide to the rear to chamber a round. He then tucked it into the small of his back as he walked around the front of the car. Albert pulled his out from between the front seats and carried it in his hand as they started across the street.

CHAPTER 10

There is something in the way men who are accustomed to violence carry themselves that is instantly recognizable to other men of the same breed. Flavio, Buto, and Guerro had just stepped out of the Suburban when they saw the two men step out between the buildings. Julio had opened his door but had still not shifted his tender torso around to swing his legs out. All five men looked into each other's eyes and instinctively knew that they faced an opponent.

The two police officers were at a slight disadvantage as they tried to yell "police" while drawing their weapons. The three cartel thugs had no qualms or hesitation in pulling out their guns and opening fire.

Brian realized that with their vests and heavy artillery in the trunk of their car, they were going to be at an extreme disadvantage. He took off like a shot, sprinting across the driveway towards the Crown Vic. He hadn't even taken two steps when he heard gunfire behind him. Brian twisted his body and fired two shots towards the large man who was shooting at him. Both shots missed and hit the car behind him. He noticed more men drawing guns from the second vehicle, and he sent two more rounds their way. Again, both rounds missed the men but hit their vehicle. *Great, Doudt, you sure showed those cars what's up!* Brian thought as he felt a burning in his side.

Jim drew his pistol and took a step back so that he was between the two parked cars they were next to. He hoped that by spreading out, they would be able to provide a base of fire that would keep them from being out flanked, even though he was uncomfortable being too far away from his partner.

Buto had immediately drawn his 9mm and started shooting, first at Brian as he sprinted across the driveway, and after missing twice, he turned and fired at Jim. Although he had a high-capacity pistol, it did have to be reloaded, something he had failed to do after the excitement in Lemon Grove. After firing several rounds, Buto pulled the trigger and heard the loudest lack of sound he ever would. He pulled on the trigger again and, after receiving the same result, stood up slightly and tilted the pistol up to see the slide locked back on an empty magazine. He had to stop and think about this turn of events for a second then began scratching at his side for a spare magazine.

The wasted time cost him a world of hurt. Jim put his front sight on the center of his chest and fired a controlled pair into his sternum. The two rounds rocked him back on his heels but did not drop him. Jim immediately initiated a failure to stop drill and fired a round at his head. The bullet impacted the cartel member on the right side of his forehead and muscular reaction caused him to spin away and go down.

Guerro had taken two steps back to get next to the door of the Suburban. He fired three shots at the man sprinting past in front of him, striking him once in the side. As the man stumbled behind what was obviously an unmarked police car that they had failed to notice on the way in, Guerro turned his attention to the man who was shooting his childhood friend to pieces. He attempted to aim at the head and arms that were visible, but Buto jerked violently into his line of fire and fell past him.

Flavio had been able to take a step to his left and get between two cars. He had his pistol out and was going to circle around the front of the car to try to flank the officer in front of him when he felt a slight tug and his arm went numb. Flavio looked down to see his shattered humerus and the exposed meat of his bicep hanging out. He looked up and saw Guerro retreating back between the Suburban and the Acadian. Esteban and Damien were rushing forward from the Acadian with their pistols blazing.

Flavio tried to raise his arm so he could transfer the pistol to his other hand, but that arm just didn't work anymore. He turned to go back to the GMC when a load of buckshot crushed in the side of his head. Flavio's body flopped forward and then fell out from between the cars.

Brian had stopped behind the Crown Vic, and having pulled his set of keys out while running to the car, unlocked the door and reached in to pop the trunk, he hit the red 11-99 button on the VDT and rolled out to the back of the car. As he was coming back around to reach into the trunk, he saw Flavio trying to flank his partner.

Not feeling any pain from the wound in his side, Brian took aim and pressed off one shot. He saw it hit the guy's right arm, so he reached in and ripped out his shotgun. A quick flick of his wrist chambered a round and his trigger finger flipped off the safety as he brought the 12-gauge up to his shoulder. The guy he had shot was still standing, so he put the circle reticle on the side of his head and sent nine .32-caliber lead balls crashing into the side of it. The man dropped out of sight. Sweeping the sight left, Brian heard Jim cry out, "Cover, reloading!"

He saw a black male walking forward, shooting with one hand. Brian fired a load of buckshot at him. The pellets tore into the man's right upper chest and arm, causing him to stagger into a parked car and then trip over Flavio's body.

Brian was continuing his sweep left when he was slammed back against the car behind him by a bullet that entered just below his right nipple and shattered his rib. The bullet was deflected enough that it didn't enter his lung, but several pieces of the shattered rib did.

He tried to maintain consciousness as he slumped down between the cars, but he lost the battle and fell over on his side. The last thing he saw was Jim's worried look as his vision greyed out.

Esteban considered himself somewhat of a shootist. He had attended a couple of shooting courses and practiced regularly. He was very observant at the range and had listened to cops as they talked about technique. Then one day he had seen a Marine teaching his son how to shoot and had been blown away. The man could draw and fire in a flash and was incredibly accurate. He soaked up every word he said, even following him out into the pro shop afterwards.

He purchased the same type of .45 that the Marine had been shooting, along with a similar holster and other accessories. He practiced what little he had learned and found himself to be one of the better shooters at the range in short order. Those skills kept him alive this day as the people all around him were dropping like flies.

Esteban had to hop over the bodies and move around open doors to get a field of fire on his enemies. As soon as he heard the shotgun go off, he turned to engage the officer, especially since the other one had dropped out of sight. The shotgun boomed again just as he got a sight picture on the officer firing it. Esteban squeezed the trigger and saw his bullet hit home. He turned but didn't see the other officer. As he was taking cover behind the cars, he was hit in the ankle by a bullet.

Jim had flopped down on his side and fired one well-aimed shot at the moving feet three cars down. The bullet chipped off a piece of Esteban's ankle and knocked him off his feet. As he fell down, he heard the GMC reversing out of the driveway. Esteban looked back and saw another set of legs coming from the Suburban in the aisle between the next two cars over. Another shot skipped off the asphalt next to his cheek. He rolled over and scrambled to the front of the vehicle. After looking around, he hobbled for the opening between the buildings leading out to the front.

Jim saw the suspect disappear between the buildings. He popped his head up and looked around quickly before ducking back down. He moved a little further between the cars and did it again. After the second time seeing nothing, he sprinted across and hopped over Brian's body to the open driver's side door of their car. He reached in and hit the 11-99 button on the VDT keypad, noticing too late that the red light was already flashing, then grabbed the mic.

"Eleven ninety-nine, officer down; shots fired at 615 E Street in the parking lot out back!"

"All units, 11-99; David Two is reporting shots fired at 615 E Street. David Two, cover is code three!"

Jim turned back around to see a bloodstained Julio pointing his Glock at him. The wounded man had climbed out of the car and started to hobble to his apartment, but when he saw the officer with his back to him, he staggered out to the driveway and fired at the officer as he turned around. The bullet caught Jim in the collarbone and punched him over on his back.

Julio didn't stay around to check on the results. After watching Guerro hop in the Chevy and drive away, he decided to get his family and get south right away. He went to the breezeway between the buildings to find his wife staring at him with a look of horror on her face. He grabbed her by the arm and spun her around.

"Get the children and get in the car! Now! Come on, vamanos!"

"Julio! You are hurt! Let me ..."

The slap stunned her.

"Now! You must hurry." He bent to pick up his daughter, but the pain in his side wouldn't let him stand back up. He settled for pushing the crying little girl in front of him towards Luna's car. Luna picked up their son and opened the back door. She was putting him in his car seat when Julio pushed her out of the way, slammed the door, and shoved Luna into the driver's seat. He rolled his body into the passenger seat and pulled his daughter up into his lap.

"Go! I will tell you where!"

Luna backed the car carefully out of its space, mostly to avoid the gathering crowd, then drove slowly out of the front driveway and onto E Street.

CHAPTER 11

Charlie Cooper's phone began emitting a sonar ping, telling him that he had a SWAT callout. He was pulling it out of its holder and standing up at the same time. His father gave him a quizzical look.

"I guess the good city of Chula Vista just doesn't want you to have company today, Dad." Chuck threw his jacket over his shoulder and nodded at the table. "Can you take care of this?"

"Yeah, go on." His father waved him away. "Check on your brother too."

"Copy that," he said over his shoulder as he headed to the door. He looked down at the phone and called up the emergency message as he stopped at the door to his unit. He saw 11-99 and got a sinking feeling in his gut. He slid into the driver's seat and picked up the mic.

"Zebra Two!"

"Zebra Two, code 10," the dispatcher came back immediately, confirming the SWAT callout.

"I'm 10-8."

"Zebra Two, shots fired at 615 E Street, back parking lot. Officer down."

"Zebra Two copies; I'm eight blocks away."

Chuck had the siren going on his Crown Vic as he squealed out of the parking lot. He was busy driving for a minute until he got on E Street then once he was headed south, he began pulling up the call on his VDT. The requesting unit came up on the screen.

"Oh shit!" he said and slammed his foot down on the gas. He had to swerve around an ambulance that was itself turning onto E Street. He slid up to the front driveway and cussed vehemently when he realized he couldn't drive through to the back. He dropped the car into reverse and looked over his shoulder only to see the ambulance filling his rear window. Cussing even louder, he slammed the car into drive and spun the wheel to the left, punching the gas as he did so.

The car spun a 180 in the street; he went back to 6th Street and turned left. Two patrol cars were blocking the driveway with officers pointing their guns into the complex. Chuck slid to a stop behind them and climbed out of the car. He ran around to the trunk, which was still swinging up from his popping it from the inside. He pulled out his vest carrier and shrugged into it. He spent twenty-three seconds snapping and securing his gear to his body and putting a Kevlar PASGT helmet on his head.

While he was doing that, another SWAT officer slid to a stop and ran over to meet him. They both grabbed their M4 carbines and rushed forward. They could make out the bodies all over the lot. Spying Detective Doudt's head next to a pair of legs by Jim's car, Chuck's stomach clenched.

"Any movement?" he asked the two officers who had been there when he pulled up.

"Negative, but there's bodies, weapons, and shell casings all over the place."

"Okay, Chris, let's go!"

The two SWAT officers began a fast tactical walk up the driveway, the barrels of their rifles tracking everywhere their eyes went, sweeping between every two cars. They paused at the black Yukon and cleared it, then checked each of the bodies, zip-tying their hands before rushing over to Jim and Brian. They stopped at the rear of the car, almost back-to-back, and again swept the parking area for threats.

"Cover!" Chuck said and crouched down next to Jim and his partner. "Jim—ah fuck! Hey Jim!" He shook his brother's shoulder gently then felt for a pulse.

"Ow … shit! Hey, I'm shot in that shoulder, you dumb ass!" Jim said through a haze of pain. "Check on Brian! Get medical in here! The last two suspects ran out front. First one is an Asian male, wearing a button-down yellow shirt. Second one is an HMA, black, brown, wearing a blue Dickie's shirt over a white T-shirt and jeans. He's the one who shot me!"

"Zebra Two to all responding units. At least two suspects are in the area." Chuck broadcast the descriptions and began coordinating the perimeter as the two paramedics came through from the front of the building. They shoved Chuck out of the way and moved Brian out so they could work on him. The chest wound was their biggest concern, so they cut his shirt off and sealed it.

Chuck was applying gentle direct pressure to Jim's shattered collarbone with a field dressing. As soon as they had Brian on the stretcher, one of the paramedics had to run around the outside of the building to the front and get the ambulance, then drive it back around because the SWAT team was still clearing the apartment complex.

By now, the neighborhood was crawling with cops. Chuck walked Jim to the ambulance and waited as Brian was pushed in on the gurney, and then helped Jim into the back.

"I'll be there in five minutes; you understand?" Chuck was giving his brother a stern glare. "I'm calling Dad and the rest of the family."

"Have Caroline meet Kelly please. Oh wait, shit; she's down with Kate at SDSU. Okay, I'll call her but she's gonna need to be there. Brian's kids will have to be told too. They're at their mom's house this week." Jim was slouching over and his speech was starting to slur. "I need to tell you about the Stanfords too! Someone needs to get over there ..."

The medic had finished securing the gurney and was trying to close the door. Jim fought with him while Chuck tried to yell at Jim to cooperate. Jim finally shoved the medic back and leaned out the door.

"Listen to me! These guys are after the drugs that the Stanfords have!"

The medic had recovered from the shove. "We have to go now! Either sit down, or I'm throwing you off!" the red-faced young man said. "This guy has a sucking chest wound! Sit!"

Chuck nodded and pushed both of the ambulance doors closed. He watched the boxy vehicle drive away then pulled out his phone. He debated with himself on who to call first then dialed his father.

"Hello, son; that was fast," Hal Cooper said. "I'm still here watching the ball games if you want to come on back."

"Dad, Jim and Brian were both shot. Jim's okay, but he took one in the shoulder. Brian is in bad shape—multiple GSWs with a sucking chest wound."

Chuck paused to wave away a uniformed officer who was approaching him. "Can you call Caroline and have her meet Kelly before she gets to Scripps? It's a bad scene here. Bodies all over the place and about a million rounds of spent brass. It was one helluva fight."

"Oh Christ!" As the father of two police officers, this was the phone call Hal had dreaded. A lump formed in his throat. "Okay, what about you? Are you all right?"

"I'm fine, Dad. I got here after all the shooting was over. Don't get the girls all upset. I walked Jim out to the ambulance under his own power. We still have a couple of armed suspects on the loose." Chuck paused and looked around at the increasing chaos. "I told Jim five minutes, but I may be longer."

"Okay, son; be safe!"

"I will dad, see you at Scripps."

Chuck hung up the phone and turned to the patrol officer who had been waiting impatiently a few yards away.

"Sorry, what's up?"

"Lieutenant Emmerson is out back and wants to see you. He just came from the shootout your brother was in, in Lemon Grove. He wants to see you five minutes ago."

"What shootout? In Lemon Grove? Today?" Chuck started jogging towards the back of the complex, mumbling to himself about two shootouts and how his brother was going to pay dearly for all this.

He ducked under a piece of crime scene tape that was being stretched across two poles to keep people out of the back lot. He looked around at all the carnage and saw Emmerson by Jim's car. He trotted over, walking up just as Emmerson finished talking to someone on his phone.

"… yeah, yeah … okay … I'll have one of my D's talk to them ASAP, but they're both en route to the hospital with serious gunshot wounds, so don't count on anything quick … Okay, I'll get back up with you in about an hour, after I get my head around this." He closed his phone and turned to Chuck.

"Hey, I'm sorry about your brother. Did you see him before they took him?"

"I walked him out front, Lieutenant. He was hit pretty good, but he tried to tell me what was going on. Something about 'The Stanfords have the drugs.' One of the patrol guys said they were in a shootout in Lemon Grove? I thought they were working a homicide down here?"

"Oh man—it's a long story. But tell me again about the Stanfords and drugs. Did they find out something here about drugs?"

"That's what Jim said. 'These guys are after the drugs the Stanfords have.'" Chuck leaned back against the car as his cell phone vibrated. He looked at the screen then said, "Let me take this, Lieutenant. My family is being notified about Jim."

Emmerson waved him on, took a few steps away, and made a call of his own.

"Hey, babe, are you on your way?"

"Yes, your dad called, and I had to do something with the kids. Kelly and Kate are on the way up from SDSU. How bad is it?"

"Well, Jim just got hit once in the upper chest shoulder area that I could see. He walked to the ambulance under his own power and I spoke with him. His partner, Brian Doudt, I don't know if you remember him?"

"Of course I do! He was at the Chargers tailgate party."

"Oh yeah; well, he got it pretty bad … multiple gunshot wounds to the torso, sucking chest wound, the whole nine yards. It's pretty bad out here, and I was just told this was the second one they were in today! Apparently, they were in one in Lemon Grove earlier."

"Oh my God! Was that them? It's all over the news! They're saying two people dead out there and a cop is in critical condition! What were they doing in Lemon Grove?"

"Babe, I have no Idea. I'm just getting caught up on stuff here." Chuck leaned back against the car. He was immediately shooed off of it by a technician. "I'll see you there. Love you."

"Love you too."

Emmerson was waiting for him when he turned around. He spent ten minutes going over everything from South Bay to Lemon Grove back down to where they were standing. There were still a lot of variables to figure out. They didn't know if this Julio guy was a victim or a suspect. Witnesses said he was injured when he packed up his family and fled. They now believed that the Stanfords were in possession of someone's drugs and were probably suspects. Data was going to be slow coming because they had two crime scenes in their jurisdiction and one outside that needed coordination. Three officers were shot. It was looking like a long night ahead.

By the end of the day, it would be the bloodiest day for law enforcement in San Diego's history.

CHAPTER 12

Sheila grabbed the coffee filters from her pantry and set them on the kitchen table. She turned and opened the fridge to put the groceries away when she saw movement through the open doorway to the garage. She saw a shadow move past the door, and then saw what looked like a teenager looking at the boxes stacked along the wall.

"This is just the shirts, man!" Richard hissed loudly to Albert. "I don't see the other boxes here!"

Albert had moved closer to the door to the interior of the house and turned to shush Richard. "Quiet, or she'll hear us!"

The sentiment was wasted since Sheila had heard every word. She stepped back and tried to move around the kitchen table. She had planned on making a break for the master bedroom, grabbing her purse along the way. They had a landline phone in their bedroom, but she wanted her cell phone with her in case they disabled it by lifting the other receiver. She realized that she had left the purse and cell phone in the car. *Not good, Stanford, not good!*

Just as she was rounding the table, a scuffling sound in the garage made her glance at the doorway. The momentary distraction caused her to lose sight of the stack of filters on the table. She brushed it with her arm, causing the stack of plastic-wrapped filters to fall over.

The noise was just loud enough for Albert to hear and realize that whoever had made the noise obviously heard his and Richard's last exchange. Albert swung through the door just in time to see Sheila bolting around the far side of the kitchen island towards an interior hallway.

"Fuck! She's running!" Albert took off after her as Richard ran in through the door.

Sheila made it down the hall to her bedroom ahead of Albert but did not get the door closed and locked before he slammed into it, sending her staggering back a few steps. He stepped forward and extended his right hand to point his pistol at the off-balanced woman.

Tom and Sheila had met while they were both in the Marine Corps. Tom was a gunnery sergeant with 1st Force Recon, and Sheila was a sergeant and helicopter crew chief. They had met at the SERE school in Warner Springs, where Tom was an instructor and Sheila was in an instructor development course. The two had run into each other again at the gym on Pendleton, where Tom worked out regularly and Sheila was a Judo instructor. They had recognized the athleticism in each other and a relationship began.

Sheila demonstrated not only her Marine heritage, but her martial arts background as she easily swept the extended arm away from her before reversing it and turning the sweep into a hip throw. Albert, who had no martial arts training whatsoever, found his arm wrenched back and soon saw his own feet flying past his face.

Albert's head impacted the wooden bed frame that surrounded the four-poster bed in the center of the room. The edge of the board was sharp enough to lay open a three-inch gash along the back of his head. His right arm reversed direction again; he heard his wrist crack before his fingers went numb then seemed to catch on fire. Albert let out a scream as the pain rocketed up his arm to his now out-of-socket shoulder.

Sheila tried to wrest the gun from the man's hand as she heard footsteps pounding down the hallway. Albert's hand had gone limp and the pistol was falling out of it as she tried to grab it. It landed on the floor between her feet and his hip. She was bent over, picking it up as Richard came through the door.

Richard was tempted to just shoot her, but he hadn't seen the money boxes in the garage, and he couldn't take the chance that the husband knew the whereabouts of the boxes. If she had stored them somewhere and he didn't know the location, then they were screwed. He settled for trying to knock her out. He swung his pistol at her head just as she was swinging Albert's, towards his crotch. They both connected.

Sheila was driven to her knees when Richards's pistol smashed into her head just above her left ear. Richard had turned the pistol so that the magazine tore a gash on her scalp from up in her hairline above her temple down to her cheekbone. She saw stars and her ears began to ring.

Her hand had slammed the top of the slide up between Richard's legs into his crotch. Pain exploded upward from his crotch to his stomach and caused him to double over. He was able to keep from falling face first into the bed by grabbing one of the corner posts.

Sheila tried to stand, but when she put her left hand down to help push herself up, it landed on Albert's hip, which shifted under her weight. This caused her to lurch to the side, moving her head out of the way of a weak follow up by Richard.

Unfortunately, it moved her head into the range of Albert's left hand. Although his right arm was sprained above the wrist and he had a dislocated shoulder and tendon damage, his left arm was fine and he landed an awkward blow to her temple with his fist. It was strong enough to stun Sheila long enough for the two men to wrestle her onto her stomach and pin her to the ground.

"Puta whore!" Albert was using his left arm to wrench her left arm up between her shoulder blades. "You fuckin' broke my arm! Now I'm going to break yours!"

Sheila let out a yell of pain. Richard was lying across her shoulders, holding her right arm down with both of his, so that he could get to the pistol she was still holding. Richards's body was preventing Albert from cranking her arm all the way past the breaking point, which he would have gladly done. He was in so much pain he wanted to just kill the woman and be done with it.

Sheila realized what he was doing. She pointed the pistol at the floor— the neighbors had kids, and she didn't want to risk injuring an innocent— and pulled the trigger three times in the universal distress code. The loud reports startled Albert, who couldn't see what was happening on the other side of Richard's body. He loosened his grip momentarily, and that was all Sheila needed to roll to the left and jerk her right elbow down and free from Richards grip. Her elbow slammed into Albert's nose, breaking it at the bridge.

Sheila rolled her body into a fetal position and then snapped her head back and straightened her legs. Her head smashed into Richards's nose, and although she didn't break it, it began bleeding just as much as Albert's. The action got her free of Richard's grasp, and she was able to break free from Albert, who was just about out of fight. She tried to roll over and bring the pistol to bear when Richard slammed his pistol into her skull again, and she lost consciousness.

They all three lay there, breathing heavily. Richard was the first to get to his feet. He remained hunched over because of the intense pain radiating out from his stomach and crotch. Blood ran freely from his nose onto Sheila and the floor. Albert rolled off of Sheila, onto his back, and cradled his wrist as blood poured from his nose. It began running down his throat, which caused him to sit up and cough violently, sending a spray of blood all over the wall and carpet.

Richard recoiled from the fluid that hit him. He began looking around for something to secure Sheila with. He hobbled over to the walk-in closet and looked inside. His attention was immediately drawn to a huge standing safe. It was three feet wide, six feet tall, and two feet deep. It was definitely big enough to hold a good chunk of the missing cash. He tugged on the handle, not really expecting it to open. He was surprised when the handle turned, but the disappointment set back in when the door refused to open. He continued his search, finally coming up with a two pairs of Sheila's nylons from a drawer in the bathroom.

He went back out to find Albert sitting on top of the woman, who was regaining consciousness. They quickly tied her wrists behind her back using both pairs of nylons. Then they flipped her over and sat her against the foot of the bed. The rough handling brought her the rest of the way around. She shook her head and glared at the two men standing over her.

"What do you want?" she ground out from between gritted teeth.

"Bitch! I want your fuckin' head cut off!" Albert raised his hand to slap her, but Richard grabbed his arm.

"What is your name? Is it Stanford?" Richard asked.

"Why? What do you want?" The gunshots had been loud, and Sheila was hoping to stall these two long enough for the police to get there.

"I am going to explain something to you, and you need to listen to it very carefully." Richard was doing his best to imitate Guerro from the storage unit that morning. "I will ask you a question once, and only once. If you do not answer me right away, my friend here is going to cut off a finger. Do you understand?"

"Yes."

"Good, now is your name Stanford?"

"Yes."

"What's in the safe in the closet?"

"My husband's military stuff, including his guns."

The honesty of the statement caught Richard off guard. He stared at Sheila for a second, blinking his eyes.

"Open it."

"I can't—"

"Bitch! I swear to God I'm going to—"

"I can't open it!" Sheila screamed, drowning out Albert. "My safe is in my closet. It has a gun in there and some jewelry. I'll tell you the combo to that one or I can open it for you. That one is my husband's. I'm trying to cooperate here!"

"Bitch, don't lie! What, your husband doesn't trust you with the combo to his safe? Bullshit!" Albert turned to Richard. "She's fucking lying!"

Richard looked around and saw the other closet door. He walked over and looked in. There was a smaller four-by-four-foot safe on a shelf. He doubted that it could hold even one of the boxes of cash.

"Where did you get those boxes that are in your garage?" Richard knew the answer, but he was trying to see how much honesty he was going to get from Sheila.

Unfortunately for him, Sheila's experience with interrogations put her way ahead of Richard's game. She could meet his expectations and still get what she wanted.

"I bought them at an auction just a few miles from here. The auction was held at South Bay Self-Storage. They have an auction there—" Sheila's verbal torrent was cut off by Albert grabbing her face.

"We know about the auction, bitch!" He punctuated the statement by shaking her head. He shoved her face back. "Just answer the question."

"I was!" She looked at Richard. "I don't know what you guys do or don't know! You said answer your questions and when I try to give you complete and accurate answers, you get mad! I'm just trying to help! What is this all about?"

Richard made soothing gestures to Albert and turned to the bound woman at his feet. He had just opened his mouth to speak when the phone on the nightstand rang. He turned and looked at it. He was going to just let it ring but figured it would be a distraction. He walked over and yanked the cord out of the wall. They could still hear two other extensions ringing in other parts of the house, but at least they could finish their conversation.

"Okay, we know about the auction; we know you bought our unit by mistake. What we want to know is where all the boxes are. That is not all of them in your garage. Where are the rest of them?"

"No, we didn't buy it by mistake. We bought the shirts to give to the kids down in Mexico." Sheila realized that the other boxes might be the only thing keeping her alive. "We went to buy a trailer. The unit we bought was just an afterthought. We saw the shirts and got them for the kids. Why are you so concerned about the shirts? You can just have them—all of them. The rest are at our church, I think, or already in Mexico. You'll have to ask my husband where he put them. They were—"

"Someone's here, Rich." Albert had walked away from the two of them and had been watching out the bedroom window. A man was walking towards the house. He had a cell phone up to his ear and was talking to someone animatedly. "Fuck! And he's on the phone with someone!"

The man turned and looked at the street. He saw Albert's car and walked to it, staring at the license plate. He stopped and turned back to look at the house. He said a few more words and then hung up. He began walking in the direction of the garage slowly. He stopped halfway up the driveway and stared into the garage at the still idling Audi with its open door. He began looking closely at the windows along the front of the house and noticed the movement when both Rich and Albert ducked away.

"Hey, Sheila! You all right in there?" The man was yelling towards the front of the house, but they could hear his voice from the open garage door. "I just talked to Tom on the phone, and he's on his way here. And the police too."

"Fuck it! We're out of here!" Albert turned away from the window. "You tell your husband we will be calling you soon. If you know what's good for you, you'll play along. We own the cops, so don't even think about calling them. You won't know if the cop knocking at your door is one of us or not!" He lashed out with his pistol and knocked Sheila down flat on the floor.

Both men ran through the house and out through the garage door. The man in the driveway stumbled back as Albert rushed him and pummeled him to the ground. They both ran past him and jumped into Albert's car. Richard had his phone out and was dialing Guerro's number as they sped down the street. He had just hit send when Albert, who was quite panicked, ran the stop sign at the end of the next block over. The minivan was only doing 45 MPH, but it was a perfect T-bone impact on the Altima. The car was almost broken in two as it wrapped itself around the front end of the Chevy Astro van.

As far as mini-vans went, the Chevy was the biggest of them all and carried a lot of mass. The bumper pushed the driver's side door to the middle of the car, bruising Albert's pelvis and snapping his left thigh like a matchstick. Rich was thrown back and forth but managed to remain conscious as the smaller car was spun around and pushed up on the curb.

It took a moment for the pain to set in, but when it did, Albert screamed. His body had suffered so much trauma that he only had one good one in him. The sound trailed off into a series of semi-conscious grunts as his head flopped forward and the blood running out of his nose joined that from his compound fracture. He lost all consciousness and slumped the rest of the way forward.

Richard had to tug on the handle of his door several times before he realized it was not going to open. He managed to roll out of the car window and stagger to the side of the road before collapsing on the ground. He took several deep breaths and was rolling on to his side to try to sit up when the first car that came upon the scene stopped to help.

The man who got out was jogging up to Richard when he saw the gun in his hand and slowed down. Richard gestured him forward with the pistol and croaked, "Are the keys in it?"

The man froze, then just nodded. Richard kept his gun pointed at the man as he staggered to the car and got in. He only had to make it to the mall so he could get picked up. He put the Camry in gear and drove away.

CHAPTER 13

Guerro was in a rage. He had lost his entire crew to two gunfights and had to ditch the ride he was in. He called the warehouse that they used to store vehicles and told them he was coming in. He would get a new car there and get his thoughts organized.

He was just about to call Richard when his phone rang. Seeing the number, he pulled to the side of the road to talk. The one thing he didn't want was to get pulled over for talking on a cell phone. The news he got from Richard had him pounding on the wheel in frustration. He agreed to pick up Richard at the mall and threw the phone in the cup holder.

Richard looked like an absolute wreck as he staggered to the SUV. His eyes were beginning to swell shut, and he walked with a pronounced limp while holding his hands pressed to his lower abdomen. This, combined with the gore smeared on his lower face, made him look like something out of a George Romero movie. He staggered to the SUV and almost collapsed into the passenger seat.

"What the fuck, Esse? You look like shit!" Guerro looked Richard up and down. "What's up with Albert? Are you sure he's dead?"

"I don't know, man; he was bleeding from where his leg was tore off!" Richard was slowly getting into a more comfortable position to put on his seat belt. "We got T-boned by a van on his side of the car. He was pretty fucked up already from the Stanford bitch. He bled out for sure, and they're going to have to cut him out of the car."

"What do you mean he was 'already fucked up'? What did she do?"

"I don't know; she used some kind of martial arts and put up a fight. She hit me in the balls too." Richard still had his hand pressed to his stomach.

Guerro looked over and stared at Richard. The gaze was unsettling, especially since the car was doing 35 MPH along Bonita Road. Guerro finally turned his eyes back to the road and sighed.

"So where's the money?"

Richard spent the next ten minutes telling him of the events at the Stanfords' house and how the money was probably already in Mexico.

Tom flew up the street and barely missed his neighbor, Malcolm, as he skidded to a stop in his driveway. Malcolm had stood up after being knocked down and made his way to the trunk of the idling Audi. Tom took one look at his still dazed neighbor and dashed into the house. Other than the knocked over stack of coffee filters, nothing appeared out of place. He called Sheila's name but received no answer.

He found her lying next to their bed with a small blood stain spreading out from the two lacerations on her head. He was careful to feel along her neck for a spinal injury before going to the bathroom and getting a washcloth. The cool cloth cleaning her cuts brought her around.

"Hey babe, are you hurt anywhere else?" he said, looking for other injuries.

"Ohh, I'm sore all over. I haven't been this sore since I was competing." Sheila sat up groggily. "There were two of them. Did you see them?"

"I saw them at the church, and I even spoke to the one who looks like he's in high school." Tom helped her lean up against the bed as he continued to clean the blood off her face.

"Yeah, that's them. They wanted their shirts back. They said that we stole them. I told them they could have them back." Sheila was shaking her head in confusion. "Was there anything in the other boxes in the trailer?"

Tom rubbed his neck as he thought about it. "Nope. I mean, we didn't open any more of them, but the ones we looked in were just shirts."

"Well, maybe we should ... Oh my God! Malcolm, are you all right?"

Malcolm had stopped in the kitchen and wrapped a bag of ice in a towel. He finally made his way through the house to the bedroom and was standing there with it pressed to the side of his head. He took one look at Sheila and handed her the ice pack. "Here; you look like you need this more than me."

"Thanks, there's a first-aid kit in the bathroom below the sink; could you grab it?" Tom asked as he took the pack and placed it against the side of Sheila's face, which was already starting to turn purple. "What happened after we talked, Mal?"

"I have no idea. I looked at their car, the Altima, and turned towards the house. Then I heard some loud bangs, so I got closer." Malcolm walked over and sat in a chair. "I had just called out to Sheila when these two guys rush me and one of them sucker punches me. I fell down and cracked my head pretty good."

They all stopped and listened to the sound of sirens approaching. Tom turned to Malcolm and raised an eyebrow in query.

"Did you get a chance to call 911?"

"No, but I'm sure someone heard the gunshots." Malcolm looked out at the street from one of the windows. The sounds continued to grow in volume, but no emergency vehicles ever came in sight. After a few minutes, the sounds stopped.

"Babe, the one young kid said that we shouldn't call the cops. He said 'We own the cops.' I don't think he was lying, or at least I think he believed it when he said it." Sheila had eased herself up to the edge of the bed and was now leaning over, holding the ice pack to her head. "They sounded like mobsters. I really want to know what's in the boxes."

"I do, too, babe. Let's get you to a hospital and get you checked out," Tom said as he glanced at the window again. "Where the hell are those cops, if they got called out?"

"I'll be just fine, hon." Sheila was slowly standing up. "Let's go look in the garage."

All three of them went out to where the boxes were stacked along the wall. Tom turned off the Audi then started opening the boxes. He used his pocketknife and slit the tape on the few that were sealed completely. They emptied all of them onto the floor and went through every piece of clothing, finding nothing.

"Well, that wasn't very enlightening," Tom said as he folded the last few shirts and put them back into a box. "I'm going to call Doug and ask him to look in the boxes in the trailer."

Tom took out his cell phone as Sheila and Malcolm pushed the last of the boxes against the wall. Doug answered on the third ring.

"Hey, what's up?"

"Are you anywhere near my trailer?" Tom asked.

"Right next to it. Why, did you forget something?"

"Can you do me a favor and look into the boxes in there and tell me what's in 'em?" Tom asked as he put the phone on speaker.

"You don't know?" Doug was walking towards the door.

"Well, it's supposed to be shirts for the kids down in Mexico, but we think there was a mix-up and there might have been some other stuff stored in there by mistake." Tom looked over to see Malcolm holding a shirt to his face and inhaling deeply. He looked at Sheila, who just shrugged.

"Where did you leave the keys?" said Doug.

Tom's face took on a contrite expression as he patted his pants pockets, feeling the lump of the keys.

"Ahh crap! I have them right here!" he said, digging them out.

"All right give me a second to jimmy the lock ..." There was a sound of clanking in the background. "Okay, got it. Just a sec ..."

Again they waited as more background noises came through.

"Okay, the first box, which is open has ... shirts; the next one has ... shirts ..."

"Open one of the sealed ones." Tom covered the mouthpiece and whispered to Sheila, "What's he doing?" He gestured with his chin at Malcolm.

Sheila again shrugged and went over to quietly ask Malcolm what was up with the sniff test.

"All right; I just opened one of the sealed ones and it has nothing but shirts. You don't really want me to open all these boxes, do you? There has to be a hundred of them. I can see in a few more of them, and it's all clothing as far as I can see." Doug was moving some of the clothing around and looked into two more sealed boxes. "Yeah, nothing but shirts, Tom."

"Okay, Doug, thanks. Just lock it up for us, would you?"

"You got it, buddy." Doug stepped out of the trailer and locked it. "When are you coming by to pick it up?"

"I'll be by later today to grab it. Thanks," Tom said as he hung up.

"Well, as far as Doug can see, all the boxes there are full of shirts too. What in blue blazes are you doing, Mal?"

"I'm smelling them to see if they are full of cocaine!" He had another group of shirts up to his nose and took a deep breath.

"Do you even know what cocaine smells like?" Sheila had a doubting look on her face.

"Well, not exactly, but I saw this show once where the drug cartels made the cocaine into a solution and impregnated clothing with it to ship it north, then they soak the clothes in some chemical rinse and get cocaine. These shirts don't smell like chemicals though." He looked at the shirt he was holding and frowned.

"I think we need to call the police on this, babe. We'll give them the shirts and let them figure it out." Tom had the garage tidied up, and he closed the overhead door as they went inside to call the police. Before Tom could dial, the house phone rang.

"Hello?" Tom asked, picking up the receiver in the living room.

"Did your wife give you our message?" The voice had a thick Hispanic accent.

"If you are the guy who was just at my house, know this: I will find you and I will fuck you up to the point that God himself will not recognize the mess!" Tom's drill field voice was coming out.

"Do not make threats to me; you are already a dead man. The only thing that you need to decide is whether or not you want your wife to die a slow death with you. If you give us our belongings back, only you will pay for the trouble you have caused. If you do not, I will kill you and every member of your family that can be found ... and I have a lot of resources." Guerro did not like the tone Tom had used; no one—since he was a kid—had spoken to him like that and lived.

"What is the big deal with these fucking shirts? We just went through the boxes and that is all there is! I could give a shit less if you want your fucking shirts back, but I am going to the police and if I ever see you again, I will crush your little throat in my hands!" Tom spoke fiercely into the phone as Sheila went into the living room and picked up the other extension.

"First of all, we have never met; those were some of my companions that were just at your house. You have never seen me, nor has your wife. So you will not know who I am until after I have walked up and put a bullet through her skull, or yours, for that matter. Secondly, you lying about my belongings has me a little disappointed. If you are man enough to make threats, you should be man enough to admit you have stolen my money. Since we seem to have come to the understanding that we are not in agreement, I tell you this—you will not see us coming; there is nowhere you can hide that I cannot find you. I own the police, and I have resources that you cannot fathom. Give me back my money and it will go easy. If I have to come find it, more people than you and your wife will die."

"You know what, fuckstick? Come get your damned shirts, but if you are looking for money, you will be sadly disappointed because there is none! I'll be right here, and I don't care who you think you own; you just pissed off the wrong Marine!" Tom slammed down the phone and went stalking down the hall to the bedroom. Sheila and Malcolm followed behind.

"Mal, I don't want you involved in this, so I'm going to ask you to leave. Those guys that were here believe for some weird reason that I stole money from them. I am telling you I did not. I do not want to endanger you, but the asshole on the phone said that he owns the cops, so please be careful if any of them come around asking questions." Tom had his safe open and had pulled out an AR-15 carbine and inserted a magazine. He pulled out a pistol and some other gear and began putting things on his belt. A Colt National Match .45 ACP went into a Blade-Tech holster on his right hip, and a quad magazine pouch for it went on his left. He attached a one-point sling to the rifle and began pulling stuff off of the shelf over his head.

"What the hell are you guys going to do?" Mal asked as Sheila went to her closet and began doing the same thing, only she put a Glock 19 on her hip with just two spare magazines. He stood there looking back and forth between them.

"I'm serious, Mal. Whoever these people are, they mean business. How the hell we got caught up in it is beyond me, but I'm going to find out. You really need to just lie low; I wouldn't want you getting hurt over this."

"Okay, but you know where to find me. I'll call you if anyone comes around," Malcolm said as he headed to the door.

"Hey, Mal, I would keep a gun handy if I were you." Tom turned to his wife and said, "Well, this is what we're gonna do …"

CHAPTER 14

The emergency room was madhouse. Although things got a little chaotic at times, this was an all-time record for the staff. Three of the suspects had still shown signs of life and had been transported in. A police guard had to be set over each of their rooms, although two of them would die eventually. This along with Brian and Jim, and half the department made the ER a little crowded.

As the word got out and people from the community heard about the shootings on the news, friends of the officers' family and other well-wishers began to show up. Jim's entire family including his parents, his wife and daughter, and his brother had all tried to get in to see him. Only by physically shoving them out into the waiting area was the nurse able to clear enough room to get to work.

Herb Johnson was a six-foot four-inch monster who had been a weight lifter since high school. Herb had grown up in Chula Vista, graduating from Chula Vista High and then joining the Navy. After four years, he had gone into the reserves and went to college. One criminal justice degree later, and he was working for his hometown PD. Herb was now head of the investigations division and a commander in the naval reserves. The massive cop loomed over Chuck, who was not a small man in his own right.

"Okay, so we still have no idea who the Stanfords are? We just know that they have some quantity of drugs that these guys are after. The 187s at the self-storage was these guys looking for the drugs, right?"

"From what I can gather, yes." Chuck hadn't taken any notes. "My brother said we need to look at the Stanfords when I put him in the ambulance."

"I have to give the LT something for the press and we need to get some info on these people. Did he have anything else?"

"Nope, I'm waiting until he gets out of surgery."

"All right; I'm going to do a search on the Stanfords, and see what I come up with. Tell your brother I said get well."

"Okay, I'll see ya."

Herb turned and walked down the hall, the huge man cutting through the crowd like an icebreaker. He nodded at a few folks before pulling Lieutenant Emmerson off to the side.

"Well, so far we have two dead at South Bay Self-Storage, both of them employees, two dead in Lemon Grove, one of them the guy who runs the auction company for the storage place. Two dead now and one critical from over at E Street, all of them we are considering suspects. We have several shooters missing from each crime scene. There is apparently some sort of connection to the cartel. Jim said something about the Stanfords having the drugs that these guys are after. I'm tracking down the name now. We think that the drugs were stored at the self-storage and were somehow stolen." Herb finished looking at his notebook and flipped it closed.

"Be careful approaching these Stanfords; they seem to be pretty important to the cartel. Make sure you …" Emmerson was cut short by his phone issuing an emergency tone. He looked down at his screen and muttered, "Shit, another officer down!"

"What? Where?" Herb's phone started beeping at him as he asked the question.

"Come on, let's get this sorted out."

CHAPTER 15

Albert had not bled out. He was in terrible shape but regained consciousness just as Richard drove off. Swearing softly, he tried to take stock of the situation. His left leg was broken for sure, but his right was only sore. He was applying pressure to the wound on his left leg when he noticed a man peering in the window at him.

"Can you help me please?" The pain in Albert's voice caused the man to flinch back a little.

"Fuck you! Your friend just stole my car and the police are on the way. You can just sit there till the cops show up!"

Albert let his head fall onto the steering wheel. He noticed his pistol was still wedged between the seat and center console. He was so furious that he pulled the gun out with his left hand and shot the man looking through the window right in the chest.

After watching the body fall away from the window, Albert began working his way out through the passenger side window. He almost passed out twice from the pain but finally managed to drag his body out of the car. He had made it up onto the sidewalk when an ambulance pulled into the intersection, followed closely by a police car. The two paramedics grabbed their boxes and were heading towards the body lying next to the driver's side while the police officer got out and looked around.

A woman up the block yelled something incoherent and pointed at Albert. The young officer nodded and began jogging in his direction, thinking he was just an accident victim. He slowed and turned as the volume of the shouting increased. Just as he figured out that they were telling him to be careful, two things happened. One of the paramedics yelled out to him that the victim they were working on was shot, and a bullet tore into his right hip. The bullet shattered the pelvis right above the hip socket. A second bullet hit him in his bulletproof vest. The vest stopped the round, but it still felt like getting hit with a baseball bat in the small of the back. The last bullet entered his neck on the left side from behind. This bullet tore out a chunk of muscle but missed the major blood vessels.

The paramedics and everyone else on the street began running for cover as Albert continued to drag himself to the sidewalk. As he hitched himself around the side of a car, he came face-to-face with a young Asian kid trying to get into it. The teenager stopped moving as he looked at the gun pointed at him.

"Give me the keys and run!"

The frightened kid dropped them and took off at a sprint. Albert picked up the keys and managed to drag his body into the driver's seat without passing out. He started the Civic and got it rolling down the street, thanking God that it was an automatic.

Behind him, the paramedics rushed to the downed officer and called in the shooting to dispatch.

CHAPTER 16

"Babe, we have to call the cops sooner or later." Sheila was trying to get comfortable in the seat of Tom's Toyota as they drove to Doug's house. Her injuries were making this impossible and the Motrin hadn't kicked in yet. "This is crazy; they can't have all the cops in their pocket."

"No, but I need to make sure we contact the right cops. If these guys are for real, then we may wind up having some very real problems. I want to go through all the boxes in the trailer and then I want to call in a favor." Tom drove calmly but made random turns and kept a close eye on his rearview mirror. After feeling comfortable with his back trail, he made his way to Doug's. They pulled the truck through his side gate, and Doug closed it behind them.

Doug was waiting for them by the trailer by the time Sheila gingerly climbed down from the cab. They all started hauling out the boxes. Doug went inside to get a box cutter, and as Tom was shoving one of the last boxes towards the door, he heard Doug yelling.

"Hey you guys, come here! You have to see this!" Doug was gesturing frantically for them to come into the house.

Tom and Sheila went inside of the house to Doug's living room. The TV was paused on a local news station.

"Let me rewind a second …" After a few seconds, the breaking news story started over again. The story covered the deaths at the self-storage and the shootout in Lemon Grove and then the shootout on E Street. The police lieutenant giving the press conference in front of the hospital told of the injured officers then stated that they were looking for shooters from all three crime scenes. He went on to explain that they believed the shootings were related to the cartel's search for the Stanfords, who had stolen a large amount of drugs from them.

Tom, Sheila, and Doug all exchanged dumbfounded looks. The man on the screen said they were to be considered armed and dangerous. More details would follow as they became available.

"Shit, this is not looking good for us, but he got the armed and dangerous part right!" Tom marched back out to the trailer and began opening boxes. The first three again resulted in nothing but shirts. The fourth was entirely different.

"Hey guys! I think I found our problem!" Tom said as he pulled out the plastic wrapped bundles of cash. There were ten in all. Each bundle was clearly marked as an even million dollars.

"Oh wow!" Doug said with eyes as big as pie plates. "That doesn't look like drugs to me, but it sure looks like drug money."

"Come on; let's see what else we've got." Tom was opening the next box with his folding knife.

"Hon, if we find drugs, we are calling the police immediately!"

"Yes, babe; I promise."

Opening the rest of the boxes resulted in them finding the other sixty-three boxes of cash and the last of the shirts.

"Holy shit, Tom! If those packages are marked right, that's 640 million dollars! And you say you bought the locker legally? Whoever didn't pay the storage rental on that is in serious trouble with his boss." Doug was looking at the packages of cash that they had stacked back in the trailer. "I mean, you paid for the locker, right? So everything in it is yours, right?"

"I think so. I'm going to have to talk to an accountant and a lawyer, and I'm sure we'll have to pay income tax on it. But we have to deal with these cartel people first." Tom was fingering a plastic wrapped bundle. "We now know that the threat from them is real. People have been killed for a lot less than $640 million, and I think these guys mean business. We have to find a safe way to get a hold of an honest cop. Now that we know what's at stake, I firmly believe that they probably do have a few cops on the payroll."

"Why don't we call someone at the base? I doubt that someone at PMO has been compromised." Sheila was constantly looking around the yard. "We could even store the trailer at MWR and it would be a lot safer than here."

"Uh, what's PMO? And what and where is MWR?" Doug had a confused look on his face.

"Sorry, bud, Jarhead speak there. PMO is the Provost Marshalls Office or Military Police for you civilians. MWR is just the storage lot on base." Tom was slitting the plastic wrapper on the bundle he was holding. He looked at the well-worn bills and figured them for the real thing and not counterfeit.

"What are you doing? You don't want to mess with that!" Sheila was staring at Tom as he began laying out the banded packs of bills. Although most of them were hundreds, there were banded fifties and twenties as well.

"I most certainly do. We are going to need some resources of our own to get through this." He handed a couple of stacks of bills to Doug. "Here's a hundred grand. I need you to get lost for a month. I'm going to give you some instructions, and I want you to follow them very carefully. These guys will have all kinds of folks looking for us, and I want you to be safe. You need to follow these instructions to the letter, got it?"

Doug just kept staring at the money in his hands.

"Hey! I'm serious! I need you to focus, Doug! These guys already managed to track us to the church. That means …" Tom paused as Sheila began pulling out her phone. "What are you doing? Hey! Stop!" Tom placed his hand over the phone screen as she attempted to dial.

"Helen is at the church still! And what about the Boy Scouts?" Sheila didn't try to pull it away, but she didn't let go of the phone either. "My God, if they were already there, then they could be going back!"

"I know, babe, but we have to be smart about this. From now on we don't make any calls on our own phones. We use burner phones that we'll get at a grocery store. We'll keep our phones for the contacts, but no calling out, got it?" Tom was pulling his own phone out from its belt holster. "In fact, we need to turn them off and keep the batteries out of them."

"I've called Helen three times today, and I'm sure a quick call to warn her is okay." Tom reluctantly nodded and turned to Doug as she walked away to make the call.

"Doug, come on, I need to use your computer for these instructions and you need to pack some clothes. You were almost ready to head south anyways for two weeks, right?"

"Yeah, I wasn't going to leave till Friday though."

"Well, you're leaving today!"

"But my reservation isn't till Friday night."

"You're not going to Mexico, goofball! You are going on a nice long sightseeing trip across America!"

Tom picked up another plastic wrapped bundle and shoved it into Sheila's hands as she rejoined them. He thought for a second and shoved another 100K in Doug's as well.

"Make it a nice trip!"

"Uh thanks, I guess."

They all trooped into the house and began their preparations. Sheila helped Doug pack and make arrangements for his early departure while Tom sat at the computer and wrote out a set of instructions that would hopefully keep Doug alive. It took them twenty minutes to get everything packed and into Doug's car. They then unloaded the steel lockbox in the bed of Tom's truck and stored the tools in Doug's garage. Another ten minutes had a majority of the cash stuffed into the lockbox. There was still another seventeen boxes worth of cash left over. After repackaging it back into the boxes, they were able to get ten of them into the bed of the truck. They didn't want to have anything sticking above the side of the bed, so they hid the last seven boxes in Doug's garage. They left with Doug following in his car.

Their first stop was the pharmacy, where they bought three pay-as-you-go phones and every minute card on the rack. They then went to an office supply store and bought three laptops with extensive software suites and air cards. Sheila began setting up the accounts as they slowly made their way towards downtown San Diego.

Sheila got on Craig's List and began looking at a specific section. She found what she was looking for and made a phone call. After a brief conversation, a deal was struck and she hung up the phone.

"Okay, it's all set."

"All right, I think this will be a clean enough break to get him on his way."

CHAPTER 17

This was Emmerson's third crime scene of the day, and it was just as bad as the first two. The officer who had been shot was gone by the time Emmerson and Herb got to the scene. The Altima that had caused the wreck was a mess on the inside, with blood smeared everywhere. The small pool of blood from where Paul Asher, the police officer who had been shot, was smeared from the paramedics. This was not going to be an easy scene to process.

There were plenty of witnesses to interview though, and their stories ranged from one pretty credible account from a woman, to a wild tale of gangsters shooting it out on the street Chicago style from the teen whose car had been stolen. They were going to have to wait for the crime scene investigators from the sheriff's department to arrive since their own teams were still busy with the other two scenes.

As they were putting out a BOLO for the stolen Honda, dispatch reported that they had received reports of possible sounds of gunfire from just two blocks away. Because of the huge amount of activity, no unit had been dispatched yet. Herb and Emmerson looked at each other and climbed into the Crown Vic.

"Can it get any worse today?" Emmerson muttered as he put the car in drive.

"I think we're about to find out."

It only took them two minutes to get to the address of the reporting party. They pulled up to see a woman just walking out her front door. She came to a complete stop when she saw the two officers getting out of their car with their hands on their guns. And even though Herb's badge was in plain sight and Emmerson was wearing a police Polo shirt, she was taken aback.

"Ma'am, we're responding to a report of shots fired in the area. Were you the one that reported them?" Emmerson slowly approached the startled woman.

"Oh yes; I did about forty minutes ago." She was staring at Herb, who was looking around the neighborhood and still had his hand on his gun. "There were three of them and they came from down the street." She pointed further along the street at a nice grey house with a neatly trimmed lawn.

"Did you see anything else?" Emmerson asked as Herb positioned himself on the far side of the car from the house. The lady noticed this and began backing up to her front door.

"Is there someone on the loose? My kids are inside." She stepped up onto her front porch step.

"Well, we've had some activity in the area and we want to be careful." Emmerson looked over to Herb. "Hey Herb! Roll Chuck and his guys out this way!"

"Copy."

Herb leaned into the car and typed a request into the VDT and hit send. He didn't want to make the SWAT callout verbally, so as not to alarm the woman. The VDT responded by making a series of beeps. Herb typed in a few more instructions and stood back up.

Chuck's phone made a sonar ping; every member of the family in the waiting room froze and slowly looked at him. He pulled out the phone and began reading the text message. His wife stepped closer and looked up at him as several other officers in the room had their phones make various noises ranging from an obnoxious alarm horn to "Hey! Yo mama's calling you!" Cop humor knowing no boundaries.

"All right, gents. Let's go! I want everybody to jock up before getting into your cars. Let's not have another incident with officers having to fight their way back to their cars for their shit!" Chuck looked at the other officers as they nodded.

"You be safe now, you hear?" Hal had stepped up next to Kelly and put his arm around his daughter-in-law. He turned to the rest of the guys as they began to file out. "All of you be careful, and Godspeed."

CHAPTER 18

After stopping at two more stores to buy six more phones and some more airtime cards, they stopped at a postal store and had several sets of passport photos taken. They also made a photocopy of Doug's license. After making one more stop, Tom and Sheila, followed by Doug in his car, made it to the San Diego Airport. They used Doug's credit card to buy a ticket on Southwest Airlines to El Paso, Texas. Doug checked in and went through security. Once in the passenger waiting area he made his way to the restroom and changed his clothes from the carry-on bag he had with him. He stuck a ball cap on his head and called Tom from the stall he was in.

"Okay, I'm feeling like Jason Bourne here!" he whispered into the phone.

"Your flight should be boarding now. As soon as it shows departed, I'll text you and I want you to come on back out. We're in the cell phone waiting lot."

"Okay."

It took them twenty minutes to get him out of the terminal and into the back seat of the truck. They then drove up to Vista in the northern part of the county. They followed the GPS to an address just off the 78 Freeway. There was a 2005 Winnebago Adventurer RV parked in front of the house.

They walked up to the door, which opened at their approach. A well-groomed elderly lady held open the screen and said, "You must be Michelle? I'm Meredith."

"Yes, ma'am. This is my husband, Eric, and this is Doug." Everyone shook hands all around.

"Well, come in; I have everything ready." She ushered them into the living room. "I will need to make a copy of your license, Doug."

"Oh, I made one for you and have the original here." Doug produced the copy and pulled the actual license out of his wallet. Meredith looked at both then handed the license back. "Thank you; I could have done that on our scanner."

They all sat down around the table, and Doug completed the private rental agreement. The substantial deposit was made in cash. Meredith was told that Doug was only planning to use the RV for a week but it could go longer. They paid for a month's rental just in case and that, coupled with the large deposit, had Meredith staring at Doug.

"You know, I was going to sell that beast when my husband died, but every once in a while, my grandson borrows it to take his kids camping. I would probably sell it to you for not much more than you've already given me." She waved the stack of cash. "Why didn't you rent from one of the big rental places?"

They had discussed this before arriving and they had their stories straight. They did not want to buy an RV because then the DMV would be notified of the sale and they had not had time to get Doug a fake ID. They obviously couldn't rent one from a place that required a credit card deposit after leaving a trail at the airport.

"Oh, I always try to rent privately. It keeps the money in the local community, and the coaches tend to be in much better shape." The sincerity in Doug's voice was quite convincing. "And since the soil tests we do can sometimes take a while. The rental agencies tend to not be as flexible if we need to extend."

"Oh, I see. Well, that makes perfect sense." Meredith pushed a receipt form towards him. "So you'll need this …"

"Okay, well, I guess I can show you the coach now." She picked up the keys and headed to the door.

Doug shot a glance at Sheila, who just grinned at him. Having a little old lady "show" Doug, who worked on them for a living, how to operate the RV's systems was one of the most amusing things they had ever seen. The coach was remarkably clean and everything worked. After the tour, Meredith wished them good night and safe journey then went back into the house.

They said their goodbyes and Doug got into the RV. He was going to wander around the country for a few weeks until it was all over. They had agreed to not tell each other where they were, but they had opened new e-mail accounts and would be keeping in touch. They also had two phones each and were planning on using them on alternate days.

Tom and Sheila watched the RV drive down the street then got into their car. They then spent the next two hours purchasing pre-paid Visa and Master cards. They found one card carrier that allowed them to load up to $5,000.00 for a low fee. They bought five of them.

It was almost midnight when they got checked into a hotel room, using the pre-paid card. They told the front desk clerk that it was a gift from their kids. After dragging their bags up to their room, they both flopped down on the bed and turned on the TV. What they saw had them both sitting right back up.

CHAPTER 19

The callout was issued Code 2, which meant no lights or sirens. The SWAT team met up around the corner from the Stanfords' house. The snipers were given nineteen minutes to get into position and then another ten to observe the target. When no activity was observed, the entry team approached the house. Members of the perimeter team began contacting neighbors and moving them to safety.

Malcolm was sitting on his couch when the knock came. He had been watching one of his favorite TV shows and almost just got up and walked to the door. He stopped and grabbed his .38-caliber revolver at the last second though. He looked out his front window to see several dark shapes moving across his lawn as well as the Stanfords' yard across the street. He didn't even bother looking through the side window at whoever had knocked. He turned and began running up the stairs to his room.

On the front stoop, Glenn Mitchell, one of the tactical team members, was looking through the side window into the foyer when he saw a man with a gun in his hand run past and head towards the back of the house. He immediately put the call out on the radio as he ducked to the side for cover.

Once Malcolm reached his bedroom, he slammed the door shut and picked up his phone to dial 911. He heard muffled shouting as the 911 operator came on the line.

"Nine-one-one, what is your emergency?"

"My name is Malcolm Diehl; I live at 18544 Calle Luna in Chula Vista. My neighbors had some guys try to break into their house today, and I tried to help. They attacked me in their driveway, and I just saw them on my front lawn! I have a gun, but these are serious bad guys!" Malcolm was beginning to shake he was so scared.

"Okay, stay on the line with me. I'm connecting with Chula Vista police right now." There was a series of clicks and another dispatcher came online. After explaining his situation again, the dispatcher informed him that it was probably the police due to activity on the street.

"Yeah, well, those cartel guys said they own the police so they better not come in my house!"

Martin Fuller was at the end of a long day that started with the call to the self-storage unit. He had a few more minutes till his shift was over and then he wanted to get home. Two officer-down calls in one day had him worn out. The statement by the man on the phone made him sit up straighter in his chair.

"Sir, what 'cartel guys' are you talking about?"

Malcolm then began to explain the day's events to Martin. When he was done, Martin asked him to stand by.

"Lincoln One, David One. Priority traffic."

Both Herb and Emmerson were down at the rally point that the SWAT team had set up. The ERT trailer was just pulling up, and the noise from the diesel motor drowned out the call on Emmerson's radio. Herb heard it, however, and moved away from the noise.

"David One."

"David One, I am on the line with a man who says he has armed men outside his house. RP states that he had contact with members of a drug cartel at the address where you are currently conducting operations. RP address is 18544 Calle Luna. Subject has barricaded himself in his room and is armed. Subject claims he is concerned that any officers at his door could be corrupt."

"Fucking great!" Herb mumbled before keying the mic. "Central, tell him that I will be at his door in five minutes. We are trying to approach the 18523 address covertly and cannot be lighting up the neighborhood."

"David One, standby."

Martin explained what was going on to Malcolm, who in turn informed him that the Stanfords had left their house over an hour earlier. After a few more minutes the situation was sorted out and Emmerson and Herb were at Malcolm's front stoop. Several team members concealed themselves and watched as Malcolm came to the door. He let the two officers into the foyer.

"Okay, Mr. Diehl, could you please tell us what is going on?" Herb said as they stood in a small circle.

"Well, earlier today, I heard what sounded like gunshots across the street. I called Tom's phone to ask if everything was okay, and he told me that he had just called Sheila to see if some guys in a blue Altima had followed her. I told him there was a blue Altima parked right over there." Malcolm pointed to the curb on the other side of his driveway. "He said 'Oh shit, I'm on my way. Make sure she's all right.' So I went into the driveway and yelled that Tom was on the way. These two guys come flying out of the house and one of them knocks me down. They jump in their car and take off." Malcolm was pointing up the street towards the accident scene.

"So Tom gets here, and we go inside and Sheila is pretty beat up. While we're trying to figure it out, some guy calls them and threatens them. They took off about ten minutes later." There was a hesitation in Malcolm's voice that both officers picked up on.

"Do you know where they went?"

"Nope."

"Is there anything else you'd like to tell us?" Herb could see that the man was shutting down and he couldn't understand why.

"Well, the guy that called stated that the cops worked for him." Malcolm had a hard time meeting Herb's eyes in the first place. Now he just stared at the floor.

"The guy who called them and threatened them said that we work for him?" Emmerson was giving Herb a concerned look.

"That's what Tom said. I only overheard his half of the conversation."

"Mr. Diehl, how well do you know the Stanfords? What kind of folks are they? What would make these people chase them?" Herb asked.

"Oh, they're the best! Good, honest, church-going people. They are both retired Marines. Both really involved with the church. No kids. Sheila has a niece and nephew that have visited before." Malcolm finally looked Herb square in the eye. "But I'll tell you this, they don't have the drugs that the guys wanted. We checked all the boxes, and there was nothing but shirts. Then Tom called his buddy, who checked the rest of the boxes and he didn't find any. So whoever is going after them has got the wrong people."

"How do you know about drugs being involved?" Emmerson asked as he walked to the front door and flashed four fingers at the men outside. They began to head over to the Stanfords' house after receiving the all-clear signal.

"Because that's what they were after. But there weren't any in the boxes. Go look for yourselves; the boxes are in their garage." Malcolm gestured across the street.

"Thank you, sir. Here's my card, and I'm sorry if the officers in the front yard startled you. I can assure you that we do not work for any drug dealers." Herb handed him a card and Emmerson did likewise. "We are going to check the house across the street, and we may have a few more questions for you."

"Okay. I'm glad to help, but that was pretty sketchy over there. Those guys meant business."

The two officers went outside and met up with Chuck Cooper, who told them that the house had a solid perimeter around it, and they could make entry any time.

"Hold up on that. I want to get a solid warrant first. The Altima that was involved in the shooting down the street was here just prior to that incident. According to the RP over here"—Emmerson gestured over his shoulder at Malcolm's house—"the owners are long gone, but there is definitely a crime scene inside. Make sure to tell your guys that we need minimal disturbance of the scene. I don't know where we're even gonna get a CS crew. They're all tied up at the other scenes!"

It took them almost an hour to get the warrant and assemble an investigative team. Malcolm even came out and told them where the spare key was and the code to the alarm. The team finally made entry and quickly and efficiently cleared the house. Chuck walked out and gestured to Herb and the lieutenant.

"You guys were right; something happened in here. There are bullet holes in the master bedroom and several blood stains." Chuck stepped aside as the two others went past him into the house. "And there are boxes of shirts in the garage, just like your RP said. Techs are going to test for residue."

Emmerson went to the garage while Herb went to the master bedroom. There were two distinct puddles of blood, both of which had been smeared several times. There were also spray patterns and more smears throughout the room. Trying to piece together what happened was going to be very challenging without a witness. Herb looked into the closet and saw the safe. There was an open ammo can sitting on top of it. Inside were two empty boxes of Cor-Bon .45 ammo and six empty boxes of Federal Match .223 in 69 grain. There were two empty, soft long-gun cases on the upper shelf. There were two more ammo cans up there as well, containing a couple of hundred rounds of 12-gauge buckshot.

Herb let the crime scene people start processing the area and went to look at the rest of the house. He was met in the hall by Emmerson, who did not look happy.

"Come here; you gotta see this." He did an about-face and they walked back down the hall to a large room that had been converted into an office. The entire room was full of Marine Corps memorabilia. Pictures and awards lined three of the walls, while the fourth had a built-in wall unit that had shelves full of martial arts trophies and more pictures. The books were split evenly between horror novels and those of a military history nature. There were two shadowboxes mounted behind the desk, showing the careers of Tom and Sheila.

"Look here." Emmerson was gesturing to a row of picture frames. They held awards for a Silver Star and two Bronze Stars with 'V' devices. The citations were in frames underneath each award, telling of some pretty astounding feats of heroism performed by one Thomas Stanford, once in Iraq and twice in Afghanistan.

"Holy shit!" Herb exclaimed as he admired the display. "Well, I think we can pretty much assume that whoever tried to fuck with these people picked the wrong ones to mess with."

"Yeah, well there were some pretty disturbing things in the garage." Emmerson looked at his notebook. "There were gunsmithing tools and a couple of those AR-15 lower receivers that you mill out on your own. A whole bunch of parts kits for them, some of which I think might be able to be converted to full auto."

"Well, it's not illegal to have the parts; it's just illegal to install them," Herb said as he continued to inspect the rest of the room.

"Yeah, and if you had some guys show up at your door and beat up your wife, looking for drugs, would you install those parts?" Emmerson was staring at Herb's back. He slowly turned around and looked the lieutenant right in the eye.

"I sure as hell would!"

CHAPTER 20

Sheila was up well before Tom and had been busy on one of the new laptops. She had made copious amounts of notes in a spiral binder and had breakfast delivered by room service. The smell of coffee roused Tom from the bed.

"You know, I met this Marine once who was sooo gung ho to start his day, he was always up before the crack of dawn and ready to go," she said over her shoulder to her husband, who was still sitting on the edge of the bed, looking like a four-year-old woken too soon from his nap.

"Yeah? Well, that guy got old and he never got any beauty sleep to begin with, so he's making up for it now." Tom stood and walked to the bathroom. "What have you gotten done so far, my Internet queen?"

"I rented us a plane hangar for the next month at Palomar Airport. It should be big enough for us to store whatever vehicles we need to swap out while we get set up. I've chosen three vehicles we need to pick up today. A Toyota Sequoia, a Ford F-250, and a 2007 VW Passat. All of them say the registration is current for at least three months and will take cash." She looked at her notes. "I looked into converting some cash into negotiables so it would be easier to carry around, but that will require some pretty good ID and would put us on the radar. I have a couple of RVs for sale that we could use if we decide to go the camping route like Doug. I've been looking at twenty-eight- to thirty-two-foot-long units. Weren't we just looking at these two weeks ago and saying how nice they were, but we could never afford one?"

"Yes, my dear, we were, but since I made a very judicious investment that has since paid off and ruined our lives, I feel that we should splurge a little. In fact, an airplane hangar makes me think of getting an airplane!" He walked over to the breakfast cart and poured some coffee.

"I believe it was my idea to buy the locker."

"Okay, so I can blame all this misfortune on you!" After adding an obnoxious amount of sugar and cream to his coffee, Tom picked up a croissant and had half of it in his mouth in one bite. "I don't know how hotels always get the softest croissants, but these are great!"

"You didn't have to buy the damn thing; it was your money!"

"Can't win no matter what," he mumbled around a mouthful of croissant. He grabbed a plate of bacon and eggs and plopped down on the bed.

The news was full of the stories from the day before. There was even mention that their home was now a crime scene and that they were being looked for. One station had them as "persons of interest" and another had them as "drug dealers and the suspects in a series of murders throughout the county."

"Ahh shit! I didn't know that many people were hurt and killed! Dammit—I'm going to have harsh words with these guys when I get a hold of them." Tom was shaking his head as he scanned back and forth between news channels. "Let's have the money all pre-sorted when we go to get the vehicles. I don't want to be pulling bills off of some huge roll after trying to negotiate."

"Why are we negotiating? We have plenty of money."

"We don't want people thinking we have a ton of cash. In fact, we want them thinking we're broke like everyone else. And let's get this done before our faces start to show up on the news." He finished mopping up some yolk with the last of a croissant and stood up. "I'll be ready in five. Where are we going first?"

"I say we pick an RV first, then the cars. We can't get the truck until tonight. The guy who owns it is working till 4:00 this afternoon." Sheila stood and began putting on her belt slide holster and other gear. "The Passat is closest to here."

Three hours later, they pulled a nice Allegro RV and the silver VW into a large hanger at Palomar Airport in north San Diego County. The hanger had a small bathroom in the corner and plenty of room for at least two RVs the size of the one they purchased. The tags on the vehicles were all good for at least another six months. They parked Tom's truck in the far back. It was no longer safe to drive. They transferred the majority of the cash to the RV but put stashes in the VW as well. They picked up the Sequoia and then went by Doug's and picked up the last of the money they had been forced to leave behind. Cash was not the only thing stashed in the vehicles. They had stopped at an Adventure16 and purchased several backpacks.

Each of them was made into a "go bag" or "bug-out bag," the term used by survivalists to describe a pack that had all the necessities to "bug out" at a moment's notice. Each of them had underwear, socks, first-aid kits, changes of clothes, hiking shoes, a pistol and ammo, hygiene items, and of course some of the cash that they had so much of.

Tom spent the rest of the day organizing the items and getting the vehicles in shape. He had the vehicles serviced and cleaned. He had the tires on the Sequoia changed to a more aggressive off-road type. After replacing the floor mats, he considered them good to go.

Sheila went into the bathroom and lightened her hair. She had also purchased extensions in the new color. When she was finished, her light brown, shoulder-length hair was blonde and down to the middle of her back. The addition of some sunglasses with large lenses and loose clothing had her looking like a million other Southern California women. The glasses and some judiciously applied make up covered the bruising and swelling that had left her looking like a pro boxer after losing a title fight.

Tom, who had always kept his hair short, had to settle for a baseball hat and sunglasses. Fortunately for him, Oceanside and Carlsbad were full of Marines and he definitely fit in. The clothes they purchased, however, were all subdued colors and the pants were jeans or cargo shorts. They had also purchased sturdy low-quarter tactical boots. They actually had fun buying as many pairs of Oakley and SPY sunglasses as they could. Each vehicle got a couple of pairs of those as well.

The one bad thing about the hangar was the fact that it was a huge open space with a corrugated tin roof. There was no air conditioning and the September sun had the inside temperature in the upper nineties by late afternoon. They wound up retreating to the RV and, after plugging it into the wall socket, used the A/C to keep cool.

They ventured out early in the evening to buy the truck. The 2009 F-250 4x4 had been lifted and had 35 BF Goodrich all-terrain tires. The XLT Lariat was the top of the line for Ford, and it set them back $34,000.00. It was, however, in very good condition with a Power Stroke V-8 diesel engine.

They drove back down to Chula Vista and parked at Plaza Bonita. They turned on their old phones and began checking their messages. Both of their voice mailboxes were full. Most of the messages were friends and church members who had heard about them being suspects and wanting to know what was going on. There was one from Malcolm describing the events that happened after they left. They each had a message from a gruff-sounding detective, asking them to please call him on his cell phone anytime. They also had a message from someone who said it was in their best interest to call him back. It even had a phone number at the end.

"They got our cell numbers pretty quick," she said, frowning at him.

"Well, if they're willing to throw a couple million at us to get back a couple hundred, that makes sense." Tom had written down all the numbers left for them to call. "So, do we call the good guys or the bad guys first?"

"I say bad guys; that way if they give us anything good, we can relay it to the supposed 'good guys'." Sheila was keeping a vigilant eye on their surroundings.

"Okay, bad guys it is ..." He put the phone on speaker and dialed the number.

"Mr. Stanford, where are you?"

"I'm at Disneyland. How can I help you?"

"You are to bring all of the boxes you stole from us down to the parking lot of the Factory Outlet Center in Imperial Beach. You will park at the southwest corner and call me back. You will return every dime that was stolen. You have one hour to do this, or you will spend the rest of your very short life being hunted by men who have no compunction about torturing little children to get what they want." The Spanish accent was barely noticeable.

"All right, but I'm not bringing my wife. She is somewhere safe, and I'm not putting her at risk."

"I really don't care about your wife; just be there." The line went dead.

"Well, he was a cheery fellow." Sheila was looking at the Google Earth image of the Factory Outlet Center. "Quick access to the I-5—five minutes and they're in Mexico."

"Yeah, I have an idea." Tom was dialing the detective's number.

"Detective Johnson." The voice still sounded gravelly.

"Good evening, detective. This is Tom Stanford. I got your message; how can I help you?"

Herb was at his desk and motioned for one of the other officers to get the tech guys on line. The department had the ability to parasite trace any call to one of the department-issue cell phones. He also put the phone on speaker and leaned it against his pen and pencil holder. He grabbed one of the pens and began taking notes.

"Sergeant Major, I believe we need to discuss some things that have happened in your life recently."

"I would love to, but first I'm going to give you some information that you can use. This is real-time intel, so record it if you can or else take notes."

Two other detectives had come closer to the desk and were listening. They both pulled out notebooks and prepared to write.

"Go ahead, sir."

"First of all, my wife and I have done nothing illegal. We purchased a travel trailer and one storage locker legally from an auction at South Bay Self-Storage. We paid for these items in cash at the time of the auction. The travel trailer has had the proper paperwork mailed to the DMV. The other locker contained boxes of shirts, not drugs as you have alleged repeatedly on the news. There was not one speck of drugs in the unit, to the best of my knowledge. However, some of the boxes did contain cash, lots of it. Since I legally purchased the locker, it is legally mine. Two men showed up at our church yesterday looking for us. They followed my wife back to our house, where they attacked her. She managed to injure them both, and even got a gun away from one of them, which she used to fire three shots. She did not hit either one of them, and they fled our house. We have since received two very threatening phone calls from them demanding their money back. The person who made these demands also informed us that no matter what, he was going to kill us. In light of yesterday's events, I am taking this threat quite seriously. I just got off the phone with this individual, who has told us to meet him at the Factory Outlet Center in Imperial Beach. I am to park in the southwest corner of the lot. He gave us one hour to be there exactly three minutes ago ..."

"Do not go there ..." Herb started.

"Please do not interrupt me, detective." Tom raised his voice to talk over Herb's. "What I am going to do is call them at the allotted time and tell them that I have left a car with the money in it at the mall off of Palm Avenue and 805. Tell me the make, model, and color of a car that you want to plant there and I'll pass it on to them, along with the license plate. If you are smart, you will get someone down to both locations and be prepared to take them into custody. After the violence yesterday, I hope you will be very careful."

"When will you come in so we can clear this up?" Herb had everyone running to get the operation coordinated.

"You are wasting time, detective; we can work on that later." Tom was starting the car. "The man I spoke to also stated, 'the police work for me.' And I have a feeling that may have some merit to it. Bag some of these bad guys and we'll talk."

Herb gave him the info on one of the bait cars that the auto theft taskforce used and tried to ask him more questions, but he wound up speaking to a dead phone.

"Cell tower down here, east of 805 ... probably Plaza Bonita Mall. GPS on the device just went off. He must have taken the battery out," one of the detectives said, hanging up a phone.

"Rick, did you get a hold of the sheriff's office in Imperial Beach? We're going to need them in on this." Herb was grabbing his jacket from the back of the chair as he headed to the door.

CHAPTER 21

Octavio Flores had seen how much money his older brother Juan made working. He was always impressed by the nice clothes and rolls of cash he flashed around. So when his brother offered him a chance to do some work for his bosses, he jumped at it. The sixteen-year-old was excited to find out he was going to be doing some real spy-type stuff. And a grand for one night's work! He was so excited he could hardly sit still.

They had taken him to a warehouse in south Chula Vista, where they told him exactly what he was expected to do. He was given an iPhone and told to get over to the Factory Outlet Center and wait in the food court. They even gave him a hundred dollars for the food. He was to sit so that he could see a certain section of the parking lot. He was to have the ear buds in at all times and keep up a running commentary. He was supposed to act like he was listening to music while he ate. They gave him a picture of two old people, a guy and a lady. He was told to be on the lookout for anyone who looked like a cop too.

Octavio got into his car and filled the tank up with premium—something he had never done before—and headed on down to the outlet center. He parked his car out in the area he was supposed to be watching, figuring it would give him an excuse to go outside and check his surroundings if it looked like he was getting something out of it.

He walked inside, bought a carne asada burrito, and sat down to wait.

Dawn Burleson was a dirty cop. She had always been just a little too bent for walking the straight and narrow. She was the daughter of a Navy man and her mother had been one to take advantage of her husband's long absences to bring men over. Something that she did little to hide from her daughter.

Dawn had graduated high school with mediocre grades and lucked into a job at the city's parks and recreation department. While there, she had seen an internal job posting for meter maid. This had gotten her into the police department. She had found that she had a flair for writing tickets and was soon one of the top-producing employees. She even made employee of the month.

Dawn made friends with one of the community service officers and soon thereafter was hired on as one. She still continued to write more tickets than anyone else, though some of them were not always legit. Two years later, she interviewed and was hired internally as a police cadet.

Again, her mediocre grades kept her from really shining at the police academy, but she did graduate and get assigned to the traffic division. Because of her propensity for writing scrip, she was soon out-producing the rest of the officers and made corporal ahead of her peers.

Her rapid rise came to a screeching halt when a local news station, reacting to complaints from citizens, placed hidden cameras at a school bus stop and recorded Dawn writing tickets to several vehicles for passing a school bus while stopped, even though the bus had not put out its sign or turned on its lights. She could be seen waving the cars over without even looking up to see if the bus had its lights on. The video footage was completely damning and the resultant investigation saw her demoted.

A few weeks later, while sitting at a bar, she had been approached by a guy who struck up a conversation, complaining about politics at work. He said that he had seen her story on the news and thought that she had gotten the shaft. He told her that if she ever needed some extra work doing some consulting he knew some guys who would pay her more than enough to make up for her loss in pay.

It started out as asking her about police procedure and security issues. Then she was asked about how patrol officers did their jobs. Pretty soon she was supplying the cartel with watch schedules and taskforce operations orders. In return, she was given some intel to make a few high-profile drug busts from competitors. Soon she was back in the good graces of the department. She would never see her dream come true of making lieutenant in charge of traffic, but after five years, she was a detective in narcotics.

The information she supplied to Guerro was used sparingly and only to limit their losses. Dawn continued to get envelopes full of cash, and Guerro got more than enough information to make it a profitable arrangement for him. Very rarely did she get a call asking for specific information. She had gotten one yesterday.

Dawn was briefed with the other units heading down to the arranged pick-up points. Once she was in the car, she called Guerro and let him know that Tom Stanford had made the whole thing a setup and that he should ignore the ruse about the car being at the alternate pick-up spot. Guerro thanked her and told her there would be something extra for her this month.

Guerro decided to leave Octavio in place, just in case, and see how things turned out. He pulled his other assets in the area away, just to make sure they weren't at risk of being observed. He had just confirmed that everyone had left the area when Stanford called.

"Are you in the lot? Because I don't see you," Guerro asked.

"You and I both know you are not in the lot either. And you're a fool to think I would walk right into an ambush. But I did do you a favor. I put your stuff in a green Ford Expedition, license number 5FTE441. It is parked over at the Costco mall off of 805 and Palm Avenue, between the gas pumps and the tire store." Tom had driven to that area and was sitting in a lot less than a mile away.

"Very well; you had best hope that it is there, or you will ..."

"Save the threats, puss nuts. I'm still kicking your ass for hurting my wife if I ever see you. You would be best advised to piss off and leave us alone, or you will be the one regretting his decisions. Go get your money and leave us alone. Last warning!" Tom clicked off and they immediately got on the road headed back to Carlsbad.

The members of the San Diego Sheriff's Department investigations unit, as well as several detectives from Chula Vista, set up at both locations. Some SWAT guys were able to set up on the factory outlet center from over half a mile away and keep the parking lot under observation with their spotting scopes.

Everyone waited with a heightened sense of anticipation for over two hours. The observers watched Octavio's attempts to act cool while checking out the parking lot. He came out twice during that time and looked around. After another hour, everyone was convinced at both sites that it was a bust.

Herb's phone rang just as they finished their third hour of boredom. He looked at the caller ID and saw a blocked number. Tom had used his personal phone before and the caller ID had shown his name.

"Detective Johnson."

"Well, did you get some bad guys?" Tom asked in a somewhat cheerful voice.

"Negative, and if you're just messin' with me …"

"Detective, I am getting very tired of people threatening me. I gave the guy the exact information you gave me. This leads me to believe that either he didn't believe me, or you are compromised and someone told him about the sting. Neither of these things inspires trust in me, so I am going to let you know that I am planning to go off the grid for a while. I will check in with you and try to be of as much assistance as I can. Unfortunately, you have placed me in the position where I cannot trust you. If I come in, you have already established that I am involved in the drug trade, and it would be very easy to come up with a justifiable homicide." They were parked at the beach in Del Mar, watching the moon rise over the water. A seagull began making noise next to the car, and they tried to roll up the windows, but it was too late.

"Well, enjoy the beach. Just understand this, if you come in we can protect you until this is all figured out. If you guys stay on the run, you are going to be on your own. I've already started a background on you two, and I believe that what you are telling me is true. Just come in so we can close out these murder investigations, and I swear we will protect you."

"My time is almost up, Detective Johnson. I really do hope you believe me, but my wife and I have to survive after the investigation. We're not as alone as you might think. I'm truly sorry for your officers who were hurt. I wish those who were injured a speedy recovery, and I wish the families of the slain ones peace. We'll be in touch." Tom ended the call, took out the battery since it could be used in the next phone he used and tossed the old phone into a trashcan next to the car.

They drove back to the RV and crashed right away.

CHAPTER 22

Guerro had a full-blown command post established at the warehouse. Juan had told him that he could put out a bounty of 10 percent of whatever was recovered. Even if nothing was recovered, the reward was ten million dollars in cash. A sixty-four million dollar payday would truly inspire some monumental effort on the part of the hitmen and bounty hunters that Guerro had assembled.

He set up a technical workshop where a staff of computer experts and techno-geeks could coordinate tracking the Stanfords down. There were three of them in there now, working on tracking Tom and Sheila's iPhones. They had been able to determine the cell tower that had been used during the phone call, and it drove Guerro nuts that Tom had been just a few miles from where he was standing. If he would have had an exact location, he would have sent twenty men to get them or die trying, cops or no cops.

Detective Burleson had given them as much technical information about the police department's computer system as she could, including her password. The hackers had been able to get in and write a backdoor program to access most of the department's files. This also included their Tap/Trace system. Unfortunately, they weren't coming up with anything.

Everyone froze when the burner phone that Guerro had been using to talk to Tom rang.

"Dead man, you just blew your last chance at survival." Guerro was having a hard time not swearing at the phone.

"That's dead woman," Sheila said as she laughed into the phone. "Hey, I'm just calling to see how my two friends are doing. I heard they got into a little fender bender when they left my house."

"Bitch, when we get a hold of you, I'm going to give you to them to carve up. You will pay for your arrogance." Guerro was seething now.

"Ooohh, talk nasty to me some more, little man. How do they feel knowing a woman kicked both their asses? I truly pity you when my husband gets a hold of you. You little girls don't even know what a real man looks like. I just thought I'd tell you that we've decided to stick around and see if we can find you. Because when we do, you won't have to worry about the police kicking in your door, you'll have to worry about your throat getting slit in the middle of the night. You tell those two fairies that came to my house that I will beat the crap out of them before my husband kills them. Good night, tough guy."

Richard, who had been standing next to Guerro and overheard the conversation, was spluttering mad and his face was bright red with embarrassment. He had lost his limp, but the bruising his body had taken was in full bloom. He had purple welts on his arms and face from both the damage Sheila had done and from the car accident.

Albert had shown up directly at the stash house, in direct violation of the rules. He was half-dead from blood loss and it was inconceivable how he lasted all the way down to Rosarita Beach in Mexico. He was still alive when he got there. Both he and Julio were being tended to by a private doctor. Esteban had made his way back to the warehouse and had his foot wrapped with ice and propped up on a chair. The other members of his crew that day had perished in the gun battle at the apartment complex, or were in police custody.

Guerro also had one more weapon in his arsenal. Mike Beltran was a retired FBI agent and private investigator. He had no qualms with working for Guerro, gathering intel. He just would not commit murder. Mike had one of the best analytical minds in law enforcement. He had a degree in forensic psychology from John Hopkins, and he was worth every penny.

Beltran had been reviewing the information that they had gathered on the Stanfords for most of the day. He was quite intrigued by their behavior. On the one hand, they were known to be law-abiding, church-going, and upright citizens. Yet they also had shown a strength of character and almost a disdain for the danger they were in. He could understand this with Tom Stanford; his military record spoke for itself. But Sheila had been a helicopter mechanic and crew chief. She was an outstanding Marine and apparently quite an accomplished martial artist, but her attitude surprised him.

Their taunting behavior was so out of place for how people in their position should act, that Mike felt he was missing something. After retiring, the couple had spent most of their time doing missionary work for the church. Sheila taught a women's self-defense class at both the church and at a Dojo. Tom was an avid fisherman and hunter as well as a recreational pilot. He would also compete in some local shooting competitions.

Sheila had a niece and a nephew, the latter being deployed in the Army. Her niece was married and living in a suburb of LA. Other than that, all other immediate family had passed away. Her brother had succumbed to some illness and their parents had perished in a car accident years ago. He had the hackers looking for the location of the niece and nephew. They would be collected and used as a bargaining chip.

"What do you think? Do you believe that they are going to stay around?" Guerro had his hand on Mike's shoulder as he looked over it at the computer screen.

"I'm still working on it. They are not acting like scared people should. They did not run to the police right away. They show a great deal of independence and self-reliance. Tom had no qualms lying to you about returning the money, yet by all accounts, he is the most honest man to ever walk the face of this earth, according to his military records and the way people talk about him at the church."

Mike shook his head and rubbed his eyes. He was tired of sitting at the computer screen all day. "Sheila shows the same disdain for her situation. If they were smart, they would hole up in some cabin high in the mountains with no phone, no internet, and no contact with the outside world. They would last about a year that way. This sticking around, if they do it, would be counterproductive to survival, but they are so over-confident that they just might stay. I need to see more to develop a better picture."

"I care nothing about pictures, my friend. I just want a location. I'll paint a picture then." Guerro turned and walked towards several of his regular crew. The threat from the Stanford bitch had him feeling uneasy, and it was something he was neither used to nor comfortable with. He set up a watch schedule, which included an extra guard. As he was doing this, one of the hackers came in and gestured for him to come to the computer room.

"We accessed their AT&T account, which includes their cable, internet, and cell-phones. Their iPhones are only being used sporadically, but the cell tower and GPS hits we are getting are still local, all South County." He bent over a screen that had a map with several points plotted on it. "They fully disable the phones so we can't use the ESS tracker from 911. We will get notifications the next time they even install the battery in the phone. I suggest you have a few people around the South Bay, in these areas." He pointed at a few places. "They are the most likely. Then when something pops up, we can just alert them as we send more people. It's probably the best chance we have of getting eyes on them."

"Okay, send this to my phone. I'll tell you who else to send it to once I have a crew figured out."

"Already done."

Guerro walked over to a couple of the hired hands they had brought in. Most of them were gang members trying to make a name and move up the food chain a bit. He gave them marching orders and sent them out to cover the places marked on the Google map they had been sent. With nothing left to do, he left the warehouse for a steak and some sleep.

CHAPTER 23

"Detective Johnson." Herb was at the police station gym, on the weight stacks. He was breathing pretty heavy.

"Herb, it's Jim Cooper; you got a few minutes to talk?"

"Hell, yeah. How are you feeling? I've just been waiting on word for when I can come down and talk to you. How's Doudt?" Herb sat up from the bench and began wiping his face with a towel.

"I'm still pretty sore. At least two more surgeries to repair the shoulder. Brian is still down hard. They haven't even brought him around, and he goes back under the knife today."

Jim adjusted the hospital bed to sit up a little straighter. Carol and Hal both began adjusting pillows and trying to make him more comfortable. They resembled a NASCAR pit crew and he frowned at all the fuss. "Listen, the reason I'm calling is, you guys are way off base about the Stanfords. What I was trying to tell Chuck was that they were in danger. The former owner of that unit, guy said his name was Ben on the phone, is the one who showed up in Lemon Grove and killed the guy out there. We think they unknowingly took some drugs from the cartel."

"How do you know the Stanfords are innocent?"

"The employee at the self-storage place left us a note in Sharpie pen while they were roughing him up. Said that both Jerry and the Stanfords were in danger."

"Well, I guess that's why I'm having such a hard time reconciling their involvement with their background. Everyone we've talked to says they are the next thing to Mother Teresa, and we should be ashamed of ourselves for even thinking they had something to do with it. What do you know about this Doug guy from the church? He's missing too."

"I have no idea who that is, but if these suspects got a hold of him, he's either dead, or wishing he was."

They talked for another ten minutes, going over the events from that day, and Herb promised to get down there later in the day to go over the case. After he hung up the phone, Herb sent a text to Tom Stanford. "Believe you now. Give me a call."

After sending the message he lay back down and started his set over.

Tom and Sheila spent the next day running around turning over two million dollars into usable negotiables. They had stacks of pre-paid Visa cards that they loaded to $5000 each. They didn't want to risk some IRS notification, so they stayed well away from the $10,000 mark with anything they bought.

Tom made a few phone calls to some fellow Marines and explained his situation. It almost started World War III as they all, to a man, wanted to go after the men responsible for attacking a well-respected sergeant major who took care of his troops. The offers to kill anything and everyone were numerous. His two best friends made plans to meet up with him. After giving them instructions about being careful, Tom checked his text messages.

"Well, Detective Johnson says he believes us now."

"Okay; how does that change our situation?" They were sitting at an outdoor café in Julian.

"Let's find out." Tom used the day's burner phone to call him.

"Hello, Detective. To what do I owe your change of heart?"

"The detective that was shot while investigating the murder at the self-storage is out of surgery, and he told me about the auction."

"Yeah, it had us kind of confused because for a day all we found were shirts. We couldn't figure out why these people were after us. We didn't find the cash til yesterday. Unfortunately, by then, these guys had painted a target on our backs. I don't think anything we do can get things back to the way they were. Did you get any bites last night?"

"One kid may have been watching the parking lot at the outlet mall. No one showed up at the other location." Herb was back at his desk and looking at the surveillance report from the night before.

"Really? Well, what does that tell us about the bad guys?"

"Not a whole heck of a lot. I doubt they believed you."

"Yeah, but don't you think they would have at least checked. The chance to recover that money would have been worth sending a minion or two, don't you think?" Tom was frowning. "If I thought for one second that returning everything in that locker would get them off my back, then I would have gladly done so. But they had already attacked my wife, and we hadn't found their money yet. We need to know why they didn't even at least try for the car."

"If you come in, I can help you. You're right about them playing hard ball. But we have witness protection." Herb leaned back and noticed several of the other detectives looking at him. One of them held up a piece of paper that said "Trace?" on it. He shook his head no. "How much money did you find, if I might ask?"

"The locker held 107 boxes, sixty-four of them were packed with $10 million each in various denominations from twenty- to one hundred-dollar bills. The other forty-three boxes held misprinted T-shirts. There were absolutely no drugs in any of the boxes. When the locker came up for auction, we saw the shirts and decided to buy them for the kids down in Mexico. We also purchased a trailer to use while we stay down there. I purchased the locker for $140.00, which I paid at that time. So I believe it is mine. I promise I'll pay the income tax if I survive."

Herb started laughing out loud at the last statement. It took him a few minutes to regain his composure. "You know what Tom … if I may call you by your first name?"

"You may."

"Thank you, please call me Herb. You know, Tom, I believe you would pay every single dime. Just make sure you write off every dime you spend protecting yourself."

It was Tom's turn to laugh out loud. "You know, I sure will! I notice that we are still listed as suspects though. Is there a chance that may change?"

"There will be a news conference tomorrow. Make sure you watch it."

"We will.' Tom was stretching as he asked. "Is there anything else we can do for you, Herb?"

"As a matter of fact, yes. Do you happen to know the whereabouts of your friend Doug? Our interviews at the church turned up that he has disappeared. I hope he is with you; I fear for his well-being if he is not."

"Oh, please do not worry about him." Tom was still chuckling as he watched Sheila pay the check. "We sent him on an all-expense paid vacation to Acapulco."

"Acapulco! No shit?" Herb hadn't meant to be so loud and immediately lowered his voice and leaned forward. "Well, if you say he's safe. I'll take your word for it."

"I'll be watching the news tomorrow, and I'll be in touch."

"All right; good luck and stay safe."

"We're trying."

"I see that …" And this time it was Herb who hung up the phone.

"Okay, we can kill the search for Doug Blankenship. Tom Stanford said he is on an extended vacation." Herb picked up the file on his desk. "I want to start working these guys from the Altima shooting. We have a ton of DNA and fingerprints to work with; let's make something happen."

After everyone was back at their desks, Dawn approached Herb and gestured for him to talk with her outside.

"So what's the deal with Blankenship? Why are we not looking for him?"

"Well, he's not a suspect, and Stanford just said that he sent him on an all-expense paid vacation."

"To Acapulco? Isn't that what you said?"

"Yeah, I didn't mean to be so loud. I guess they think these cartel guys will go after him because they stored their trailer at his house—at least that's where we found it."

"Did it have the drugs in it?"

"There never were any drugs. The Stanfords bought a locker at an auction. These guys that are shooting up our city were storing cold, hard cash in it. The Stanfords bought it for some shirts that they were going to give to poor kids in Mexico. They didn't find the cash until after our suspects showed up and attacked them."

"Wow, how much cash was there?"

"Stanford says $640 million in packaged, used bills. He even told me he was going to claim it on his income taxes." Herb grinned. "I told him to write off the security measures he's taking."

"Six hundred, forty million?" Dawn had her mouth open. "What security? How can he claim stolen money on his taxes?"

"Whatever he spends on avoiding getting killed is a cost of business and a legal write off. What do you mean 'stolen money'? He purchased the locker legally at auction. It's all his."

"No way! Christ! I never thought of it like that." Dawn was trying to wrap her head around that amount of cash. No wonder Guerro was willing to kick down some money to her. She decided on the spot that she was going to get her hands on that money.

"Yeah, well, he says he would have given it up to avoid all this, but now he's looking at being on the run for the rest of his life." Herb shook his head. "Any word on the street from this? If it is the Canton gang, some word may be out on the street."

"Nothing I've seen yet, but it would take a little bit to filter down to us. I'll talk to the guys over at the taskforce office."

"Thanks."

Dawn left the building and headed over to a local Starbucks. After making sure there were no other cops in the shop, she pulled out her iPad and, after connecting to their Wi-Fi, began typing. She sent out three e-mails. One of them to Guerro.

CHAPTER 24

Eddie Palceck was the State Department DEA liaison for Mexico. He had received a request for information from a local police department in San Diego regarding a Douglas Blankenship. The information was entered into his BOLO file, and he pretty much forgot about it. He was sitting at his desk when he got a call from one of the special agents down in Acapulco.

"Palceck, how can I help you?"

"Hey, Eddie, it's Robbie down here in Acapulco."

"How's the hard life treating you?" Ed leaned back in his chair. Robbie was always good for a few laughs.

"Well, aside from the fact that my margarita was a little too slushy at lunch today, things are okay. Hey, I'm calling about this BOLO you have out on a Doug Blankenship. One of our CI's said that the cartel is doing a full-court press on trying to find this guy down here. I mean, they're hitting the hotels, checking flights, everything for this guy. Is this important?"

"I think it was just a request for info from a local PD." Let me give them a call, and I'll get back to you."

"Okay, but don't make it too late. We have a pig roast tonight."

"Smartass." Eddie put the receiver down and went into his BOLO file. He found the request from a Detective Johnson and called the number.

"Detective Johnson."

"Detective, this is Special Agent Ed Palceck with the DEA. I'm calling about an RFI you guys sent us for a Doug Blankenship."

"We sure did. We were looking to see if he fled the country, but we have an idea where he is now."

"That idea wouldn't be somewhere near Acapulco, would it?"

Herb sat bolt upright at his desk. He looked around at the people in his office, and then said, "Agent, can I get a number for you and call you right back? I need to get on a secure line."

After getting a direct callback number from Palceck, Herb went to his car and thought about things for a minute. He then told dispatch he was going downtown. He drove his car to the federal courthouse and asked security if he could check in his gun at the lockers they kept just for that purpose. Once given a key, he put his gun and cell phone in the locker. He then went upstairs to the DEA field office.

After checking in with reception, he requested that he be able to make a secure call to their Washington office. He was ushered into a conference room and the door was shut. He called Palceck's number and got an answer right away.

"Hey, it's Herb Johnson CVPD. How did you hear that Blankenship was in Acapulco? Please don't tell me he's turned up dead."

"Not as far as we know. We received your BOLO and distributed it. I just got a call from one of my agents down there who says that there are known cartel operatives scouring the city for this guy. According to him, they are checking hotels and airlines."

"Oh shit! So we don't know if they've found him?" Herb had some real issues to deal with now. "Was the BOLO sent just to Acapulco for some reason?"

"Nope; it was an all-posts bulletin. It went to all our overseas desks. There is no attachment for a specific area. Is there something we need to know about this guy?" Ed opened a new page in his notebook file on his computer.

"He went missing after a series of homicides out here. We are pretty sure the Canton Cartel is looking for him because he helped some other folks that they are interested in."

"Is that the Stanfords that are also listed?"

"Yeah, but I hope it was an intel leak on their side. Otherwise, I have a leak in my department. That's why I'm calling you from your field office."

"Ahh, I see. Well, if you want, I'll code this and make just you the POC for any further."

"I would appreciate that." Herb was thinking furiously. "You may get a call from the taskforce guys out here. Could you cc me anything that comes up? I'll have my chief get with your SAC out here."

"Okay, I'll flag this for my inbox only." Ed typed for a few seconds. "I'll call my guy back down in Mexico."

"Thanks, Agent Palceck; I'll be in touch,"

"It's Eddie, and no problem."

"Thanks, Eddie; it's Herb. I appreciate it."

Herb used the phone to call his department. After using the phone tree and waiting for three minutes, he was talking to Dee, the chief's receptionist.

"Hey, Dee. Is Ol' Bill in?"

"Herb? What are you doing on this line? Yeah, just a second and I'll put you through."

"Hey, Herb, what's up?"

"Chief, we may have a problem with these homicides. Can I get you to call me on a non-department phone? Can you call me at 619-438-1081?"

"Non-department phone ... why am I not liking this?" Bill got out his personal non-department cell phone. "Okay, give me the number again."

Herb did so and hung up. The phone rang six seconds later.

"Okay, what's going on?"

"I think we have a leak in our department. We may not, but until I know different, I have to act like we do." Herb went on to explain how the cartel was looking for Blankenship in Acapulco.

"Couldn't Stanford have a leak on his end?" Bill had always ferociously defended his cops. "We don't know it's us, right? It could have been anything."

"Yes sir, but the reaction time was pretty quick. And the suspects made statements to the effect that 'they owned the cops' to both of the Stanfords. With the amount of money involved, I wouldn't doubt the cartel's involvement."

"How much money is involved? I thought we didn't find any money or drugs so far?"

Herb spent fifteen minutes bringing the chief up-to-date and then hung up. He then went to the SAC's office and asked for the name of a liaison officer that he could coordinate with for further communications. He then left the building, and not having a personal cell phone that he kept with him, he walked across the street to Horton Plaza and went into a cell phone store there. He purchased the cheapest pay-as-you-go phone he could and sent a text to Tom Stanford.

"CALL ME AT THIS NUMBER WHEN YOU ARE SOMEPLACE SAFE AND CAN TALK. URGENT!"

Tom didn't get the text for several hours. He had been busy contacting a few more Marines and arranging to meet up with them on Camp Pendleton. He almost missed the news broadcast where Lieutenant Emmerson announced that the Stanfords were no longer suspects and that the police now believed they had been victims of a crime. Afterwards, he drove out to the east side of the base and put the battery in his phone and checked messages. After reading the message from Herb, he took the battery out of his phone and drove further east off base and into the city of Escondido. He turned on one of the burner phones and called the number the text was sent from.

"Hey, Tom, did you tell anyone else that Doug was in Acapulco?"

"Huh? What are you talking about?" Tom was confused since he had spoken to Doug that morning, and he was just leaving Salt Lake City. He hadn't told Tom where he was heading.

"Yesterday you said you sent him on an all-expense paid vacation to Acapulco. Did you tell anyone else where he is?"

Tom let out a bark of laughter as he realized what he had said the day before. "No, Herb, I did not tell anyone else where he is. Can I ask why you need to know this?"

"Well, we had put out a BOLO for all three of you. I got a call from a DEA agent who said that the cartel is looking for Doug in Acapulco."

Tom's laughter died on his lips as the full import of what he had just been told sank in.

"Detective, no one knows that Doug is in Acapulco, because he isn't. I was being facetious when I said that yesterday. I spoke to Doug this morning and he is nowhere near there. I made up the location on the spot while speaking to you yesterday. As part of his security, we agreed that we would not tell each other where we were. If these guys are looking for him in Acapulco, then you have a leak on your end." Tom gritted his teeth in frustration. "You are the only person I ever mentioned that location to, so you better clean up your own house. I would suggest you implement some operational security. Is this number secure?"

"It's a pay-as-you-go phone. I got it today."

"And sent me a text to my old phone, which is compromised, which means both the phones we are talking on now are compromised!"

"Shit, you're right."

"Toss the phone you're using; I'll get in touch with you to set up secure communications. Your house is dirty, Detective. I promise, you are the only person I ever mentioned Acapulco to."

"Okay, I'm sorry about that. You're sure he's all right?"

"I spoke to him this morning, and he is enjoying the all-expense paid trip. You'll forgive me if I don't say where, especially since I don't know."

"I understand. I'll be waiting to hear from you."

"It will be soon, out!" Tom shook his head at the waste as he took the battery out of the cell phone. He drove out of the lot he was parked in and headed back west. He stopped at an ARCO to fill up and smashed the cell phone with a hammer and tossed it in the trash as he waited for the tank to fill.

CHAPTER 25

Beltran was hard at work trying to track down any link he could to the Stanfords. He had started backgrounds on most of the members of the church they attended, and had the geeks running a social media search on anyone who interacted with them. He had dozens of pictures of them, and Guerro was preparing an operation to snatch Sheila's niece.

He was also building a portfolio of military contacts. People they had served with in the Corps over the years. Between the two of them, that covered forty-seven years of service. Tom was relatively easy since he had been in the Special Operations community, and that was a pretty tight group. Sheila was much harder. She had served in all three air wings and had more overseas deployments than her husband.

He kept the search local to San Diego and tried to cross-reference as many contacts as he could. The amount was overwhelming. He was getting blurry eyed and frustrated when one of the geeks let out a shout.

"Got him!"

Beltran walked over and stood behind the man, who was furiously typing on his keyboard.

"He turned on his iPhone and picked up his messages. I captured his queue. Right here." He gestured at his screen. "He has a ton of messages we can go through."

The screen they were looking at minimized as a Google map appeared. A red pin indicated a spot near the back gate to Camp Pendleton. As they watched, the pin turned black.

"Shit! He unplugged the battery again."

"Who is closest?" He turned to the tech who was in charge of monitoring where the kill teams were throughout San Diego.

"Ummm, nothing north of Mira Mesa. Half hour to get there at least."

"Well, send them up that way!" Beltran waved his hand at the screen then turned to the first tech. "James, look through those messages and see what you can come up with!"

"Already on it. Let's see ... VMs over here, texts over here ... Wait, what's this?" James began writing strings of numbers down. "This message says 'Call me at this number when you are somewhere safe and can talk. Urgent' Let me track that phone number ... okay, number was assigned today ... Here we go! Got a lock on the phone that sent the message! No GPS; going to have to use towers. Umm ... phone's not in use right now. Its search signal has moved south from downtown towards us. That phone is down here in Chula Vista. I have a line trap on it. Whatever number Stanford calls from we'll have it and can run a trace."

"You still want the guys to head north?"

"Yeah, get them in the area—maybe Vista or San Marcos, somewhere around there. In fact, get another team moving up that way too. Shit, we should have homeless people sitting outside every gate to the Marine Corps and Navy bases watching for these people."

People were making calls and the center was hopping as Guerro walked in. He looked around and made his way over to Beltran.

"Anything?"

"We got a hit off of his cell phone. We're doing a back trace on a line that sent him a message. He was on the east side of Camp Pendleton. We have two crews headed that way." Mike gestured at the goings on.

"Tell the crews alive. Fucked up is okay, but they have to be alive." Guerro looked at the map. "I am heading up there."

He didn't bother to tell them to keep him updated. They were paid well, and most were aware of the consequences of failure. He nodded at his crew as he headed to the door. They all scrambled to get out to the two SUVs that were waiting in the garage.

They were on the 805 heading north when James called.

"Yes?"

"They're talking. The phone that sent him a message is somewhere in central Chula Vista. The other phone is ... just a sec ... Okay it's in Escondido! Just east of the 15 ... Localizing ... Looks like he's right off of the 78. Signal is not moving. He's somewhere in a box between the 15 to the west, Center City Parkway to the east, and south of the 78."

"Javon is near?" Guerro was gesturing for the driver to speed up.

"Yeah, he's just getting off the 15 onto the 78. He's two minutes out." James was pacing back and forth between the computer screens. "Still talking. We have Hector coming up. I'm having him get off on Valley

Parkway ... Okay, Javon is on surface streets; we're within two blocks of him. Signal is still not moving."

"We are approaching the 15 now ..." Guerro was cut off by James swearing.

"Shit! They just hung up ... and the battery is out!" James pounded the desk. "Well, you're close, no signal anymore."

Beltran grabbed the headset off of James and held it up to the side of his head.

"He'll be moving now; get close to the freeway onramps! Look for him exiting the area!"

Javon Williams had been given pictures of Tom and Sheila and Tom's truck. Everyone in his van had their heads going back and forth as they tried to peer into cars and looked at every white guy they saw. They were coming up Center City Parkway when they were told to head back to the freeway. They made a U-turn at Mission Road and went back. Two blocks away, Tom Stanford pulled out of the lot of a little strip mall he had been parked in and went west on Mission. Both parties were unaware of how close they had gotten to each other.

CHAPTER 26

Sheila had spent the day wiring some pretty substantial amounts of money to various people. The amount of cash they had found in the boxes was proof that the people she was dealing with could throw some assets at them. Because Tom and Sheila had such limited family, it made it easier to try to help them out. Tom's first wife and his son had been killed in a car crash in Los Angeles very early in his career.

Her nephew, Reese, was a sergeant in the Army. He was currently deployed to Iraq, and she doubted that anything these clowns could do would place him in more danger. She sent him a message on Facebook to let him know what was going on. She also mailed him a care package with instructions only he would be able to decode. The instructions told him where and how to access a large amount of funds.

Her niece, Bree, was a different case altogether. She was a young mother who worked as a financial analyst at a bank. Her husband was also in banking and they had a seven-year-old boy and a five-year-old daughter. One of the first calls she had made once they knew the nature of the threat was to her. Although they were doing well, they could not afford to hire twenty-four-hour security for even one member of their family, let alone four.

The manpower issue was solved by Tom's network of friends in the Corps. He had twenty former Marines who were very capable operators and had volunteered to help protect his family. The money he gave them was well appreciated too. Retirement from the military was not what it used to be. They were also able to recruit a couple of men who had just finished enlistment tours and were hungry for work. Equipping them was almost a non-issue since between all of them, they had enough weapons and ammo to take over a small country.

David William "Bull" Toliver had retired from the Marine Corps two years earlier. He had taken some time to just relax, ride his Harley to all the tourist places he wanted to see, and drink beer. The nickname 'Bull' was just as much a description of the man as it was a moniker. At five feet, eleven inches and 240 pounds, he was as solid as a brick wall. He had taken over as the team leader for the Whitakers.

The day had been spent overseeing the installation of a state-of-the-art security and monitoring system in the house. They had assigned one man to stay at the kids' school, and another drove Bree and her husband, Brad, to and from work. Bull himself stayed at the house during the day. He worked 'Port and Starboard' with another man, who covered them throughout the night. One final man was stationed outside during the night. He would drive around the neighborhood and check the small strip mall a few blocks away.

All of the men were experienced operators who knew that their number-one enemy was boredom and complacency. A rigorous communications protocol was established and the men were constantly playing "what if" mind games to look for weaknesses.

Bull was standing at the back door, looking out at the backyard, recovering from a very intense session of "Why" with Bree's daughter, Lynn. The child had managed to win the battle by bringing the huge man to his mental knees. He had finally had to give up and say "just because," conceding defeat to the five-year-old. Bree had rescued him from the gloating child by taking her upstairs for her bath.

He had just taken a sip of coffee and heaved a sigh of relief when the radio bud in his ear whispered.

"Bull, got a van with a couple of guys in it at the 7-Eleven. I see a total of four that are visible. It's a Ford Econoline just like ours. No front plate and I can't see the rear one."

"Copy, let me know if they move. The guys should be here soon, and we can hang out a bit to see what's up."

"Roger that. Steve and Duane said they'll be here in about five mikes."

"Copy." Bull went to the foyer closet and got out an M4 Carbine. He inserted a magazine and chambered a round, making sure the safety was on. He shrugged off his jacket and pulled a tac vest on. He was putting an oversized windbreaker on when Brad came down the stairs with a wet-headed Cody in tow. He pulled up short when he saw Bull pulling the jacket over his gear.

"Should I be concerned?" He had put a hand out to stop Cody from barreling right through to the den. They had a *Halo* challenge planned and the seven-year-old had been pumping his friends at school for tips on whipping his dad's butt.

"Nothing yet, sir. It's just getting dark." Bull had set the rifle back on the shelf in the closet, out of reach of the kids. He eased the door most of the way closed and smiled as they went by him to the den. Most of the lights were dimmed, and he slowly walked the rest of the ground floor. He had just returned to the front of the house when his radio came alive again.

"Steve and Duane just went by me; they'll be there in one mike."

"Copy."

The two relief men were walking up the driveway when the radio sounded again.

"Bull, an SUV just pulled up next to the van. There's nine guys total I've had eyes on. Getting the creeps about them too."

"Okay, Frank; we're jocking up!"

Bull met the two Marines at the side door and told them to get their gear on. They both had "Go" bags in the garage and had their gear on in twenty seconds. They opened the sliding door to their own Econoline that was parked in the garage. They placed the keys in the ignition and disconnected the automatic garage door.

Now they just had to wait. If the threat turned out to be nothing, then the family would continue its regular nightly ritual. If the men in the parking lot turned out to be up to no good, then things would get interesting real quick. The house didn't have a basement or safe room, so they were going to shelter in a hardened garage and escape if they had to.

"Okay, I have a white male just climbed out of the SUV and is walking a little yip dog. Man, he looks like someone fucked him up. Guy can't be more than twenty years old."

"That matches the description of one of Sheila's assailants." Bull let out a piercing whistle. Brad and Cody immediately put down their game controllers and went to the garage. They had clothes there ready to go, and Cody scrambled into a pair of jeans and a dark sweatshirt, pulling on a well broken-in pair of sneakers when he was done. Brad changed into similar clothing and a pair of hiking boots. They were just finishing up when Bree and Lynn came through the door. Lynn was wrapped in a towel from her interrupted bath. The men all turned their backs and gave the women some privacy to get dressed.

Once everyone was ready and in the van, the Marines moved out into the house. They had two men stay near the garage door while Bull moved to the front of the house. He took up a position in the Whitakers' den. He called up the security system cameras and began checking the perimeter.

"Okay, our subject has turned down the street. I'm eyes off. Still on his buddies at the 7-Eleven."

"Copy. Man, I'd love to snatch this little fucker." Bull saw the young man dressed in a sweater, walking a dog, come into view on the screen.

"Gun! I have a long gun at the van!" Frank whispered urgently into the mic.

"Good enough for me. Activate the plan." Bull typed a command into the computer and hit enter. He went back to the closet and got his rifle and his helmet. He put the helmet on and secured the chin strap. He dropped the night vision goggles down over his eyes and turned them on. The house was dark, and they all waited.

Rich walked the dog past the house, hoping it would stop and piss on a bush or poop in the front lawn. It did sniff along the edge of the grass but did not loiter too long. He didn't notice anything out of the ordinary and continued on past the house. After circling the block, he went back to the 7-Eleven and told the team that everything appeared normal. He rejoined Guerro in the Expedition.

Guerro gave a few quick orders and three men took off on foot. The rest loaded up into the van. The men on foot began working their way to the house, two heading for the front and one of them heading for the house that shared the back fence with the Whitakers.

"Two tangos headed for the front, one headed for the back. The van is still parked in the lot. I estimate at least five in the van and another two or three in the SUV; can't tell for sure with the windows tinted." Frank updated the rest of the team as his phone buzzed. He looked at the text message and continued. "Back up is three mikes out."

"Copy all." Bull had received the same message.

It took the gang member coming over the back fence another two minutes to get there. The two who had gone around the front were waiting when he called them and told them he was ready. Duane could hear the whispered conversation from his location in the family room. They all three rushed the house in a somewhat coordinated attack. The van started up and began heading to the house.

"Van's rolling."

"Copy."

"We're one out." The rest of the Whitakers' security team had scrambled from their hotel in an SUV.

"Copy." Bull said again.

The house was now dark except for a light in the kitchen and a light on in the master bedroom. Bull watched as the man in the backyard rushed up to the door and attempted to kick it in. The locks had been replaced earlier that day, and it took him three kicks to get it open. When he finally got through, he stepped inside and turned towards the kitchen. He took exactly one step forward and fell face down with a hole in his head.

"One down hard," whispered Duane.

One of the two men who rushed the front door pulled out a very short 12-gauge shotgun and fired a round of buckshot at the lock. It destroyed a four-inch section of the door and put a bend in the metal frame. His partner had a little better luck with a damaged door and was able to boot the door open. They both bumped into each other as they swept through, trying to look like TV bad guys.

The one with the shotgun turned right to Steve, who was waiting for him in the living room. The *pop, chutt,* and *clack* of the weapons action cycling was the last thing he heard as his head was snapped back by the impact of a 5.56 mm round.

"One down hard," Steve whispered.

The last man alive was just turning to tell his partner to head upstairs when he realized something was wrong. He turned his head in time to see his partner falling back his direction. As he continued to turn, he felt a presence at his back. The alarm bells were starting to go off when he lost consciousness. The blow to the base of the skull was supposed to kill him quietly, but he let out a grunt instead and collapsed.

"One down, still alive," Bull said. "Help me get them out of here."

The three men were hauling the bodies into the downstairs bathroom when Frank told them the van had rounded the corner.

"We'll go loud this time!" Bull whispered to the two men as they headed back to their ambush positions.

The Ford van pulled up right in front of the house and six men rushed out and up the front walkway. They burst through the already open front door and looked around. Two of them immediately headed for the stairs, figuring that the family was being trussed up for them in their bedrooms. Two of them headed towards the kitchen. The other two stood in the darkened foyer and looked around.

Bull hit the button on the alarm panel and closed his eyes. He already had earplugs in so was not deafened by the screaming of a 200-decibel alarm. Also, all the lights in the house came on full bright. Then they started flashing at exactly eight flashes per second. This cacophony went on for five seconds, then the lights went out and the house was plunged into darkness. The alarm continued for another two seconds.

As soon as the lights went out, the Marines flipped down their NVGs and turned them on. The alarm continuing for the extra two seconds covered the sound of this. The now completely blind and disoriented gang members did not hear the series of clacks as the actions cycled on the Marines' weapons. In less than four seconds, all of them were dead.

The driver, who had remained in the van, was startled by the siren and immediately dialed Guerro to tell him an alarm had gone off. He felt, more than heard, a presence at his window and looked up to see a silenced pistol barrel pointed at his head. The HK MK23 Mod 0 pistol is a large and scary looking piece of gear, especially when pointed at your head. He immediately tried to talk his way out of his bad situation, but the gun spit a .45 hollow-point right between his eyes. The phone fell to the floor of the van as the driver slumped over.

Lights were starting to come on around the neighborhood from all the commotion. Frank calmly reached in and undid the driver's seatbelt and shoved the body between the front seats. Steve came running out the front door and bolted over to the van. They didn't see that the driver's phone was lit up because the body was on top of it.

"Let's go get those fuckers at 7-Eleven!"

"On it!" Frank drove the van around the block at a reasonable speed and headed towards the 7-Eleven. They were just turning onto the street when Frank saw the SUV tear out of the parking lot at a high rate of speed.

Steve was securing the dead driver when he saw the phone with an active call. He immediately shut the phone off, holding it up for Frank.

"Shit they heard us!"

"Can we follow them?"

"Sure as hell gonna try. Get some of the guys up and see if we can get a good tail going." Frank had the tan Expedition in sight as it headed for the I-10 Freeway. They were able to get the last of the security team diverted into the pursuit before they made it to the house.

Steve got on the radio and started to coordinate a tail.

Bull, in the meantime, had to do something with his prisoner before the cops showed up. The unconscious man was trussed up with flex cuffs and tossed into the back of the van. The Whitakers were hustled to Duane's suburban and driven away. The bodies were left where they lay and a note was left for the police, telling them to contact a Detective Johnson at CVPD.

CHAPTER 27

Sheila and Tom were sitting on the bed at a Marriot Hotel when they received the text that Bree's family had been attacked. They had checked into the hotel using a pre-paid Visa card and one of Tom's friend's IDs. The clerk hadn't bothered looking at the picture to see if it even looked like Tom—which it did, kind of—and had checked them right in. They both had laptops open and were typing away when the phone they had set aside for emergencies beeped.

Tom looked at the text and then showed it to Sheila.

"Bull says they're fine and moving. Let's go." They had made up a set of rules for survival. One of those rules was always be mobile when using a cell phone. They were going to be talking quite a bit right now, so they jumped in the Sequoia and got on the road. Sheila put batteries in two of the burner phones and waited to call until they were a good five miles from the hotel.

She called Bull first to get an update. After he filled her in on the events at the Whitakers, he told her that they had been able to follow the SUV with the person they think attacked her to a house just south of downtown LA, next to the I-10 and 110 freeways. Four of the guys were hanging out in the neighborhood. One of them got into some raggedy clothes and was acting like a homeless person to keep the place under surveillance.

Next, she sent a text to Herb's department cell phone and told him to expect a call from LAPD about the bodies at her niece's house. She explained what had happened, leaving out the names of the Marines who had been there. As soon as she hit send she took out the battery and busted up the phone.

"Well, shall we send a message to our lil' fren'?" she asked, imitating Al Pacino.

"If you insist, my dear."

"Okay, here goes." She dialed the number she had for Guerro. It was answered by a different voice.

"Do you want to return what is ours and save yourself a lot of trouble?" Beltran was pointing to the phone and gesturing for the skeleton crew of technicians to get back to work.

"Let me speak to your boss."

"I am the highest ranking person you can speak to at this time."

"Really? Then tell me how you liked the results of your little screw up tonight."

"I don't know what you are talking about, but I assure you these people are nothing to be trifled with." Beltran was gesturing for someone to call Guerro.

"So you are not a part of the group that attacked my niece's house tonight?"

"I am a consultant of a sort to them. Look, if you would just—"

"We are not going to 'just' do anything! You have attacked me and my family for something you could have had just by asking. Do you know that if you had just called us and asked us, we would have given you the boxes back? Instead, you have killed multiple people, and injured more. You have threatened to hunt us til the day we die, so no I will not 'just' do anything you ask. What we will do is respond just like tonight to every attack on us. By the way, we'll burn that money before you'll ever see a dime! Tell your boss he can call me at this number for the next two minutes, then we're gone again!"

Beltran shook his head at the truth of the statement she had just made. They probably would have returned the money. No questions asked. Unfortunately, they were way beyond any kind of reasoning with Guerro or Alfaro; both had egos too big to allow the affronts to their pride to go unpunished.

Beltran took the phone that had Guerro on the line.

"I just got a call from Sheila. From what I gather, things did not go well."

Guerro was seething mad. After fleeing from an unknown adversary, he had been forced to stay inside this smelly house. Rich had retired to his bedroom with a young girl. He dared not go somewhere until some more reinforcements could be gathered. They were starting to trickle in now, but he wanted to get back to San Diego.

"What did she say?"

"She said you have two minutes to call her at this number." Beltran read off the number they had copied down.

"Are you tracking it?"

"Working on it now."

"All right; I'm calling her."

Guerro dialed the number and took a deep breath.

"Ohh ... is this the boss man finally?"

"Puta whore! What do you want?"

"Oh, I wanted to ask how your attacking an innocent family went tonight. You wouldn't know though, would you? Because you ran like a little coward. So I'll tell you what happened to your crew. They are all dead or captured. I hope none of them know where you live because the guys that have them are experienced at making the Taliban talk. So you just think about that, and remember what I said about that throat of yours being slit. Could happen any day now!"

"Bitch! I'm going to ..." And Guerro was talking to a dead line again. He hurled the phone across the room, regretting it when it flew apart upon hitting the wall. He was swearing vehemently and almost dancing on the balls of his feet with rage.

One of the local gang members stuck his head into check on him. When Guerro saw him, he pointed a finger at him and motioned him forward.

"I want a list of those who were with us tonight. Next, I want you to call everyone you know to come here. And I want them to bring guns."

"Okay, Holmes. I'll do it now." He started to shrink back out the door when Guerro froze him in place with a look.

"It is Señor Guerro or Sir!"

"Yes sir!" the young man said over his shoulder as he beat feet out of there.

Bull had parked in a Wal-Mart parking lot and made sure that the wide-eyed young man lying in front of him was thoroughly gagged. The van was a cargo type, which they had installed ballistic panels in to protect the occupants. There was a bench bolted along each wall and a corrugated floor that had to be uncomfortable. It was about to get a lot more uncomfortable for Javier Mendoza.

"So let's talk about your decisions in life so far. What has led you to the point where you're sitting in the back of my van about to have your fingers cut off? Hmm?"

Javier tried to reply, but the rag being held in his mouth with duct tape barely let out a muffled grunt. Javier had a goose egg on the back of his head, and his neck burned where pieces of broken vertebrae were like little coals of pain.

"I'm sorry, did you want to say something?" Bull leaned over and grabbed his face, squeezing it painfully. "This is how we are going to talk. I am going to ask you a question. You are going to answer me by nodding yes or shaking your head no; got that?"

He let Javier's face go and his head fell back to the floor with a *thunk*. He stared at the kid for a moment and after receiving no response kicked him.

"That was your first question, asshole. I suggest you answer it!" After a few seconds, Bull noticed the young man squeezing his eyes open and closed. Bull reached down and felt his neck. The lumps and bulges told him that the kid had suffered a severe neck injury.

"Are we having trouble moving our head? Blink once for yes, twice for no."

One blink.

"Okay, then; do you know the address where the rest of your group is staying?"

One blink.

"Is it over by the 10/110 intersection?"

Javier got a panicked look on his face but blinked once.

"Do they have a lot of guns there?"

One blink.

"Well shit! I guess I really don't need you anymore except to hang your body up as an example for the other guys. Can you think of one good reason why I shouldn't carve you up like a turkey?"

One long slow blink and Javier tried to struggle against his bonds. Another kick to the ribs calmed him down.

"I didn't think so." Bull pulled his mic down in front of his face and pushed his transmit button.

"Frank, the kid here says that you are at their safe house. I'll be en route now."

"Okay, we have eyes on two guys outside. Both of them can barely keep from finger fucking their pistols, they touch them so much. Steve is dressed in rags, sitting on the corner. There are four of us here."

"Copy, out."

Rich had finally finished with the young girl and come out of the back room. Guerro just snarled at him and went into the kitchen. He was pouring his second cup of coffee when he heard the front window break.

He was turning to walk out there when Richard came barreling into the kitchen.

"Cops! They just shot the guys out front!"

Guerro hadn't heard any gunfire so he doubted it was the police. He turned and followed Rich out to the garage. The house had been equipped with an escape tunnel. They slid a tool chest forward on its casters and went down a ladder into a hole. Guerro had a hard time keeping up with Rich's slender frame as he ran unhindered through the tunnel, while Guerro had to keep his torso turned sideways to navigate the narrow confines of their escape route.

The tunnel terminated in a garage on the backside of the block, three houses down. They climbed up into the garage and into the Chevy Impala that was waiting there. Rich pushed the button for the garage door and slid behind the driver's seat. They drove out onto the street. It was the first time in a long time that Guerro had been on the street without a security element to escort him. The feeling was not nearly as unsettling as the thought of what could have happened, had he stayed back at the house.

They drove to the end of the block and turned towards the freeway. They had a three-hour drive back to San Diego. They both sat through it in stony silence.

The Marines had waited until they could see both of the men out front and another through the window. On Duane's command of go, three rounds were fired and the team rushed the front door. A body was seen running past the window on its way to the back of the house.

"One going left!" Steve whispered.

"I saw him." Bull was trying to gain a field of fire on the left side of the house. They had not been able to approach while the two sentries were out front. Bull heard a door slam and some kind of movement in the garage. He tried the door and it was locked. He tried to work his way around the side of the garage but was brought up short by a fence. He decided to stay put and secure the garage as the rest of the team cleared the house.

Steve, Duane, and two others went through the front door and broke off in pairs. The dead gang member in the front room wasn't going anywhere with the side of his head missing, but Steve put two in his torso just to be sure. Duane and Ben went down the hallway towards the rear of the house, clearing rooms as they went, the soft calls of "clear" and "coming out" drifting over their radios. Ben opened the last door on the left and found a naked young Latino girl sitting up in bed. She took one look at the skull-faced mask covering the bottom of his face and screamed. He rushed forward and tried to slug her. She cringed and rolled away from the assault. As she finished her roll, she looked up and saw Duane, who slammed the butt of his rifle into her forehead.

"Dude! She was good looking before you did that!" Ben continued to pan his rifle around the room.

"Good! I hope it leaves a mark! Teach her to not hang around with bad folk!" Duane's country accent coming out almost made Ben chuckle. They checked the closet and flex cuffed the young girl, leaving her lying on the floor naked. "Back of the house is clear."

They stuffed a dirty sock in her mouth and duct taped it in place. They found an oversized sweatshirt that they pulled over her upper body, leaving her hands cuffed and the sleeves empty. A quick search turned up a pair of booty shorts that Ben held up.

"Better than nothing," Duane said and they began pulling them on the girl's legs. She only kicked once. When Ben raised his rifle butt and lifted an eyebrow as if to say *Do you really want to do this?* She immediately settled down.

Steve and Chris moved through to the kitchen and eventually made it to the garage door. They were stacked just outside of it when the girl's scream echoed through the house. They got ready to kick the door and asked Bull where he was.

"I'm right next to the fence on the other side of the garage from the house." Bull backed off a ways. "I heard movement inside a while ago, but I can't get a view on the backyard."

"Okay, we're making entry, if you can get clear."

"Go ahead; I'm back around the corner of the house."

The two men went through the door and swept left and right. They covered each other as they carefully cleared the garage and found no one. They did, however, find a cabinet full of cash. The Saran wrapped bundles had been kept there because Guerro and Rich were coming up.

"Holy shit!" Chris exclaimed as they pulled the packages of cash off the shelf. "How much do you think is in there?"

"A shit ton more than my last retirement check, that's for sure," Bull said as he walked in the door from the house. He looked in the Expedition that was parked in the garage. Seeing the keys dangling from the ignition, he popped the rear hatch and said, "Load that shit in here!"

They loaded all the cash into the SUV while Duane and Ben hauled the bodies of the two sentries into the house. They then began searching both buildings. Another cabinet contained several bundles of a crystalline white powder.

"Anyone want to guess what that is?" Bull smirked.

Everyone just shook their heads and continued searching. The house turned up a variety of weapons, most of them junk. They did find a Bushmaster AR-15, in good shape, and several pistols, mostly Beretta 9mm and a Tec-9 with an unbelievably long magazine stuck in it. A nice .45 ACP by Nighthawk Industries was found, which almost resulted in a fistfight between Ben and Steve when Bull asked who wanted it. A serviceable AK-47 and a Remington shotgun rounded out the list. All of the weapons and ammo were gathered and placed in the garage next to the Expedition as well. Just as they were finishing up, a car pulled up and a guy got out with a duffel bag. He looked around, and not seeing anyone, frowned. He walked through the front door and started talking before his mind could take in the scene in front of him.

"Man, who's supposed to be outside ..." He stopped in mid-sentence as he realized that the people who were facing him were not what he expected.

"Who's supposed to be on first, motherfucker?" Duane said as he slammed his rifle butt into the side of his head. The Abbot and Costello reference was not lost on the other two men, who grinned at the joke.

The blow rendered the man unconscious instantly. They cuffed him and removed the gun in his waistband. His duffel bag yielded an Uzi carbine with the barrel cut down and another brick of cash wrapped in plastic.

"Put that in the car too while I call Tom." Bull stepped away from the group and dialed that day's cell phone number.

"You guys all right?" Tom asked.

"Oh, were just fine!" Bull proceeded to tell him about the three prisoners, the cash, the drugs, and the fact that the young-looking guy got away.

"Shit! I really want to have a conversation with that guy."

"We got a picture of him at Bree's house. I'll have Frank send it to you in a minute. What do you want to do with the meat sacks and cash? We're not touching the drugs, bub."

"Do you think any of them knows anything that would be of use to us or the cops?"

"We got a shitload of intel from these guys ... cell phones and a laptop. We recovered some weapons too. I bet they could solve a bunch of crimes with the ballistics from that alone. I don't know how we'll get it into the hands of a cop legally though. Also, anything we get from interrogating these guys wouldn't be admissible."

"Yeah, but it might allow us to point them in the right direction. Is the girl part of it, or is she just scrum?" Tom caught the look of annoyance that Sheila shot him at the derogatory term that Marines use for women who are only good for sex and nothing else.

"I think she's worthless. She was naked in a back room with the FFL look on her."

Tom busted out laughing at the statement but kept the comment about the "Freshly Fucked Look" to himself. He didn't totally escape the glare from his wife though; Sheila had a pretty good idea where the conversation was going. Tom cleared his throat and got back to business.

"So how much cash was there?"

"Hell, we didn't count it! I'm thinking a couple of mil, at least. All yours as far as we're concerned. Pay for your troubles. We've already been given a generous salary." Bull nodded to Steve as he signaled that they were ready to leave.

"How about we split it? We are burning through cash at a pretty horrendous rate. You let me know if you think you can get some good intel from these guys. They haven't seen your faces, right?"

"Nope. We were in Halloween mode." Bull watched as Steve began to water the side of the house with the hose. He ran around to the other side of the house and started hosing down that wall as well. "We'll get back to ya in the morning."

Ben pulled up the van; the prisoners, all of whom were awake now, were carted into the vehicle and stacked like cordwood. A small flicker could be seen in the back room, and Duane came running out the front. Steve got an alarmed look on his face and dropped the hose.

Their plan was to torch the house and garage, but they didn't want any bystanders to get hurt. They got in the van and waited until they were a block away before calling 911 and reporting the fire.

The responding police found most of the guns a safe distance down the front drive and the duffel bag full of the coke from the cabinet in the garage. The note on top said courtesy of your local patriots. The fire in the middle bedroom was intensely hot and fueled by accelerant they had found in the garage. It burned the bodies to ash. The skeletal remains were all that was left for the forensic experts to go through. Several slugs were found and entered into the ballistics database of the FBI.

CHAPTER 28

Daniel Klein ran a small but profitable law firm in Orange County, California. After serving in the JAG Corps, he left the military and began his practice. Before being an officer, Dan had been an enlisted man in the infantry. He had been a fire team leader under one of the best sergeants in the Corps. He was sitting in his office when the door flew open and a loud voice said, "Dammit, Corporal Klein! How many times do I have to tell you to stack the grid squares face up!"

"Please tell me that you have not frightened my poor secretary to death! I am somewhat fond of her, you obnoxious ape!" Dan leaned back to see Tom Stanford peering around the edge of the doorframe. "Come on in! I'm not going to shoot you … yet!"

"I was not cowering in fear, sir! I was shielding yon maiden from any return fire. Since she is well off to the side and you are just as likely to hit there as anywhere else you aim, it was an act of chivalry; I swear!"

The aspersion about Dan's marksmanship brought a smile to his lips. He had shot "Expert" since boot camp. Tom marched pompously into the room, carrying a small briefcase. He was followed by his wife and, finally, Dan's secretary.

"Michelle, please hold all my calls. If the Sergeant Major is here, then cats and dogs are probably sleeping together and the world as we know it is about to end!" He waved Tom and Sheila into the room. Michelle bobbed her head and backed out the door.

Dan stood up and came around the desk to pump Tom's hand and meet Sheila. He looked her up and down, then looked at Tom, then back at her.

"You cannot seriously be hanging out with this mouth breather!" He looked over at Tom and said, "Okay, what's wrong with her? She has to have some kind of deformity."

He lifted Sheila's lip and peered at her teeth. "Is he blackmailing you? Because I know this really good attorney who can get you out of whatever he's holding over your head to make you stay with him ..." Dan was about to start feeling her legs for deformities when Tom slugged him.

"Knock it off, you leech!" Tom had to speak up over Sheila's laughter.

They all sat down with smiles on their faces. Sheila took in the room and all the Marine Corps memorabilia. She noticed that a great majority of the pictures showed Dan as an enlisted Marine. There were even a couple of pictures of him and Tom together.

"Okay, please tell me he did something wrong. Anything wrong. If he did, I'll die knowing that the saying 'No one is perfect' is true." Dan was leaning back and looking directly at Sheila. He acted like Tom wasn't even in the room. "I'm sorry I missed your wedding, guys. I was on deployment."

"Oh, he stepped in it, all right. He stole millions of dollars from a drug cartel, is on the lam from the police, and keeps trying to launder money!" Sheila said with a smile on her face.

It took a minute for Dan to recover from laughing. Tom spent that time scowling at both of them, which did nothing to stop them from laughing. When he finally got control of himself, Dan literally had to wipe tears out of his eyes.

"All right, seriously, what can I do for you folks?"

"Well, smart ass, you can help us get out of this jam!" Tom glared at him. It was almost enough to start him laughing again.

"What jam?"

"The *we have millions of dollars of cartel money and they are trying to kill us* jam! Did you not hear her?" Tom's serious look brought Dan up short.

"No shit?"

"No shit."

"Oh, wow." Dan leaned back and took a deep breath. "Okay, tell me about it."

Thirty minutes later, Dan was staring at the pile of cash in the briefcase.

"So let me get this straight. You want to retain me to set up this corporation, and acting as its director of operations, use it to purchase some land and build a house on it that is secured better than Fort Knox?"

"Yup, there will also be tax returns to file, charitable donations to make, a substantial payroll. Some of it will have to be invested to maintain enough cash flow to pay for the security we need. It will be a lot of work."

Tom looked him in the eye and asked, "How much money would it take for you to retire right now?"

"Huh? What do you mean?"

"Right now, how much would it take for you to walk away from this?"

"I was planning on another thirteen years, with the kids and mortgage and stuff. I don't know ..." He looked at the ceiling and did some calculations in his head. "Probably 1.3 to 1.6 million. I owe almost 600K on my house and another 80K just in our three cars. My retirement and investments will cover me after that."

"Done! Here's 1.8 million and another two hundred thousand for your office staff for severance pay."

"Holy crap!" He looked at Sheila. "Excuse my language ..."

"I was a Marine too; I've heard worse." She grinned.

"I can't take that much money from you guys. You said sixty-four million, right? A property like that, with a trust to cover expenses, after you pay income tax, you aren't going to be able to afford it. Hell, after taxes, you guys should just run. If those guys have the kind of assets you're talking about ... Man." Dan was shaking his head.

"Puss nuts! I said there were sixty-four BOXES! They each had ten million in them!" Tom turned to his wife. "I'm sorry babe; he usually has to take off his shoes to count higher than ten ..."

"Six hundred and forty million?" Dan's mouth wasn't quite on the floor, but the desk was the only thing keeping it from hitting it. "No wonder they're after you!"

"Well, smart man, can you do it?"

"Hell yes, I can do it! And you purchased this locker legally?"

Tom pulled out the receipt and showed it to him.

"I'm going to have to do a little research." Dan turned to his computer and began typing. "We'll have to list it as income but, wow are you going to have some write offs!"

"Once the corporation is established ..." Tom started.

"You're going to have to use a shell if you don't want your name on any paperwork."

"Whatever. We want to have the house and land set up exactly like I have designed. That's going to mean spending time with the contractors to get it right. This place needs to make Saddam's bunker look like Legos, got it?"

"No problem. It will take me two days to get everything set up. Are you guys okay? In the mean time?" He gave them a concerned look. "You have to be living off grid, right? What about your house?"

"You can just purchase a cashier's check, right? And pay it off?" Sheila asked.

"Not really. Since they know your address, if they have the resources you say, they'll be able to back trace any payment." Dan was shaking his head. "We could probably do it through an off-shore account. This is going to take some time. I have an idea though. How do you pay your mortgage?"

"Our retirement checks go into our Navy Federal Credit Union account, it is automatically paid out of that."

"All right then, this is what we're going to do ..."

Herb, Chief Owens, and Emmerson jogged slowly along the path next to Bonita Lake. The chief was feeling the pressure, as two other agencies had called him asking why notes had been left at two more homicide scenes with Herb's name on them. Apparently, Tom Stanford was taking on the entire West Coast drug network, and winning.

Herb had received a FedEx package with a phone and specific instructions on how to contact the Stanfords. The package had also contained $2,000.00 in cash with instructions on how to buy new phones and a lesson on communications security that was more of a chastisement. He notified the chief in a confidential memo about receiving the cash, per department policy.

Herb was now determined to weed out the leak in their department. He had done his best to recall everyone in the room when he had spoken with Tom Stanford on the phone that day. The list had eight names on it, including Detective Burleson, the lead narcotics detective. The three men were discussing how to identify the traitor, when Herb's phone went off.

"Hi, Herb. Just calling to let you know that Doudt is out of surgery and is doing well." Chuck Cooper had a much happier tone than he had had in the past few days. "Do we have anything solid on what's going on?"

"Oh, that's great! I'm with the Chief and Emmerson; I'll let them know. As for what's going on, the fucking Canton gang has apparently bitten off more than it can chew. Sheila Stanford's niece's family was attacked at their home up in LA County. The result was a bunch of dead gang bangers and a burned down house near downtown. Someone left a bunch of cocaine and weapons on the front porch with a letter telling them to contact me. The guns are being tested for ballistics. I bet they are matched to a few crime scenes."

"Well, alrighty then. I would seriously like some stick time on the guy who shot my brother."

"Doubt it's going to happen soon. Border camera shows Julio Paez and his family heading south into Mexico. The neighbors said he was bleeding

Sell your books at sellbackyourBook.com!
Go to sellbackyourBook.com and get an instant price quote. We even pay the shipping - see what your old books are worth today!

00074723132

when he left with his wife and kids. Might have had a little domestic violence in the driveway before leaving. We're pretty sure he was with the Canton guys, but he might be running too."

"Okay; well, let me know if you need anything. My crew is ready for some payback. The service for Dean is day after tomorrow."

"Yeah, this has been an interesting week."

"I think there is a Chinese curse that goes something like that."

Brian Doudt was sitting up in his hospital bed when Chuck Cooper walked in with two FEDEX boxes under his arm. He looked at them and then handed one to Brian. He managed to find a seat by putting two potted flower arrangements on the floor. It only slightly changed the veritable jungle of flowers in the room.

"These just arrived at the station for you and Jim; thought I'd run them over. How you feeling?"

"I am sore as hell but the meds are wonderful!" He held up the remote control for the self-administered pain meds and smiled. "They wheeled Jim in here this morning. We spent an hour going over the shoot. Herb came by and confirmed that my version of events matched his statement. Man, I'm sorry he got hurt."

"Hey! That's enough of that bullshit! You guys did fucking awesome, taking on that many suspects at once." Chuck was about to get choked up. He watched as Brian opened the package and looked through it.

"Holy shit!" Brian exclaimed "Look at this!"

Inside the box was a plain white envelope with a letter. There was also a package of bank documents held together with a rubber band. He handed the letter to Chuck.

Dear Detective Doudt,

I want to thank you for your service and your sacrifice while working on the criminal case at the South Bay Self-Storage. My wife and I were horrified to hear of your injuries while trying to protect us, and for that we are eternally grateful.

I hope you will accept this small token of our gratitude and know that your heroism is a rare thing that few people would appreciate. My wife and I will always hold you in the highest regard.

Enclosed is a receipt for a deposit into the medical fund set up by members of your department for you. There should be enough to cover any and all medical expenses related to your injuries. Anything left over is yours.

We have also established an education trust for each of your children in the amount of $250,000.00.

We cannot thank you enough and it is with great regret that I cannot shake your hand to say thank you. Perhaps one day I'll have the honor.

With our deepest thanks,

Tom and Sheila Stanford

Chuck finished reading the letter and looked up at Brian.

"A million dollars! The receipt is for a million dollars!" Brian waved the piece of paper at Chuck. He looked through the other paperwork. "All three kids got $250 thousand. Oh man … 750 thousand dollars for college!"

Chuck looked down at the other package in his hands.

"I better give this to Jim. I have a feeling he's going to want to see what's in it."

"Hey, do you think this is legal? Will I be able to keep it?" Brian had a frown on his face.

"I'm pretty sure you will. I'd call the POA attorney, though, just to be sure. The medical trust is legal for sure, but I'd still talk to the POA."

"Yeah, I will … a million dollars." Brian was gazing at all the zeroes on the deposit receipts.

Chuck left him mumbling to himself and went next door to his brother's room. A few minutes later Brian heard Jim's shout.

"Holy shit! A million dollars!"

CHAPTER 29

"Hello."

"So, how is your LA operation going? I heard from some friends of mine that you had some problems. I just wanted to tell you that the LAPD has your cocaine. You going to go after them? I don't think so."

Tom could hear the breathing on the other end of the line getting heavier. Then the man finally spoke. "I am going to speak plainly to you. There is no reconciling this between us. You have a multi-million-dollar price on your heads. There will be no rest for you ever, for the rest of your life. I am going to find every member of your family and kill them."

"Yeah? How did that work out for you this last time?" Tom laughed out loud. "You can tell that we are shaking in our boots. I told you once before, you pissed off the wrong Marine. If I ever get a hold of you, I am going to disassemble you piece by piece. You are a coward, going after innocent women and children."

"Well, know this, if you think you Marines are so tough. We have a complete file on you. Every Marine you ever served with. Anyone we can connect to your service, we will find them and kill them. I will make sure that their bodies are left so that their families know that it was because of you that their loved ones are dead." Guerro was clenching his teeth. "I doubt that you can warn them all. But they will start showing up dead, I assure you this."

"You had best be ready to bury a lot of your people, because the men I served with are not the kind you want to mess with. Why don't you just write this off and go away. There is no benefit in it for you now. Oh, by the way, the police officers your men shot appreciate you paying their medical bills."

"The money is not as important as making you pay for offending me."
Guerro could tell that the statement about killing Marines had hit home
with Stanford. "Watch the news."

"Harm one innocent person ..." Tom was speaking to a dead phone. He
sat staring at the disposable phone and the recording device that he had
attached to it. He disconnected it and dialed a number.

"Yo," Bull's bass rumble answered.

"We got a serious problem."

"Talk to me, brother. But to be honest, I was kind of aware of the
difficulty you're in."

"Listen to this." Tom played the recording of his and Guerro's
conversation.

"Shit, you'd need an ALMAR to alert everyone you served with!
What? Is he going to just start killing Marines on the street?" Bull was
fuming. "I wish we had discovered that fucking tunnel when we took the
house."

After the fire department had put out the fire at the LA stash house, the
news had reported the existence of the escape tunnel. The family that
rented the house where it came up claimed that the garage was not part of
what they paid rent for and had no idea that the garage was used by drug
dealers.

"How do we go about getting the word out? I have twenty-six years'
worth of friends I have to worry about now." Tom was worried that the
cartel would just start killing young Marines outside of military bases.
"We need to at least warn their commands."

"Relax, Devil Dog; I've got an idea," Bull said in a soothing voice. "Do
you mind if I give your detective buddy a call?"

"I didn't want you guys involved in the first place, Bull. If you get ID'd
for any of that stuff in LA, you could spend a hitch in jail and they will get
to you in there." Tom was shaking his head as Sheila drove them through
Ramona out towards the desert in East San Diego County. "They also have
a leak in their department. Come on, man; you're stressing me out here!"

"Stressing you out! Thanks for the concern, but I'll tell you what. You
send him the recording you just played for me, and I won't need to call
him."

"Are you going to tell me your plan?" Tom didn't like not knowing
what was going through his friend's head.

"Like the dirt bag said, 'watch the news.'"

CHAPTER 30

Sergeant Major of the Marine Corps, Cole Janches, was sitting in his office when the voice of the young lance corporal who served as his administrative assistant told him he had a phone call. He put down his pen and took off the damn eyeglasses that he had to wear now. He rubbed his eyes and picked up the phone.

"This is Sergeant Major Janches. How can I help you, sir or ma'am?"

"Hey, Corky, you fat fucker! You can help me by answering a simple goddamn question. It's an easy one, so you won't have to ask the hard-working PFC in the front office the answer."

"I don't know who you're calling fat, Goat Boy! And I rate a Lance Coconut for an admin!" Janches laughed out loud. "Do you need to clear your Etch-a-Sketch so you can record the answer to whatever knowledge I can shed on your pathetic existence?"

"Do you still get to have words with the CMC on a regular basis, or are you a hide-in-the-closet sergeant major? I know how much trouble you got in when you tried to come out of the closet last time. In fact, wasn't that the whole reason we have *Don't ask, don't tell?*"

"I'm pretty sure he'll talk to me, but I'm not asking him to read you bedtime stories or cuddle with you. Besides, I know for a fact you're more comfortable with farm animals." Janches leaned forward. "Tell me what you need, Leatherneck."

"Check your e-mail. I just sent you a file that is a recording of a conversation between Tom Stanford and a member of the Canton Cartel. The e-mail has a long explanation of exactly what has happened and there is a contact number for a Detective Johnson at Chula Vista Police. You can verify the e-mail contents with him. You should also take the threats as

100 percent serious. These guys have killed multiple innocent civilians and even a couple of cops. They even went after Tom's niece. I'm talking groups of armed men shooting up innocent civilians here." Bull avoided telling his old friend about his direct involvement. "To put it in simple terms that even you can understand, this cartel is about to start killing any Marines that they even think knew Tom when he was on active duty."

"Oh, fuck me to tears! I'm calling bullshit! Do they even know what would happen if some kind of crap like that happened? They would bring the world down on them!" Janches started calling up his e-mail. "Let's see … Okay, I have it. Hold on …"

Janches took seven minutes to read the e-mail, then he listened to the recording.

"Jesus Christ on a crutch! What a shitty deal. No chance to give it back and walk away." Janches started typing his own e-mail. "That's a hell of a lot of Marines he served with. I'm going to have to notify NCIS and the FBI about this threat. CMC is not going to be happy. I'll call him right now."

"Thanks, Corky! I knew I wasn't going to regret cutting you out of that Hummer." Bull laughed.

"I may regret you cutting me loose … Can I reply to this e-mail?"

"Yeah, but I'm kind of under COMSEC right now, so here's the number you need to call me at. All others are bad."

"Why the hell are YOU under COMSEC? Wait, never mind; I don't want to know. You know, this shit was easier when we just had to hide the fact that we lost a Hummer to 'Naval Action' from the first sergeant."

When Bull and Janches had been in the Middle East they had often found themselves with too much time on their hands. And idle hands being the devil's playground, they had managed to come up with several ways to entertain themselves. One of them was to drive a HMMV out into the surf and verify that the engine's snorkel worked. The problem was that the beach in that area was manmade with concrete blocks. About twenty yards from the shore, the bottom dropped off and went from five feet deep to thirty feet deep.

One day, as the young Marines were splash testing the snorkel on a Hummer, they managed to drive it off this underwater precipice. Three of the four Marines were able to get free from the Hummer and make it to the surface.

Janches got his seatbelt twisted and wound up thirty feet down, out of options, and out of air. Bull had seen that they were missing a man and immediately dove back down and cut Janches loose. Janches swam to the surface so fast, he shot out of the water to his hips. The Marines on the beach said that Janches popped out of the water like a cork. The name

"Corky" had stuck to him ever since. Bull's actions sentenced the Marine Corps to its future sergeant major and himself to Janches's undying loyalty and friendship, said sentence not really being a bad thing for either the Corps or Bull.

"Yeah, but I don't miss the ass chewings!" Bull was having the same memories.

"I'll be in touch, Bull. Stay safe."

"You got it, out."

There were few people who could call the commandant of the Marine Corps up and ask him to clear his afternoon schedule. Corky was one of them. As the senior enlisted Marine, it was his job to keep the general up-to-date on troop welfare issues. A slew of dead Marines turning up was something he needed to know about before it happened.

There were three loud knocks at the door. Since his secretary would have announced anyone other than Janches, General Christian Leo was pretty sure he knew who it was.

"Come!"

Corky marched into the general's office and stopped eighteen inches from his desk. In a parade ground voice, he pronounced, "Sergeant Major Janches, one each, reporting to the General that all is well until he hears what the Sergeant Major has to say!"

Leo looked at Janches with a confused expression but was smiling.

"At ease, Sergeant Major. What can I do for you?"

"Sir, I need you to look at the e-mail I just sent you and listen to the recording that is attached." Corky relaxed and took a seat across from the general. He gestured at the computer terminal. "I will explain further when you're done, sir."

Leo opened the e-mail and began reading. He looked up with a frown on his face and then played the recording. He frowned some more and played it a second time. When he was through, he reached over and hit the intercom button on his phone.

"Sir?"

"Lynn, have Colonel Felton get over here as soon as possible. Once you've done that, get me the director of NCIS, please."

"Right away, sir."

"Okay, Corky, Tom Stanford was a squared-away Marine when he worked for me. How did he get involved with this cartel?"

Janches spent several minutes relaying the information that Bull had given him and what he had also learned from a phone call to Herb Johnson of CVPD.

"Six hundred, forty million, huh? I guess that's clean living for ya."

The commandant called up some news accounts of the violence on google. He was scrolling through them when his secretary notified him that Colonel Felton was there. Felton was admitted and shook hands with Janches. Less than a minute later, the phone beeped and he had the director of the Naval Criminal Investigative Service on the line.

"Hi Garrett. I've got you on speaker phone. I'm with Colonel Felton and Sergeant Major Janches."

"Sorry for the delay, General. I was on another conference call with Admiral Cates." The Director of NCIS was sitting in his office across town. "What can I do for you gentlemen today?"

Janches spent the next twenty minutes going over everything he had been told. The recording was played several times. Once that was done, a round-table discussion broke out on how to secure what was pretty much an entire third of the Marine Corps from being attacked in a criminal manner.

"I think we need to break this down into manageable chunks, gentlemen." Felton looked at Leo and Corky. "We need to identify who is most at risk, and in order to do that we need to know what this cartel knows."

"And how do we know what the cartel knows?"

"Well, sir, it's like this—if they googled Stanford's name, then they got some intel on him. If they did any kind of a background, then it will be easy to find out what information they have." Felton gestured at the computer. "In the recording, this Ben guy says that they did a full background. I'm going to assume they got access to his military records. We need to look at them and start finding out what they found out. That will give us a probable target list."

"Okay, let's get on it. I want my people taken care of. Anyone who shows at risk, fellow squad mates, COs, XOs, whatever, I want them notified of the threat. Concentrate in San Diego at first. I think they will stay local, but I may even issue an ALMAR. I do not want to see my men turning up dead." Leo looked Felton in the eye. "I want someone on this yesterday, and I want it finished today by noon!"

Felton took it to mean that he should act with a sense of urgency since it was already three o'clock in the afternoon.

"Aye, aye sir! I have just the Marine for the job."

"Very well, Garrett, is there anything you need from me?"

"Only copies of that correspondence, please, General. I will begin working on it from my end."

"It's in your in box now." Leo hit send to forward the e-mail. "Gentlemen, I would like to have a meeting tomorrow at 0900 to see where we are."

It was well known that when the CMC stated he *would like* anything, what he really meant was *It damn well better happen*. They all confirmed that they would be in his conference room the following morning. The meeting broke up with Felton striding quickly down the hall.

He turned the corner into his office and said, "Clark, get me O'Malley in here now, please. I don't care where he is; I need him in my office via fastest means possible. Send out the SRT team in a bird if necessary!"

"Yes sir!"

Felton went into his office while PFC Clark dialed the cell phone of Greg O'Malley, the lead investigator for the Marine Corps CID—or Criminal Investigation Division—in Washington.

The Washington Redskins had few fans more loyal than Gregory O'Malley. The team hadn't gone to the playoffs in years, but O'Malley was at every game when he was in the States. He was just putting his cooler in his trunk to head to the game when his phone rang. Seeing the number on the caller ID made him wince.

"O'Malley."

"Gunner, please hold for Colonel Felton." A series of clicks later and Felton was on the line. "Hey, Gunner, what are you doing right now?"

"Giving CPR to a twenty-three-year-old virgin Redskins cheerleader on the beach in Tahiti, sir! I got my leave papers cleared last week." O'Malley knew they were going to have some work for him that might infringe on his football, so he did not feel bad about laying some guilt on the colonel.

"Oh, is that so? Well, get off her and get your ass into the office. There is a briefing package here for you. You have a meeting with CMC tomorrow morning at 0900 and he wants the case solved." Felton was waiting for some kind of reaction.

"Copy, sir; solve the world's problems by 0900, got it!" O'Malley pulled the cooler back out of his trunk. "Is there anything else the good colonel would like me to accomplish before then?"

"Get CMC some answers before 0900, and I will consider you to be an outstanding Marine. Fail and you're fired. That is all!"

"Aye aye, sir!" And with that, O'Malley slid the cooler into his garage and hit the button to close it. He jumped in the car and drove over to HQMC. The night duty gave him a funny look as he signed in and went into the secure wing wearing his "Skins" jersey.

O'Malley stopped at the vending machine and got a few snacks and drinks, went to the restroom, and having taken care of all his biological needs, sat down at his desk and opened the packet he found there. He looked through it once and turned on his computer. He logged into the NFL network so he could keep track of the game, and then went to work. He was still there at 0700 the following morning when Colonel Felton walked in the door.

"Shit! Have you been here all night?"

"Yes, sir. I've almost got this wrapped up."

"What? You're shitting me!"

"It is my duty to inform the Colonel that the Chief Warrant Officer would not shit him since the Colonel is the Chief Warrant Officer's favorite turd ... in all due respect ... Sir!"

Felton looked over O'Malley's shoulder at the notes and printouts. There were copies of two search warrants signed by judges and a slew of other correspondence. The stacks of papers were organized and set out in a logical order.

"Would you like to know how we are going to dig these guys out?"

"Enlighten me." Felton pulled a chair around the desk and sat down.

CHAPTER 31

Sheila Stanford usually loved to shop. Right now she felt like a purchasing agent for some shipping company. The items she was purchasing were all bought in bulk amounts, some of them literally in tons. Rice, beans, salt, spices, flour, baking soda, canned goods, and countless other items had to be ordered. The items then had to be organized and space allotted for each one.

She did get to do some fun things with all the money. She sent very large checks to several of her favorite charities. Tom had reined her in on giving away too much since they would be needing some substantial resources to survive. His argument became somewhat invalid when, after checking the books and accounts that Dan had set up, they realized their fortune was growing faster than they were spending it.

Bull and his crew had brought back twenty-three million from the LA mission, giving half of it to Tom and Sheila. The $11.5 million was more than they had spent thus far.

Even with everything they had spent, they now had over 643 million dollars. They had taken care of the families of the officers who had been killed or injured by the cartel. They had also sent substantial checks to the families of Brad and Tina, the self-storage employees.

She did get to have some fun spending the money on new clothes, although there weren't too many nice dresses. She did hit Victoria's Secret and blow a wad that was more than she had made in the previous year. The fashion show she gave Tom in the cramped bedroom of the RV kept his comments to a minimum. She couldn't say it kept his mouth closed because it hung open most of the time she was parading around in the rather revealing negligee.

Tom did grumble a little bit the following day about how he hadn't been able to spend any of the money. He vowed to change that soon enough though. The Internet had endless possibilities.

CHAPTER 32

The conference room adjacent the commandant's office was big enough to seat fourteen people around the table, and chairs lined the outer wall for another ten. A large flat screen at one end was hooked up by a single cable to a laptop. The old days of maps and charts were being supplanted by an anti-climactic little computer. Most of the room's space was wasted, as there were only seven people there.

Leo had just walked in and sat down when O'Malley, still wearing his Redskins jersey walked in with a bunch of folders. He staggered to the front of the room and started laying them out in a specific order. Once he was done, he looked up and realized the commandant was staring at him. He looked at his watch and blanched, realizing it was 0850 and any chance of changing clothes was out of the question.

Other people had begun to trickle in, and everyone who was supposed to attend watched as O'Malley began to stutter. He looked at Felton, who mumbled something about "favorite turds" under his breath and grinned.

"Um, sir, I was going to change really quick before the briefing. I can ..."

"Does your uniform have anything to do with protecting my Marines?"

"No, sir!"

"Then it's not important."

"Aye aye, sir!" O'Malley stood up and turned on the flat screen.

"Gentlemen, if I could go around the table and introduce everyone, it will make understanding what has happened easier, and it will help us address how we are going to solve this problem." O'Malley started on his left. "Colonel Felton, Head of Marine Corps Criminal Investigations Division. Garret Aylsworth, Director of NCIS. Sergeant Major Janches.

General Leo. Tate Mitchell, FBI Cyber Division. David Logan, from the Attorney General's Office."

Everyone nodded as they were introduced. Several produced cards and put them out on the table for others in the group after the meeting.

"Yesterday, a very credible threat to a number of our Marines was brought to Sergeant Major Janches's attention by a fellow Marine he had served with …"

O'Malley spent thirty minutes briefing the room on the occurrences to date. "Any questions so far?"

"So this Sergeant Major Stanford is a straight shooter?" Logan asked.

"Yes, and in more than just the literal sense. He honorably retired after twenty-six years of impeccable service. Former 1st MARDIV sergeant major. He should be sitting at my desk. Outstanding Marine," Janches said, his look daring anyone in the room to argue.

"A quick look at him after his retirement shows him to be living within his means, active at his church, does missionary work with his wife. Hell, I can't find a soul who will say a bad word about him," O'Malley confirmed.

Logan looked back and forth between them and said, "Okay."

"What we are up against is a well-known, very organized, criminal cartel that has massive resources. The DEA estimates their profits in the hundred-billion-dollar range …"

"Christ, that's half my budget!" Leo said.

"Yes, sir, very well-funded." O'Malley acknowledged the general's interruption. "And membership in the cartel is estimated at three to five thousand individuals, most of them in Mexico. Their distribution is mostly through Arizona and California. According to Sergeant Major Stanford, the threats to him, his wife, their family, and any Marines he served with are quite credible, as you saw in the news footage.

"To address this threat, I have requested and received a warrant for all FOIA requests that have been received for Stanford. If someone is running background checks for the cartel, we are going to find out who they are and try to trace it back to them.

"The local police department that initially handled the homicide investigations has been compromised by a leak in their department. The FBI cyber-crimes folks are going to work on that.

"We have determined that someone is making calls to find out the whereabouts of Stanford's friends. Two Marines that I got a hold of stated they had received calls asking if they knew Stanford or his whereabouts. Several of Stanford's friends have dropped off the face of the earth and no one seems to know where they are."

"I don't know where they are, but I can tell you they are okay," Janches said.

"And how would you know that, Sergeant Major?" Leo asked as several questioning looks were directed at him from around the room.

"Sir, I have been informed by a couple of the individuals that the Gunner is referring to that they are helping Stanford to stay alive. They are practicing OPSEC to keep off the grid."

"I'm assuming you are talking about that miscreant 'Bull' Toliver," Leo said with a grin.

"Sir, Master Guns Toliver, is a known associate of Sergeant Major Stanford. It is not too far of a stretch to think that he would come to the Sergeant Major's aide, especially as one of the Sergeant Major's two Bronze Stars is for 'Running through fire-swept terrain, ignoring the rounds impacting around him to recover a seriously wounded fellow Marine.' Said Marine being one Gunnery Sergeant—at the time—Toliver."

"Okay. So Gunner, you were saying?"

"Well, sir, I have a Marine going over to review FOIA requests right now with a warrant. That will get us headed in the right direction. I also suggest that this briefing packet be included in the President's DOD daily, sir. He will want to know and he might have state put a little pressure on the Mexican Government to get the word out that harboring these guys would be detrimental to our goodwill or whatever. Slightly above my paygrade, sir.

"I have received some intel from 'other' sources, but since the cat is out of the bag about Toliver, I will tell you that we have received phone numbers and contact info for a substantial amount of the Canton Cartel's southern California Network." O'Malley looked at Tate. "The FBI and DEA are processing as much of this as they can and using it to attack their operations. This should slow them down some and give us another avenue to track them down.

"The one major issue we still have is that they could follow through on their threats and start attacking our Marines anytime now. So anything to push along the inter-agency cooperation would be of great benefit, sir," O'Malley finished and looked at the group.

"I'll get the packet to the White House. I am also going to issue an ALMAR. If someone so much as touches one of my Marines, I will make a mess of their house." Leo looked at Felton, Janches, and O'Malley. "I'll expect daily briefings."

"Aye aye, sir!" they all said in unison.

CHAPTER 33

"Hey, goat fucker, are you still alive?"

"Corky, they have not yet found a way to kill me, so I guess I am!" Bull leaned back from the hotel room table, where he and Steve were counting the cash from the LA safe house. "Did you get a warning into the CMC's ear?"

"Shit, I got one into the CIC's ear!" Janches was also leaning back in his office chair.

"Good because these guys are untrained, but they are definitely serious about doing harm." Bull got up and walked out onto the hotel room balcony. "So is there any good news besides our fearless leader being in the loop?"

Janches took a few minutes to tell Bull what had happened in the meeting. "And here's a tidbit for you. There was a FOIA request for Stanford's service records. It was sent to a company called Telcor Investigations in Atlanta. We served a warrant there this afternoon and took everyone into custody. The owner, John Marino, started squealing like a stuck pig when the AG's office threatened him with an aiding terrorists charge and a grand jury subpoena. Turns out, he was a cutout for a company called Beltran Investigations out of, wait for it ..."

"San Diego?" Bull said hopefully.

"The service record was express mailed to a P.O. Box in Chula Vista." Janches was on a roll. "Beltran is a former FBI agent who left after he was turned down for the top spot in the NY field office. I guess he was an excellent investigator but played really poor politics." He gave the address to Bull and said goodbye.

Bull walked back in and gathered the troops. He went over the conversation he just had while Ben got on the computer and started researching Beltran. There were several articles about high-profile cases he had solved.

"Well, the guy is good," Ben said, looking through the articles. "In fact, if I needed to track someone down, I'd hire him."

They all let that soak in for a while.

Guerro was just sending some men to look into the first of the "examples" he intended to make for Stanford when Beltran walked in with a phone to his ear.

"Okay, just send the whole thing to my box. I'll get you a check right away." He hung up and turned to Guerro. "Some more info on Stanford coming in tomorrow."

"Well, I'm going to make him start paying tonight."

"I don't want to know about it." Beltran had still technically not done anything illegal. Except for the conspiracy to commit murder and aiding and abetting part. Why he still insisted on acting as if he was separated from the activities of the rest of the group was beyond Guerro.

Guerro had not had any good news to report to Juan Alfaro so far. His report, substantiated by the news reports had Juan writing off the money. It was a huge loss but not the biggest they'd ever had, nor would it be the last. He was, however, more upset about the twenty-three million in cash and the almost seven million in product they had lost in LA two nights before. That was not a trend he wanted to see continue.

Beltran left the warehouse for the day and went home. He changed into some workout clothes and went for a run down by the bay. He finished back in the parking lot of the yacht club and grabbed a duffel bag out of his car. He walked to the gate leading to the docks and entered the proper code to get in. He walked down the slips to a sixty-five-foot sailing yacht and climbed on board.

The Seetracker was his dream boat. He was close enough to having the money put aside to just sail down through the Panama Canal and spend the rest of his life cruising the Bahamas. Unfortunately, he wanted a lobster and champagne lifestyle and that was expensive. He figured it would take a liquid ten million dollars to achieve this. *The Seetracker* had almost seven of the ten stashed in secret compartments around the hull.

Beltran put his latest deposit in one of those compartments and decided to shower on the boat. Afterward, he put some chicken on the grill that was mounted on the railing by the cockpit. Salad and some wine to go with the chicken and asparagus on the grill made up his repast. He sat in the cockpit with his feet up on the steering wheel and watched the sunset.

The boat was owned by a shell corporation that he owned offshore. A few more jobs, or even completing this one, and he was gone. He went to bed with the sounds of the harbor soothing him into a deep sleep.

The Cessna 420 was a beautiful aircraft. The owner had babied it and it had always been stored in a hangar. The avionics package was the latest by Garmin with a programmable digital dash. The annual inspection had been done two months prior and the engines still had 1200 hours before they would need an overhaul.

Tom and Dan looked the plane over carefully and had it inspected by a reputable mechanic. They didn't even haggle over the price. Dan wrote the owner a check and drove him to the bank to cash it.

Tom had been a recreational pilot for several years but did not have his multi-engine rating. He hired a private flight instructor whose first lesson was flying the plane back to Palomar Airport with Tom. He would spend the next week studying and flying to get his license upgraded.

He just stood there and smiled when Sheila walked in the hangar.

CHAPTER 34

Lieutenant Colonel Rich Coffman tossed the carwash mitt into the bucket of dirty water. He picked up the bucket and carried it to the door of his garage and set it out of the way. Then he picked up the hose and turned to spray down his 1965 Corvette. The classic white-and-red hot rod was his pride and joy. As he turned around, he saw two Hispanic males walking towards him.

Coffman had been in enough tight spots to know that he might be facing one now. The realization did him no good as the two men opened fire with the pistols they both had in their hands. As soon as Coffman's body hit the ground, the two men each grabbed an arm and pulled the body up onto the hood of the car. One of the men used a folding knife to slit open Coffman's shirt and then used it to pin a note to his chest by slamming the knife into his ribcage. The note read *Tom Stanford did this.*

The two men walked down the driveway and got back into their car. The entire encounter took less than sixty seconds. Several neighbors saw the car drive away, and one even got a license plate number. The city of Oceanside and the Marine Corps just suffered the first casualty in the cartel's war.

"Hello?"

"Sergeant Major, this is Gunner O'Malley. We have our first victim."

"Ahh shit! What happened?" Janches was at home just getting ready for bed. He stopped putting on the shorts he usually slept in, and began reaching for a pair of jeans.

"Lieutenant Colonel Richard M. Coffman. Just recently retired. Former XO in First Anglico when Stanford was there. Image search on Google pulled up a pic of the two of them together." O'Malley was packing up a suitcase for a flight to San Diego. "Two Hispanic males walked up to him in his driveway and gunned him down while he was washing his car. They pulled the body up onto the hood and used a knife to pin a note that says 'Tom Stanford did this' right into his chest."

"Shit! CMC is not going to be happy about this."

"Colonel Felton is notifying him now." O'Malley was glad he didn't have to face that chore.

"Okay, what do you need me to do?"

"It would be great if I could talk to Stanford or your other guys when I get out there. I'm on a 0720 flight."

"Those guys are pretty security conscious. When you get there, buy one of those pay-as-you-go phones and send me the number. I'll have them call you." Janches didn't think any communications between Bull and O'Malley would result in any friendships. Bull was an operator and O'Malley was a cop.

"All right; I'll e-mail you in the morning."

"Hey, did Coffman get the warning?" Janches asked.

"I have no idea."

CHAPTER 35

The FBI Cyber Division had some of the best hackers on the planet. Recruited for their love of all things electronic, most of them saw their job of tracking down the rest of the talent as the most fun challenge of all.

Upon being assigned to the Stanford case, David Gaines, whose cyber-handle was "Lofty," began looking at CVPD's files. It took him nine hours to find the back door program and another seven to figure out a hack for it. He was able to determine which original access code was used to gain entry. After putting a monitoring program in place, he sent his report to Washington.

Special Agent Mitchell didn't open the e-mail until 11:30 the following morning. He immediately sent it to O'Malley and Felton. O'Malley checked his e-mail when he got off the plane but missed receiving it by about twenty minutes. He was talking to Bull on the phone when it notified him of the e-mail. He forgot about it and didn't check his messages until later that night. The information could have saved a couple of lives.

CHAPTER 36

Ben and Steve were staking out a Mail Boxes Etc., looking for Mike Beltran and discussing what they were going to do with the money they had made. The haul from the LA stash house was almost twenty-three million dollars. Neither man had even dreamed of possessing near the amount that they received after Bull had divvied it up. Even with half going back to the Stanfords, the seven-man security team was still dividing up 11.35 million bucks. Bull kept out a couple million to hire some more guys, but that still came out to just under a half million apiece. Add in the 200K that Tom had already given them, and it was more than enough to occupy their minds as they waited for Beltran to show up. Bull had more Marines arriving every hour and the team would soon number over twenty individuals.

"I'm going to take a cruise around the world," Steve said, looking at a thick pamphlet put out by one of the nicer cruise lines.

"Man, with your luck, the ship will break and you'll wind up on the 'poop cruise'." Ben couldn't help ribbing his fellow Marine. There had been a story in the news recently about a cruise ship having mechanical difficulties. The passengers had been stranded for days with overflowing toilets. "I'm getting a damn Ferrari or something. Some bitchin' ass car that I can just drive the wheels off it."

"You'll wreck it in a week. You need to go back to driving Hummer hoods. That was the last time you drove something and didn't wreck it." Steve and Ben had stolen the hood from a Hummer out of Motor-T once, and using the attachment points for lifting, had tied it behind another Hummer and used it like a sled for Christmas. The desert sand had scraped the hood down to shiny metal and when they replaced it in the motor pool, it looked like the hood from a DeLorean. They both cracked up at the memory.

"Movement." Steve nodded towards a guy getting out of a BMW.

Mike Beltran did not fall under the rules for the crew that worked for Guerro. He drove a nice 7 Series BMW that befit a successful owner of a small company. He didn't bother setting the alarm as he walked in to the postal service store.

Ben got out of the car and walked towards the store. He ran into Beltran as he was exiting with a manila envelope in his hand. The envelope had a strip of blue tape wrapped around it. He held the door open for Beltran as he walked out and even exchanged a nod with him.

He continued into the store as Beltran got into his car and drove off. "That's him. Positive ID on the package."

"Yeah I saw it." Steve pulled out of the driveway and followed the BMW. "Car is heading east on Telegraph Canyon."

Ben waited until they were gone then walked outside as Duane pulled up in a Dodge Durango. He slipped his gear over his T-shirt and pulled his rifle from a case between the seats. Two other cars were already on the road and everyone was talking to each other, getting cars in front of the BMW.

They managed to not be seen, even though the car did several counter surveillance maneuvers. The problem with them was that they worked on a single- or two-vehicle tail and only slowed him down enough to allow the cars from a four-vehicle tail to get ahead of him.

They followed Beltran to the entrance of an industrial park. Everyone noticed the abundance of cameras as they drove by. They set up a loose perimeter around the park and got on the laptops to start doing research. Every vehicle and their occupants that entered or left the property was photographed and the license plate recorded. Beltran and the BMW left two hours later.

"Leave me a couple of OPs here to watch all the exits. Everyone look for this Ben guy that messed with Stanford's wife," Bull said as he set up another tail for the Beemer.

"Copy."

"On it."

"I'm rolling after the car."

"I think he's heading back to the 805." The radios were going full tilt as the operation turned into a two-part challenge.

Beltran drove straight to his yacht and went right aboard. He disappeared below deck and wasn't seen for almost an hour. When he came back up, he was wearing a Hawaiian shirt and khaki pants. He walked to the clubhouse and had dinner on the patio looking out over the harbor.

"If he lives on the boat, it will be a little tougher to take him. The neighbors are mighty close." Duane was walking along the boardwalk, keeping the sailboat in sight. "It looks like the boat to port is lived in. The one on the starboard side has the covers all over it and doesn't look very used."

"Copy that." Bull was parked at the far end of the lot and was updating a Google map on his iPad. He had the industrial park and the yacht club marked with pinpoints and was entering data about both sites.

The team observed Beltran taking one phone call and chatting with the waitress and that was it. He paid his check and got up and left. He went back to the boat for another half hour before returning to his car and leading the team to his house. Once inside, he stayed there for the rest of the night.

CHAPTER 37

"Detective Johnson." Herb was at his desk getting ready to leave for the day.

"Detective Johnson, my name is CWO-4 Greg O'Malley. I'm with the Marine Corps Criminal Investigation Division."

"Ah yes, Gunner, I was told to expect your call." Herb picked up a piece of paper from his desk. It was a copy of a letter from the commandant's office to his chief asking for the department's cooperation in the investigation into the terrorist threats received by the recently retired members of the Marine Corps. At the bottom, the chief had written *Whatever they want!*

"Are you a Marine?" O'Malley had noted the use of the familiar term for his rank.

"I am a commander in the US Navy Reserves," Herb said. "My instructions are to assist you in every way possible."

"Would it be possible for me to come down and meet you to go over some of this? You are aware that the cartel followed through on its threat to Sergeant Major Stanford and killed one of his former XOs last night?"

"No, I wasn't. I'm sorry to hear that." Herb clenched his teeth. "I am getting really tired of hearing about innocent people dying over this whole thing. Does Tom know?"

"I am not in contact with the Sergeant Major. I don't know if he is aware of the homicide, and to be honest I hope he remains ignorant for a while," O'Malley said.

"Why is that?" Herb asked a little surprised by the statement.

"Because from what I know of the Sergeant Major, if he thought he could save just one Marine's life, he would gladly sacrifice his own."

O'Malley took a deep breath. "I have to hope I can make enough of a dent in their operations to make it not worth their while to continue this."

"You're probably right about Tom; from what I know of him and the limited interaction I've had, I believe he would gladly sacrifice himself in a heartbeat to save another Marine." Herb was nodding. "Or anyone else, for that matter."

"So when is a good time for you?" O'Malley asked.

"Are you familiar with San Diego?"

"I was stationed at MCRD once awhile back."

"Okay, well, I'm going to bring our lead narcotics detective and we'll meet you downtown." Herb was texting Burleson. "You see there's this bar ..."

Dan Klein looked at the huge plot of land. The flat 177-acre parcel was located in the Anza Borrego Desert, just south of State Route 78. The huge rectangle of land was completely level. He walked the perimeter with the owner of the construction company that he had chosen to build the next iteration of Fort Knox.

"Well, what do you think?"

"You're going to want to put an eight-foot-high wall along the road there if you don't want bullets hitting innocent people. Also, I would curve the road and put in Jersey barriers. And you're serious about an airstrip and helipad?" Chris Tully had been a Marine, and came recommended by a mutual friend. The combat engineer had gotten out of the Corps and used his GI Bill to get his contractor's license.

"Yep, has to be built to plan for the house and tunnels. I welcome all other suggestions to make it as secure as possible. The site will be used for stashing high-wealth clients for extended periods of time. Speed is also of the essence; I need the facility as soon as humanly possible."

"Well, you agreed to an incredibly expensive labor rate. And if your money is good, I'll get it done on time or ahead of schedule."

"Here is a cashier's check for the initial installment plus 10 percent. I really don't want to have phone calls for incidentals; if you can justify the expense, do it. If it is more than the overage I just gave you, I will get a check to you within twenty-four hours." Dan handed him the cashier's check. "I cannot emphasize speed and quality of the building."

"Sir, twelve-inch-thick concrete walls. Steel shutters and these reaper lock things. Man, I don't know what kind of trouble you're expecting, but you'll be able to handle just about anything short of a military assault." Chris looked around one last time. "My trucks will be on their way out here in an hour. We'll have the pad for your security trailer ready tomorrow morning and the first connex boxes here by the afternoon."

They walked back to their parked vehicles. As they shook hands to leave Dan said, "Hey Chris ..."

"Yeah?"

"More important than speed, though, is discretion."

"Got it!"

CHAPTER 38

Herb and Burleson were seated at the Black Crow in San Diego's Gas Lamp District. Herb had a soda water and Burleson was nursing a beer. It was hard to miss O'Malley when he walked through the door. The six-foot-tall Marine was very well muscled. Although his red hair was shaved on the sides of his head, the freckles on his face and arms gave him away as a ginger.

Herb lifted a hand and O'Malley noticed it immediately and made his way over. Herb and Dawn stood and introductions were made all the way around. After sitting down, the waitress took O'Malley's order for a coke and left.

"Well, Gunner, what I've done is put together a complete case file and timeline for what we believe has happened so far. There is a synopsis on top with references to the specific files." Herb handed over an accordion file. "The files from the other agencies are in there as well. I got a hold of Oceanside PD and they have agreed to share their file with us. I talked to their deputy chief and brought him up to speed about what is going on, since Oceanside is probably going to be the site of more of this."

"I'm sorry, what happened in Oceanside?" Dawn asked.

"Two Hispanic males walked up to a former officer that Tom Stanford served with and shot him in his driveway. They then pinned a message to his chest with a switchblade saying it was Stanford's fault."

"Oh wow!" Dawn exclaimed. No one on either side had told her about that.

"Yeah, I just found out about it a while ago," Herb said.

Dawn wasn't quite mollified but it set her at ease that she was part of the team. She had been feeling a little ostracized lately at the department.

But some of the other D's felt it too and had mentioned it. They hadn't put together that certain info was not being shared with them. Herb had been juggling a fine line.

"Well, we may have a line on the cartel's operations. We were able to track down the guy who is working for the cartel, doing some of their intelligence. I have some information on a probable location of an operations center." O'Malley leaned forward slightly. "Some retired Marines have been helping the Stanfords with their problem."

"I figured as much," Herb said. "The deal in LA was too easy. They wiped out half of the main supply network for the city."

Dawn was taking it all in. If they were getting ready to move on the warehouse, she had to let Guerro know. If she saved their bacon, she could demand a healthy chunk of change. Guerro had never turned her down when she had asked for some cake after keeping them out of trouble.

"Stanford was a recon guy. It's a very tight-knit, close community. The men who have dropped off of our radar are all tier-one guys. They are capable of doing things that would cause great harm to the cartel if they are left to their own devices." O'Malley leaned back again. "I'm of half a mind to let them. It would end this problem quickly, but there would be a lot of bodies to account for."

"I hate to tell you this, Greg, but the last time I checked, we had laws and rules for that stuff." Dawn had a look of disgust on her face. "I'm not a big fan of vigilantism."

"Detective, I said 'half a mind.' I too believe in the law. However, you have to admit that sometimes the law gets in its own way and is incapable of moving at the speed necessary to mitigate a threat that is as fluid as this one." O'Malley noticed Herb looking at Burleson. "Please remember, the Stanfords—who as far as I can see, are the most righteous people on the planet—did not ask for this. Every action they took that got them into this mess was an act of kindness towards others. The thanks they are getting for their actions is a life on the run from some very dangerous criminals. I, for one, think justice would be served tonight if those criminals disappeared. I would hope that you folks would be tired of your fellow officers being shot by these same criminals."

"Have no doubt, Greg. We want to see them brought to justice, and we sure don't want to see anyone else get hurt," Herb said, sipping his soda water. "We do, however, play by the rules. So, within those boundaries, what can we do to help you?"

"I could use a full brief on their operations. Any files on the members you've identified would be helpful. You guys are about to receive a huge influx of federal involvement."

"You do realize that too many people can be a hindrance. Our taskforce office has been very successful in developing intel on the narcotics trafficking into the US through the Southwest region." Dawn was getting fired up. "You want to help us, get the AG to prosecute the cases we develop."

"Detective, I am here to address one problem: the cartel's attacks on Marine Corps personnel." O'Malley turned a not too friendly look in her direction. "I can solve those other problems at a future date if you wish. In the meantime, it is my intention to track down the murderers who started all this. They are killing innocent Marines. I will stop this from continuing to happen. It may be a moot point after tonight, but we will see."

"What's going on tonight?" Herb was getting a bad feeling in his gut.

"The operations center I mentioned earlier is under surveillance right now. If those men can get me a location of the shooters from any of the crime scenes, the NCIS will serve a warrant. I guarantee you that they will be prosecuted." O'Malley nodded to the waitress as she asked if they wanted another round.

"Just one more." Dawn nodded and smiled at the waitress as well. "Excuse me while I make room for this one."

Both men started to stand as she excused herself from the table and made her way to the bathroom. O'Malley noticed that she pulled out her phone just as she made it to the restroom door. He turned back to Herb.

"She's a little protective of her turf," he said, tilting his head in the direction of the restrooms.

"She's been pretty effective at turning up leads on trafficking. Nobody likes Feds coming in and upsetting the applecart. That said, I wouldn't mind letting you jarheads clean up some of the more violent members of the cartel. These guys just started killing everyone that was in their way. A good cop is dead and two of my best friends are in the hospital."

The appetizers they had ordered arrived, and the two men talked about the military as they waited for Burleson to return. O'Malley had never been deployed on a ship, but they had both shared a duty station earlier during their careers.

Dawn had her phone out and was scrolling through her contacts as she entered the women's restroom. She went to the far stall and sat down on top of the toilet. She was typing furiously trying to get as much information to Guerro as she could. She hit send and waited. She wasn't going to be able to have an extended exchange, but she was going to try to wait for instructions.

She didn't have to wait long to receive a reply, and she answered the question it contained. Two more quick exchanges, and then she deleted the messages from her phone. She stood up and went to the sink where she washed her hands and then made her way back to the table. The food had been delivered and she sat down. She was somewhat calmer as they discussed the cartel's activity.

After an hour, they agreed on a tentative course of action and called it a night. O'Malley had parked in a pay lot on the next block. Burleson had used a valet out front. After retrieving his car, he was driving back past the front of the restaurant when his car was stopped by a traffic light. He overheard Burleson tell the valet, "Sorry, can you hold on to it for a minute? I have to go to the bathroom. I should have gone during dinner."

The statement sent a jingle through O'Malley. He put the tidbit away for later.

CHAPTER 39

Guerro was coordinating a new delivery schedule with Juan Alfaro, when one of his phones beeped. He took one look at the message and told Juan he would call him back. He sent a question back to Burleson and waited for a reply. Once he received it, he started yelling orders at his crew.

The whole crew inside the warehouse began breaking down their computers and packing things up. Guerro sent Beltran a text and told him he might be under surveillance. He then sent two men out to comb the neighborhood and grab anybody who looked out of place. Several boxes of equipment were loaded into vehicles that were parked on the warehouse floor. After everything was packed, the techs all got into cars and waited for the order to leave.

Guerro had twenty-three soldiers at the warehouse. All of them were armed with pistols, and some also had shotguns or AK-47s. One of them had an HK G3 battle rifle he had taken with him when he deserted from the Mexican Army. They all took up positions around the building and started looking out windows. Guerro sent four more men out to check the surrounding area.

"Lead, Ghost One. I have movement. Two males walking around, looking in bushes." Dillon Remke had done ten years in the Corps and loved it. He had given it up though when his special needs child became too much of a burden for his wife to handle alone. He had gotten out and was working an underpaid security job when Bull had called him and offered him a chance to get out of the financial hole that seemed to be sucking him down.

The money was enough for him to fly his parents out to help care for his son Rick while he was working. Dillon had been a scout sniper in the Corps and was set up on a hill almost a half mile away when he observed a substantial amount of activity at one of the buildings in the industrial park he was watching.

"I also have a lot of activity at the ..." He checked his map. "Five-twelve building. Lights going on and off, lot of bodies moving past the windows."

"Lead, Ghost Three confirms the activity. I have people moving between 512 and 514 buildings." Pete Horn was even farther away on the other side of the complex.

"Lead copies." Bull was parked at a shopping center two miles away. He was sitting in the back of the Econoline van they had taken from the cartel up in LA. "Let's make sure we can follow any vehicles that leave."

Several replies came back confirming receipt of the order. They had ten men and six vehicles watching or staged next to the industrial park. They had several other Marines who were off on a different mission, so they were running a little short on personnel.

"Lead, Ghost One. I have two more males out looking through the complex. Subjects are looking into cars with flashlights." Dillon had not seen the last two of Guerro's men because they were moving around the far side of the building.

"Okay, something has got them riled up. This may be what we were looking for." Bull was staring at the map. He was waiting for Ben and Steve to call him back from the yacht club. They had six men down there looking into Beltran's boat.

They had kept the industrial park under observation since they had followed Beltran there earlier in the day. They had identified Beltran as a probable cartel operative when the owner of Telcor Investigations forwarded a supplemental information package to him. The package contained information made up by Greg O'Malley that would allow any action taken to be easily identified by the law enforcement agents assigned to the case. The package was sealed with bands of highly visible blue tape.

After tailing him for the rest of the day and identifying the warehouse, the boat, and his residence, Bull had set up full-time surveillance on all three locations. Steve and Ben were doing a sneak and peak on the yacht. Duane and two others were watching his house, while everyone else was watching the park.

"Lead, Dog Two; Beltran is up and moving around as well."

"Dog One confirms. I saw the light come on, but it's off again. He may have just been taking a piss." Duane didn't see any other activity at the house.

"Dog, keep an eye out, we have a bunch of activity at the industrial park that just started; timing is right if someone is calling these people." Bull was starting to get that pre-combat rush where his mind got sharp and things started to click into place.

They waited for a few more minutes when all of a sudden an urgent call went out over the radio.

"Bear Three you have two men behind you! They just came out from behind the building!"

Tim Westbrook was Bear Three. He was parked two blocks away from the closest driveway into the industrial park. He saw the two men who were over two blocks away in front of him, but he didn't notice that two more had come out onto the street behind him. He was slouched down in a Dodge pickup with his eyes barely above the dash. He watched as the men behind him started looking into every car on the street with flashlights. As he was watching, he noticed that one of the men had a gun in his other hand pressed up against his leg.

"Lead, Bear Three! One of the guys behind me has a pistol in his hand! They're going to be at my truck in about two mikes!" Tim pulled his Colt Commander out from his holster. He slipped a Surefire X300 light onto the frame rail and swept the safety off.

"Bear Three, get out of there; we're blown!"

Tim leaned forward to start the truck. Unfortunately, one of the men behind him saw the movement and gestured to his partner. They both rushed the truck with guns out and flashlights on.

Tim had switched his pistol to his left hand to turn the key in the ignition. He saw the lights hitting his cab and had a sight picture out the passenger side window as the man on the curbside appeared there. The two men fired at the same time. Both of them hit their opponent. The cartel thug fired through the pickup's door and the bullet was slowed substantially from passing through it. It still hit Tim just below his Tac vest and entered his lower abdomen. Tim's round went out through the passenger side window, blowing it out into the man's face. The glass, however, was the least of the damage as the .45-caliber Federal Hydra-Shok bullet impacted him right above the upper lip and punched a hole in his face. The damage was catastrophic as the bullet tore through the sinus cavity and up into the brain. The man collapsed where he stood, dead before he hit the ground.

Tim had only had a chance to say "I'm hit" over the radio before the man on the driver's side opened fire. He fired nine rounds through the door post and window. The last six were unnecessary as the third round hit Tim in the back of the neck and severed his spinal column. His head fell forward at an unnatural angle.

Arturo Torres slowly stepped up to the cab as the two other soldiers from down the street came running up. One of them was on the phone yelling in Spanish. Just as Arturo was leaning in close to the cab of the truck, a 5.56mm slug tore through his upper back and burst out through his chest. A second round followed less than a third of a second later. His body slammed into the truck and then fell back out into the street.

The two men who were running up the street stopped in their tracks. One of them stared at Arturo as he slid to the ground. The other man had seen a slight flash in some bushes and pointed his pistol at the general area and opened fire. His partner turned to look where he was shooting just as two more flashes signaled the arrival of two more slugs, this time in his own chest.

The last man standing tried to dodge away but only prolonged his life by a second at most. Two more flashes, and he fell to the pavement. The street went quiet. After a few seconds, a man emerged from the bushes with a rifle held at the ready. He was whispering into a microphone as he approached the truck.

"Where's the last two guys? Bear Three is down! Ahh man, he's fucked up bad," the man said, looking into the cab quickly. "Bear Three is KIA, say again Bear Three is Kilo India Alpha. I took one in the side on my plate. I'm mobile but am going to need medical."

"Bear One, Lead copies all; Bear Four is coming your way." Bull was trying to get his guys some help when his radio crackled again.

"Lead, Dog Two, subject is out of his house and moving through his backyard. I have him on the motion sensor."

"Keep on him!" Bull had too many things happening all at once to be a coincidence.

"Lead, Ghost One, all hell is breaking loose in the industrial park and the surrounding neighborhood." Although it was just coming up on nine o'clock, most of the neighborhood had settled in for the night. Porch lights were coming on in the area and people were stepping out onto their front lawns. Guerro was counting on the noise and presence of the surrounding populace to help him escape.

Two of the garage bay doors rolled up and five cars and trucks all drove out all at once. The vehicles went straight out of the industrial park and scattered. The Bear surveillance team followed a van and a Range Rover, figuring them to be the highest-value targets. If there hadn't been so many civilians on the street, they would have engaged all of the vehicles with suppressed rifle fire. As it was, they had to settle for following two vehicles. They totally ignored the blue PT Cruiser that drove sedately out of the complex.

The van and Range Rover drove to the Mission Valley Mall, where a movie was getting out of the AMC Theatre. They parked and both subjects vanished into the crowd as the Marines tailing them held back. They kept eyes on the vehicles and waited.

CHAPTER 40

Michael Beltran had called it a night and was debating with himself on whether he should watch Letterman or not. He opted for climbing into bed and if he fell asleep, so be it. He was just nodding off when his phone beeped out an urgent tone. He swiped his finger across the phone and opened his text messages. The message from Guerro was to the point:

You may be under surveillance—get clear and call me.

Beltran sat up and went to his closet. Unable to see, he had to turn on his light for a second to grab his "Go Bag" that was inside his closet. His bachelor's mess made it difficult without the light. After grabbing the bag, he put on some jeans, hiking boots, and a dark flannel shirt. He turned off the light and started looking around.

There were no strange cars on the street. He went to his nightstand and pulled a device out of the drawer. He plugged it into his phone receptacle and then plugged the cord into it. The device measured any current draw on the wire and would tell him if there was any unusual current flow along the line, a sure indicator that the line was tapped. The reading came out normal and he started to breathe a little easier. His alarm panel showed all green.

He sent Guerro a text to ask if he was sure, and how he knew. Guerro's reply was that Burleson had just found out about it.

Not wanting to take any chances, he decided to slip any tail he might have and go down to his boat. He would sail it out of San Diego Bay and head towards Mexican waters. He could sit off the coast and see anyone coming for miles.

He slipped downstairs and again looked around; nothing appeared out of place. He considered just getting in his car and seeing if he could flush out the tail that way. But he knew if they were good, he would never make them. He decided to err on the side of caution and slip out the back. He went out his sliding glass door and moved along the edge of his yard to the back fence. He had to go over the wall kitty-corner because the people directly in back of him had an annoying little dog. The yard he went into belonged to a quiet older couple who were never seen after eight o'clock at night.

He made his way to the front yard and looked carefully up and down the street. Still nothing. He waited two full minutes up against the bushes before deciding the coast was clear. He stepped boldly out onto the sidewalk and turned right. He only had to go six blocks to a parking garage, where he kept a BMW GS1000 Dual Sport motorcycle. He made it to the garage without seeing anything suspicious.

He walked up to his bike and opened one of the saddle bags. He pulled out a riding jacket and unlocked a full-faced helmet. It took him another minute to get his backpack stored and his gear on. He started up the bike and rolled out through the security gate with his eyes scanning every car he passed.

Once on the road, he began to feel that Guerro—or more importantly, Burleson had made a mistake. He had always held the woman in low regard. She seemed a little trashy to him. He took a few precautions to identify surveillance but nothing set off any alarm bells, so he headed to the yacht club.

He pulled into the member's lot and parked his bike over by the rack that the Junior Sailing Club used to store its sabots. He stayed in the shadow of the storage area for almost five full minutes this time. Again, nothing seemed out of place, so he walked out onto the dock to his boat, stopping to chat with some folks on their boat in the next slip. He told them he was going out for a couple of days.

He climbed on board and set his backpack down next to the door as he fished his keys out of his pocket. He unlocked the security panel and stepped into the main saloon. He had just looked down and noticed a wet spot on the carpet when a hand clamped over his mouth and his head was wrenched back. Beltran was a long time out of the FBI Academy, and his reactions were a little too slow. A long and very sharp-looking knife appeared in front of his face as a second set of hands grabbed his wrists.

The knife was laid at his cheek with the point just below his eye. His hands were pulled behind him and two pairs of zip ties were used to secure his wrists. He was then lifted up and dropped on the deck none too gently. His feet were duct taped. A gruff voice spoke into his ear.

"You should have listened to whoever tipped you off. If you would have driven that pretty bike into the mountains, you'd be a free man now.

Unfortunately, I have it on good authority that you have been asking questions about my friends. The information you acquired was used to kill a very good man."

Steve leaned back as Ben wrapped duct tape around Beltran's head. "Know this, you piece of shit; your life is forfeit. There will be no grand jury, no trial, no plea bargain. You can cooperate with us, and we will let you live. You will have to go to Mexico because everything you tell us will be recorded and given to the police. But you'll be alive. Nod your head if you understand this."

Beltran's eyes were as big as dinner plates as he began nodding his head at the masked face in front of him. He was flipped back over and left lying facedown as the two men went about searching the cabin. They stayed below decks for over two hours searching every nook and cranny. It wasn't long before they had discovered his safe. They looked at it, shrugged, and kept searching. A few minutes later, Ben walked up and dropped a bundle of cash on the ground in front of Beltran's face. Again, nothing was said and the feet walked away. A short time later, another bundle landed next to the first. Then his Mossberg 590 Mariner shotgun was unloaded in front of him and set up on a shelf. One, and then the other of his hidden pistols were unloaded and joined the shotgun.

"Well, let's see what you had with you, hmmm …"

His backpack was dumped out and rifled through. His passport was photographed and his keys were pocketed. Another twenty minutes of ransacking his boat, and then one of the men stood up straight.

"Copy," he said and the two men nodded at each other.

"It looks like your neighbors are finally all tucked in for the night," one of them said as the other one went up on the deck and cast off. The powerful Cat Diesel came to life and the boat slid forward out of the slip. Once clear, it made a gradual turn to the north.

No one spoke to him for another forty minutes. They then hauled him up on deck and took him to the back of the cockpit. The cutting board from his galley was set next to the grill. His zip ties were cut off and he was manhandled over to the edge of the boat. His left arm was wrenched behind his back while his right hand was held next to the cutting board. He struggled, but the two men holding him controlled him with ease.

His fingers were put on the board and his right pinky was hacked off with the large knife. The digit made a soft *plop* as it hit the water and sank out of sight. He looked off to the north, seeing the lighthouse at Point Loma passing by on the right as the blunt pain shot up his arm. He tried to scream, but the duct tape kept his scream to a muffled moan.

The men pushed his stub against the outside of the grill. The sound of his flesh sizzling reached his ears before the searing pain reached his brain. Again his scream was limited to a moaning deep in his throat.

He was shoved down into the foot well of the cockpit. He was left there for another ten minutes while the boat motored further off shore. Finally, the tape was slit and pulled off his head. He lay there panting for another minute as one of the men leaned over him, staring at him intently.

"I'm not convinced," he said over his shoulder to the other man.

"You want to do another one?"

"Yeah, I think we should. I mean didn't they threaten to cut off Sheila's fingers? Fair is fair." Both Marines had been incensed when they had heard about the threats made by Albert and Richard at the Stanfords' home.

"No, wait! I'll tell you what you want!" Beltran had studied interrogation techniques, but they were for situations where there were laws and guidelines. He was out of his element dealing with these men, who were so instantly capable of violence.

"Yeah, you're right. He's still thinking."

"Huh, what?" Beltran didn't understand what was happening. "I said I'll tell you what you want!"

"Okay, let's go."

He was again pulled up and his ring finger was severed with one quick chop of the knife. This time, his scream was allowed to fly out across the water. He passed out when they cauterized his finger. He regained consciousness when they splashed water on him while rinsing the blood off the back of the boat.

"Michael, let me explain a few things. We do not operate by the rules you think we do. We operate on an even playing field with you cartel members. We do not have any rules restricting us on how we gather information. None.

"I am going to ask you questions. You will answer them completely and truthfully each and every time. If I for one second even think you are lying or concealing something from me, I am going to cut off the rest of your fingers one at a time and then move on to other parts of your body. The information I require is time sensitive, and I swear with God as my witness, if another Marine dies because of your delay or inaction, you will not survive the night. Do you understand?"

"Yes, I will cooperate fully. You didn't need to cut off my fingers." Beltran was trying hard not to cry. "I have money, I can get you lots more money, and then I'm gone! I'll disappear."

The two men exchanged another look.

"He's beginning to think again," Ben said.

"What does that mean? I swear I'm going to do what you ask!"

"What that means is the only thing you should be concentrating on is answering my questions." Steve tapped him on the forehead with the knife.

"Okay."

"Are there any more plans to attack associates of Tom Stanford?"

"Yes."

"When?" Steve leaned forward and stared into Beltran's eyes.

"Tomorrow, I believe ..." Beltran screamed as his hand was crushed under Steve's boot.

"I do not like uncertainties," Steve said when Beltran had regained his composure. He took a few minutes to bandage the abused appendage.

"I am answering to the best of my knowledge." Beltran was wincing from the waves of pain radiating up his arm.

"I know; I'm just setting ground rules." Steve's tone was almost nonchalant. "Now when and who?"

"There was a target list developed. There were seven names that were the most vulnerable."

"You developed a list of seven names," Steve clarified, emphasizing the *you*.

"I, uh, yes," Beltran admitted.

"Who is on the list?"

"It is on my tablet." Beltran nodded at the cabin, where the device sat on the salon table.

Steve retrieved the tablet and pushed the power button. After following Beltran's directions to access his files, he forwarded the list to Bull.

"Okay, so let's talk about the guys you are working for. Are they at the industrial park where you were earlier today?"

"Yes, some of them. Some are at another safe house in Chula Vista. Guerro lives south of the border most of the time. The warehouse was just set up to track down the Stanfords. It is also where they store vehicles for use during day-to-day operations." Beltran hitched himself into a more upright position.

"Who is Guerro? In fact, let's make a little chart of who's who in the cartel."

It took them an hour and a half to go over the limited amount of knowledge that Beltran had since he was only brought in on security issues. Once Steve was happy with the information on the cartel's operations, they started on the Stanford issue. They relayed all of this information to Bull as well.

"Okay, so now let's talk about you." Again the knife was tapped on Beltran's head. "You see, once we were on to you, we did a background of our own. FBI, PI license, the whole nine yards. What I want to know is why I should let a traitor like you live. It's okay to start thinking now."

"Look, I can get you real money. Two million apiece if you let me go. You'll never hear from me again." He looked back and forth between the two men. "I'm out. I'm done!"

Ben looked at Steve and shook his head.

"Well, that's funny because we found more than that right here on my boat. Do you have some more stashed away? Oh wait, we still have the safe to look into. Do you want to give me the combo, or should we start with your other hand?"

"Standard right two rotations, left one, direct to number. 16-44-19." The directions flew out of Beltran's mouth so fast he almost stumbled over the words.

Ben went down and came back a minute later with a small packet of cash, a small revolver, and some bank papers. He looked at them then showed them to Steve.

"Now why would you have your offshore banking stuff in here?" He gave Beltran a curious look.

"Um. That's a trigger account. The safe is in case someone gets on the boat and tries to burglarize it. The cash and stuff is supposed to make them think they got everything. When they try to access the account, it notifies the bank personnel and they get grabbed. You have to be there in person. It's a front for the cartel so whoever tries to show up and collect is in trouble."

"Ahh, very clever. So this is to prevent them from searching and finding the rest of the stuff you have hidden away. So tell me; is there any more stuff hidden away that we didn't find?" He gestured to the table in the saloon. There were two pistols, two bundles of cash, and the shotgun lying there. Beltran had his cash spread out in four hiding places plus the small amount in the safe. He decided to split the difference in risk and go with a maybe.

"You found my cash and guns, you got the stuff out of the safe. Yeah, that's it." He held Steve's gaze. He never looked away and never blinked.

"I told you he would start thinking too much," Ben said as he pulled Beltran up by the neck. He let out a startled squawk and tried to regain his feet. He was pulled off balance as Steve re-lit the grill.

Ben released the chokehold slightly as the man struggled. Steve had to grab his legs to help maneuver him to the back of the cockpit again.

"What? I swear I'm not thinking too much! I don't have anything else." He was pleading and crying as his other hand was set against the cutting board. "I swear! That was it! What do you want?"

"Where is the rest of the cash you have on board?" Steve said as the knife came down on his other pinkie. Beltran watched, stunned as the digit flew into the water. It was a pale image as it slowly began to sink out of sight. He let out a scream as the pain hit. He inhaled just in time to scream again as the stump was pressed to the outside of the grill.

"We shouldn't be having this conversation. I told you that if you lied to me, or in any way held back, I would do the rest of your fingers, yada, yada." Steve was waving the knife in Beltran's face. "Now being a man of my word, I have to fuck you up some more ..."

"No, wait! I didn't lie! You said you found my cash. I didn't know how much you found!" He was pleading as sweat poured down his face. "Tell me which hiding places you found, and I'll tell you where the other one is."

"See? He's still trying to be smart." Ben was pushing his hand back towards the cutting board again.

"Please! Everything, I'll give you everything!"

He was flipped onto his stomach and his pants and shirt were cut off of him. He was whimpering piteously by the time he was sat back up in just his underwear. They re-taped his legs together and loosely zip-tied his hands in front of him. Ben applied a bandage to the most recent amputation, and then offered him a couple of aspirin. He was allowed to take four of them and wash it down with a bottle of Fiji water.

"How many places do you have cash stashed on my boat? We know it was more than two because we found more than two. Your little white lie tells us that you are still not being forthcoming, hence the reason your other finger is feeding the fish." The knife was set on his cheek again. "Now financial information; I want you to access your real offshore accounts right here on your iPad so I can change the passwords. I want to know where else you have cash and vehicles stashed. We know where some of it is; you will not know what we do or do not know. So the only way to be sure the rest of your body parts remain attached is to be an open book. Do you understand?"

"Yes, sir."

"Don't call me *sir*, pussnuts! I work for a living!"

CHAPTER 41

Herb received the call about the shootout in the industrial park just as he was pulling into his driveway. He simply shifted the car into reverse and pulled back out. It took him less than ten minutes to get there. Because of recent events, the SWAT guys were responding to "all shots fired" calls. Chuck Cooper pulled up at the same time Herb did.

"Man, I am going to retire early on all this OT," Chuck said, walking up and shaking his hand.

"You know the city manager is going to wind up giving us comp time off or some other bullshit," Herb said, grinning back as they walked to the building, ducking under the crime scene tape as they went.

They examined the crime scene where the four cartel soldiers had been left in the street. Shattered glass showed where the pickup had been parked. The bodies had been left alone, but the weapons had been partially disassembled and stacked near the curb. Chuck looked at Herb with a quizzical look on his face.

"I think some law-abiding citizens may have done this to prevent someone from in the community from hurting themselves," Herb said with a wink.

"Why not just take them with them, if it was Stanfords' Marine buddies?" Chuck was looking at the neatly laid out parts.

"I think the reasoning is that we will find ballistic matches to other crime scenes." Herb gestured to the warehouse set back in the complex. "This was supposedly where they were coordinating the operation against the Stanfords."

The two men walked over to the open warehouse door. They looked inside but did not enter. The overworked crime scene unit was still walking up and down the surrounding two blocks.

"We gonna look in here?" Chuck asked.

"Waiting for a warrant. One of the calls reporting the crime stated that armed men were coming and going out of here." Herb looked at the vehicles that were still parked inside the garage. One of them was the GMC Acadian that had been hit several times in the shootout over on E Street. The bullet holes were plainly visible. "I don't want anything we get out of here to be excluded if we can ever make an arrest."

"Yeah, although there may not be anyone left." Chuck was also staring at the cars inside the structure.

The burner phone in Herb's pocket rang. He stepped away and answered it.

"Yeah."

"Listen, I have some very important information for you." Tom's voice came over the line.

"Just a sec." Herb got out a pen and notebook. "Okay, whenever you're ready."

Tom spent five minutes telling Herb about the operation planned against one of the Marines who had served with him. There was supposed to be an attempt on him in the morning. Herb wrote down all the information and told him they would be there. Tom said not to bother; the Marine was warned and in hiding.

"Do I want to know how you came about this information?"

"I have no idea how I came across this information," Tom said in an official tone. "I received an anonymous text from an unidentified phone number giving me the information that I just gave you. In light of recent occurrences, I felt it prudent to notify local law enforcement of said information."

"Yes, I see," Herb replied in an equally civil tone. "You wouldn't happen to know anything about a shootout at an industrial park in south Chula Vista, would you?"

"You know what?" Tom asked. "I just might. I received another text that said there was a van and a car parked at the Mission Valley Mall. Both vehicles were seen leaving the scene of a violent encounter in south Chula Vista. I would bet that those vehicles have some interesting evidence in them."

"I don't suppose there would be any probable cause for law enforcement to search these vehicles, would there?" Herb was shaking his head at the word games they both knew they had to play.

"I'm sure there would be if you looked at them." Tom gave him the descriptions of the van and Range Rover. "Check your e-mail, Herb. There should be some interesting stuff coming your way."

"We'll check on the cars in Mission Valley. Are all of your people all right?" Herb asked in all seriousness.

"I just learned that one of my friends from Afghanistan was killed in a car accident tonight. I am very upset about this." Tom's voice was like ice over the phone.

"I'm sorry to hear that," Herb said. "Please know that we are working to end this."

"I believe you, Detective. Good night, good luck, and God speed."

CHAPTER 42

All of the Marines, except for the two watching the cars in Mission Valley and Steve and Ben, had regrouped at the Hilton Hotel. They had made arrangements for Tim's body and notified Tom. He had taken the news hard, but it wasn't the first time he had lost a fellow Marine.

They had rented out the entire floor and put extreme security measures in place. The hallway was covered by pinhole cameras and motion detectors. The rooms directly above and below the ones that were actually occupied were also rented so no one could approach from those directions. Two men stayed on watch while everyone else hoisted one in Tim's honor.

"I hope those cops can get something done with what we gave them." Bull was planning on having a few. He didn't normally let himself go, but he had really liked Tim. "That had to be some kind of facility for them."

"Yeah, those fuckers have earned my displeasure." Dillon Remke was putting a bandage on Paul Kursk's abdomen. Kursk was the one who was shot going to Tim's aid. He had driven the truck away afterwards. Kursk just grimaced and nodded. They all settled down to get some rest. They had an operation planned for the morning.

Steve and Ben brought the boat about. They had gotten a hold of a pretty substantial amount of assets from Beltran. They had found three of the four bundles of cash. By the time Beltran fessed up, they had all four bundles totaling just over seven million dollars. They had also learned that he had access to a slush fund of three million dollars that he was allowed to use in case of emergencies. His real account in the British Virgin Islands had almost a million dollars in it.

It took Steve twenty minutes to transfer all of the funds out of the institutions they were in and send them to a numbered account in Switzerland. The money was there for less than six minutes before automatic instructions triggered a series of transfers. This was done despite dire warnings that they shouldn't touch the cartel's money.

"Dude, do you seriously think we care?" Steve was shaking his head and looking down on the man, who was still sitting in the bottom of the cockpit. "I mean, you have to admit that we've been making a pretty good dent in their operations. I am pretty sure if they ever found out who we are and got us alone they would try to kill us. I say 'try' because so far, these guys have failed miserably."

Steve finally brought the boat to a stop. Ben came back to the cockpit and Beltran was hauled up to his feet. They walked him to the edge of the boat, where he stood shivering in his underwear.

"I have just a couple of questions left," Steve said as Ben went over to the dinghy winch.

"I'll answer them!" Beltran thought he was going to actually get away. A plan to explain what had happened to the cartel was already forming in his mind. Once he was in Mexico, he was going to find out who these two men were. Then he was going to send every asset after them he could. He would work for free for years to see to it that these two animals paid for what they had done.

"How much is this boat worth?"

"Five hundred, seventy thousand." The answer came out automatically.

"How are you going to make it up to Cindy?"

"What, huh?" The look of confusion on Beltran's face was genuine. "Who is Cindy?"

"Cindy is the little girl whose Dad was gunned down in his driveway."

"I uh ..."

"Don't worry; I'm going to give her everything you ever owned."

"I, uh, okay."

"Yeah, he's thinking again," Ben said. He reached up and removed the skull mask that was still covering his face. Beltran immediately recognized him as the man he had passed at the Mail Boxes Etc.

"No I ..." Beltran looked back and forth between Steve and Ben with a pleading look on his face. The size-thirteen boot connected solidly with his chest and he flew overboard.

They were nine miles off shore. The Coronado Islands were just barely visible to the south. The seas were calm.

Beltran bobbed to the surface, spitting out seawater.

"I told you I'd let you go," Steve said, leaning over the cable safety rail. Beltran still had a glimmer of hope that they would drop the dinghy for him. His hopes began to fade when Ben stepped away from the Dinghy.

"Well, good luck. A nautical man like you should be able to navigate by the stars." Steve pointed to the lights of Mexico in the distance to the south. "But here's a hint. Mexico is that-a-way!"

The diesel motor increased in RPMs and the boat pulled away. Beltran was having a hard time staying on the surface with his hands and legs still tied. His amputated fingers stung with the salt water. The aspirin combined with the soaking caused the wounds to bleed again. The tape around his legs had him in a panic. He kept thrashing to keep his head above the water. Had he kept still and taken in deep breaths, he would have floated. He also would have avoided sending out shock waves through the water. Shock waves that were noticed by a fourteen-foot-long predator.

The mako shark was pregnant and hungry. She had hit a tuna earlier in the day, but another shark had grabbed the back half of the fish before she could turn around and grab it. The thrashing on the surface signaled prey in distress. She turned towards the impulses and began to zero in. A minute later, her nostril detected the copper scent of mammal blood. Her tail began to propel her forward at greater speed.

She was not the only creature to pick up on the dinner bell. A blue shark and a black tip also began to head in the direction of the struggling man. They were no match, however, for her speed and aggressiveness.

The first thing that told Beltran he was not alone was a hard bump against his leg as he snapped his head back to breathe. He almost let out a scream, but he was learning that if he kept the air in his lungs he floated better. He bit down on his shout and looked around. No fins cut the surface; the ocean was calm in every direction.

He had just settled down again when he felt a tug on his leg this time. Now he knew he was in trouble. He tried to kick out at whatever was down there, but the realization that he had been bit hit him as the pain radiated up from his right thigh. He let out a scream this time. It didn't last long though, as his mouth went under the surface of the water.

He reached down with his hands and felt along his leg. The right one was still attached but there was a ragged tear on the outside of the thigh. He porpoised his body violently to get his head above the water. Just as he took a deep breath, he was slammed from behind, and he felt a crushing pain in his ribs. The mako, detecting that other sharks were closing in, had taken his torso in her mouth. She shook her head violently until a section of his abdomen and rib cage tore loose.

Mike Beltran's last thought was a line from some old black-and-white movie about sleeping with the fishes. He closed his eyes as his body began to sink. Moments later, it was pulled violently sideways. The black tip had arrived and wanted his fair share. Fifteen minutes later, there was nothing but scraps of flesh that the smaller fish flitted about consuming.

CHAPTER 43

Sheila Stanford walked up behind her husband and placed her hands around his neck. She began gently massaging the muscles along his shoulders. He put a hand on one of hers and sighed.

"He was an outstanding Marine."

"Of that, I have no doubt, honey." Sheila continued to rub. "Does he have any family?"

"Yeah, he has an uncle in some nursing home that he wanted to take care of. I guess the conditions there are pretty bad. That's why he jumped on board."

"Is there something Dan can do?"

"Yeah, that's the next thing I'm putting him on."

"Is the new house taking up that much of his time?" Sheila looked at some papers that Tom had been going through. "It seems to be moving along."

"Yeah, might as well put something else on his plate." Tom picked up a phone and dialed a number.

Dan Klein was having a late breakfast with his wife and discussing a vacation trip with the kids, when one of the phones on the table rang. He excused himself and stepped away from the table.

"Hey, Devil Dog, how are you?"

"Tim Westbrook was killed last night while staking out the cartel's operations center."

"Ahh shit, man. I'm sorry." Dan shook his head. "Is there anything I can do?"

"That's why I'm calling you …"

Five minutes later, Dan said, "Consider it done," and hung up the phone.

The trucks arrived by the dozens. Piles of construction materials were laid out in neat rows. Lumber, rebar, aluminum bracing, and scaffolding were all placed in specific places.

Giant backhoes scraped and leveled the ground. Various pits and trenches were cut and dug into the desert soil. Pipes were laid and electrical wires were pulled through conduits. The project was the most activity that Ocotillo Wells had seen in years.

Chris hired as many locals as he could out of Borrego. The security company was operating out of a portable office building installed at the entrance. A big sign read *TMN Security; all vehicles must check in prior to entering the property.* Chris had thought he was going to have issues with the company when he was told he couldn't use any of the trailer office space. But aside from them refusing to let him use some office space, they had been friendly and efficient, going out of their way to facilitate the smooth flow of traffic.

Chris found the reason for them keeping the office to themselves one night when he showed up and was met by a security officer carrying a rifle and wearing pattern disruptive clothing. The combat vest and M4 carbine told him that they meant business.

The footings and underground tunnels had been scraped out, leveled, and the concrete poured. The crews were tying the rebar for the walls and foundation. His only problem had been getting a plumber to take him seriously about how fast he needed to get things done. After the second time he had to hold up a crew, he fired his original sub-contractor and brought in another. He promised a 10 percent bonus if he never had to wait again. Things had moved along nicely since.

The plans called for a 5800-square-foot main house with two out buildings and an airplane hangar. The main house was two stories, not counting the subterranean level. The ground floor had a great room and dining room that took up the entire front half of the house. A modern kitchen and "mud room" were to the rear left and two bedrooms and a bathroom were to the rear right. Upstairs was a massive master suite, which looked out onto the roof, which formed an upper-deck Jacuzzi area. Because of the sandstorms that were frequent in the area, the Jacuzzi would be built up on the roof to help prevent dust from getting into it. There was a cabana bar as well to provide shade and a place to drink.

The airplane hangar was built on top of a thirty-six-inch concrete wall base. The hanger had a fuel bower with hoses that could refuel a plane or helicopter both inside and outside of the structure.

The first of the two outbuildings was a huge forty-foot by sixty-foot garage. It was connected to the house by a covered breezeway. The roof of the breezeway formed a walkway from the roof of the main house to the roof of the garage. The entire roof of the garage was a solar farm. Four wind turbines rose from the corners as well. Under the breezeway was a tunnel connecting the main house to a hidden access door in the oil change pit inside the garage. A small bathroom with a shower took up one corner of the open space.

The drive-in door of the garage was a steel roll-up door. This was reinforced with cement-filled steel barrier posts. The posts fit into steel sleeves set in the concrete floor. It would take an armored car to crash through it. The side door from the breezeway was a steel-cased monster with wire reinforced glass.

The roofs on all of the buildings were crenellated like a castle. The thick balustrades would provide excellent shooting positions with fields of fire in all directions. Because the house was in the desert, it had extended eaves to help keep it cool. Each corner of the house had a small circular viewing platform. Each of these had a celestial telescope set on a tripod. These scopes were able to provide a visual resolution of less than an inch anywhere on the property.

The perimeter had an eight-foot-high wall on four sides. The south side had some barbwire at the top. There were various types of large cactus plants planted all along the wall.

The driveway had two curves in it. One was designed to slow a vehicle down so it could be examined at a distance, and the other forced it into a vehicle trap. The split-rail fence was actually made up of steel posts camouflaged to look like wood. The tops were designed to break, off revealing large metal hooks. The posts were connected to each other by thick wire cable under the ground and through the faux split-wood railings. Any vehicle trying to leave the driveway would be brought to a halt in short order. There were secret places where a car could go through the fence without a problem.

The vehicle trap was right before the fence ended. It was a twenty-foot-long steel plate that was buried under the road's surface. When triggered, two hydraulic pistons would open and cause the far end of the plate to drop into an eight-foot-deep pit. Anything short of a tank was not getting through unless the occupants of the house wanted it to.

The entire build was going to cost just over 4.3 million dollars. Dan Klein had approved every security measure and expense he had recommended.

Chris was going to have a good Christmas.

CHAPTER 44

Hubert Dean Paulson was seventy-two years old and still sharp as a tack. He had little use for the simpering weaklings and crybabies he was forced to live with. None of these people would have lasted two days in the Chosin, much less the three months Hubert had spent slogging in the ice and slush.

The facility that housed him was a state-reimbursed institution that was one step above a prison. He had no family left, except for a grandnephew who he adored. Tim had turned out to be a fine young man and excellent Marine, in spite of his mother's shortcomings.

Hub could always count on a couple of visits a week from Tim. He was always taking him to ball games and dinner. Hub knew it had to be hard on a junior Marine's salary, but Tim had always managed to be there, unless he was deployed.

Tim had told Hub that he had a job coming up that would allow Tim to get a bigger place and maybe Hub could move in with him. Hub had refused, saying Tim had to get on with his life and not spend his time taking care of an old fool who was good for nothing but war stories and had to go to the bathroom every ten minutes.

Hub was in the sunroom, looking out at the back lawn when he noticed the room getting quiet. He looked over his shoulder and saw three Marines in dress blues being escorted by one of the attendants towards his couch. The look on their faces was all he needed to see to send a lump of cold lead up from his stomach to his throat. He stood up to face them.

"Mr. Paulson? My name is Sergeant Major Stanford and this is Master Gunnery Sergeant Toliver and Master Sergeant Derry." Tom indicated the other two men with him as they all shook hands. "Sir, I have some bad news regarding your nephew, Tim."

"Tell me he died in an honorable fashion, Sergeant Major." The tears were starting to run down the old man's face. "That's all I need to know."

"Sir, he died defending his fellow Marines." The tears were starting to run down Tom's face as well. "He was one of the finest Marines I ever served with, sir!"

"Please just call me Hub ..." And with that, the old man collapsed back onto the couch and gave into the sobs that wracked his body. He seemed to age twenty years before their eyes.

The three men in uniform were all sitting around the old Marine talking in subdued voices when Dan Klein entered the room with the facility administrator. They walked over and Dan was introduced by Tom.

"Sir, I'm here to tell you that your nephew made arrangements for you in case anything happened to him. Tim's new employer had a very substantial insurance coverage for his employees, and I'm here to inform you that he indicated how his insurance was to be used in your care." Dan gestured at Mr. Lennard, the facility manager. "Mr. Lennard here has been served transfer paperwork for you to be moved to a different facility."

Hub looked at the Marines in confusion. He was on a fixed income and this place was the best he could do. Care facilities were very expensive.

"What? I can't afford much more even if he had SGLI or VGLI." Hub referred to the two most common forms of insurance carried by service members.

"Hub, I give you my word as a Marine," Tom said still wiping the moisture from his eyes. "You will never have to worry about money again for the rest of your life. Come on, let's get you out of here. There are some of Tim's friends that are really looking forward to meeting you."

"You know, I'd like to see his friend Dillon again. I liked that young fella." Hub was starting to show a little more life and he wasn't as hunched over.

"As a matter of fact, Dillon is waiting for you at your new place. He said he wanted to make it just right," Bull said as he helped the elderly man to his feet.

"You wouldn't be 'Goat Boy,' would you?" Hub said, peering into Toliver's eyes. "Tim told me about a Marine they called 'Goat Boy.' He told me about a fireplug of a Marine who molested a mountain goat while they were out doing some mountaineering."

"Yeah, well your nephew talks too much!" Bull's face started turning red. "It was all in good fun until a couple of young Marines took it too far!"

"Uh huh, I thought so." Hub was smiling finally. "Well, I can tell you a few stories about Lewis Puller."

All of the men present stopped and stared at the mention of one of the Marine Corps legends. Lewis B. "Chesty" Puller was one of the most revered Marines in the Corps.

"You served with Chesty?" Bull asked.

"Hell yes! I even had some choice words for him once at the Chosin." Hub nodded at the statement.

"Oh man! The guys are going to want to meet you! Come on!" Bull had Hub's arm and was hustling him out the door.

They took him out front, where a limo was waiting for him. The Marines overrode his protests about needing a few things from his room, telling him that they were being brought along.

The limo ride took an hour and twenty minutes with all of the passengers exchanging stories along the way. When they pulled up in front of the Remington Club in Rancho Bernardo, they were all laughing uproariously.

Hub stepped out of the limo and looked at the manicured lawn and beautiful buildings. He hesitated for a moment until Tom whispered in his ear, "It's all been paid for, for the rest of your life, Hub."

They walked up to door and were met by a concierge, who took them to a two-bedroom suite. Tom opened the door and gestured for Hub to enter. As he stepped across the threshold, he saw Dillon Remke standing in the living area. Hub looked around at the spacious room. The walls were filled with his and Tim's awards and decorations from their time in the Marines. A newly created shadowbox showing Tim's service was placed next to Hub's old box, which had been cleaned and polished.

Hub took a few steps forward and hugged Dillon, who winced at the pressure on his wound. Hub noticed and stepped back.

"I think you all need to let me know what went on," Hub said to the men standing around him.

"Yes sir; you see, it all started with the Sergeant Major there trying to do a good deed ..."

CHAPTER 45

The US Ambassador to Mexico walked into the President of Mexico's ornate office and smiled at the men in the room. The President had agreed to meet with the ambassador and have certain members of his government present for it. The meeting took just under the half an hour that it was scheduled for.

The ambassador left with a smile on his face.

Inside the President's office, several of the people who had been in attendance were making urgent phone calls. These calls generated a wave of other calls. In less than an hour, there was a call back.

Miguel Rodriguez Canton was sitting on his veranda looking out over the Pacific when his assistant brought a phone out to him. He took the call and listened to the person on the other end for over a minute. When the man on the other end was done speaking, Canton was silent for a moment.

"I will look into it. I have not been happy with the things that have gone on in southern California lately. Please relay that I will send out the word to stop all reprisals until further notice. But please tell them that these people have been stealing from me, and I consider them criminals." He pressed the END button and placed the phone back on the tray. He then pulled out his cell phone and sent out a text message.

Juan Alfaro was trying to make sure he could get his product to the right people for distribution. With the virtual destruction of one of his two main routes, the network was in shambles. He was relying on the other half to pick up some of the slack. This meant routing some of the product through Arizona. The conservatives there were far more intolerant of his activities than the people of California were.

He had just confirmed delivery of a shipment and was going to send a text to El Jefe, when he noticed he had a text from him. He read the message and responded to it. He then sent a message to Guerro. One that he was not going to be happy to get.

CHAPTER 46

Detective Burleson was watching the security footage from South Bay Self-Storage. It had taken the department over a week to get the recordings from the security company. Since the footage had been erased that day, the department had been forced to subpoena the footage from the company.

She was shaking her head at the screen. Guerro and the others all had been recorded. The footage clearly showed each face at some point. Rich, Guerro, Esteban, and Julio could all be seen in the footage. The others could be seen as well, and that was a problem since their bodies had been recovered at the crime scene on E Street and identified by Jim Cooper.

The vehicles that had been recovered from the industrial park were also on the footage, and some of the slugs recovered matched the ballistics from Doudt's gun. Julio's blood was found at the crime scene in Lemon Grove at Jerry's house and in one of the SUVs. The chain of evidence linking the crime scenes was rock solid.

There was no way she could edit or delete the footage. The department would just subpoena it again. Guerro's free access across the border was about to come to a screeching halt. They would have his biometrics in the system in the next twenty-four hours, and then he would be screwed if he tried to travel north back into the country.

The only good thing to come out of all this was that none of the suspects had any kind of record. It made it easy for her to claim that they had never popped up on her radar.

She closed the file on her computer and was just turning away when she noticed a new icon on her screen. She looked at it more closely and, not recognizing it, clicked on it. Nothing happened. She double clicked and when she got the same result, she ignored it, assuming it was some department program.

She went to the bathroom and then out the side door and made her way to the Starbucks. After ordering, she sat down and began sending out e-mails. She didn't notice the pretty blonde girl sitting two tables over who had an inconspicuous black box next to her laptop.

"Are you getting it?" a voice said in her ear.

"Umm hmm," she murmured, keeping her head down as she typed.

Herb was in a van parked a block away. It was normal to borrow officers from other agencies when working corruption cases. Cops obviously recognized cops from their own department.

Jordan Berry was a lateral hire from a small department in northern California. She had been on the job with SDPD for less than a month. She was the perfect fit since she only lived a few blocks away. She had also minored in computer science, so she wasn't too lost when the cyber-crimes geeks explained the sophisticated programs she was going to be using.

The information that the cyber-crimes unit had given Herb was enough to point him at Burleson, but it wasn't enough to convict her in any way. She could have had her password stolen. Herb had doubts though, as several conversations and other small things began falling into place. The fact that both times she had come across actionable intelligence for the cartel, they had somehow gotten a hold of it, set off the alarm bells in Herb's mind. Her early history with the department just confirmed his feelings.

After receiving the information, Herb had approached the chief and laid it all out. A call to the DA's office had produced a wiretap/electronic device warrant. The small box that Jordan was using was the equivalent of a keystroke monitor for wireless transmissions. Every time her laptop communicated with the Wi-Fi in the Starbucks, the signal was caught and analyzed. The e-mails Dawn sent were displayed only seconds later on Jordan's screen. She was immediately forwarding them to the other agents in the two vans parked nearby.

The third e-mail Dawn sent to a friend, talked about seeing a movie this weekend and how it would be really good to see their face again. She complained about how expensive movie tickets were getting.

"Shit, if that wasn't some James Bond spy craft, I'm a Jewish Rabbi." Herb looked at Chuck Cooper, who was in the van with him. There were four SWAT officers in the area because taking an armed police officer into custody tended to be a little dangerous.

"I believe the term is 'trade craft'." Chuck was looking at the e-mail. "Yeah, that could be seen as a warning, never hold up in court though."

"Yeah, but I think we have our girl." Herb considered just pulling her in and sweating her. But in the end, if she stuck to her guns and denied everything, they really couldn't do a thing to her. They needed to catch her delivering intel, or they had to find something in her financials that indicated a source of income outside of the department. Her bank statements were clean and she didn't live outside her means. If she was getting paid she was hiding it well.

Hiding was exactly what Dawn was doing with the money. She never kept more than a few hundred dollars out of any payment she received. She used those small sums to eat just a little nicer, and buy clothes just a little more expensive than she would otherwise. The bulk of the cash she received she washed straight through her mother.

Her mother was into crafts. Knitting, beadwork, and knickknacks. She spent a tremendous amount of time making all sorts of things that she sold at the swap meet every weekend. Dawn's cash bought hundreds of thousands of dollars' worth of junk. Her mother claimed the income and paid taxes on very little of it. An unscrupulous accountant had given them some advice about write-offs. The company showed a solid income but pretty extensive expenses, since they used it to buy gold and valuable gems, which were supposedly used to make more jewelry but were instead just stored like savings.

Dawn had accumulated a pirate's stash that would make Black Beard jealous. As soon as she was eligible for retirement, she was going to sit on a beach somewhere and drink. Until then she spent very little of the extra money she received, and the gold was appreciating in value all the time.

Burleson finished sending her e-mails and stood up. She stretched and looked around before walking over and dropping her empty cup in the trashcan. She strode out the door and never looked back.

"We got all the info off of her computer. We'll do an e-mail search and start looking into the rest of it." Jordan shut off the device and closed her laptop.

Outside, the teams in the vans watched Burleson take her time wandering back to the department.

CHAPTER 47

Guerro was not happy with the text he had received from Juan. He was told, in no uncertain terms, that he was to stop going after Stanford's active-duty military affiliates. The US Ambassador had told Mexico's President that if there was not some action taken, a multi-billion-dollar aid package was in jeopardy. Although there were several people in the NPRC party with close ties to the Canton Cartel, none was willing to risk the aid being cut off over what to them was a cost of business loss. The thinly veiled threats of military reprisals were also good motivators.

The cartel's number-one enforcer was sitting in the spa at La Auberge in Del Mar. He was sitting in a steam bath considering whether or not to call off the operation to execute another Marine. The men had already left to do the job and he could say that he had received the message too late.

He was pondering this as the sweat poured freely out of his well-toned body. He had worked out in the hotel's gym and was preparing for a long afternoon at work. He took a shower and put on a robe to head back to his room. Guerro hated being dirty. He had grown up on the north side of Mexico City. The squalid apartments and filthy alleyways had been his training ground as he struggled to survive long enough to make it out of there.

Guerro had gotten his first job as a lookout for a kidnapping ring at the age of six. After moving up to armed robbery and burglary, he had finally found his way into the drug trade, bringing several of his friends with him. Once he had seen what it was like to have a nice home and car, he was determined to never go back to the filth he was raised in. His retirement plan called for a Spanish villa looking out over the ocean. He didn't ever want to feel unclean again.

Once he entered his room, he sat down and opened his computer. He went into his e-mail and noticed an alert that Beltran had accessed some of the cartel's slush fund. Hopefully he was using it to set up another operations center. All of the crew from the warehouse had escaped except for the ones who had been shot and killed. They had scattered per the plan and he hoped Beltran was getting them all back together.

He got to the e-mail from Burleson and got a little concerned. Transiting the border was important but not that hard. He didn't think the film would be good enough to keep him from moving about at will. He did catch the reference to needing some more money and made a note to drop some serious (for her, anyway) cash on her. She had been instrumental in saving them some grief and had a good paycheck coming.

Guerro checked his watch and figured the team was past the point of no return so he sent Hector a text telling him to abort if he could. He sent another text to Beltran to tell him to call him when possible.

He had just finished knotting his tie when his phone rang. He looked at the caller ID and slid his finger across the glass.

"You are setting up a new operations center, I see." He spoke into the phone as he was pulling his sport coat off its hanger.

"Is this Ben?" the bright and cheery voice on the other end asked.

Guerro pulled the phone away from his ear and looked at the screen again. After confirming it was Beltran's phone he put it back to his ear.

"I'm sorry, who is this?"

"Ben, Ben, Benny, Ben, Ben," the voice mocked. "You don't want to know who this is, but I can't help myself since we have the same name. This is Good Ben. You can have the name Bad Ben."

"Whoever you are, my name is not Ben and I do not know anyone by the name of Ben." Guerro was puzzled by the conversation. He thought that perhaps there was a computer error and someone was calling him by mistake. The next statement from the voice at the other end of the line blew that theory right out of the water.

"So, is it Guerro then? Are Ben and Guerro the same person?"

"Who is this?" Guerro was getting a sinking sensation in his stomach. "I do not know why you are calling me Ben."

"That's the name you gave to Jerry the auction guy after you killed Tina at the South Bay Self-Storage."

"Ahh ..." Guerro sighed as he remembered the ruse. "Is Mr. Beltran there with you? I would like to speak with him please." Guerro went back to his laptop.

"Isn't going to happen there, buddy. Mike is taking a nice long swim in the Pacific Ocean right now." There was a faint rushing of wind in the background. "But man, this is a nice boat he gave me. Oh, and thanks for the cash there, buddy. He said you wouldn't mind if we gave it to Tom and Sheila Stanford. We're also making a contribution to the family of the Marine you had killed the other day. You know this is getting pretty profitable. You keep making screw-ups and we'll all be rich!"

Guerro was trying to track the money that had been accessed. Once he saw the coded receipt for the Swiss account, he knew the money was as good as gone.

"I do not know who you are, but know this. I will find you and I will kill you," he snarled. "You can count on there being more Marines dead until I have Stanford in my hands. I am sure your name is in my files somewhere in relation to him. I will keep killing every one of you until there are none left."

"I wouldn't try it on the list that Mikey gave you," Ben said. "Every one of them has been notified and are expecting you. It is one thing to attack someone like a coward; it's a whole 'nother ballgame when a Marine knows you're coming."

"Well, I would watch the news if I were you ..."

"Actually, I would have you watch the news, pussnuts." Ben laughed out loud. "But there won't be anything on the news about the five guys you sent to kill an innocent Marine today. Why don't you try calling them? Give me a call back afterwards and tell me how it goes."

Guerro had to keep from throwing the phone at the wall as it went dead.

CHAPTER 48

Hector Gutierrez was in a world of shit. He thought he had planned this hit to perfection. His target was some military guy who ran in marathons and triathlons and stuff. The guy was always running on the footpaths around Lake Hodges and Lake Poway. It had been easy to establish a pattern and put a plan into motion.

Hector had placed a lookout at the end of the guy's street and when he came out of his house in his running gear, they followed him to the Lake Hodges Open Preserve. Hector waited until he saw which path the guy was running on and then went to hide alongside the trail. He had a .22-caliber pistol and a knife. The plan was to wait for him to come back along the trail, and then step out and shoot him. He had some rope to tie the body up to a tree. He was supposed to display it in a certain manner.

Things went wrong when a bush grabbed him as he was looking for a place to hide along the trail. He was so startled that he didn't have time to react as the landscape around him literally came to life and threw him to the ground. His hands were zip-tied, and a gag put in his mouth. He was professionally searched and then hog-tied with his own rope.

The guy he was supposed to kill came walking back and stood over him, shaking his head. The man looked at the bush and asked.

"Am I clear?"

"They're just grabbing the last one now," the bush growled. "Give 'em a few to confirm."

"You got it. Hey, thanks guys; I really appreciate it."

"Keep it on a swivel, brother—this isn't over yet."

"Roger that!" And the man started jogging away as Hector felt his legs being lifted up. He was soon being dragged further into the brush. Once they were a good thirty yards off the trail, he was flipped over on his back and his silenced .22 was held right over his eye.

"Listen to me," the green face under the foliage said. "I already know who hired you. I want to know how you were going to get in contact with them to let them know you finished the job."

His cell phone was waved in front of his face by the other bush. He had a hard time following it because the barrel of his pistol being jammed into his eye kept his head from turning. Hector mumbled something through his gag and closed his other eye.

"I think he just told us to fuck off," the bush holding his phone said.

"Okay." The bush holding the pistol was about to pull the trigger when the other one stopped his hand.

"Do you really want to trust that homemade silencer? That thing doesn't look all that safe."

"Yeah, but it's just a .22."

"Okaay." The one bush moved back a ways.

Hector knew his rights and knew that the guys holding him were violating them. He sat there with a smug look on his face as the pistol was placed over his eye again. He was thinking about how much trouble these guys were going to be in as the tiny bullet plowed through his eye and entered his cranium.

"See, it worked!"

CHAPTER 49

The white Styrofoam panels went together like children's building blocks. Little black plastic webs were inserted between them and then rebar was laid in the channels. Plumbing and wiring were pulled through and put in place. Once the walls were built up all around the first floor, aluminum and steel braces were placed. Another wave of cement trucks arrived and the concrete was pumped into the walls.

The concrete was vibrated down into the walls by men with long metal rods, who made sure there were no air pockets to weaken the concrete structure. The bottom thirty inches of wall was two feet thick, requiring extra cement to fill it in. Security windows with redundant steel shutters were installed.

The first floor of Fort Knox west was coming along nicely.

Greg O'Malley hit the end button on the phone he had been given and leaned back in his chair. He had some decisions to make on how to handle the information he was in possession of.

During Tom Stanford's career, he had been an honorable man and outstanding Marine. He had never been in trouble and was regarded by everyone as one of the most ethical men to walk the face of the earth.

Bull Toliver was the epitome of a mission-oriented Marine. He apparently had no problem killing anyone who was a threat to him or his fellow Marines. The cartel was now down about thirty-five men. Although Bull had not said what had happened to these people, or even admitted to being involved in their demise, he had "come across" information that several members of the cartel who had been planning to harm innocent people had suffered mishaps resulting in their untimely exit from this world.

The conversation had gone something like, "Hey, I just heard that the guy who was going to shoot Gunnery Sergeant White tripped and fell on his pistol, which happened to discharge right into his eyeball, resulting in a cranial collapse leading to his death." Although O'Malley didn't care one bit if the criminals from the cartel met untimely deaths, he did have a feeling of guilt—however slight—that he had facilitated what may have been a criminal action by the individuals who may have had something to do with said untimely deaths. He was conflicted on how he would communicate the mishaps the cartel was suffering without exposing them all to a conspiracy charge.

He decided to continue the "rumor has it" charade and keep his communications up the chain of command in the hypothetical realm. He thought about what he was going to say, and then called Felton.

"Good evening Colonel, O'Malley, Gregory, one each reporting as ordered."

"Gunner, tell me you have some good news for me."

"Well sir, that is relative. The cartel made an attempt on a Marine that was on that list that we compiled of potential targets. I heard from a friend that he was pretty sure that the assassin tripped and fell, causing a negligent discharge into his right eye, killing him instantly." O'Malley took a deep breath. "No one was harmed except the poor man who tripped."

"I see." Felton was digesting this. "You know, I was wondering if any of Stanford's friends had been reached yet. I was hoping to have a discussion with them."

"I have not yet been able to locate those Marines, sir. The threat posed by recent criminal activity has caused them to stay off the grid. Is there anything you would like me to relay to them if I should come across one of them, sir?"

"No, Gunner; I think Corky can get a message to them if necessary." Felton looked at his watch and sighed. "I wish I could tell the CMC that we had this wrapped up."

"Well, they're still at it, sir, so I don't think the message has gotten out to the bad guys yet."

"State Department said to let them know if it continued." Felton was writing notes as they spoke. "I'm letting CMC know now."

"I'll be in touch, sir." O'Malley rubbed his tired eyes. "I've heard that the cartel's distribution network has suffered mightily. Also, I think we identified the police leak. Their internal affairs division is on it."

"Very well, keep me in the loop."

"Aye aye, sir!"

CHAPTER 50

Tom and Sheila were going stir crazy. The couple had been very careful to stay out of sight as much as possible. This meant spending a lot of time in the hangar that they had rented. The RV they were staying in was nice, but the honeymoon was getting a little old.

Tom had another couple of days' worth of flying to do before he upgraded his license. They were planning to take off and fly around the country for a couple of weeks before heading out to their new fortress being built out in the desert.

Tom had finally allowed Cole Janches to coordinate with the US Marshalls Witness Protection Program to get them new IDs and passports. They weren't planning on doing anything that would require the use of the documents, but they were there just in case.

Tom finally had enough of being cooped up and decided to call Bull. There was the sound of laughter and glasses clinking in the background when he answered.

"Well, I'm glad to see you guys are having so much fun on my dime!" Tom said. "Corky always said you could skate better than anyone he knew."

"Hey, hard charger!" Bull's jovial voice boomed out of the phone. "You need to hang out with Hub; he has some great stories about Chesty."

"Since you have failed to bring an end to the hostilities, Sheila and I were thinking about getting out of this hot box."

"Come on down here! We have plenty of extra rooms, and you guys could use a night out." Bull got serious for a second. "Things have been very quiet since they went after White. We could run a PSD detail while you guys went out for a nice dinner and a movie or something."

"I think we just might do that." Tom was gesturing to Sheila to grab her bag. "We'll be there in about an hour."

"Great! You really should spend some time with Hub though. The guys haven't given him a minute's rest. We'll be expecting you. Out."

Tom informed the two Marines and one former Navy Corpsman who were serving as their security that they planned on going downtown and meeting up with the rest of the crew. The cars were made ready, weapons checked, and radio communications established with the guys on watch at the hotel.

One of the Marines stayed on at the hangar, while the other two drove the Sequoia as a chase vehicle behind the VW. The drive down was uneventful and they made it into the hotel without incident. They rode the elevator up and were met in the hall by Bull himself.

"What's up, nasty?" he said with a sneer at Tom. "And MY lady!" he said, bowing gracefully to Sheila.

They walked down the hall and entered the big suite where Hub was holding court. He was sitting there, enthralled, as Steve was telling a story.

"... and so this asshole says 'Who's on first, motherfucker!' and pops the guy right in the head." Steve pointed at Duane. "And he does it with an Abbot and Costello voice!"

Everyone in the room started laughing while Duane grinned sheepishly. Several of the men saw Tom and Sheila and a cheer went up. After several minutes of backslapping and hugs, drinks were poured and everyone settled back down into their seats. Tom looked over at Hub, who had a tumbler half full of something in his hand and nodded.

"Here I go and get you a nice place to live, and you come down here to hang out with this bunch of losers." Tom gestured at the room full of men. "I thought you'd have found a wahine at the new place."

"What the hell am I going to do with a wahine?" Hub shrugged then winked at Sheila. "My mortar tube was shot out a long time ago! Excuse me for sayin', ma'am."

Sheila only blushed a little at the modest admission.

"I do appreciate the help though, Tom." Hub lifted his glass in a toast. "Tim was always trying to take care of me. He was a good boy, and I'll miss him."

"To Tim!" The toast was repeated by all as they lifted up their glasses.

"Semper Fi!"

"Ooh Rah!"

They spent an hour chatting and remembering Tim. After a bit, Hub got a serious look in his eye and pinned his glare on Bull.

"Okay now, it's time for you to come clean on the 'Goat Boy' moniker. Tim told me something about it, but I want to hear it from the horse's, or in this case, the goat's mouth!"

Bull was about to open his mouth when Ben stood up and yelled, "Oh hell no! He won't come clean! I'll tell ya the truth, seeing as I was a witness to the whole sordid affair!"

Bull was frowning at Ben and began mumbling something about it not being too late to throw a certain somebody over a cliff. Ben studiously ignored the threat and charged forward.

"You see, we were with FAST Co. 11th MEU doing our work-ups before we go on float. We go out to do our rappel quals, and head out to some cliffs in the national park. We get all our lines and gear set up and we are running every one through no problem. Late in the afternoon, this herd of mountain goats comes wandering along the side of the cliff. I mean these fuckers are just walking along the vertical face on these tiny little ledges. It was unreal.

"So anyways, Bull is a third of the way down on this one rappel and he decides to stop and take a piss. So there he is with his fly unzipped pissing off to the side, when this little black goat gets curious about what he's doing and walks along the ledge Toliver is standing on and goes right up and sticks its face right in his crotch!"

Everyone in the room started to chuckle as Ben continued on.

"So Bull gets all flustered with this thing about to knock him loose. Remember he was still on the line but had to undo the front part to get at his little man ..."

"I don't know what you're calling little ..." The rest of Bull's comment was drowned out as everyone booed him into silence for interrupting.

"Thank you," Ben said to the crowd before continuing on. "So where was I? Oh yeah, so Bull is trying to redo his harness while this goat is butting into him and trying to smell his piss. I have no idea what he drank the night before, but the goat sure thought it smelled good because he was right there on that shit!

"Now once Bull gets his shit buckled, his harness not his pants, he turns towards the goat, which can't really turn around on this ledge, and it starts backing away. Toliver, who is feeling a little violated, decides he wants some payback. So he grabs this thing, turns it around while it's kicking and bleating, then holds it by its back legs and starts acting like he's jamming it from behind. I mean he's got this things legs spread out by his hips like this." Ben stood in the center of the room and demonstrated. "And he's pumping his hips like there's no tomorrow. The goat is screaming rape, and we are all just fucking dying laughing."

Even Bull was laughing at the memory at this point.

"So he abuses this thing for like two minutes, and it must be pretty fucking confused, because instead of running back the way it came, it jumps on this other tiny ledge and just starts bleating its fucking head off! I mean this thing is crying foul!" Ben had to stop and catch his breath for a second before carrying on. "So Bull finishes his rappel and we keep sending guys over the edge, and this thing is just fucking stuck. The other goats have kind of gathered off to the side and are bleating back at this thing.

"So Barr decides to rescue the little guy and bounds over there. He gets it all tied up in a sling and rescue rappels the thing to the bottom. Now seeing as the commandant has published several letters about Marines not leaving family behind without financial resources, we decided to make sure that Bull's new life partner, it was a boy goat by the way ..."

The hoots and catcalls aimed at Bull were not very complimentary.

"Hey ... Hey, don't judge! Don't ask, don't tell, remember!" Bull said in mock defense of his actions.

More catcalls at the notoriously unpopular rule were heard.

"So Bull leaves and Barr has this goat and we decide that since Bull doesn't have a date for the Ball, and seeing as he already knows the goat in the Biblical sense. We decide to arrange a blind date.

"So we're at the hotel for the ball and Bull gets shitfaced drunk. He makes it back to his room and falls asleep. We tie the goat's legs up and sneak into his room, which was quite a feat of daring do, I might add, since I had to climb across from the balcony next door." Ben took a bow.

"So it was you! You asshole, I'll remember ..." again the catcalls shut him up.

"I let the guys in and we put the goat in the bed with him and start taking pictures of them spooning!" Ben had his hands together like a pillow next to his face. "Everything is going fine until the goat decides it's had enough and starts thrashing around. It kicks Bull right in the nuts, and that finally wakes him up."

By now everyone in the room was laughing uncontrollably at the look on Bull's face. Steve walks over and holds up his laptop with a picture of bull spooning with the goat. The laughter got even louder when he changed the picture to one that had been taken of Bull and the goat on the side of the cliff with Bull holding the goat by the rear legs.

Hub looked at Bull.

"Yup, that'll get ya a name"

CHAPTER 51

Herb and Emmerson were sitting in Emmerson's office venting their frustration about not being able to get evidence on Burleson. No matter how hard they looked, they couldn't find Burleson's money. She paid her bills on time, her bank statements matched her paystubs, and aside from the fact that she was able to transfer a good portion of her income into savings, there was nothing to indicate she was on the take.

They looked at her mother's business, and it showed a small but healthy profit. Again, Burleson claimed the income she got from that as well. Nothing they could dig up was going to convince a jury. And surveillance didn't show her in any kind of relationship with anyone. With no financial and no personal motive, they were going to have to catch her red-handed giving the cartel information.

"Well, we could set up a sting," Emmerson suggested. "It's either that or get some false intel into her hands that we can observe the reaction of the cartel. I don't know what that would be unless we use the Stanfords as bait."

"I don't think they want to risk any more exposure than they already have." Herb was shaking his head. "Maybe set up a fake meeting with the Stanfords though. That might expose her if we set it up right."

"That could also be dangerous if these guys show up trying to collect on Stanford's scalp."

"Yeah, but if we don't even involve them, it won't expose them." Herb leaned back in his chair. "But it will definitely be a high-risk operation. Jim Cooper said these guys had no problem just going for their guns, and one of them was a pretty good shooter. He thinks prior military or maybe even a competitive shooter."

"What about former cop?" Emmerson deadpanned.

Herb met his gaze and they both started laughing out loud. Two years' prior, the department had closed a case after two officers had flat out lost gun battles to documented gang members. Interviews revealed that the gang had hired some former military guys to coach them in shooting. The chief had implemented an officer survival program to address the shortcomings in his officers' tactical training, California standards for the training of police officers being notoriously lacking in shooting skills department. Of course, every cop who wore a badge thought they were Wyatt Earp when in actuality, most were substandard marksmen.

After the laughter subsided, they put their heads together and came up with a plan.

CHAPTER 52

The first floor of the main house was finished, along with the garage and other outbuildings. A series of semi-trucks began arriving with huge water and fuel tanks. Two large diesel generators were unloaded and installed in underground revetments. Wind turbine towers were delivered and erected. Solar panels and a battery bank were installed.

Fort Knox west came to life as the wind turbines started to produce power.

Guerro met with Juan Alfaro on the patio deck of the Hotel Del Coronado. They sat out on some couches looking over the Pacific Ocean and discussed the state of the network.

"The boss is not happy with the call from the Presidente's office." Juan sipped on his mojito. "Now although he has said no more killing of random Marines, we are not averse to your finding of the Stanfords and their immediate friends. With them, you can do as you please. El Jefe does not have a problem with that, nor do I."

"I understand. I was just trying to flush him out. The attempt on the second Marine was underway when I received your message, not that it matters, Hector was found this morning. I was told where to look for him by one of Stanford's associates." Guerro had to keep from gritting his teeth as he explained the taunting phone call he had received from Ben. "He was killed with his own gun."

"And what of Beltran?"

"He is missing. According to this Ben, they took him out for a swim in the Pacific. I think we can consider him gone as well."

"I am starting to really dislike this Stanford fellow." Juan considered their next move, then remembered something. "You said they accessed our accounts?"

"Sí, Beltran must have given the account information up under stress. We know from the people that were allowed to live in LA that these cabrons will extract information through force," Guerro said. "They have no problem just killing our men either."

"Ahh ... yes," Juan mumbled. "The shoe is not so comfortable on the other foot."

Guerro was so incensed by the way things had gone thus far that he was literally ready to explode. These things were not supposed to happen in the US. In Mexico maybe, but not here. He was down a significant percentage of his "security personnel," and he was way behind on getting a new distribution center set up.

"My friend, I have known you for twenty years," Juan finally said. "I am hoping you will just take my advice for a moment. Take a vacation from this." He made placating gestures as he saw Guerro getting ready to blow up.

"Just concentrate on getting distribution back online. I'm not saying forget about these people; I'm just saying let it go for a little and let's get back on task. Let them think we have given up. Then when our heads are clear, and they are complacent, we will put every effort into tracking them down and killing them. In fact, we can have someone looking for them while we focus on our jobs."

"Keeping the shipments safe was my job!" Guerro seethed. "I had never lost a shipment before this! And now we have lost money from three places!"

"Yes, but we do not hold it against you when the police intercept a shipment randomly. That is what this is, my friend. It was just the loss of a random shipment. That is the way El Jefe sees it. Do not trouble yourself over it. Your loyalty was never questioned." Juan placed his hand on his friend's arm in a calming gesture. "Like I said, we are not through with these men. We will be prepared for them in the future."

"Sí, mi amigo, I understand." Guerro's blood came down to a simmer from the boil of a few minutes before. "But I swear, I will put Stanford's neck in my hand and squeeze the life from him." Guerro was holding his fist up and demonstrating.

"I believe you my friend, I believe you."

Bull was having the time of his life screwing with the cartel. Being an expert at unconventional warfare, but hardly ever being allowed to put his full talent to use while in the Corps, he was now using his skills to the utmost of his ability.

Ben and Steve had brought back a wealth of information from their pleasure cruise. They had made Beltran sign his signature on several pieces of paper so that it could be easily copied or forged. The Marines had taken over his holding company and sold off all his assets. His home was listed through a realtor, and his two BMWs—car and bike—had sold on Craig's List in hours. The boat was listed with a yacht broker who was willing to buy the yacht for the listing price of $450K if it didn't sell in a month.

Some information that they had recovered was fed to a grateful Herb at the police department. Some was kept and was going to be used to track down the other safe house in Chula Vista. They hoped to get their hands on Guerro and sweat him for enough intel to get to whoever made the decision to go after the Stanfords. Their lives would forever be tinged with paranoia, anything that could be done to reduce that would be helpful.

Beltran had also been another boon to their finances. Between the cash, house, boat, car, and motorcycle, they would wind up clearing almost ten million dollars. Add in the three million they took from the cartel's account, and they were making more money than they could spend. So while the number of soldiers that Guerro had was diminishing, Bull had hired a platoon's worth of combat-proven, Special Operations-qualified Marines and Sailors.

Ben and Steve had taken on the mission of going after Guerro. They had gotten the names and phone numbers of several of Guerro's security people. Through a series of cutouts, O'Malley had been able to get the lines tapped and they had established surveillance on two of the men who were believed to be security for Guerro. They had been followed to a house in Eastlake that they were pretty sure was the stash house Beltran had told them about (he hadn't known the address), but the house was in a quiet neighborhood with little traffic. So other than doing a couple of drive-bys, they had not been able to get good eyes on the target. It was right in the middle of an upscale housing tract that was well lit and full of nosey retirees and yuppies. Any unusual activity was sure to be noticed.

Steve merely considered this a challenge to his stealthiness. After doing extensive research on the computer, he had come up with a location that he thought would provide a good observation point. The neighborhood was on a mesa with no real terrain features close by to allow someone to gain an elevated view.

There was, however, a ridge about a mile and a half away that had just enough elevation to allow someone to see into the backyard if they had a powerful enough viewing device. Steve had discussed the celestial telescopes Tom was getting for the desert house and decided he would get one early and try it out on the suspect house.

There was an optical warehouse on Mission Avenue in Oceanside that provided him with a Celestron telescope. After painting the bright-white tube with some earth-tone spray paint and draping the tripod with some camo net, he set it up on the ridge. He made sure the lens would not reflect any light at the house and began trying to see into the windows.

His search was fruitless since all the shades were drawn, but he did see several different men go out on the back patio to smoke. He hooked up his digital camera to the telescope and began taking close-ups of anyone who came into sight. He also managed to get most of the license plate numbers of the vehicles that came and went. When they had enough men available, they ran tails on the cars or trucks as they left.

Over the next five days, they developed a database that included pictures, vehicle ID, and addresses of all the people who were coming and going. When they had enough evidence to convince them that they were looking at the right place, Bull called a meeting at the hotel suite.

"Take a look at the faces in here." Steve started off the briefing by handing out file folders to everyone. "I need to know if any of these guys are people we've seen during any of our contacts with these clowns."

Several of the men ID'd one or more of the pictures as subjects who were seen at the industrial park. Bull then had to decide how best to deal with the information. If he gave it to the police, then they might be convicted, and some more of the cartel's operation disrupted, but it would do little to improve the safety and security of Tom and Sheila. If they took direct action, however, they ran the risk of facing criminal prosecution themselves, but he was pretty sure they would eliminate the men who had been involved in attempting to track down the Stanfords. But there was no guarantee that they would get them all—at least not without extracting information from the men in methods that were sure to violate their civil rights.

Bull and a few of the others who had served in Iraq and Afghanistan had no illusions about how to deal with people who had no moral compass. Those people had no problem killing indiscriminately but cried foul when they got caught and wanted those considerations they so blithely ignored when attacking other people. Bull, Steve, Ben, and a few others had no problem slitting the throat of those kinds of people, but some of the team still had a little too much civilization left in them to be comfortable with fitting the punishment to the crime.

"None of the subjects we've seen at the house match the description of Guerro." Ben flipped the file back onto the desk. "He's the one that has a hard-on for Tom and Sheila. If we can just get our hands on this guy, I think we can end this whole situation."

· "My understanding is that none of these guys knows where he goes off to." Rudy was one of the former snipers who had been recruited for the duration. "But we got close, both in LA and at the industrial park, so we know he takes part in the operations himself. According to the 'interviews' Bull conducted among his staff, Guerro is never very far away. We also know that he likes to stay in nice hotels and has a bit of a grooming fetish. We should be able to predict his movement patterns if we can get him to go after Tom at a place of our choosing."

Bull stared at the slender man sitting in one of the overstuffed chairs. That was about the longest speech anyone had heard him make.

"Using Tom as bait is off the table. We will not do ..." Bull started.

"I didn't say Tom had to be there. I just said he had to go after Tom at a place of our choosing," Rudy corrected. "You are absolutely correct; Tom shouldn't even be in the same county."

"So how are we going to get them to believe that Tom is going to be in any given place at a specific time?"

"We tell them in a convincing manner."

"Okay, convince me first ..." The men gathered around as Rudy laid out his plan.

CHAPTER 53

Tom and Sheila began moving into the desert house. First they drove the RV out and hooked it up to the side of the garage. Dan introduced them to the security staff and the construction foreman. They then spent the day driving around the town of Borrego. They found a small house on the outskirts of town for sale and had Dan begin the process of buying it. They then went over to Salton City and did the same thing, buying a house that butted up against the State Vehicle Recreation Area. They now had two options to run to if things got bad.

They made two more trips back to San Diego to pick up their belongings. Herb had sealed their house after it had been cleared as a crime scene. Dan had asked the security company to place an agent on their house for the time being. The agent was trained in counter-surveillance and was instructed to report any unusual activity.

Bull had a well-armed team of men go to their house and pick up a long list of items ranging from Sheila's clothes to Tom's weapons and ammo. Bull had also sent men out to every gun store and PX in the area to buy up all the ammo in the calibers the men carried. They also made several huge purchases online. In fact, one of the online distributors found the purchase so large that they notified the ATF. It took a phone call from the Marine Corps CID division to clear it up. Bull decided O'Malley was beginning to come in handy.

The garage and first floor of the house were finished. The solar farm and windmills were producing power and the kitchen was done so they could cook out of it. A trip to Barbeques Galore for two huge propane grills and all the accessories had Tom ready to be the cook for the foreseeable future. Bull had a few of the guys put bunks in the garage and they slowly started to move the base of operations from the hotel to the house.

By the second night, Tom changed the construction priority and had the massive fire pit moved to the top of the list. That next night they all sat around a huge bonfire, eating grilled steak and lobster with mashed potatoes and corn on the cob. Tom and Sheila loved hosting the men who had risked their lives for their safety. The men, for their part, were grateful not only for the work and the hospitality, but for the feeling of camaraderie as well. The stories got more colorful and the boasts got bigger as the night wore on. A few beers were lifted in honor of those lost, but everyone drank in moderation.

Bull and Tom sat off to the side as the night was winding down and discussed the future. They were leaning against the short stone wall surrounding the pit, watching the young men get scolded by Sheila. They kept cleaning the dishes and picking up the mess, which she was attempting to do by herself. Finally, one of the younger men told her that if she didn't sit down and let them work, he was going to Kung Fu the hell out of her. This made everybody stop and stare before the whole crowd busted out laughing. Sheila sheepishly sat down and let them get the area squared away.

"We can't thank you guys enough for what you've done, bud," Tom said, gesturing towards the two guys putting away the grill. "I wish we could make it up to you with something more than a meal."

"At ease with that shit, Devil Dog! You have no idea what you've done here." Bull gestured to the two men who were walking out of the garage fully jocked up. "These guys were pulling down barely more than minimum wage or going into debt for their schooling. They feel like they've done a good thing here. It's a noble purpose, and that's something most of us haven't had since the Corps. Now they feel like they've done something good, and they're making money commensurate with their sacrifices. You've given them, and even me, a sense of accomplishment. But to be honest, I would have been here on my own dime for you, bud; you know that. I owe you more than I can ever repay, so let's kill that line of thinking right now."

"Doesn't mean I don't feel bad for Tim and his uncle though."

"I think Tim would be very happy with where Hub is right now." Bull grinned. "Shit, these kids can't wait to visit him when they get off. Old bastard holds court like a medieval king in that big common room. These guys sit around listening to him talk about Chesty like he was a boot! They love it."

"Yeah, he's a pretty funny old guy." Tom looked at the unlit cigars he and Bull were both chewing on. "So what's the plan now? How are we doing?"

"Well, Steve and Ben have made it their personal mission in life to find this Guerro fella. They have what we are pretty sure is the cartel's stash house under observation. O'Malley came through for us with the video from South Bay Self-Storage. I e-mailed you the video. He's a pretty cold-hearted fucker. He killed those people out of hand. Do not hesitate brother. I'm telling you, just drop the hammer on him if he ever gets in your sights. He killed the manager with a blade slowly; he's not someone to fuck around with, copy?"

"I hear ya," Tom said, meeting the serious look in Bull's eyes. "I'll end him if I ever get the chance."

"Okay, I just don't want you being all in touch with your feminine side when you're dealing with him." Bull playfully slugged his old friend.

"Pull my tampon out, got it." Tom was grinning back.

"If you two are done with your testosterone fest, you can go get a pot of coffee ready for the night watch guys!" Sheila said over her shoulder as she leaned back in her folding chair.

"Yes, ma'am! Right away, ma'am!" Bull said, saluting her as he pushed off the wall. "Is there anything else I can do for you, ma'am?"

"Carry on, recruit!"

"Aye aye, ma'am," Bull mumbled as he walked into the garage.

"Come on, commander, let's go to bed since you took away my playmate," Tom said with a lecherous look in his eye.

"Thomas Allen Stanford, if you didn't revert to a barbarian every time you got around that over-muscled ape, you would find me a little more willing to be your playmate." Sheila was grinning.

"Cover!" Bull yelled from the door to the garage. Marines immediately began drawing weapons and looking around. "She used his middle name! Shit just got real!"

Several of the Marines who had jumped to their feet and begun to scatter at the word "cover" stood up and shot dirty looks at Bull. A few seconds later, everyone was laughing.

"Toliver, you asshole! I almost spilled my beer! You must enjoy pissing people off!"

"Shit, Master Guns! Cut that shit out!" One of the Marines was dusting off the knees of his pants as he stood back up.

Several others grumbled at Bull, who showed absolutely no remorse at his prank.

CHAPTER 54

The taskforce conference room was packed with officers from several different local and federal agencies. The only people in the room who knew about the investigation into Burleson's activity were the SAC for the DEA, Herb, and O'Malley who was presenting the intel that had been fed to them by Toliver and associates.

Dawn was seated next to a border patrol agent she had known for several years. They were laughing at some inside joke as the last of the group trickled in. Herb made a note of everyone Burleson had a private conversation with.

Once everyone was comfortable, the taskforce commander gave a brief overview of the situation in regards to Stanford and the cartel. He then turned the floor over to O'Malley, who powered up his laptop, which was already plugged into the plasma screen TV on the wall. A PowerPoint graph showed up, and he began briefing everyone on the cartel's command structure.

Dawn was caught a little off guard when a close up of Beltran came up during the course of the presentation. Her shock only got worse as several pictures of Guerro were posted. She almost blew out a sigh of relief when the box for Juan Alfaro showed a big question mark. The pics of the cartel members who were killed and captured in the shootout on E Street were shown and the people present were asked if anyone knew them. No one did.

After O'Malley finished with the background information, he presented a huge amount of intel on the workings of the cartel. This included a bulk of the information given up during Beltran's interrogation on the boat.

Several agents questioned the source, but O'Malley just said it was classified as "reliable."

"The cartel's operations against the Stanfords should begin to fall off." O'Malley was using a laser pointer to circle Guerro's picture. "We don't think the vendetta against them will be sustainable. The state department has put pressure on Mexico, and the Stanfords have agreed to turn themselves into witness protection. They have said that they will turn over the cash to the DEA, and they just want to disappear. They will be coming in later this week; we will be able to interview them at that time. Sergeant Burleson and Agent Heller from the DEA have been selected to conduct the interviews, so send them a list of questions if you have any for them."

A few grumbles of *Yeah, I'd like to know how 600 million bucks feels* and *Man, what's it feel like to have a million-dollar price on your head?* drifted across the room. The meeting broke up the way meetings do, with small groups forming to discuss things. Dawn and Bruce Heller, from the DEA, wandered over to O'Malley as he was putting away his computer.

"So where are we meeting the Stanfords?" Burleson asked. "And how the hell are they gonna turn in all that money? I don't think they can carry it all in by themselves."

"Well, it turns out that they were staying in an aircraft hangar," O'Malley said as he turned to face them. "They bought an RV and have been living in a hangar at the Palomar Airport. They have a few things left they want to take care of, and then we'll go pick them up day after tomorrow in the afternoon. They are going to leave the cash there in their truck. We'll do the interviews downtown. The US Marshalls will take them away from there."

"Hangar, huh?" Heller said. "Well, I never would have thought of that."

"Yeah, well, Stanford is a pilot," Dawn said, looking at her nails. "What time do you want to meet to go up there?"

"Stanford said not before 1400. But I don't want to be too much later because then we'll hit traffic on the way back downtown." O'Malley picked up his case and faced them. "So let's meet at 1200 for some lunch then we'll head over there to pick them up."

"Okay."

"Sounds good."

CHAPTER 55

Marisella Gutierrez was one of the lead housekeepers at the Hilton Hotel downtown. She had worked hard to get where she was, but the salary she brought home was never quite enough to get ahead. She had grown up in San Ysidro, just a hundred yards from the border with Mexico. While her brothers were always getting into trouble, she had been a good girl and studied in high school.

She had heard her brother, Victor, talking about how the men he worked for were looking for a group of military guys who had stolen money from his work. She knew he was involved in the drug trade, but he seemed adamant that these guys were crooks who were just stealing from them. She listened to his conversation for another twenty minutes. When Victor went into the house to use the bathroom and get another beer, she followed him inside. She was waiting for him in the hallway when he came out of the bathroom.

"Vic, were you serious about the reward money? For those guys you were talking about?"

Vic stopped in his tracks. He loved his sister dearly and did what he could to keep her away from the life he was leading. His sister was off-limits for his friends to date as well. She had never been interested in his gang, being involved in school. Her question caught him by surprise.

"Why do you want to know? You going to use your super brain to figure out where they are?" Vic's teasing was good natured.

"I need some more money for school, and my classes are taking more time. So I had to drop one of my shifts." Marisella lowered her voice. "Mom doesn't know and I know she can't afford it, anyway. I just want to know if I find them, would your boss kick down some of that reward money?"

"Mija, if you locate these guys, he'll pay for a Harvard education. These guys been costing us money and killing our homies." Vic grabbed her by the arms. "But they don't play, girl. Give them bad information, and they'll fuck me up, for real."

"All right, let me check on a few things then I'll call you."

"Don't be talking to no one about this, Marisella; I ain't playin'."

"I won't, mijo."

Marisella watched as one of her girls pushed her cart down the hallway of the fourth floor. She noticed that the same doors still had "Do Not Disturb" signs stuck in the card slots. She checked her rooms list and made sure that all of the rooms that didn't have the cards posted were serviced. She made the appropriate notations on the sheet and noticed that four of the rooms had not been serviced in a week and a half. Either they had hygiene issues or no one was staying in the rooms. These rooms were rented by the same group of men staying on the floor below. It was this odd behavior that had caught her attention originally.

She had also noticed one of the small cameras on the third floor. Those rooms had Do Not Disturb signs on some of the rooms, but they had gone into some for cleaning. She had noticed several military-looking bags and long cases. There was always someone in the room while it was being cleaned, and the laptops were always closed. All of the occupants were men who looked dangerous, in spite of the fact that they were always polite, and they all had a rugged air about them.

Marisella decided that she would tell her brother about the men and see if she could get some reward money. She waited til she was on her break and then called Victor. He told her he would pick her up at work instead of her having to ride the trolley home. He said he would be waiting for her in the lobby.

Ron Parsons was handling the lobby watch when Victor walked in and sat down. He watched as the Hispanic kid immediately put his face in his phone and began to act like there was something there. Ron picked up on the kid eyeing everyone who came through the lobby.

"Lead, lobby, I got a Mexi-kid down here looking everyone over."

"Lobby, copy, I'll send down some back-up."

"Negative, hold off for a bit. He's just sitting there. I'll let you know if anything changes."

"Lead copies, out."

Ron was sitting at the lobby bar, sipping on a ginger ale. From this vantage point, he could see the front doors, the check-in desk, and the alcove to the lobby restrooms. He watched as the kid gave everyone who entered the once over. This went on for half an hour, and Ron was just considering having the guys come down so they could start a tail on the guy, when one of the housekeepers came out and gave him a hug. After a brief conversation, the two of them walked over to the elevator bank.

"Lead, subject was just met by one of the housekeepers. He looks like a family member. I don't think there's anything to worry about."

"Copy"

Inside the elevator, Victor pushed the button for the third floor. Marisella slapped his hand away but it was too late. She told him about the extra cameras she suspected had been installed in the hallway. She then pushed the button for the fourth floor. When the door opened on the third floor, they both stayed to the rear of the elevator car and waited for the door to close. They rode it up one more floor and they both stepped off.

It took Marisella about five minutes to go over her suspicions with Victor. She pointed out the camera placement on the floor below and showed him which rooms were being used, and which were empty. Vic had her use her master key to let him in to look at one of the rooms. After knocking and announcing herself, they went inside.

The room was being used for storage, and there were some luggage and duffel bags neatly placed against one wall. They looked the bags over and found two with names stenciled on them. Vic snapped pictures of the baggage and close-ups of the names.

They made sure everything was just as they found it and left. Neither one of them noticed the small piece of scotch tape that was hanging from the top of the hinge side of the door.

They went down to Vic's car and he drove Marisella back to her parents' house where she lived. After dropping her off, he went to the new warehouse that Guerro had rented and asked to speak to him.

"What can I do for you?" Guerro looked up from the desk he was using.

"I think I've found the people we've been looking for." If Vic was expecting a reaction, he was disappointed because Guerro's face remained impassive. The silence stretched out for a few seconds.

"Would you like to tell me where they are?" Guerro only knew Vic by name and had not had much interaction with him. If he had, then Vic would have known to start explaining himself right away.

"Ah, um, sorry. Yeah, well, you see my sister works at the San Diego Hilton Bay Front downtown, and she noticed some things about some guys staying there that made her wonder about them. They are all military guys and they have some rooms rented out that they don't even use, and some others that they only allow housekeeping into while they watch them." Vic swallowed nervously. Guerro had a very intense stare that was quite unsettling. "So my sister let me into one of the rooms that they had rented and there were some military bags. I got these names off of the bags."

Vic showed him the pictures he had taken of the luggage and the name tags on it. Guerro looked at the pictures closely then wrote down the names from the luggage tags. He stared at them for a minute then pulled open one of the desk drawers. He pulled out a file and began running his finger down a list of names. He stopped on the second page and looked back and forth between the name he had written down and the one on the list.

"Victor, what made your sister tell you about these men?"

Vic didn't want to admit that he had been talking out of school at a backyard BBQ. They had been told not to discuss business with anyone outside of work. Vic had a story ready to go.

"She just mentioned it at home the other day. She said these gringos acted weird at work. So I asked her some questions and decided to check it out for you. She's hurting for money and I thought if we found them for you, I could help pay for her college, you know?"

"I see." Guerro reached into a briefcase and came out with two banded stacks of currency. "Here is $20,000.00. You have earned this for being observant and coming to me right away. I am going to follow up on this. If these are the men I am looking for, your sister will not have to worry about school or even working for the rest of her life."

"Thank you, sir!" Vic looked at the money on the desk. "If there is anything you need, my sister and I will do whatever we can to help."

"I would like to meet your sister, please." Guerro's mind was already developing a plan.

"She is either getting ready for her night class, or she is already there. I can go get her right now though, if you would like,"

"No, let her finish class, and then I will meet you somewhere." They made plans for meeting later in the evening at a restaurant.

CHAPTER 56

Dawn Burleson had decided that she needed at least one other person to help her get the money and take off. She decided her mom would be able to act as a lookout and getaway driver. She made a few phone calls and did a little Internet research before picking up her mother and heading up to Palomar Airport.

Once there, they drove around looking at the various hangar facilities. The only one they had a problem with had a security guard at the gate and her badge got them in without any fuss. They looked around and finally found Sheila's Audi parked at the end of a row of hangars. After a little nosing around and asking a few questions, they found out which hangar belonged to the Stanfords.

The hangar had a man-sized door set to the side of the main roll-up door. A quick inspection showed that it just had a regular handle and not even a deadbolt. There was no visible way to open the big doors and she didn't even want to try. She had her mother pull up right outside the door and told her to wait.

Dawn knocked on the door and waited. She figured the Stanfords had been given her name and would allow her in when she presented her badge. She had it ready in her left hand. She had her body bladed slightly to the right to conceal the silenced 9mm she held in that hand. She waited a minute, and then knocked louder.

A head popped out of a hangar halfway down the row and looked in her direction. She waved at the man and continued waiting. The head disappeared.

After waiting a few more seconds, Dawn went to the car and got out a hooligan bar. She inserted it into the jamb and hit it once with a mallet to set it. A quick heave and the door popped right out of the frame. She took the time to put the tools back in the car before entering.

The hangar was dark, but enough light came through the open door and a skylight to allow her to see Tom's truck with a camper shell on it. She walked over to it and saw that it was full of boxes. She tried the hatch, expecting it to be locked and was pleasantly surprised when it wasn't. This was going to save her the trouble of pulling her car inside while she broke into whatever the money was stored in.

She dropped the tailgate on the truck and pulled a box out onto it. She slit the tape and opened the top, revealing the plastic wrapped currency. She gave it a pat and began folding the box flaps closed. She set the pistol down on the tailgate to do it.

"She put the gun down," Herb told Emmerson, who was sitting with him in the hangar three spaces down. They were watching multiple video feeds from hidden cameras in the Stanfords' old hangar. It had been one of the DOJ agents with them who had stuck his head outside earlier when she was banging on the door.

"Wait until she's got her hands full and is walking towards the door," the agent said. "Wait until she puts at least one box in her car. Then we'll have intent established."

"Bravo, move up to the end of the building. She doesn't have anyone with her besides her mom," Emmerson said into his radio.

Two rows over, an armored car pulled out of an empty hangar and drove to the end of the building. Two Suburbans with tactical team members standing on the running boards pulled up on the other side of the aisle. Everyone checked in that they were ready just as Burleson returned for the third box. She had to climb into the bed and work the next one out. She was tugging it out onto the tailgate when Emmerson gave the go command.

The two Suburbans rounded the corner and were almost at the hangar door when Dawn's mother noticed them in the rearview mirror. She was able to honk the horn two short beeps before she was looking down the barrel of an MP-5. The other team members were able to get through the door before Burleson could do more than drop the box. She didn't even bother to go for her service pistol as she realized she was looking at a bunch of cops coming through the door.

"Don't shoot! I'm a cop!" she yelled as the classic red dots appeared on her chest.

"Not anymore, you aren't!" Herb said as he and Emmerson walked in through the door.

Burleson was taken into custody without a fight. She was handcuffed and searched. Her ID, badge, and both guns were confiscated and placed in a bag with her cell phone. After she was properly secured, Herb Mirandized her. When he was finished he asked her, "Are you willing to talk? The AG is here and might be willing to make a deal if the information you give us is good. We understand that your information may be timely. We have your e-mails and texts. If you give us the info to end this, they'll cut a deal and you will probably get off with just a few years' prison time. If you do not, we are going to run conspiracy charges on you for the four murders, at a minimum; we may add more. You will get life in prison without parole for that, possibly even the death penalty."

"What about my mom?" Burleson wouldn't look up to meet Herb's eyes.

"All we have on her is accessory to burglary," the AG said, looking at Herb. "We cut a deal, and she walks as a fourth waiver."

"What do you want from me? I don't have any real information. And I never told anyone anything really important."

"Really? You didn't inform the cartel that the drop Stanford set up was a fake? You never told them about the videos from the self-storage?"

Her head snapped up at that.

"You never fed operational intelligence from the taskforce to your contacts within the organization? We've been onto you for a while. Why do you think the cartel has failed at everything they've tried?" Herb was stretching the truth, but it didn't hurt to keep her guessing. "We have your text messages to Guerro—all of them. So you just think about how many that is. Our charge sheet will be over twenty counts."

"I still want my POA attorney present before I make any deal."

"Your choice, but understand this, the offer expires the second the cartel takes any more action. And I will make sure that they know you came here to steal their money and bail on them. We know you didn't notify them."

The AG leaned in closer. "I bet they would be a little pissed at your lack of loyalty."

Burleson began to shake. She was, for the most part, a tough character. The options she was looking at were pretty terrifying. She wanted her brain to kick out an answer to her troubles, but it kept going back to the fact that she finally got caught. She wanted to cut a deal right there, but she knew if she did and had to spend more than a week in jail, she wouldn't be alive to get out and spend the money she did have stashed away. She really needed to talk to a lawyer.

"I don't think I have enough useful information to be of any assistance to you," she mumbled. "I'd like to speak with my attorney before answering questions."

"Very well." Herb shook his head in disgust. "You are going to be booked back at the station. You will be allowed to contact the POA attorney of your choice. We have a gag order that will place you in seclusion until your indictment proceedings are over."

They placed Burleson and her mother in separate cars for the trip back to Chula Vista. The gag order they had did not cover the mother, and they didn't want Burleson giving her mother any instructions. The boxes of cash, which were actually full of paper, with just enough cash on top to make it look real, were loaded and taken down to be logged into evidence.

Herb stepped away from the rest of the officers and sent Tom Stanford a text message. FEELING LIKE A PLUMBER TODAY. MY LEAK IS FIXED.

CHAPTER 57

Tom and Sheila were furniture shopping when they got the message about Burleson's arrest. Since he was checking messages, Tom checked his old phone number and found a message from Guerro.

MY BOSS HAS DECIDED THAT YOU ARE NO LONGER WORTH OUR TROUBLE. DO NOT INTERFERE WITH OUR OPERATIONS ANYMORE AND YOU WILL BE LEFT ALONE.

He showed the message to Sheila and forwarded it to Bull.

"What do you think?" he asked.

"It would be nice if it was true. He doesn't strike me as the kind of guy who gives up too easily."

"Yeah, I agree. I don't think we should plan on going back home just yet."

"Me neither, especially since I really like this sectional for the great room ..." Sheila grabbed his hand and led him over to the massive leather couches.

Tom sighed and followed along like the good Marine he was.

The ceiling joists and panels were all tied together and the cement trucks began rolling in again. The roof and upper-deck walls were poured while men again vibrated the concrete down into the structure. As soon as it was all poured, another crew began using floats to smooth out the rest of the roof area. It took an entire day for the concrete to be poured and formed, but when they were done, Fort Knox west was ready for the cosmetics.

The following day, a stucco crew began shooting the light-brown coating on the outer walls while on the inside, finishing crews put the mud filler on the walls and prepped it for paint. The plumbing fixtures were installed in the kitchen and bathrooms, while the flooring crew tried to stay out of the way while taking their measurements. There was some grumbling that there was too much going on at once, but Chris kept them on task and mediated any conflicts.

Another office trailer was brought in and set up as a temporary barracks for the rest of the security team. More men began moving out from the Hotel in San Diego.

One of the reasons Guerro had moved up so quickly within the cartel was his intelligence. Unfortunately, his temper got in the way sometimes. He had finally gotten it under control when Victor had come to him with the news about the Marines at the Hilton. His meeting with Marisella had convinced him that these men needed looking into.

San Diego is a military town and servicemen coming and going for various functions was quite common. The Marines' behavior wouldn't have been noticed by a casual observer, but it did get noticed by someone in the hotel industry. Guerro was ecstatic that he had finally caught a break.

He gave Marisella a list of things to look for, such as behaviors and what types of vehicles they drove. She had immediately told him that there was almost always a man in the lobby, and she often found one of them walking around outside. She told him about the small black camera that had appeared in the hallway of the third floor, and the other things that had made her notice the men with hard eyes.

One of the names Victor had given him matched a name on the list of known associates of Tom Stanford. That was the nail in the coffin as far as Guerro was concerned. He began putting the pieces in place to follow or abduct one of the men. He knew that they were skilled in counter surveillance, so he made sure to bring in some skilled labor. Although Beltran was missing and presumed dead, he had a couple of other private investigators that he used from time to time to do background checks on people. He called them all in and briefed them on the men he wanted watched. He also called in a few men from the gangs that they distributed cocaine to, only using hardened criminals with prison time.

He had given Marisella a phone and instructions on how to report any future activity. He gave her another twenty thousand dollars to secure her loyalty and told Victor to keep the money he had already been given.

Victor would drop her off and pick her up at work from now on so that people would get used to seeing him around the hotel. They were also to take lunch breaks together in various places so they could pick up on movement patterns.

One of the PIs was sent to check in and requested a room on the third floor. He was given a room on the fourth, the only room available being in the opposite wing. He set up a set of cameras on his balcony looking down into the courtyard and pool area. He was able to start picking out the men who walked through on a regular basis. He started getting high angle photos of them. Every once in a while, he would catch one looking up and get a good face shot.

It took them three days to get the teams assembled and start moving them into place.

Duane walked down the fourth floor hallway headed for the room where some of the bags were kept. He checked to make sure that all of the Do Not Disturb cards were on the right doors. He also looked carefully at each door in the upper corner on the hinge side. On every door of the rooms that the Marines had rented, a piece of scotch tape had been placed between the frame and the door. Scotch tape was wonderful stuff because it was transparent when applied firmly but became opaque when it was not attached to a surface. This made it virtually impossible to see when the tape was in place, yet was visible when the door was opened.

Although not a foolproof system, it was a good indicator that an unauthorized person had entered a room. Because a person looked at the side of the door with the knob on it most, a piece of tape on the hinge side would mostly go unnoticed.

Duane saw that the tape had been disturbed right away. He calmly walked right past the door and then stopped while patting his pockets. He mumbled a curse and turned around to head back to the elevators. He pushed a button on the side of the radio that was clipped to his belt under his jacket. This sent out a general alert tone to everyone on their net. Once back in the elevator, he got on the radio.

"Base, Romeo One, has anybody been in room 426 lately? Tape is off the door."

"Hold One; I'm checking the log."

The Marines took their security seriously and Bull had been adamant about standard operating procedures in the event of possible security breaches. At the first sign of an incursion, everyone got with their "battle buddy" and no one did anything alone. Duane stepped off the elevator on the third floor and went to the room they were using as an operations center. He went over to the desk, where one of the guys was looking through a green canvass logbook.

"Anything?"

"No one's been in there since Tuesday, and according to Rick, all the tape was in place at 0742 this morning."

"Well, it is definitely not attached now," Duane said as Chris entered from the other room. He was strapping on a concealment vest as he walked over to the chair where his suit jacket was draped across the back. Chris had to wait while Duane got his armor on and they both did a final gear check as two more guys came in from other rooms. Two men went to the elevator and two went to the stairwell. Duane and Chris rode up to the fourth floor but waited in the elevator alcove while the other two men cleared the stairwell several floors above and below the fourth. Once they got the "all clear" they walked calmly down the hall to room 426 and opened the door.

They kept their pistols in their holsters until they were stacked on the door then drew them as the door opened. Duane went left, pushing the door all the way to its stop, sweeping along the wall with his pistol. Chris went right and cleared the bathroom. The men had done several dry runs in all the rooms they had rented. This was so they knew the various floor plans. Duane and Chris moved like two ballet dancers as they checked every section of the room. As soon as they gave the all clear, the other two men came in, and they thoroughly searched the room for bugs and cameras. Nothing was found. They checked their baggage and again nothing was found missing or out of place.

"You think it could have come off by itself?" Chris asked as they finished checking the room.

"Could have, but the others are still in place." Duane put his bag back with the others.

"Well, let's check the other rooms on this floor and we'll call it good."

They inspected all of the rooms and again found nothing amiss. As they left each one, they again made sure all the doors were taped shut. They looked around at the hallway and went down to the second floor, where all was okay. They met back in the operations center just as Bull was walking in. They gave him a brief rundown of what had happened.

"Nothing weird on the video, right?" he asked.

"Nope."

"Okay, we're out of here day after tomorrow." He walked over and looked in a pelican case. "We still have a couple of cameras; let's stick one up there and we'll be careful. Let's make sure everyone acts like Boots and keeps a 'Battle Buddy' with them."

"Roger that; I'll put the camera up," Chris said as he pulled out the equipment. Duane helped him get it ready and they both went up to the fourth floor.

Across the street from the Hilton, a guy sitting on a pedi-cab made notes of what lights turned on and off. He also kept an eye on the vehicles that left the hotel driveway, looking for occupants that met certain criteria. All of this he typed into his smart phone and then sent to Guerro's team. He was able to compile a list of five vehicles.

The Marines always travelled in pairs. They considered themselves to be on a military operation, so they took the same precautions they would if they were in a hostile country. This made them difficult to follow, especially since they usually just went to one of the many local military bases. Guerro finally got lucky on the third day when two of the SUVs they had identified pulled out together and began driving east.

Using a very loose three-car tail, they were able to follow the two cars all the way out to the Anza Borrego Desert. Both vehicles pulled into what looked like a construction site. The drivers made a note of the location and called it in to Guerro. He told them to find a place close by and hole up. They were not to risk being seen by anyone.

The next day, Marisella reported that the group had checked out of the hotel.

CHAPTER 58

Tom made a standard-rate turn to bring the twin engine plane around on a downwind leg. He retarded the throttle, lowered the cowl flaps, and lowered the landing gear as the speed dropped past the max safe speed for its deployment. After making sure the aircraft was trimmed out for landing, he waited for the runway threshold to pass by his left window. A minute later he was touching down on the five-thousand-foot runway. The plane didn't even require half that distance to roll out, and he was soon at the hangar next to his garage.

After completing his shutdown checklist, he climbed out to see a group of guys sitting in lawn chairs watching him. Several of them began a polite golf clap as his feet hit the ground. Tom took a couple of stage bows before walking over and hopping on a Kawasaki MULE parked just inside the hangar door. He drove the utility vehicle to the front of the plane and hooked up the tow bar for the front landing gear. He backed the plane into the hangar and unhooked the MULE, parking it off to the side again.

"You know, if any of you want to actually earn some of the money I'm paying you, one of you could bring me the fuel hose and turn on the pump." Tom was opening the wing tank on the right wing. "Hop to it!"

Duane and Chris grinned at each other as they slowly got up and walked over to the fuel pump. They helped Tom get the plane fueled while constantly making Air Wing, and even worse, Air Force jokes. Tom endured the ribbing with a smile. Once the plane was fueled, they went back to the house to make long-term plans.

They had to pass by the horseshoe pits to get to the house. Two very intense games were going on and the taunts and jeers were in full swing. Bull had initially put in one pit for the guys to have some fun while off duty. Being A-type personalities, the competition was soon fierce with a white board tracking an impromptu tournament. A second pit followed shortly thereafter. Two corn-hole boards were also set up and that became the game of choice once the beer got flowing.

Tom noticed that everyone was armed and that there were a couple of the vehicles always parked close by. Every building on the property had a weapons safe in it. All of the safes had the same combination, and all the security team members had it. There was a field trauma pack sitting on top of each safe as well. The contract guard company was good. It was owned by a retired Marine and his officers were prior military and law enforcement. They were all well-armed and had even started doing some scenario training with Bull's guys.

The group of men all went into the main house and gathered around the dining room table. The table was made from an old English castle door. The iron-banded massive plank table could seat fourteen people comfortably with enough room for a huge feast to be laid out down the center. Tom was using the dining room as his office since the second floor wasn't finished yet.

"All right, Goat Boy, what do we have, and what do we know?" Tom started off.

"Steve and Ben are 100 percent sure that the house they are watching is some sort of safe house. They have been able to identify several of the people from the South Bay video coming and going from it." Bull frowned at him for the Goat remark. "O'Malley here says no one else has been killed, but that may be because the word is out and CMC sent out a letter authorizing all of us to carry 24/7. I'll let him tell you about it."

"We have pretty much told half the Corps about your problem children. We did a database search and cross-referenced any names of Marines that were in units the same time as you, with Google and Bing searches. After running the databases in several formats, I came up with a pretty lengthy list and submitted it to CMC." O'Malley gestured at his computer screen. "The list was just over 1200 names that came up in direct correlation through those formats. We have a 100-percent notification rate for those that are still on active duty or reserve status. We are only at 86 percent on people that are retired or left the service."

"Well, that's a pretty good percentage," Tom said.

"Yeah, I feel pretty good about it too. If we're having a hard time finding them, then the cartel's goons should too. But I don't think we're out of the woods yet." O'Malley pulled out a file and dropped it on the table. "Dawn Burleson was a detective sergeant with CVPD. She had gotten busted for falsifying some traffic tickets early in her career. After spending a bit of time in purgatory she made it to sergeant as a narcotics detective. She had a pretty good arrest record, which she admits is due to intel supplied to her by her cartel contacts. She claims they were informants. We think she was given info to help the cartel with their rivals. It worked out pretty good for both sides until she started giving the cartel operational intel. They are doing a case analysis to see if she blew any federal operations. If she did, then they'll charge her federally.

"The judge has her under a sequestration order right now. We were able to convince him that her having the ability to communicate with anyone poses a life-threatening risk. He gave us forty-eight hours for the hold on her mother, which is up in about two hours, and ninety-six on Burleson. I think we can pretty much count on the cartel knowing about two minutes after her mom gets free."

"Can't you guys threaten her with conspiracy if she calls anyone?" Bull asked.

"Sure, but if they have any kind of code system set up, we'll never prove it. And we know they used some tradecraft in their computer communications."

"Man, I'd like to exercise some 'Tradecraft' on her! It was this bitch that notified their warehouse we were coming, wasn't it?" Steve had an intent look on his face. He had been very close to Tim, who he had served with in Iraq.

"Yes, I'm afraid it was." O'Malley nodded. "We're pretty sure it was her that blew your attempted sting, Tom, and she was also responsible for notifying the guys on the video tape that we had their pictures."

"She's going to prison, right? No fucking around, no plea bargains where she gets off with two years at Club Fed, right?"

"Oh, that's probably exactly what will happen." O'Malley met Steve's gaze. "It won't be two years. Her plea deal will be for eight minimum. With good behavior, she'll be out in three and a half. We'll see who shows up to represent her. If it's some high-powered firm, then we'll know she's getting help from the cartel."

"Well, fuck me to tears!" Steve exclaimed in disgust and turned away from the table.

"I hope she walks," Bull said.

Tom turned a knowing look at his old friend, while the others at the table looked at him stunned. Steve whirled around and looked to see who had uttered such blasphemy. He was taken aback when he realized it was Bull.

O'Malley realized what Bull meant before it could sink in to the others.

"I'm not going to be a party to some vigilante squad going out to commit murder." O'Malley met Bull's gaze and everyone could tell that a volatile battle of wills was about to erupt. O'Malley was severely outnumbered but was not about to back down. Tom stepped in before any more words could be exchanged.

"Greg, no one is asking you to do anything or be a part of any conspiracy to do anything illegal." Tom made met the eyes of everyone around the table. The tension dropped noticeably but did not disappear. "Bull was just expressing an opinion, that's all."

"Yeah, I was just saying that she was probably an underpaid officer who was a victim of circumstance." The sarcasm dripped off the statement.

"I have the same feelings towards her that you guys do." O'Malley looked around, showing that he was not easily cowed. "But she'll get what's coming to her."

There were some grumbles of discontent around the table. The conversation went back to security planning for the long term. Bull had paid everyone for three months in advance so they were covered for the interim. But they could not operate at this level forever. They were going to have to reduce staff and make a long-term budget. They were going over this when Sheila walked through the front door. She looked around the table and, seeing Greg's red hair, immediately walked up to him and stuck out her hand.

"Gunner O'Malley, I presume. Sheila Stanford. I cannot thank you enough for all the things you've done." O'Malley took the offered hand and shook it. "Please tell me you can stay for dinner. It gets a little tiresome with these knuckle draggers around here. I was hoping to have some intelligent conversation."

Greg burst out laughing and returned the stares of the chastised men around the table. He stood up straighter and bowed his head slightly in the affirmative. He then turned Sheila's hand and kissed the back of it.

"It would be my honor, ma'am. At least someone around here appreciates my contributions to the war effort."

Bull and Steve glared at him while it was Tom's turn to burst out laughing. It was then that Sheila picked up on the vibe in the room. After exchanging looks with her husband, she put her arm in O'Malley's and walked him into the kitchen, asking what he would like in the way of proper food. Apparently, she was getting tired of steak and potatoes every night. Being of Irish decent herself, she began talking about food from the old country. Bull heard the words "corned beef and cabbage" just as they went into the pantry.

"Oh, hell no!" he exclaimed. "I'm going into town to eat if that crap is on the menu tonight!"

A couple of the guys agreed with him while surprisingly a couple said that they were fond of it. The naysayers agreed to go with him into

Brawley for pizza and beer, while the rest headed outside to the horseshoe pits. Tom closed his laptop and went into the kitchen to see if O'Malley needed rescuing.

He did not.

CHAPTER 59

Guerro's men had finally gotten the break they needed when one of them saw Sheila Stanford drive onto the lot of the house that was under construction. It had been difficult to make any kind of observation into the property because of the eight-foot-high wall around the outside and the security that constantly patrolled the perimeter. They had taken to planting a 4x4 truck in the state park right across the highway with two men inside, watching the gate to the property. They had seen the car leave earlier and head east. It was being driven by a hard-looking man and there was a passenger. The man hadn't looked like any of the pictures of people they were looking for. But when it returned, they were able to clearly see Sheila's face through her open window.

Guerro received the text confirming the presence of at least Sheila at the desert house. He did not think Tom would be very far away. He sent out the message to gather his newly replenished hit squad. They were going to move before the elusive Stanfords disappeared again.

He had been slowly sending members of the cartel who had been members of the Mexican Military north and putting them in a small house that he rented in Salton City. These men had experience with military-grade weapons, most of them having the HK or FN battle rifles they had taken with them when they had defected from the Mexican Army. Some of them had even been trained by American Special Operations forces for the War on Drugs and had old American M16s. This had made recruiting them even more enjoyable to the cartels. The foolish pride of the Americans to think they could change everything would someday be their downfall, but for the time being, Guerro was grateful for the higher-quality soldier he was getting.

The soldiers all put on some type of camouflage clothing, but they all wore bright red-and-white sneakers. This was a habit they had long ago developed in their wars with other cartels. It would be their identification to each other in the chaos that was about to ensue. They were organized as a military unit, and the platoon and squad leaders gathered around an aerial photograph on the wall of the living room.

First platoon would get in position and assault through the main gate and directly at the house. Second platoon would circle the property and hop the wall on the other side of where the construction supplies were. This would give them a covered approach. They would grab any ladders they could to use to get on the roof of the main house or the garage and work their way down into the home since the second story was not finished yet.

They received word that Guerro would be there within the next two hours and to wait for his arrival. In the meantime, they were to head in the direction of the house since it was some twenty miles away. They had to stop at a sporting goods store on the way out of town to replace the LED headlamps that they were all supposed to have, but half of the men were missing them because the other half had stolen them.

Guerro left his final instructions for the crews working in San Diego and headed east. He called Richard, who was just getting back into town after working in Arizona. Guerro told him to check on the safe house operations and get up to speed with what was going on. When Richard found out that Guerro was launching an attack on the Stanfords, he immediately asked to come along.

"Not this time, my friend. I need you to get distribution back online here. We have to catch up on our work. I promise you though, if I get the Stanford woman alive, I will bring her back to you in chains. This seemed to mollify him somewhat and he headed over to the stash house.

Ben and Rudy were the two men who had observation duty at the stash house. They were sitting on two lawn chairs, looking at the sun as it set across the horizon. Both men had the patience of Job. They were accustomed to waiting for hours for the right shot.

They both noticed when Richard's car pulled into the driveway. Ben was on the celestial telescope and Rudy had a smaller spotting scope set up. They both got a look at the skinny red-headed kid as he got out of the car and went into the house.

"That's our guy," Ben said as he snapped photographs with the attached high-resolution camera.

"Yup."

Ben picked up his phone and got on the line with Bull.

"Hey, we just ID'd that Richard guy that attacked Sheila and helped kill those folks at the self-storage."

"No shit?" Bull was just getting into the car to head into town. He told the guys to head back into the house.

"Yeah, his car is in the driveway," Ben said, and then described the car and its license plate.

"Okay, let me go see what Tom wants to do. I'll get back with ya in a few mikes."

"Copy, out."

Bull went back inside and told Tom what the guys in Chula Vista had observed. He immediately got on the horn with Herb.

"Hey, a little birdie just told me that if you hurry, you can catch one of the guys who killed those folks at the South Bay Self-Storage in a house out in Eastlake."

"Oh really?" Herb was sitting at his desk and began frantically snapping his fingers at one of the detectives in the squad room. "And did this little birdie happen to get the address at which this felon is staying?"

"You know what, he sure did." Tom gave him the address and then said, "We have eyes on the target building now. I will advise you of any changes."

"Your guys aren't going to be in danger if we serve a warrant on the house, are they?"

"Nope, the observation is from a distance, but I would advise haste. I think if he is parked in the driveway, he's not staying long, and my guys aren't in a position to follow him if he leaves. The best you'll get is a direction of travel from us. Expect a call from a guy named Ben at this number if anything changes."

"I got it. We're rolling five minutes ago."

Tom called Ben back and gave him Herb's special cell phone number.

"Things are about to get interesting down there," Ben said to Rudy.

"I can't wait for the show. Did Tom call the PD?"

"Yeah, and I bet they're itching for some payback."

"I imagine they are." Rudy adjusted himself behind the scope and made sure nothing of note had changed. They would keep a close eye on the house until whatever happened was over.

Chuck Cooper got the alert tone just as he and his wife were walking out of the grocery store. He took one look at the pager and rushed home the three blocks to his house so he could throw on his gear and head to the scene. He got a call from Herb while he was en route. Herb told him who they were after and he got a chill down his spine. He got on the radio and made sure that everyone stayed back until the warrant was in hand.

They had several patrol cars get into position in the area so they could initiate a traffic stop if Richard went mobile. The two observers on the hill were able to see some of the activity. The department's armored car was staged at the closest firehouse. The SWAT team met there and got ready. Herb rolled up a few minutes later and waved a piece of paper.

"It's a go!"

"Can your D's start making contact with the surrounding residents? There could be serious gunfire when we take these guys down," Chuck asked as the tactical team members began mounting the armored car.

"You got it. Let me see who has a POV here and I'll get them going," Herb said as Chuck returned to his preparations. Herb found Allen Young and they took off for the block that the stash house was located on. Keeping out of sight of the house, they contacted the residents of the first house on the block. Up on the hill, Rudy watched through the telescope as Ben was peeing on a bush.

"Well, it looks like things are going to get interesting now," Rudy said as he watched the detectives escort the occupants of another house around the corner where they had a van to whisk them away to a Carl's Jr. four blocks away.

"Why what's going on?"

"They started the neighborhood evacuations. The warrant team won't be far behind."

"What?" Ben said in a panicked voice. "Let me see!" He pushed Rudy aside and put his eye to the telescope.

"Oh shit!" He began pulling out his cell phone as he cussed vehemently.

"What the hell is the matter with you? You don't think they have IEDs, do you?" Rudy now had a look of concern on his face.

"That is a real possibility with these guys, but I'm more concerned about tunnels." He had the phone out and was hitting the redial. "The house in LA had an escape tunnel. If these guys try to evacuate the house that the tunnel comes up in, how much you wanna bet that the guys in the main house get a warning?"

"Ahh shit, you're right."

Ben held up a hand to quiet him down as Herb answered the phone.

"Have you got movement?" he asked. He was worried that someone would walk out and see what was obviously an evacuation.

"No, but you forgot about the tunnels!"

Herb stopped in his tracks. "What tunnels?"

"When we took down the LA house, it had an escape tunnel. That's how this guy got away from us in LA. If you try to evacuate the house with the escape tunnel, your suspect is going to get warned at best, or your two guys that are doing the evac are going to get whacked at worst." Ben realized that one of the men had stopped and was talking on the phone. "Oh, is that you doing the west side of the street?"

Herb looked around but couldn't see anyone.

"Yeah, that's me. Shit! No one told me about any tunnels!"

"Well, you're committed now," Ben said, wishing he could get down there.

"Yeah, you're right. Thanks for the info; wish I'd had it sooner."

"I thought you did," Ben said. "We'll keep an eye out at the surrounding houses for unusual activity."

"Copy, thanks."

"Out."

Herb got up next to the house he had just evacuated and got on the radio.

"Central, David One, code ten broadcast. Intel reveals that this individual may have a tunnel from his house to one of the surrounding houses."

"David One, Central copies all."

"Tac One copies," Chuck's voice came over the radio. "Any idea which one?"

"Not a clue!" Herb said.

"David Five copies," Allen acknowledged from across the street.

Herb looked at him and nodded back towards the end of the street. They both calmly walked back around the corner and met Chuck. He was sitting in the grey passenger van that they were using to transport people away. An older couple that Allen had just brought out, were still sitting in the middle seats.

"We're going to have to re-think this whole thing," Herb said as he walked up. "If they have a tunnel to one of the surrounding houses, or even out into the open area, we're going to have a hard time containing the scene."

"We can back the perimeter out, but there's no way the warrant is going to cover a house-to-house search." Chuck thought about it for a minute. "We'll do that and hit the house hard. Give me a few to get some eyes out on a logical perimeter. Let's get back to the CP and we'll look at good ol' Google Earth."

"Um, excuse me, young man?" The gentleman from the middle seat waved his hand to get their attention. "My name is Jay Hooks. I bought my house twenty-two years ago when I retired from the Coast Guard. We were one of the first people to move in when the tract was finished. I know just about everybody on the block."

Chuck and Herb exchanged a look. Herb and Allen went around and got in the van.

"Perfect!" Chuck started the van. "Mr. Hooks, would you please come with us to our command post so we can ask you a few questions about your neighbors?"

"Sure, although you'd be better off asking my wife's friend, Annie. That old bat has her nose in everybody's business on the block." Jay lifted his shoulder as his wife hit him. "This is my wife, Becky, and I want you to be my witness at the abuse I take."

"I didn't see a thing," Herb said, grinning over his shoulder as everyone laughed. They drove back to the fire station after stopping at the Carl's Jr. to pick up the old bat.

CHAPTER 60

The drive out to Ocotillo took Guerro just under two hours. He spent that time coordinating the attack with his computer team and his soldiers. The tech guys had looked at the adjacent properties to see who owned them. It was still the beginning of the desert season, so most of the properties were unoccupied. They also looked up local law enforcement assets. The property was just inside of San Diego County and the closest sheriff's station was miles away on the S-2. The State Vehicle Recreation Area (SVRA) had a small contingent of park rangers, but Guerro didn't think they would be much of a threat.

He met the two platoon leaders at the junction to a small side road off of the state highway. They went over the plan and Guerro approved it. Guerro and his men strapped on bulletproof vests and got out their long guns. Guerro pumped a shell into the chamber of his Mossberg 12-gauge and looked at the men around him.

"All of them dead, except the woman. Her, I would like alive. But the rest … kill them!"

"Sí, Jefe!"

"Yes, Jefe!"

The men trotted off to their cars and the second group began walking out into the desert in order to get around to the back side of the property. Three vans were packed full of men and they prepared for a frontal assault through the main gate.

Duane was up on the roof looking out over the desert when Steve brought him up a plate of food from the kitchen. He took one look at it and made a face that caused Steve to crack a grin at him. He set the plate on the ground and pulled out a set of binoculars before plopping down on a patio chair.

The two men sat in silence for a bit before Duane snapped upright. He grabbed the telescope and turned it out to the highway. Steve noticed the movement and turned his binoculars in the same direction.

Coming up the highway at a high rate of speed were three vans, driving in a close formation. There were two SUVs following a short distance behind.

Steve said, "Oh shit!" just as the seismic alarm for the south wall started beeping. Duane hit the panic button and pulled up his sniper rifle. Throughout the compound little red LED lights started flashing in the upper corner of each room. An alarm sounded at the front gate, telling the security there to drop the steel barrier into place.

Steve grabbed one of the suppressed M4s that were kept on the roof and pointed it in the direction of the south wall just as several figures scrambled over it and dropped to the ground. He lost sight of them as they hustled behind the construction supplies that were still staged there. They were moving slow from having dropped right on the cactus that was planted along the wall.

"Contact right! Tangos over the south wall!" Steve shouted in his loudest Marine Corps voice. He chambered a round and put the cross hairs on the next head that popped over the wall. A *chut clack* later and the head snapped back. Next to him he heard Duane's CheyTac boom out a round. The two of them began putting out a steady stream of fire as all hell broke loose below them.

At the front gate, the security officer on duty threw his ballistic armor on over his torso and grabbed an AR-15 rifle. He stepped out of the trailer, just to be hurled back inside by a shotgun blast to the chest. The buckshot didn't even make it to his body armor plate because most of the energy was absorbed by two of the 30-round GI magazines on the front of his vest. The blow did knock him on his ass, however, and he fell back into the trailer as he felt a burning in his right forearm. He looked down at his arm and saw a hole that was just starting to show blood. He was surprised at how little pain he felt.

He rolled out of sight of the doorway and began crawling towards the back office as automatic fire rippled through the front of the building. He stayed low and began calling for help on the radio.

"Dave, I'm taking fire at the front gate!" he screamed into the radio as he got behind the weapons safe in the office. The sturdy block of metal made the occasional ping as a round hit it. He stood up and got his rifle pointed back out at the front door. "I'm hit; I've been shot in the arm!"

"We're taking fire from the south too!" Dave had been walking the north side of the property and was all the way at the west end when the first shots were fired. He started jogging towards the main house when a voice came over the radio.

"Dave, you are Security Two! I need you to maintain a lookout along the north and west edges of the property. Break. John you are Security One! We are covering you with rifle fire now. Stay behind cover!" As if to emphasize these words, another boom sounded in the distance. It was followed by the sound of a solid impact on metal, which was followed by screams just outside the trailer. The *boom chunk* was repeated ten times. There was the sound of rending metal and cars crashing into each other.

John stayed right where he was with his rifle pointing out the door.

Most of the team was sitting at the massive dining room table when the LED started flashing red in the corner. Everyone immediately stopped what they were doing and began sprinting to their assigned location as they drew their sidearms. Several men followed Tom as he went and opened the safe and began passing out the equipment there. Several men ran out of the back kitchen door and sprinted for the temporary barracks trailer. They got there just as a couple of guys came spilling out with their rifles in hand. They all heard the "Contact South" call and ran towards the breezeway between the garage and the main house. They scrambled inside the two walls and faced outward in both directions as the intensity of fire picked up.

There were eighteen members of the security team on the property; this along with Tom, Sheila, and O'Malley brought the number of defenders to twenty-one. Guerro had sixty men plus his personal security team, which put them at sixty-four. It took the defenders less than thirty seconds to get equipped and behind cover. Guerro's second platoon was still trying to get the second half of their force over the wall in the face of Steve's precision rifle fire. The squad leaders finally had them all rush at once and that got them over at the cost of four men.

Six more men joined Steve and Duane on the roof. They began laying down a devastating cover fire. One went to the northwest corner and began watching their backside. Two went to help Duane as he continued to engage the vehicles that had rammed through the front gate. The last three went to help Steve pin down the force that was attacking from the south.

The vans that had crashed the gate were in a sorry state. The driver of the first van had been hit with Duane's very first round. The .300 Win Mag. smashed through the front windshield and slammed into the driver's chest. The round had enough energy to punch through the bulletproof vest he was wearing and out the back, lodging in the seat back. The driver's body rebounded forward, and he wound up draped over the steering wheel.

The second van in line rammed the first one and pushed it the rest of the way through the barricade. The soldier riding in the front passenger seat of the first van shoved on the driver's body to try to get a hand on the steering wheel. This only caused the wheel to turn to the left and the van was pushed violently against the split-rail fence by the van behind it. More bullets smashed into the rear passenger area and men began to scream and push their way out of the vehicle. The van lurched as it hit the faux wood fence and rebounded back. The second van continued forward until the first curve in the road, where it ran head on into the fence again and came to a stop. Of the twelve men in the van, only eight made it out unscathed. One was wounded and the others were killed. That number dropped by one when one of the men jumped out too far and got hit by the third van in line as it passed them.

Duane just shook his head and inserted another magazine as he watched the man bounce off the front left fender and fly into the guardrail. He did not get up.

"Eagle One, can someone get a 107 up here? I have four ... correction, five vehicles coming through the front gate!"

"On the way!" Bull's voice came over the radio.

Downstairs, there was an air of urgent efficiency. O'Malley and Sheila were assigned to guard the interior of the house. Tom and Bull set about coordinating the defense. Members of the team had drilled repeatedly for this exact event and their quick response showed it.

Once every man was equipped, they made their way to the nearest open defensive position. The only exception to this were the designated marksmen. These men were equipped with sniper rifles and made their way to the roofs of both the main house and garage. Once there, they began to systematically engage anyone who appeared in their sector of fire. Donald Layman was the heavy rifle sniper and took his Barrett M107 to the roof to support Duane.

Donald flopped down next to Duane and extended the bipod on his rifle. He slapped in a magazine and pulled the charging handle to the rear before letting it slam home. He put the rifle to his shoulder and sighted in on what was now the lead van as it came around the second curve in the driveway. He put the cross hairs on a point just in front of the driver, on the hood, and squeezed the trigger. The massive .50-caliber bullet left the barrel and punched a hole clean through the hood, the steering rod, and part of the dash before slamming into the driver's left leg above the knee. The now mangled bullet and a substantial amount of debris from the steering column shattered his femur and added bone fragments to the shrapnel that was shredding his leg. The femoral artery was severed in multiple locations, but only the one closest to his hip mattered.

The driver managed to stay conscious long enough to straighten out the van and punch the accelerator with his good foot. The van started to shoot forward when all of a sudden it became weightless as the earth dropped away underneath it. A pit had appeared as if by magic and the van slammed into the concrete of the far wall. The crash broke bones and knocked several of the occupants unconscious. Those who were fast enough to get out of the rear doors were fortunate; they heard a voice yell "frag out!" and watched as a small black object arced through the air and landed in the pit next to the trapped van. Since it was just after twilight, there was a subdued flash and thump. A cloud of dust rose out of the pit.

The third and final van stopped at an angle across the drive. All of the occupants managed to get out and scatter. Some tried to take cover behind the van as they began returning fire at the roofline of the house. The van would have been good cover from pistol rounds and maybe even fair cover from the 5.56 rounds of the Marines M4s, but it did little to slow down the bullets from the two sniper rifles. Donald sent the next nine rounds straight through the vehicle, hitting and killing three of the five men hiding behind it.

On the other side of the roof, Steve was making his second magazine change when the man next to him slumped back with a .308 round through his head from one of the FN rifles carried by the attackers.

"Medic, I've got one down, south side of the roof!"

"Copy!"

Two members of the security team were qualified medics, one of them being a former Navy corpsman, and the other was an EMT. Bull ran upstairs with the medic to help bring the wounded man down. It was a fruitless gesture, as he was dead already. Bull let the medic drag the body down and took his place on the wall.

The three squads that had taken cover behind the construction equipment had taken a pasting. The only thing that had saved them was that there was still some heavy equipment parked there and the Marines didn't even bother to try to shoot through it. The survivors were able to regroup and get ready for their next assault.

The remaining men barely made up two squads, so they split in half and rushed forward, with half heading for the hangar and the others conducting a frontal assault on the house. The men heading towards the hangar only suffered two casualties, as the structure blocked the shooters on the roof from getting a good field of fire on them. The men running in the direction of the house were subjected to a heavy volume of fire. Only

four of them made it to the front door of the house without getting hit.
Three more made it with minor wounds. The rest of their compatriots lay
out in the open, most dead, some screaming or moaning in pain.

The ones who made it to the front door huddled under the eaves where
the men on the roof could not shoot down on them. They attempted to
reorganize themselves, but panic was starting to set in. Most of them had
been in gunfights on the streets of Mexico, but none had faced a
disciplined enemy with superior training. One of the men placed his 12-
gauge shotgun against the lock and pulled the trigger.

There are specially made rounds for breaching a door. These use
powdered lead and zinc compressed into a heavy slug that uses kinetic
energy to blow open the lock. The slug then disintegrates into dust,
preventing injury to those around the door. The buckshot round fired by
the cartel soldier shattered the doorknob but didn't penetrate the steel-
cased door. The buckshot did, however, ricochet back and strike several of
the other men huddled in the entryway. Several screamed as the lead balls
hit them in the legs. This caused one man to collapse against another, who
fell out into the front yard. He was immediately shot by one of the Marines
on the roof of the garage. He tried to crawl back under the eaves, but by
the time he was behind cover he had been hit in the torso and twice in the
left leg. He lay there screaming at the top of his lungs until one of his
fellow attackers turned and shot him in the head to shut him up. They
shoved the body back out into the yard.

On the east side of the house, Guerro was having a tough time getting
his men up to the house. He had anticipated a stiff resistance and had
procured an RPG-7 just to be sure he could get past any obstacle they
might encounter. He could not maneuver his men out in the open to get a
square shot at one of the buildings walls. He settled for an oblique attempt
at the back door. He directed his gunner to aim at the door and fire.

The man leaned out around the side of the suburban and placed the
sighting reticle on the back door, which led into the kitchen. He pulled the
trigger and watched the rocket head towards the door. He had to duck back
behind the car as rifle rounds began impacting around him.

Three Marines had taken cover behind the wall that surrounded the fire
pit facing the entrance drive. Another man was farther around the curve of
the wall to secure their rear. This put him much closer to the rear door. He
barely had time to register the shouts of "RPG!" and look around to see the
telltale smoke trail heading his way before the round struck.

This is gonna hurt! Dan Burns thought as he flopped onto his belly and
covered his ears. He didn't have his hands all the way sealed against the
side of his head when the round detonated against the door behind him.
The blast overpressure slammed his body violently against the retaining

wall. The pressure almost blew in his eardrums. He made sure that his mouth was open so the damage wasn't catastrophic, but it did hurt. He lay there on the edge of consciousness, trying to get his body to respond to simple commands—like *breathe.*

The RPG uses a focused cone of explosive energy to drive a jet of plasma through light armor. While the 12-gauge shotgun was pretty much ineffective against breaching the steel-cased doors, the RPG was overkill. The explosion blew away a three-foot section of the doorframe on the hinge side. It also turned the door into a twisted mass of metal that was left hanging by the bottom hinge. The blast splashed through the opening and destroyed the mudroom along with four feet of Sheila's new granite countertop.

Bruce, the Marine who was at the rear window firing slit, had seen the round coming and taken cover. As soon as he was sure that the blast effect had dissipated, he got up and dusted himself off, then began covering the three men in the fire pit area.

On the roof, Duane cursed as he rolled on top of the plate of corned beef and cabbage as he tried to shift around to get a field of fire on the enemy rocket. He low crawled past Don's legs and moved up to the next opening in the wall. Don had shifted his fire and was shooting the SUVs to pieces. Duane scanned the vehicles for movement but had to duck back several times as automatic rifle fire impacted the embrasure around him.

He had just pushed his rifle forward when Donald let out a curse and reeled back with his hand covering the side of his face. Blood was running freely between his fingers. Duane got on the scope just as the RPG gunner was lining up his second shot. Duane fired just a split second before the gunner did. His bullet struck the actual round itself and ricocheted away into the night.

The impact caused the gunner to flinch as he triggered the round. It flew to the right of where he had been aiming, but it still impacted on the back wall adjacent to the hole created by the first round. Duane's bullet had deformed the warhead enough that it did not form a symmetrical blast cone. Even though the round did not strike with its full destructive potential, it still blew away another section of wall, making the opening bigger. The house was now breached.

Out at the northwest corner of the property, Dave had flopped to the ground and was trying to watch both assaults at once. He had seen the men behind the last SUV fire the rockets at the house. He had just enough of an angle to see them behind the car reloading the RPG. He figured this to be the biggest threat, so he turned his rifle towards it and sighted in on the movement there. The 3.5x scope on top of his rifle gave him just enough of a sight picture to aim at the man holding the launcher.

He slowly began to press the trigger, but felt resistance. Cursing himself for a rookie, he flipped off the safety and sighted in again. The man had turned slightly away to face another person, so the only part of his body that was clearly exposed was the back of his shoulder. He put the reticle right on the center and pulled the trigger.

The bullet just caught the edge of the gunner's vest. It still penetrated his left scapula and blew out the front just under his collarbone. There were only a few drops of blood that splattered out and hit Guerro in the face. He wiped his face in irritation and looked to see where the shot had come from. His gunner slumped to his right, dropping the RPG and clutching his wounded shoulder.

Guerro yelled into his phone and the last ten men, who he had kept in reserve, jumped the north fence. They immediately rushed at the house, firing at the roofline. Guerro grabbed one of the other men with him and shoved the RPG into his hands. He pointed at the roofline and told him to take out the snipers up there. The man poked his head out and pulled it back just as a bullet snapped by.

This time Guerro and several of the men who had just hopped the north fence saw where the shot came from and several turned towards the low mound of sand that Dave was using for cover. He rolled away from the incoming rounds and tried to make himself small.

This gave the new RPG gunner a chance to lean out and fire the last round up at the roof line. The rocket hit just above the eaves and destroyed one of the raised sections of the roof's edge. The blast threw chunks of concrete and rebar across the rooftop. Duane and Don were the two closest to the blast and both were knocked unconscious. The other men were all wounded. The defensive fire from the roof immediately stopped on the north side.

On the roof of the garage, Dillon Remke was having a tough time getting a shot at the attackers by the hangar. Tom was going to be pissed because he was pretty sure that the new airplane had some holes in it. Dillon went to the north edge of the roof just in time to see Dave rolling away from his cover. Dillon took up a good firing position and began shooting at the exposed men to the north. He called across to Paul Kursk to let him know they had trouble coming from that direction. Kursk grabbed a box of loaded magazines and crouch walked over to the northeast side of the building.

The group of men who had come over the north wall were almost to the fire pit area. Over half of them were down, but their numbers got them up to the edge of the pit. The defenders had been rendered almost ineffective by the two RPG blasts that slammed into the back wall. Once they were able to stand over the defenders, it was only a matter of seconds before they were all down and the attackers were attempting to enter the kitchen through the huge hole in the wall.

The first person to stick his head through the wall had a hole punched right through it. The body flopped right back out at the feet of the others gathered there. The second man up had an old military grenade hull that had been packed with black powder and had a commercial blasting cap stuck in the top. He pulled the tab on the ten-second fuse and threw it through the opening. The bomblet bounced off the counter and rolled across the floor, where it sputtered and spit for several seconds.

Bruce saw it come through the hole in the wall and immediately took cover while yelling "grenade!" at the top of his lungs. He waited for a count of five, and then heard it sputtering. He was going to count to five again before approaching it. No one else had attempted to come through the doorway so he maintained cover and watched the hole in the wall.

The black powder inside the grenade hull was not packed tight enough to have a full-force detonation. Although the homemade bomb did explode, it was a low-order detonation. The fragments of the steel case were sent in all directions with flaming chunks of powder still stuck to them. These set the curtains on fire and embedded themselves in the wooden cabinets. A couple of fragments flew through the dining room arch, resulting in some swearing as the people there had to grab one of the many fire extinguishers that had been placed throughout the house and douse the flames.

As soon as the grenade went off, several of the attackers ran through the hole in the wall, spraying rounds wildly. Although they were not trained to the level of the defenders, they did throw out a lot of lead. Bruce was behind cover but still got hit twice. One round hit his vest, knocking him out from behind cover, the other slammed into his shoulder, spinning him around. His right arm went numb and he lost his grip on the rifle. He put his back against the fridge and was trying to pull the rifle across his chest with his left arm when one of the attackers stood over him and fired into his chest several times.

Bruce was snarling at the man as the world went dark.

CHAPTER 61

Chuck and Herb were facing a bit of a dilemma as they listened to Annie Meyers describe every person and thing that had occurred in front of the stash house for the last two years. She was able to confirm that a landscaping truck had removed a substantial amount of dirt from the house. Several of the neighbors had thought it was for a pool.

The house had minimal traffic on most days, but on occasion, there would be a group of vehicles that would arrive and depart together. The men all wore sport coats or were otherwise well dressed, and none of the vehicles played loud music. They also drove at a safe speed.

Annie looked at some photos taken from the security feed at the self-storage and confirmed that the men in the pictures were regular visitors to the house. She was able to positively ID Richard, since she had met him on the street once and he had seemed like such a nice boy.

After receiving much more intel than he really wanted from Ms. Meyers, Chuck decided that they would conduct a no-knock entry and see if they could flood the house before anyone could escape. The team would use the department's armored car to make a rapid approach. A breaching team would "Break and Rake" the front windows while the armored car would breach the garage.

Herb told Chuck about the Marines up on the hill and gave him the number to Ben's phone. Chuck requested that they notify him if they observed anything that looked like escaping felons. He received their assurance that they would.

Once everything was ready to go, the armored car and SWAT van drove rapidly to the house. The van stopped on the street as the armored car pulled into the driveway, scraping a long gash in the Honda Accord

Richard had parked there. The breachers attached chains to the security bars over the front windows and stepped back. The driver put the armored car in reverse and pulled the bars off the front of the house. Two team members used rakes to pull the curtains aside while other team members aimed their rifles through the opening. Still others ran around the side of the house and had to hop the fence into the backyard.

The armored car drove back into the driveway and pushed its nose against the garage door, slowly driving forward until the sliding door track popped away from the doorframe. The driver continued to push until there was a gap large enough for a man to fit through.

"Structure is breached!" Chuck yelled into his microphone as he watched the breachers throw flash-bang grenades into the garage and living room. Just as they did so, there was a sound of gunfire and the curtains on the front window began to jerk as bullets passed through them. There was also a series of *pings* as rounds came through the garage door and ricocheted off the front of the armored car.

"Shots fired!" several of the team members called out as they ducked their heads and waited for the flash-bangs to go off.

The Def-Tec nonlethal munition they deployed emitted a blinding light and a 200-decibel bang. This was sufficient to disorient the occupants of both the garage and the front room of the house. The detonation caused the two men in the front room of the house to turn away and raise their arms. Two entry team members popped up and immediately fired controlled pairs of shots into their torsos. The man in the garage was lucky in that the flash-bang landed on the other side of a tool chest. The blast was far less effective and he was able to fire at the officers who were pushing their way through the gap between the garage door and its frame. The first one made it through without getting hit, but the second man through took two rounds in the side plate of his body armor.

"I'm hit!" Alex Minton cried out as he felt the crushing pressure against his cracked ribs. The blows caused him to bounce off the frame and into the door track that was still hanging loose. The magazine pouches on the front of his vest got caught in the track and held him up, preventing him from getting through the gap. He was stuck in place, trying to free himself when a series of rounds stitched across his torso and up to his face. His head snapped back as the last round slammed into his cheek, blowing two teeth into his mouth before skidding out behind his ear. He collapsed in the opening, preventing anyone from getting in behind him, and trapping his partner inside.

Audie Volkdering was lying on his side, returning fire at the man who was firing at his partner. After putting two bursts into the man, he got to his knees and faced the interior of the garage. He glanced over his shoulder to see hands pulling Alex out of the gap then returned his attention to the doorway into the house. A face appeared there for a second, but before he could command the person to freeze, it disappeared.

Outside, Chuck and another member of the tactical team had lifted Alex out of the gap and carried him to the back of the armored car where the team medic began to work on him. As soon as they set him down, they turned and rushed back to the garage door.

"Coming in!" Chuck shouted as he managed to squeeze through the narrow opening. He stepped to Audie's side and pointed his M4 at the open door that led into the house.

"Cover!" Audie said in a loud firm voice.

"Go." Chuck picked up his field of fire.

Audie dropped the magazine out of his rifle while pulling one out of the pouch on his chest. He slammed it home in the magazine well of his rifle.

"Ready!"

"Up!" Chuck said and stepped further off to the side as Audie popped to his feet. Two more men came through the gap and cleared the room while the other two officers covered the door. The sound of gunfire could be heard from somewhere further in the house. It took the officers more than ninety seconds to clear the garage because of all the cabinets. A veritable lifetime in a gunfight, but they couldn't continue without securing the area behind them. Finally, one of the officers came up behind Chuck.

"We're clear, Sarge."

They stacked up at the door leading into the house and got ready to enter.

Rich was sitting in the downstairs office talking to Alejandro about vehicle issues. With the loss of the warehouse, some of their cutout protocols needed to be modified until they could get replacement vehicles. They were almost done when they heard one of the men in the living room yell.

"Shit! Cops!"

They had a predetermined evacuation plan for Rich or other people of importance. He got up and hurried to the kitchen. The refrigerator was rolled forward on its casters and a very well-concealed trap door was lifted up. The linoleum had been cut so that the edge of the trap door was flush with the cabinetry on either side. The hinge side was furthest from the wall and the linoleum covered the joint. With the door fully open, Rich had to squeeze by the counter to get into the opening. He was almost through when they heard glass breaking in the front room.

Once he was in the hole, Alejandro closed the door and scuffed some of the crud that always accumulates under fridges across the joint where the hinge side was. He was just shoving the appliance back into place when he heard a loud bang and saw the strobe of light from the living room. He turned away from the opening in time to see shadows moving across the closed blinds of the rear patio door.

He was debating whether he should go for his gun in the den, or just surrender. He had no record, and there weren't any drugs in the house. His mind was made up for him as gunfire broke out in the garage and front room almost simultaneously. He was cussing the fools for firing at the cops when one of the patio chairs crashed through the sliding glass door. The heavy wrought-iron chair was part of a fire pit set that Richard had gotten them at Costco. It crashed through the glass and rebounded from the kitchen island, slamming into one of the stools and knocking it over.

Alejandro had just raised his hands as two black-clad figures pushed their way through the hanging blinds and began screaming at him.

"Put your hands up!"

"Let me see your hands!"

"Turn around!"

"Get down on the ground!"

The various commands came at him so fast that he got confused and only half turned, tried to still show the palms of his hands, then turned back.

The two officers had to push through the hanging blinds then get past the toppled stool and patio chair, before they could get to Alejandro. They were each trying to go around the island and cover him, while also covering the doorway to the living room. There was another doorway that led towards the main hallway and stairway to the upper floor. Neither of them saw Esteban lean out into the opening. He fired one shot at each officer's face. Both shots hit their target, one killing the officer instantly while the other shot shattered the jaw of the second man. His head snapped to the side, spinning him to the ground.

Esteban frowned at the next set of shadows that were moving past the blinds. He snapped off two more shots through the blinds and began a reload. Outside, one of the backup officers began cussing as he fell to the ground with a hole punched in his bicep. Although the wound was a clean-through shot, the slug was a Federal Hydra-Shok .45 ACP. The massive hollow point removed a tunnel of flesh before travelling across the yard and through the back fence. Both officers dove to the ground.

Alejandro looked at the officer on the kitchen floor, who had both hands pressed to his face. There was a stream of blood and saliva, mixed with a few teeth, running through his fingers onto the floor. Alejandro figured "In for a penny, in for a pound!" and delivered a vicious kick to the side of the man's face. He slumped over unconscious.

Esteban spun around as he heard the garage door open and fired two shots into the doorframe, causing Audie, who was the point man, to recoil away from the incoming fire. Splinters peppered all four men as the big .45 rounds impacted the doorframe. Audie leaned out and snapped off a pair of shots at the two figures running down the dim hall. He ducked back and after not receiving any return fire, poked his head out again. This time Esteban was waiting a few steps up the stairway leading to the second floor. He had a sight picture on Audie's rifle as it came through the door. As soon as he saw movement he fired, striking the holographic sight on Audie's M4.

Audie cursed and ducked back again just as two entry team members pulled up short next to the corner on the other side of the hallway. The first one had to duck back quickly to avoid the two rounds Esteban sent into the drywall next to his face.

Esteban used the reprieve to hustle back upstairs and think about his next step. He changed magazines again, replacing the depleted one in the gun with a fresh one from his belt. He replaced the pistol in its holster and hustled Alejandro ahead of him down the hall to the bedroom he was using. He went to the closet and pulled out an old World War II era M1 Garand rifle. He set it on the bed and pulled out a shotgun, which he shoved into Alejandro's hands. He gestured at the doorway.

"Keep them off my ass for a minute, and we might get out of here!"

"Dude! What were you thinking?" Alejandro whispered loudly. "Once Rich was gone, we could have just given up! Why did you guys shoot at the cops? Man, we're fucked now!"

"Because we were seen on the video from the self-storage, you ass!" Esteban pointed back down the hall again to keep the panicked man focused. "Just do what I say, or I'll shoot you myself."

Alejandro knew it was no idle threat and turned back towards the hallway. He noticed what looked like a stick poking up on the stairwell. It took him a moment to realize he was looking at a periscope. He aimed the shotgun at it just as it vanished back down the stairwell.

"Hey, man! They be lookin' at us with that stick thing!"

Esteban picked up the M1 and went to the doorway. He peered into the hall just in time to see an elongated canister come sailing towards them. He slammed the door and stepped away from it while covering his ears. He heard the thud as it bounced off the door and fell to the landing outside. He saw the flash under the door and heard the *whump* as the flash-bang grenade went off. He immediately turned around and began firing with the battle rifle.

The M1 Garand fires a .30-06 round that is substantially more powerful than the .223 rounds fired by the M4s the police were using. Esteban had studied several police shootings and was fascinated by an incident that had occurred years before in San Diego. Several police officers had been ambushed on Crandall Drive by a man armed with an M1 loaded with .30-06 armor-piercing rounds. Some of the slugs recovered in that incident had penetrated six houses before coming to a stop.

Esteban began firing the black-tip rounds through the door just as Audie was coming up the stairs. He angled his fire downwards and the rounds plowed through the floor and into the stairwell, where the SWAT team scrambled to get out of the line of fire. One of the rounds caught Audie in the side of his vest and caused him to stumble back as he felt a burning in his side.

Esteban fired the final two rounds in the clip through the floor before the rifle ejected the clip with a loud *ping*. He immediately shoved another clip down through the open breach and sent the bolt forward. He fired two more rounds through the floor in the direction that he thought the SWAT team might be.

Alejandro stared as the Filipino man went to the closet again and pulled out two gas masks. He handed one to Alejandro before putting one on himself. He moved to the other side of the room and fired two more shots through the floor.

Downstairs, Chuck was facing a dilemma. He had at least two men armed with high-powered weapons up on the second floor. They were firing indiscriminately through the walls and floor. The weapon was obviously capable of penetrating the structure and body armor. He also had several wounded men that he had to consider, despite Audie's protests that he was fine. He made the decision to pull out.

"All units, power down and pull back!" Chuck began shooing team members towards the exits. "This is now a barricaded suspect scenario!"

The team began heading to the garage. They would use the armored car for cover during their extraction. The one dead officer and the two wounded ones were hustled to the garage, having to stop once as a series of rounds came down out of the ceiling. Once they were all in the garage, Chuck got on the radio to have the armored car move over to provide cover from any fire from the upper story.

As soon as the car backed out, the metal of the door sprang back closed. Several of the officers, who were a little panicked, began yelling into the radio to have the car drive back forward. Chuck told the car to continue changing position, then reached up and popped the door release for the automatic opener, and heaved the roll-up door up above shoulder height. Although the track was bent, the door screeched upwards. He grabbed a screw driver out of the nearest tool chest and jammed the door open.

The officers hustled out to the far side of the armored car and began the slow retreat down the street.

Ben and Rudy sat on the hill and watched the disaster unfold below them. They could hear the faint popping of the gunfire and couldn't help but critique what was going on. Ben, who was on the celestial telescope was focused on the back patio area. He had seen the officer get hit in the arm and go to the ground. After the second group of officers had entered, enough of the blinds had been torn down that he had a good field of view into the kitchen.

"Man that shit sucks," Ben said as he watched the tactical team retreating away from the front of the house. He noticed some movement in the kitchen and zoomed in through the patio door. He saw an individual move past his field of view. "Oh shit, better tell them about that!"

"About what?" Rudy asked, shifting his view to the back door. He saw the figure pass by again and said, "Yeah, they should know about that shit."

Ben had already been dialing Herb's number.

"Talk to me," Herb said.

"You have at least two subjects, armed with long guns and equipped with gas masks moving around the kitchen," Ben reported. "I say again, subjects are equipped with gas masks. You need to let your team know if they were planning on smoking them out, it will be a long wait."

Along the street, people were coming out of their houses and looking at all the activity. The tactical officers started to evacuate them when a series of shots rang out and everyone scattered. Civilians began running in panic as one of the officers fell to the ground.

"You wouldn't happen to have a .50 cal handy, would you?" Herb asked rhetorically. "They have some type of rifle that goes through walls like butter."

"Sorry. We are here for observation only." Ben shook his head. "We'll keep our eyes peeled for ya."

"Thanks; out," Herb said then immediately keyed his mic. "Sam Ten, David One. Our friends with the eyes report that they have minimum two subjects equipped with gas masks and rifles moving in the kitchen."

"Sam Ten copies two with gas masks." Chuck frowned as he tried to take in the reports his team was giving him. His officers reported that the entry into the living room had gone according to plan with two suspects down. The four that had gone around back had run into a gate with two latches on it. They had tried to force the gate but wound up scaling the side fence. This had resulted in them being a little behind on timing. The two who made the report didn't make it into the house until after the suspects had fled upstairs. Chuck wasn't so sure *fled* was the right term. It appeared to him that it was more of a tactical lateral movement. The suspects obviously had a plan or knew they were coming. Either way, it cost them the advantage of surprise.

They were now facing well-equipped, barricaded suspects.

CHAPTER 62

Tom Stanford was facing the doorway to the kitchen when Bull staggered down the stairs. He looked up to see his friend with blood streaming down the side of his face from multiple lacerations made by the concrete fragments that had been blown across the roof. He turned back towards the kitchen doorway just as a body went past the opening. He fired one round of 00 buckshot from the Bennelli and was rewarded with a scream and a thud as the man fell to the ground with a caved-in ribcage.

Tom ducked down and pulled two replacement rounds from his speed clip. He pushed them in through the receiver and had the gun up in less than two seconds. There was more movement and Tom sent another reminder through the doorway.

Bull turned and looked into the living room. O'Malley and Sheila had M4 carbines and were covering the front of the house. There was a banging on the front door as the men outside hammered on it with their rifle butts. The defenders could not obtain a good field of fire on the attackers and they, in turn, could not get in. They couldn't move around the outside of the house either. Although they were under cover while on the porch, they couldn't step off of it with the Marines on the garage roof looking for the slightest bit of movement. Anything that came into view wound up with a hole in it.

The attackers managed to get the last nine unwounded men they had into the kitchen. Guerro organized them and had them ready to attack when he noticed the body slumped over next to the refrigerator. He walked over and searched the body as his men began to exchange gunfire through the doorway to the dining room. He removed the grenades hanging from the man's vest and was examining them when one of his men on the other side of the kitchen let out a scream and fell to the floor next to another man who was lying there bleeding.

"Stand back, you fools!" Guerro said as he calmly walked over to the archway. He looked at the small device in his hand, and after manipulating a wire cage of some sort, was startled when it popped off. In an act of panic, he threw it into the adjoining room.

"Frag!" Bull yelled as he batted it into a corner and rolled away while trying to use his body to shield Tom. This became somewhat of a comedy because Tom was trying to shield Bull from the expectant blast with his body. They both wound up falling to the ground and covering their ears, where they waited for the bomb to go off. The expected blast never occurred since Guerro had removed the safety cage but not the pin.

After counting slowly to ten, they both got to their knees. Bull covered the door to the kitchen just as a curious face peered around the corner. He put a bullet right through the man's open mouth.

"Sheila! O'Malley! Watch the hallway from the kitchen!" Tom yelled as he sent another round of buckshot through the doorway. The other door leading from the kitchen went down a short hallway to a bathroom and the two downstairs bedrooms. It then turned a corner and came out in the back of the great room. They had barricaded the steel-core door, but Tom wasn't taking any chances.

"On it!" O'Malley shouted over the noise. He turned and sprinted down the hallway to the corner. After carefully slicing the pie he was able to see the door to the kitchen was still intact. "Still secure, Tom!"

"It's time to go turtle, bud," Bull said as he popped two more rounds through the doorway.

"We still have men outside!" Tom looked at Bull like he was crazy for even thinking that he would leave a man behind.

"That's right! And it's time to let them do their job!" Bull shoved him in the direction of the living room. "Follow the plan and don't let their sacrifices go to waste!"

Tom realized the logic and grabbed Sheila as they were hustled to the closet door under the stairs. After opening the door, Tom pushed on a section of molding and a hydraulic ram lifted most of the floor up to the slanted ceiling under the stairs. Another set of stairs led down to the escape tunnel and storage rooms that had been created during the construction of the property. They all hustled down the stairs.

Once everyone was out of the stairwell, O'Malley covered it while Bull hit the button to retract the hydraulic ram. The floor started to lower back into place when an AK-47 was shoved into the gap and jammed it open.

O'Malley sent a few rounds up the stairwell, but it was too late; the trap door was open more than thirty inches—plenty of room for a body to slide through.

"Go on, get out of here! I got this!" O'Malley said over his shoulder. "Leave the first storage door open and I'll leapfrog back."

Bull began to shove the Stanfords down the tunnel in spite of the pained look on Tom's face. He paused to push open the first door on his right, then continued to herd his charges around the first turn in the tunnel. They were approaching the next one when there was a *whummp* from a grenade going off then a series of gunshots. Bull had to physically pick Tom up to keep him from going back to aid O'Malley.

"You all right back there?" Bull screamed as the firing dropped off.

"I'm good!" O'Malley had to wipe the blood out of his eyes with his sleeve as he staggered back from the stairwell towards the storage room door. The bad guys had finally figured out how to make the grenades go boom, and one had come bouncing down the stairwell. O'Malley had managed to slam the door shut, but the blast in such a confined space had torn the solid-core door halfway off its hinges. Debris had peppered the Marine's face and the arm he had put across it to protect his eyes. "Moving back to the storage room. Come bail me out when the cavalry gets here!"

The first man Guerro sent down the stairwell had to duck back when he tried to squeeze past the broken door, two .45-caliber slugs sending him the message that he was not welcome. The next man down used his shotgun to blow the door out into the tunnel. The two men charged into the hall only to be met with a barrage of gunfire. After firing the last five rounds in his pistol, O'Malley stepped back into the storage room and slammed the steel door.

Guerro walked down the stairs and looked at the wounded man leaning against the wall. He knew better than to complain, and when he didn't, Guerro gave him a nod to acknowledge his fortitude. He turned to the other man who had his shotgun pointed at the Steel door.

"Aquí?" he nodded at the door.

"I do not know, Jefe. At least one of them is for sure."

They all looked down the hallway then heard a scuffling and the sound of another door closing. Guerro tried the handle on the door in front of him as the last of the attackers poured out of the stairwell. A small debate ensued as several of the younger men wanted to leave and refused to go further into the tunnel. Guerro sent two men to the next turn in the corridor and one back up to secure the top of the stairwell.

The men were getting ready to try the shotgun on the door when a gunshot at the top of the stairs had them looking as the body of the man who was sent to guard it came sliding down the steps. Three men rushed to the foot of the stairs when a grenade landed among them and went off.

CHAPTER 63

Rich walked hunched over through the tunnel to a point where it widened. The tunnel had a plank floor and wooden wall panels. He dug his fingers into the dirt under the edge of one of the panels and pushed up on a pin. He pushed the panel into the wall of the tunnel and stepped through into a small storage room. He turned and shoved the door closed. The door was heavy since it was dirt filled and designed to throw off customs inspectors if they pulled the wood panel off the bracing studs.

Rich sat down and began to seriously consider getting out of the drug trade. The money was phenomenal, but he was getting tired of escaping death by the skin of his teeth. He was pretty sure that the police had a perimeter set up around the neighborhood. He had no illusions about his chances if he popped out of the ground in the tool shed three houses over. If the cops outside found the tunnel entrance under the refrigerator, he was pretty much screwed and would go along without a fight.

Up above in the main house, Esteban was preparing to do just the opposite and fight to his last breath. He had moved from window to window, firing at the few police officers he could see. His plan was to let the police follow their standard practice of setting up a perimeter and then let them begin to negotiate. He would hold them off for a few hours then let the house burn down while he followed Rich out through the tunnel. He should have been well clear by now.

The M1 Garand was an awesome weapon but was limited by the 8-round clip that fed it. After firing the last round in one of the clips, it was ejected with a loud metallic *PING*. One of the SWAT team members heard it and immediately recognized it for what it was and let the other officers know what they were dealing with.

Billy Kidd was a sniper with the team and had been working his way carefully around the side of a house across the street. He was the best marksman on the team, having grown up with the onus of being named after a famous gunfighter. This was not due to any familial relationship, but rather a set of parents with a sense of humor and an appreciation of old westerns.

After hearing the telltale *ping* and notifying the rest of the team, he had slowly crawled along the side of a house until he could cover the front from his prone position, while still being well covered by the cement foundation. After getting set up, he waited for one of the suspects to expose himself. He didn't have long to wait, as he soon saw a body move past the living room window. The next time the body came into view he was ready, and as the gas-masked face turned towards him, he pressed the trigger.

The Remington 700 VBSS is a popular rifle within the law enforcement community for a reason. The rifles are incredibly accurate and the .308 Winchester is a powerful enough cartridge to put down any human with proper placement. The 168-grain boat-tail hollow-point bullet left the barrel at just over 2600 feet per second. It crossed the street and impacted Alejandro's gas mask just below the left eye. The military surplus mask uses two filters contained the cheek pads, and this is where the bullet struck.

The bullet was only slightly deflected away from Alejandro's face; it tore a hole through his cheek and blew the left side of his jaw out the back of his head, below and behind his ear. He dropped to the floor unconscious. The gas can he had been carrying fell from his nerveless fingers.

"Rifle One has one suspect down in the living room!" Billy broadcast as he scrambled back from the corner of the building. He was pleasantly surprised when there was no return fire. Billy had gone to too many schools and was too well disciplined to go back and take a shot from the same place, so he began to work his way around to the back of the house he was using for cover.

He spent four minutes crawling to his next firing point. This one was slightly more elevated and he could see further into the second-story windows. He was unable to get a shot off at the other suspect, as this one only appeared fleetingly. At least the firing from the house had stopped.

Billy backed the magnification on his scope down to increase his field of view. He kept his eye glued to the optic so he could engage anyone the moment they came into view. Aside from the few glimpses of movement, his efforts were fruitless, Esteban being too well disciplined to expose himself.

Across the street, Esteban was cursing Alejandro for the fool he was. He had heard the shot that had hit Alejandro, but was not able to see where it came from. He did become far more cautious though. A sniper was out there, and that meant he had to be on his toes, keeping behind cover and concealment. He finished placing gas cans throughout the upstairs and went downstairs where he saw Alejandro's body lying in the living room.

He barely spared the man a second look after seeing the gore on the side of his face. Figuring him for dead, he dashed past the opening to the hallway that he knew was visible to the outside, stooping to grab the gas can that Alejandro had dropped. He continued his run down the hall to the office. After dowsing the desk and couch with the fuel, he lit the room on fire and dashed back through the house to the stairs.

Once the house was sufficiently ablaze, he would escape through the tunnel. He had already called for someone to pick him up if he could get past whatever perimeter the police had set up. He continued to move with a purpose as smoke began to fill the house. The gas mask kept the smoke from really affecting him as he set the upstairs, and finally the garage on fire. He stayed low more from his need to see than to breathe as he finally made his way to the kitchen, stopping only to place the M1 into Alejandro's lifeless hands.

As the smoke level lowered to the point where it occluded the window, he pulled the refrigerator away from the wall. He opened the trapdoor, and then making sure to support the weight of the fridge on the trap door itself, tilted the appliance so it would fall back against the wall. He shimmied down into the tunnel and pulled off the gas mask. He sat at the bottom of the short ladder and waited for the fun to start.

Above him in the house, the flames spread rapidly as the gasoline in each room ignited with a *whump* and several of the windows that weren't already broken shattered outwards. In another thirty seconds, flames and smoke were boiling out of all the windows. Two minutes later, ammunition that had been scattered throughout the house by Esteban began to cook off. Contrary to popular belief, a round of ammunition that cooks off due to heat, launches its bullet at a substantially reduced velocity. It does, however, launch them and they are still dangerous.

Across the street, Billy Kidd watched the edges of the house for movement and kept up a running commentary for the command post. They were going to have to allow the fire department in or else the whole neighborhood would go up in flames. They would not risk the firefighters' lives, so a firefighting helicopter was dispatched to make water and flame retardant drops. It took eighteen minutes for the first drop to arrive and by then, the house was fully engulfed in flames. The decision was made to release the scene so the fire trucks could help extinguish the blaze.

In the command post, Herb, Chuck, and Lieutenant Emmerson were having an intense debate over how to search the neighborhood. Chuck wanted to go house to house and search every inch of the neighborhood until the suspects were found. Emmerson was not so convinced that was the right course of action.

"I know you want these guys, Chuck, but Jesus H Christ, we already have another Waco on our hands!" They were leaning over an aerial map of the area. "Wounded officers and a house burning down as we speak! The fucking press is gonna murder us as it is. If we start violating people's Constitutional rights like those dumb shits in Boston, we're going to be in some real deep kimchee!"

"What about protecting the public? These guys are going to crawl out of some rat hole and get away! How many more people are going to have to die?" Chuck had always been a straightforward guy and had always played by the rules for the fourteen years he had been in law enforcement, but he was beginning to think that the Jarheads might be on to something. "How about we ask permission to search and then just watch the houses that say no really closely? Aren't most of the residents here?"

"Yeah, but fire has to get in there first. We aren't even sure there is a tunnel." Herb had trusted all the intel he had gotten from Stanford to date, and it had all been reliable. He didn't think that the man who had told him about the possibility of a tunnel was lying to him either, but it was still just supposition. "Your call, Lieutenant."

Up on the hill, Rudy and Ben were watching the goings on with great interest. They were trading off between the high-powered binoculars and the telescope to prevent eye strain. Rudy had just gotten back on the telescope when he hunched forward and began telling Ben to look at the backyard of a house around the corner from the one going up in flames.

"Look, look, look!" he said, gesturing with his arm parallel to the telescope. "Around the corner to the north, second house to the east! That guy in the backyard just came out of that Rubbermaid shed!"

"I see him! Keep an eye on him while I call our friends in blue."

Herb answered on the second ring.

"Talk to me."

"You have a man that just walked out of a storage shed in the backyard of the second house to the east on … let me see … that would be Lakeview Drive. We didn't see any movement there prior to this. He could have gone in there in the split second we were changing out the optics between us, but we doubt it."

Herb had shoved his way to the map and was looking closely at the area.

"Okay, if the house on the corner, which faces Lakeview is one, then he is in the backyard of two?"

"That is correct."

"Description?"

"Almost all brown head to toe, and he's limping."

"Copy, all brown clothing and limping, anything else?"

"Yeah, he's walking out the east gate right now and heading east. He's walking right past a group of your officers!"

Herb looked once more at the map and dashed out the front of the fire station with Chuck right on his heels. Herb filled him in on what was happening as Ben kept up a running commentary in his ear. He filled Chuck in as they walked the block and a half to Lakeview.

Ben was able to guide them right up to the corner on a collision course with the suspect. Chuck, who was in his SWAT gear ducked into some bushes while Herb waited for word on the suspect's location before turning the corner.

CHAPTER 64

The blast from the grenade killed all three of the men who had rushed towards the stairwell. The concussion was enough to rattle everyone in that end of the tunnel. Guerro was driven to his knees, and one of the other men slammed into the wall so hard he lost consciousness. One of Guerro's men had the presence of mind to stick his rifle around the corner of the stairwell and send a burst of fire upwards. He then picked up the door and pushed across the opening, closing off most of the space and making it much harder to get a grenade by.

The grenade blast and rifle fire had Guerro's ears ringing, so he didn't hear the taunting voice from down at the other end of the tunnel at first. One of his soldiers had to tap him on his arm and gesture around the corner before he could make out the voice coming from around the corner.

"You jotos all right down there? Feeling a little claustrophobic?" Bull shouted. "My men have your way out blocked. Why don't you just give up now and I'll let you die quickly!"

"Just have Tom Stanford step around the corner, and he and I can settle our differences. Then I'll give you a chance at me, Mr. Toliver. If you are man enough to face me one-on-one."

Tom had to physically restrain Bull from walking around the corner and into a fight.

"Well, come on out then!" Tom shouted as Bull took a knee and aimed back down the hall.

Guerro simply shoved the man nearest to him out into the corridor to see what would happen. What happened was Bull put a bullet through his head but had to duck back as Guerro put his pistol around the corner and began firing and urged the remaining five men to rush around the corner.

273

All of them rushed to the next corner, where the first two to make it were brought down by gunfire from Bull and Tom. It immediately devolved into a hand-to-hand battle as rifles were knocked away and fists began to fly.

The three attackers were hindered by their numbers and got jammed up as they rounded the corner. Bull had managed to surge up from his kneeling position and use his rifle to push aside the second two men who were stumbling over the bodies of their fallen comrades. This allowed Guerro to get a clear shot at him; the 00 buckshot slammed into his vest and sent him lurching to the side.

Tom had taken a half step back to make sure he could bring his weapon to bear. He didn't want to retreat any further because he didn't want to leave Bull. He managed to shoot one more man before the barrel of his shotgun was grabbed. As soon as he felt the pull on the barrel, he shoved the weapon forward, jamming the end of it into the stomach of the man in front of him. This allowed him to trigger one final blast before a freight train ran into him from the side.

After watching Toliver slide to the ground, Guerro had turned to shoot Tom. Pulling the trigger resulted in nothing happening since he had short-stroked the slide in all the commotion and had failed to chamber a round. He immediately hurled himself at the man he had sworn to kill and tried to get his hands around his throat. The two men crashed into the opposite wall then went to the ground in a tangle of thrashing arms and legs.

Guerro outweighed Stanford by thirty-five pounds and he wound up on top. Even though he got both hands on his neck, the retired Marine was far too skilled a fighter to get choked out. Bringing his right arm across and between their bodies, Tom slammed his forearm down into Guerro's elbow joints and grabbed the back of Guerro's right hand. He simultaneously shoved up with his left hand under Guerro's right. This, combined with a twist of the body, resulted in Guerro losing his grip and getting his arm wrenched to the side.

He was in the process of trying to overpower Stanford's grip on his arm when his head snapped violently to the side from the kick Sheila delivered to it. His over-muscled neck absorbed most of the blow, but the kick brought stars to his eyes. He snarled at the woman and redoubled his efforts to kill her husband. He had just turned back to that task when he felt a burning in his side. Glancing down, he saw Toliver shoving his KA-BAR into his side. Fortunately for Guerro, Toliver's strike was at the very end of his reach, and the blade only penetrated two inches.

A second kick snapped his head backwards this time. The blow nearly killed him. Again only the muscles in his neck saved him. This time, however, the blow was much more damaging. His head was turned slightly to the right when Sheila delivered a front kick to his forehead. Two of the vertebrae in his neck splintered and sent a burning pain down his neck and into his shoulder.

The amount of damage being done in so many different areas kept him off balance long enough for Tom to shift his weight and finish the turkey neck hold on Guerro's wrist. He pulled Guerro's right elbow in tight against his own chest and used both of his hands to compress the back of Guerro's right hand until the wrist cracked.

The pain was intense and as Guerro let out a yell and tried to pull away, Sheila managed to slam the butt of her pistol down on the crown of his head. Toliver had hitched himself a little closer and shoved the knife into Guerro's back. He sliced towards the man's backbone and finally clipped the spinal cord after working the knife around in the wound.

Guerro again felt the cold pain of the knife entering his body. Although he had been cut many times in street fights during his youth growing up in Mexico City, he had never suffered such a grievous wound. He felt his legs go numb, and the pain in the lower part of his body vanished. He managed to slam his left fist into Tom's face, but as he was pulling his fist back, Sheila stomped down on it, crushing his knuckles. As he jerked the hand away, an arm snaked around his neck while another pulled back on his forehead. Once Bull had his choke set nice and deep, he rolled to the side, allowing Tom to get out from underneath.

The last thing Guerro saw was Sheila and Tom with looks of pity on their faces. As Bull pulled and twisted on Guerro's damaged neck, the splinters from the two broken vertebrae finally pierced his spinal cord and the man went limp. Bull continued to choke and twist the neck until it cracked and he was certain the man was dead.

Tom and Sheila helped their battered friend to his feet.

"Do we have any more tangos on the property?" Tom asked into the radio.

"Affirm, we still have an unknown number holed up on the front porch. I can't get a good shot into there, but they can't get out," Dillon Remke responded from the roof. "We don't have any more movement up here, but I'm sure several of the bad guys are still alive."

"All right, give me a head count," Bull said as he searched Guerro's pockets and came up with his wallet and passport. "Are the Witch Doctors all right?"

"I'm good but we need several ambulances."

"We need to get these guys some medical ..."

"Security One, I'm hit in the arm but in good shape. I've notified local law enforcement and they are on the way."

"Well, call them back and tell them to approach cautiously. We may have unexploded ordinance in the area. Everyone with a tango in sight, let's get an anchor shot on everyone we can. Break." Tom was checking Bull's chest, which was already turning an ugly shade of purple. "What's the status on those gomers on the front porch?"

"Still getting a head count, Sergeant Major," Remke said. "We've got the front porch covered and the medics are working on the team."

"Copy." Tom turned to Sheila and gestured down the hall. "Let's go get our friend out of the storage room. We're going to need him to deal with the local gendarmes when they get here."

Bull finished strapping his plate carrier back on his torso and hefted his rifle. After performing a function check, he shrugged and said, "Let's go."

"Whoever is at the top of the stairs to the basement, we're coming back down the hallway. Is the ladder well secure?"

"Affirmative, but we have movement in the area around the bottom; be careful."

"Copy."

The three survivors made their way back down to the base of the stairs. Two of Guerro's men were rolling on the ground in pain. Bull kept them covered as Sheila moved over to the door to the storage room.

"Wait a sec, Sheila," Bull said holding up a hand. He turned and fired two rounds into each of the men still moving on the ground. He returned the startled looks on their faces and shrugged. "Just avoiding some conflict."

"Mr. O'Malley, you can come out now!" Sheila shouted to the door. "I'm even wearing purple lipstick!"

Purple lipstick was the all clear code. Bull had figured the chance of his Marines using the term in day-to-day conversation being just about nil.

O'Malley opened the door and came out with his pistol in his hand. He looked at the bodies, Bull's shredded vest, and the swelling and bruising on Tom's face. He then turned to Sheila and smiled.

"Well, at least you look good," he said, grinning. He turned back to Tom and gestured at the men coming down the stairs. "We clear upstairs?"

"Negative," Bull grunted. "We have several of the attackers pinned down on the front porch. The guys upstairs are trying to get an angle on them, but we are going to have to clear the whole property. We know they used homemade hand grenades and there may be other IEDs we don't know about. As soon as we can get you to the front gate safely, we are going to need you to meet with the locals."

"Okay." O'Malley adjusted his vest and walked over to the base of the stairwell.

"Coming up!" he yelled before pulling what was left of the door away from the frame.

"You're clear!"

O'Malley stepped over the remains of the door and frame and began climbing the chipped concrete stairs up to the first floor. Tom, Sheila, and Bull followed him as he made his way to the dining room. There they righted the table so that Ed Wright, one of the medics, could work on Bruce.

The banging from the front door had ceased, and the lack of activity concerned Bull.

"Remke, can you put a frag on those fuckers on the front porch?" Bull asked as he moved towards the entry hall.

"Affirm; let me get above them, and I'll short cook one and drop it on 'em."

"Copy, give us a heads-up so we can get low."

"Roger that!"

Dillon hustled over to a point directly above the porch and pulled a fragmentation grenade off of his vest. He was just going to drop it over the side when he decided to try something.

"Manos arriba, you fuckers!" he shouted down at them. "You have five seconds to drop your shit and come out!"

"How do we know you won't shoot us?" a voice replied in a thick Spanish accent.

"You don't! But if you aren't out of there with empty hands in the air in five seconds, I'm gonna start dropping grenades on your ass. Your choice!"

"Sí, sí! Okay, we are coming out!"

"I got it covered!" Paul shouted from his position on top of the garage.

"Okay! Slowly! Show us your hands first. Any stupid shit and we waste you! Comprende?"

"Okay ..." A set of empty hands appeared around the corner followed by a face. The man took one step away from the porch when a shotgun blast threw him violently to the ground.

"What the fuck was that?" Dillon yelled as he pulled back from the edge.

"It was one of his own ..." Paul never got to finish as the remaining four men charged out from under the eave and began shooting in all directions. Paul shot the first one who tumbled to the ground but still held onto his weapon.

"Frag out!" Dillon yelled and threw the grenade as hard as he could at the last man to run out. It hit him in the small of the back before dropping to the ground and detonating. When the cloud of dust cleared, all four men were on the ground, three of them writhing in pain as the fourth lay there lifeless.

Dillon and Paul wound up putting a pair of shots into each of them and calling it done. They stayed on the roof and provided cover as a team was formed to re-secure the property.

The wounded men were taken to the security trailer by the front gate, where the first ambulance was just pulling up along with one of the park rangers from across the street. O'Malley was there to meet them and explain things. He had to repeat himself again a few minutes later when a San Diego Sheriff's Department Explorer rolled up. O'Malley informed them that it would be a federal crime scene and notifications would be sent to their agencies. He did ask them to look in the area for other suspects and the vehicles used by the group that had come over the south wall.

The two fire teams that were formed to clear the property had to take their time, clearing the far side of the hangar and the cactus bushes along the south wall. They found eight wounded survivors, three near the hangar and five who had fallen into the cactus and were in so much pain they couldn't move. The teams were able to take these men into custody without too much fuss. Most of the fight was out of them.

Tom and Sheila were snuck into one of the ambulances, just in case there was still someone out there with a gun. The staff with critical injuries were life-flighted to the regional trauma center in San Diego. Those with non-life-threatening injuries were rushed by ambulance to the hospital in Brawley. Bull and O'Malley stayed to sort out the mess, while Dillon and Paul were allowed to sneak away and pick up Tom and Sheila.

CHAPTER 65

Esteban was limping along painfully and was almost to the corner when a monstrous black man appeared right in front of him. The startled look was a normal reaction, but he took just a second too long before he tried to put on his innocent act.

"They're shooting up the whole neighborhood back there …" he said, gesturing over his shoulder.

"Oh here; let me help you, sir!" Herb said and stepped closer to offer the injured man his arm. Just as Herb closed the distance, Esteban saw Chuck in his SWAT gear covering him from the bushes. He tried to go for his holstered .45, but a huge hand clamped around his wrist while another one slammed up under his jaw, lifting him off his feet and sending him crashing over to land flat on his back. The wind left his lungs with an explosive *whoosh*, and he lay there stunned, looking like a fish out of water as his body tried to start breathing again.

Herb and Chuck flipped him over and cuffed him before his head even cleared. His pistol and other belongings were removed and secured before he was allowed to sit up.

"You know, I believe this gentleman matches the description of the guy that shot my brother, and he looks similar to one of the suspects from the South Bay Storage homicide," Chuck said, leaning in close. "Hold still for just a second."

Chuck used his phone's camera to take a couple pictures of Esteban, then sent them off via text to his brother, asking him if this was the same guy from the shootout on E Street. The reply came back almost immediately: "Definitely!"

"You know, that's the wonderful thing about technology these days—instant gratification." Herb was looking through Esteban's wallet. "Well there, Mr. Tongro. You are under arrest for suspicion of murder, assault with a deadly weapon, and narco-terrorism. There will be many more added to that list, but that will do for starters. Now, is there anyone else inside the house or in the tunnel you used to escape?"

Esteban just stared back at him with a blank look on his face.

"Okay, have it your way."

Esteban was picked up none too gently and dragged over to a cruiser. The cell phone in Herb's pocket rang as they were securing him in the back seat.

"Hello."

"You got the right guy." It was a statement not a question.

"Yeah, and we've already photo ID'd him as well." Herb waved at the hilltop. "He was one of the ones from the very beginning."

"Glad we could be of service. Just to let you know, the cartel made a move on our safe house. There were quite a few casualties."

"Oh, man." Herb leaned back against the side of the cruiser. "I'm sorry to hear that. Are Tom and Sheila okay?"

"Yeah, they're fine. Lost a couple of good men though. I'll let O'Malley fill you in. We're out of here. Oh, did you get that red-haired guy?"

"We don't know yet. The Tac guys reported several suspects down, and as you can see, we are going to have a hard time identifying any bodies we find."

The safe house was now fully engulfed in flames. A fire department helicopter was dropping a load of water on the house. Firemen, escorted by SWAT officers, were spraying the house by arcing the streams of water over the neighboring homes. A section of the roof had already fallen in and the garage wall was starting to buckle. The occasional pop of ammo cooking off was keeping everyone back.

"Well, we never saw him leave, so he should still be in there."

"Roger that; we'll see what we find in the rubble."

Herb got Emmerson on the radio and let him know what had happened. The fire department had moved up but wasn't going to risk getting any closer with ammunition cooking off. They were waiting it out as the helicopters continued to drop water from the nearby lake. Emmerson told him the warrant would probably be good on the house with the storage shed, but to wait for a supplemental, just in case there wasn't a tunnel. If there wasn't a connection between the two properties, *Probable Cause* for the stop on the street would be in jeopardy. It would be thin, but the liberal judges in California were known for making outrageously stupid calls like that.

It took the firefighters two hours to get the fire out and another before they found the tunnel entrance under the fridge. In the meantime, Emmerson had come up with an addendum to the original warrant, and they began to search the tunnel from the other end. After going through it twice, the detectives put crime scene tape around the storage shed and waited for the crime scene techs to process it.

Down in the hidden room, Rich had fallen asleep from exhaustion and slept through til the next day. He heard movement off and on for several hours and waited patiently, having to change out the batteries in the camping lantern as they got dim. He left his cell phone off since it wouldn't work down there, and he would need it right away as soon as he got above ground.

The noises finally stopped at 8:00 p.m. the following evening when the techs went home. He waited another hour before coming out. The room had a cleverly concealed peephole that allowed him to see that the tunnel was clear in both directions. After not seeing any movement for an hour, he carefully opened the door by pulling it inward then looked up and down the tunnel before stepping out and closing it behind himself. Hopefully, the police would never find the room and just fill in the tunnel, leaving them none the wiser that he had ever been there.

He made his way slowly to the tunnel's exit and climbed up the short ladder to the shed. The trapdoor had been propped open, but the door to the plastic structure was closed. Peering through the seam of the door, he could see the piece of crime scene tape that had been placed across the doors.

Rich took a few minutes to see if there was any movement in the backyard. After waiting for a couple of minutes and observing nothing, he gently pushed on one of the doors until the strand of crime scene tape popped free from where masking tape had been used to tape it in place. He again spent several minutes looking around at the vacant backyard. There were no lights on in the house since the family that rented the house were being kept under lock and key at a nearby hotel while they were interviewed and the house was processed as a crime scene.

He slipped out the side gate and stayed in the shadow of the house as he crept towards the street, which was empty. Rich turned in the other direction and began slipping across front yards until he had rounded the corner. Once there, he stepped out to the sidewalk and began walking at a normal pace in the direction of the commercial district only two blocks away. He just had to get a ride to his car at the alternate storage lot and then he was going to disappear. He had enough cash to vanish and he was almost home free. Almost.

Annie Meyers had just loaded some groceries in the trunk of her car and was ready to head back home when she looked up and saw a familiar figure walking across the parking lot and talking animatedly on a cell phone. She looked closely at the red hair and her temper began to boil.

Annie didn't carry a cell phone with her, so she considered yelling for someone to call the police. She dismissed that idea as she realized that Richard would easily make his escape before the police could arrive. Not wanting to lose him with her indecision, she climbed in the car and pulled to the end of the row so she could observe him as he continued across the lot.

He was soon out in an open area and the conversation he was having was getting even more animated. He was gesturing energetically while trying to keep his voice down. He was so intent on his phone call that he didn't notice the car bearing down on him until it was too late. He turned around and had just enough time to recognize the driver as the little old lady from across the street of the stash house before the front of the car slammed into his thighs just above the knees. His left thigh broke while his right knee popped out of joint. His torso slammed down onto the hood of the car before rebounding off and slamming down onto the asphalt. The cell phone went flying across the lot as Richard screamed in agony.

Annie backed the car, turning it at an angle before driving forward again. She rolled forward until she felt resistance and heard Richard scream again. She had rolled until her passenger front tire had pinned Richard's left ankle to the ground. She got out of the car and walked around the back until she could see the man squirming and holding his leg.

Several people were jogging across the parking lot towards her, including the shopping center security guard. She hustled in their direction and started waving her arms.

"Call the police! That man is armed! Stay back!" She continued forward as the security officer pulled out his phone and dialed 911. Several other people had their phones out and were videotaping the entire event. A squad car responded and Annie told the female officer to contact Herb, even showing her his card. The officer didn't quite know if she should arrest the crazy old lady or go check on the man who was screaming under the car. But with all the crazy things happening lately she decided to err on the side of caution and had dispatch notify Detective Johnson.

The officer pulled her squad car around so that she had a good angle on the young man who was moaning and flailing his arms. No matter how much she yelled at the man, he would not listen and follow her commands to be still so she could approach him safely. She maintained her position as another unit, the fire department, and eventually Herb Johnson all showed up.

Annie, in the meantime, had called Jay and Becky Hooks to come pick her up. Herb walked over to the group and smiled.

"I told you she was meaner than a hungry alligator!" Jay said, smiling and shaking Herb's hand. He hunched his shoulders as his wife again swatted him across the back. "And you really have to open a case of domestic abuse for me. You see what I go through!"

Herb grinned at the ongoing joke and got the story from Annie on how Richard wound up under her car. It was all he could do to keep from bursting out laughing as the tiny woman expressed her outrage, first at the fact that drug dealers were in her neighborhood, and then at the damage her house had suffered—there were two bullet holes in her walls, one of them going all the way through to her kitchen and damaging her fridge. She stated that it would be a cold day in Satan's boudoir before she let such a miscreant get away.

As they were talking, two tac-team officers were able to secure Richard, and he was removed from under the car. After placing him on a stretcher, they began to wheel him over to the ambulance. They stopped as a small force of nature stormed over and rained on the stricken man.

"You should be ashamed of yourself! Does your mother know what you do for a living? I bet she would just be mortified, MORTIFIED at your behavior. And where was your father? Huh?" Annie turned to the slowly gathering crowd. "That's the problem with our youth today! No father in the home and no parental guidance! Shame on you, young man. Shame, shame, shame on you!"

The two firemen grinned as they continued to load Richard into the rig. The tongue lashing had finally shut the man up, and he just stared at the tiny woman. The verbal tirade followed him into the ambulance and was continued to be heard even after the rear doors were closed.

EPILOGUE

The group of Marines walked slowly down the hill of Fort Rosecrans National Cemetery. The service for Tim had been a solemn affair and the Marines had several more to attend in the coming week. Walking among them, dressed in a tailored suit with a Marine Corps tie clasp, leaning on the arms of Dillon and Tom was Hub. He had shed a few tears at the service but was feeling much better now as he walked down the hill surrounded by fellow warriors. As they reached the line of limousines, Hub turned and smiled at Tom.

"I can't thank you enough for what you've done for me and what you did for Tim," he said, putting out his hand. Tom gripped it, but only to use it to pull the old warrior into a hug.

"I am the one who can't thank you enough, Hub. What you and Tim sacrificed for Sheila and me is beyond anything we can repay. But I do have one more big favor to ask of you."

"Just name it, Sergeant Major."

"I bought all of us season box seats for both the Padres and the Chargers. We would be honored if you would be in one of them with us." Tom gestured at Dillon.

"Yeah, Hub, there's a lot of guys who are still dying to meet you. Tim talked about you all the time on deployment, always saying we never had it as tough as you did in Korea. All the guys really would like to meet you. And we could tailgate before the games, if that's all right?" Dillon looked at the smiling old man.

"You fellas don't have to do all that just for me. I know you have better things to do than hang out with me."

"Actually, I don't, sir. My job is to provide protection to Tom and Sheila, and since they're going to be there, I'll be there too." Dillon waved around at the blue wave still coming down the hill. Not all the blue uniforms were Marines, several of them were officers from CVPD. Tom had paid for every plane ticket for all of Tim's friends to be there. He had also rented out half of the Coronado Beach Hotel on North Island for them to hold the wake at. "Let's talk about it at the party."

"Only on one condition ..." Hub grinned.

"Name it," several people said together.

"Someone earns a name tonight!" Hub said, grinning a challenge at the men surrounding him.

Everyone in the crowd around him shouted "Oohrah!" except for the monster of a black man dressed in the Navy dress whites of a commander. Herb just shook his head and hoped the police chief in Coronado was understanding.

ACKNOWLEDGEMENTS

This is my first full-length novel, and I could not have done it without the help of many people. I am going to go on for a bit here because they are deserving of my gratitude. Any mistakes in this novel are mine. I used my literary license as I saw fit and I alone am responsible for any errors. If there are any parts you found entertaining, it was probably due to one of these folks.

This is a work of fiction ... but having said that:

First of all, there is a real "Goat Boy." You know who you are, and I miss those times we spent hanging off of cliffs together (and a certain hotel in San Diego). To the other three Lance Corporals who may or may not know anything about a sunken Hummer in the Arabian Gulf, the cat's out of the bag now, and if Staff Sergeant "P" ever reads this book (I doubt he will, there aren't any pictures and the words are too big!), he'll know who shined up the colonel's Hummer hood!

To Coporal C. Norton, 'D' Company, 4th Recon Battalion ... man, we chewed a lot of dirt together. Thanks for being the best "Battle Buddy" ever. I love you, man.

To Sergeant James Salton Chula Vista Police Department, Sergeant Dan Olsen El Cajon Police Department, the MPs of MWSS-473, and all the other guys I've ever sat in a patrol car or on a stakeout with and watched crazy stuff. I still bust out laughing at humanity.

To my family, who first put up with my absences so I could have one of the best jobs in the Corps, and then for supporting and putting up with me while I wrote this. They are my rock and my inspiration.

To my Aunt, Merline Lovelace, the best romance writer of all time ... Don't believe me? Google her. She convinced me to get off my butt and write.

To my friends on Survival Guide, they had some ideas about fortifying the desert house and I thank them for their input. Their creativity was awesome. For the record, Kim is my #1 fan.

To all the people who served as guinea pigs for this experiment in figuring out if an ape could pound on some keys and make sense (especially Charles Hume), I thank you for your criticism and input. I must have sent this thing to twenty people to read. I think three made it through without pulling out their hair.

Finally, I would like to thank my buddy Joe Gomes ECPD and his wonderful fiancée, Yrsina Colangelo, who did my cover art. If you ever need a photographer/videographer in Southern California, look up YC Photography; they're the best.

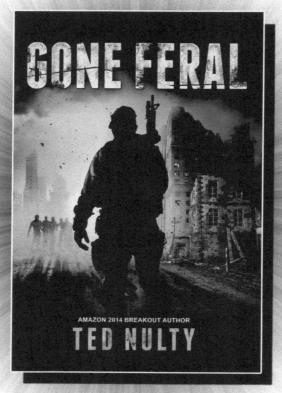

CUTTING-EDGE NAVAL THRILLERS BY

JEFF EDWARDS

HIGH COMBAT IN HIGH SPACE

THOMAS A. MAYS

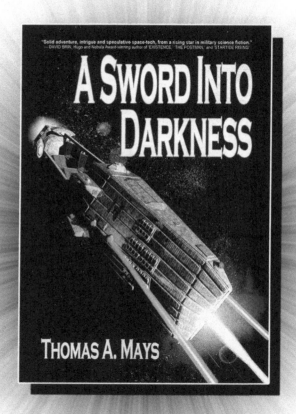

A SWORD INTO DARKNESS

THOMAS A. MAYS

**The Human Race is about
to make its stand...**

WHITE-HOT SUBMARINE WARFARE
BY
JOHN R. MONTEITH

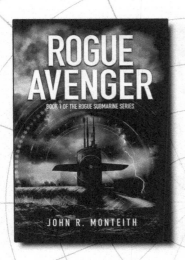

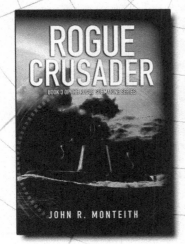

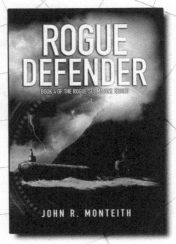

www.BraveshipBooks.Com

HIGH OCTANE AERIAL COMBAT

KEVIN MILLER

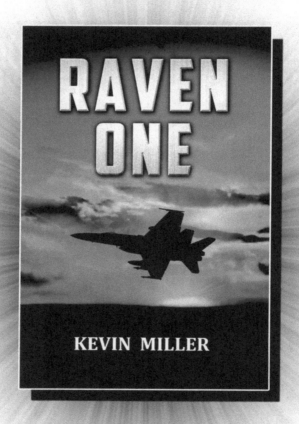

RAVEN ONE

KEVIN MILLER

Unarmed over hostile territory...

www.BraveshipBooks.Com

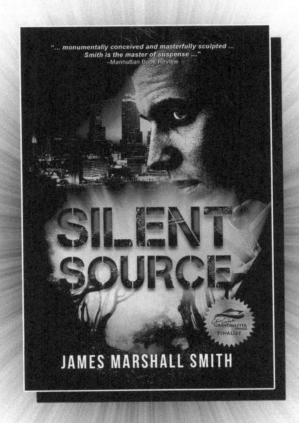